BOOKS BY KRISTIE COOK

Sun & Moon Academy Book One: Fall Semester

Sun & Moon Academy Book Two: Fall Semester

The Winged & the Wicked (with T.V. Hahn)

Havenwood Falls Short Story Anthology 2018

Havenwood Falls Short Story Anthology 2019

Havenwood Falls Short Story Anthology 2020

BOOK OF PHOENIX

The Space Between

The Space Beyond

The Space Within

SOUL SAVERS BOOK 6

UNHOLY TORMENT

KRISTIE COOK

For You, My Reader

CHAPTER 1

*A*utomatic gunfire beat out a staccato rhythm all around me. Thunder punctuated it with a loud bass sound, followed by a streak of lightning that illuminated the cracks carved into the sky and the ancient structure looming nearby. A steady rain fell, pelting my skin and drenching my hair, plastering the strands to my head.

One word drowned out the cacophony of the storm. One scream that lifted the hairs on the back of my neck.

"ALEXIS!"

One image that pushed everything else out of focus.

Auburn hair that looked nearly black from being soaked. Almond-shaped, brown eyes even larger than normal. Olive-toned skin washed out, blanched by the rain. A small and curvy, yet fit body.

Just like me.

She lunged and reached out, as though to save me from the danger.

But it was her body being peppered with the bullets. Her body that jerked and twitched with each hit. Her body that collapsed as her arms still lifted toward me, her voice again calling my name.

"*MOM!*"

The word became lodged in my throat. My mouth opened wide to let the scream out. But I had no force to make it heard. I had no power to propel my body forward. I could only stand there, unable to do anything but watch the blood mix with the rain and stain her shirt with rivers of red.

My breath caught audibly, and my hand clapped over my chest, my heart pounding against it with the force of Thor's hammer. I squeezed my eyes shut and opened them again.

My bedroom surrounded me, the misty gray of pre-dawn light leaking through the doorway to the balcony, the sheer curtain barely fluttering before it. I sat in my bed, sweat dripping down my back, trying to catch my breath.

I didn't know if you could call that a recurring nightmare, considering I hadn't been sleeping. Sleep rarely blessed me with its presence since we returned from that fatal night three weeks ago. I only came to bed at night because it was what people did. So I lay here in the dark, letting my body regenerate as best as it could, wishing sleep would wrap me in its peace and take me away from this world at least for a couple of hours. But too many thoughts and memories raced through my consciousness to allow it to shut down. Especially this particular scene. It was a nightmare, yes, but not one I could ever wake from.

The vision of my mother's death replayed in my mind day and night with just the smallest of triggers, leaving me with the same questions every time.

Why did I only stand there, stupid and useless? Why didn't I do anything?

The same answers came along with them: I was too inexperienced, too ignorant to expect such shockingly cruel behavior even from our enemy, too naïve to think my sperm-donor would murder the only woman who'd ever loved him, and too slow to act. I was not *enough* yet. Not fast enough, not smart enough, not experienced enough. Not enough of anything to be where I was now—especially not enough to be matriarch of the Amadis.

The large body under the sheets next to me stirred, and a warm, calming palm slid up my spine. I swiped at my cheeks, making sure they'd remained dry. I didn't want him to know if I'd been crying. Except for one major breakdown behind closed doors, tears usually eluded me these days, and this morning was no exception. His hand gently gripped my shoulder, and his thumb rubbed circles into the back of my neck, massaging the ever-present knot.

"I'm sorry I woke you," I whispered as I turned my head slightly to look over my shoulder. "Again."

His torso twisted toward me, rustling the sheet, and his other arm snaked across my belly. He pulled me down to him, nestling my head under his chin and curling his body protectively around mine.

"I don't mind," Tristan murmured, his lovely voice husky with sleep as he pulled me closer.

"You don't get much more sleep than I do, though."

"Don't worry about me, my love. I am always here for you, by your side, shouldering your pain with you."

Now my eyes stung, and I blinked rapidly while drawing in a jagged breath. I lived with the agony of Rina's and Sophia's deaths causing fresh breaks in my heart every day, but I didn't cry. The waking nightmare made me gasp for air with its horrific and unending awfulness, but I didn't cry. The loss and what it meant for me, the Amadis, the world, often paralyzed me, but I didn't cry. Kindness, though . . . the kindness of others always came close to breaking me. And Tristan, of course, had been nothing but kind and gentle, patient and comforting, and most of all loving. He was my rock, and I needed him to keep me anchored when the tumultuous waters of life tossed me in all directions, threatening to sweep me away.

I pressed my lips against his bare, muscular chest, letting

them linger for a long moment, and then I pulled away, wiggling out of the circle of his powerful arms.

"You're leaving me?" he asked, his voice soft and half-asleep.

"I'm going to the cliff. You try to get more sleep."

His breaths came in a steady rhythm by the time I'd dressed in yoga pants and a hoodie and stuffed my feet into running shoes. I pushed the sheer curtain aside, stepped onto the balcony, and inhaled a deep breath of the cool, salty air of a mid-September morning in the Greek Islands. Then I sprang from the third-story balcony. Even the deer on the edge of the woods didn't hear me as I landed softly on the balls of my feet. After a quick wave to the vampire guard standing watch on this side of the building, I pulled my hood over my head and took off in a sprint, past the training gym behind the mansion and through the woods.

I ran three miles straight east, through the forest and across the northern edge of Amadis Island, to where the cliffs dropped to the sea. The woods were still dark and unusually quiet as I sprinted through them. I only sensed animal mind signatures, so if any shifters or vamps had been out for the night, they were gone now, back at home in the village eight miles away at the south end of the island. When I burst out of the tree line, the sky hadn't lightened at all since I'd left—it had only been a minute or so—and it was still a dark gray. I stood on the edge of the cliff, listening to the waves crash against the bottom and staring straight outward as the breeze lifted and tossed my hair. I saw what was no longer there.

Their bodies lay side-by-side, two so tiny and one larger, all of them painfully still on the grandiose pyre built for the triple funeral and decorated with beautiful greenery and flowers. Mom's and Rina's hair were arranged in up-dos, and they wore their traditional Amadis dresses, both in royal purple. Although she'd only been the matriarch for five minutes, I had decreed that Mom deserved to wear the leader's color rather than the lighter plum shade that represented the matriarch's second. I'd also ensured Winston, her one true love who'd also died that night, lay by her side. Their arms were neatly arranged so their hands came together on their stomachs, and their eyes were closed. The peace the whole display showed clashed with the emotions that stormed through me.

A crowd of about as many Amadis as could possibly fit on the island—at least five times the normal population of 637—had gathered behind Tristan, Dorian, and me to say farewell to their leaders. Several people cried and sniffled, including Charlotte and Julia, and I thought Solomon, too, all who stood right behind us. Others, like Ophelia, the witch who had served as Rina's head of household for over a century, sobbed loudly.

I'd held Tristan's hand as he lit the pyre with fire from his palm. My power contributed to lifting the huge wooden dais from the ground and sending it over the cliff's edge, where it hung in midair. My throat tightened, and I choked on the sobs building their way up, forcing me to say my good-byes silently. The flames licked higher, sending black plumes into the air, until they swallowed their bodies. Then the entire thing disappeared as the Angels accepted my grandmother, my mom, and her soul mate to the Otherworld.

I drew in a long breath as the vision faded away and blew it out slowly. This nightmare wasn't quite as horrific as the one at the abbey, but the memory of their funeral a couple of weeks ago remained just as fresh and painful. I swallowed the lump that had formed in my throat and jumped off the hundred-foot cliff.

About a fifth of the way down, I swung my body inward and landed on a three-foot-wide ledge that jutted out two feet from the cliff side. I'd only recently noticed it, although we'd held many funerals on the cliff straight above, and nobody had ever mentioned the ledge that was almost like an altar down here. Perhaps nobody had actually discovered it before or maybe only matriarchs could see it, but I found it to be the most secluded and peaceful place to spend time alone. I hadn't ventured into the Sacred Archives yet, which would also be peaceful, I knew, but they didn't provide this view.

As though the smoke from the many pyres that had burnt over the centuries had stained the stone, the faces of hundreds of Ames women were depicted on the cliff's wall around this ledge. Including Rina's and Mom's, which were quite a bit darker than the others, because time and weather hadn't faded them yet. My fingers traced over their cheeks and jawlines as I stared at them for a long moment before turning and sitting, letting my legs dangle over the ledge.

The Aegean Sea spread before me to the horizon, where the sun began to show itself, streaking the sky and clouds with bright pinks and oranges. The water reflected the colors, and the sunrise was as stunning as any sunset I'd watched with Tristan. Two birds cawed at each other overhead as they flew by before diving down for the sea to catch their breakfast. The waves threw themselves against the cliffs and rocks below, sending spray high into the air, but not quite high enough to reach me. Still, I could taste the saltiness on my lips and tongue with each breath I inhaled.

Here in this place, I somehow felt as though I sat among my mother, grandmother, and the rest of my ancestors in Heaven, rather than on the other side of the veil that separated the Otherworld realm from our physical one. Maybe their portraits behind me provided the comfort or maybe it was something more Otherworldly, but I didn't feel quite as alone here, even though I was the last of my kind on this entire planet. In this entire realm. The Ames family line teetered on the verge of extinction, and the Amadis would follow shortly.

Somehow, I was supposed to prevent that.

"What am I going to do?" I asked aloud, not for the first time.

Mom and Rina—and even Cassandra, the very first Amadis matriarch—had promised me that night on the abbey grounds that I would never be alone. But although I felt their presence here, I also felt completely isolated. I wished they could talk to me, give me guidance and direction, tell me how to move forward. Because I was stuck. Paralyzed. At a complete loss.

"How do I lead the Amadis when I still know so little? How do I take on this war that I know is coming? How do I function without you?" I let out a guttural cry. "How can I be the mother to all of these people when I can't even handle Dorian? Please tell me what to do!"

Mom and Rina had both assured me I was ready for this role, but I most certainly wasn't. Compared to them, I was still an infant. They'd had decades—more than a century—to prepare and serve as leaders. I was still in my twenties with only two-and-a-half years of living in this strange world no Norman would believe existed. How could anyone, especially the Angels, think I was ready to take this all on?

"You are not alone."

The words whispered in my head, so quietly, I couldn't tell if Rina, Cassandra, or Mom spoke to me. Or perhaps they were just a figment of my imagination.

"But you're not here," I spoke aloud.

"But others are. You do not have to do it all by yourself." The sound came as a mixture of all of their voices, soft and multilayered.

I pressed my lips together and nodded. "I have Tristan, I know."

"Yes, you do. But not only him. You have people, Alexis. People who want to serve you."

I stared out at the sunrise as I considered this. My council.

They were telling me to form my council that would serve as my confidants and advisors.

"*Be prepared, Alexis. The Daemoni are acting. Everything is about to change!*"

"What does that mean?" I knew the Daemoni had something up their collective sleeve—Kali and Lucas had given us a glimpse of it at the abbey. But they'd been quite silent the last few weeks, and I doubted it had anything to do with them giving us time to mourn. Lucas didn't have that kind of respect in a single cell of his body. They must have been planning something big and were now ready to execute.

My ancestors didn't answer me, and I asked again, pleading. "What do you mean? What's about to happen? Tell me what to do!"

I waited quietly, but still no response came. In fact, even when I changed the subject, no more answers came to any of my questions, including what to do about Dorian. My poor son had just been an eight, almost nine-year-old child when Owen had taken him from the safe house on Captiva Island. Six months later, he'd returned taller—taller than me now—and seemingly much older, as though he'd aged four or five years while we'd been separated, complete with the broody attitude of an adolescent. I'd been letting him off easy because of everything he'd been through—from being kidnapped and kept with the sorceress-bitch Kali to watching Rina and his Mimi die violently—but I knew deep down his insolent behavior came from more than his suffering from PTSD. The Daemoni had changed him mentally and physically. I didn't know how, exactly, because he refused to talk about it and stayed to himself, rarely leaving his room as he claimed he was studying. Studying what, I also didn't know. Presumably his schoolwork, but I had a feeling he was also discovering and growing his powers. And keeping them hidden from us. *What had Kali and the Daemoni done to him?* Whatever it was, it scared the hell out of me. My baby was no longer my little boy.

I'd also been through a lot and couldn't find the answers of what to do about him within me. Tristan and I had to figure out something, though, because if my assumption was right that Dorian's powers had developed while he'd been gone, he'd become more valuable to our enemy, and they'd be after him, convincing him to change sides like all of the Ames sons before him. With the dark attitude Dorian had been harboring, it wouldn't be long before he accepted their promises and walked off to the Daemoni by choice.

"*Alexis.*" Tristan's mental voice tugged at my mind.

Yeah?

"*Are you okay,* ma lykita?"

I chuckled darkly. I often wondered how I'd ever be okay again, but I had him, so I knew I would be.

I'm fine, I answered.

"*It's almost time to meet with Scarecrow so we can get the entire lowdown.*"

The sun had risen quite a bit in the sky by now, and I'd barely noticed, wrapped up in my own thoughts. Knowing I had to push beyond my grief and take my role seriously as matriarch, I'd agreed to finally sit down with Owen today to find out everything he'd learned during his time with the Daemoni. We had a war to plan, and he had the best inside intelligence. At least, he'd better, because he had a lot of making up to do after acting like a traitor and taking Dorian from us for so long.

I flashed to the matriarch's mansion, appearing at the large, double wooden doors on the west side of the building. I entered through the three-story foyer with the stone steps that wrapped up the outer edges and fire sconces casting shadows on the walls. Rina had been a traditionalist, keeping the mansion in the past except for the media room that held all of today's technology. The only change we'd made so far was to add Wi-Fi to the mansion and electricity to Rina's and Mom's offices—mine and Tristan's now—along with all of the devices we needed to run a society and an army in today's world.

Owen arrived shortly after me, and after a quick mind-check on Tristan, I realized he'd be a few more minutes. He was in the shower, and I briefly thought about joining him, but instead decided to harass Owen again with an interrogation. Admittedly, I hadn't paid much attention to his previous recounts of why he'd taken our son, too lost in my grief. But I needed to know, so I asked every question I could possibly think of as I sat on the edge of Rina's large, antique desk and Owen sat in front of me in a wingback chair.

"So let me get this straight," I said after he'd explained everything, trying to make sure I understood. "You took Dorian to show Kali she could trust you and to be able to protect him since she was determined to have him no matter what. Kali wanted Dorian to give herself leverage with the Daemoni Ancients so she could take Lucas out and assume his position as leader of the Daemoni. You were trying to set her up with Tristan and me so we could kill her, and I could trap her soul and deliver on my so-called obligation to the faeries."

Owen's straw-colored hair shook as he nodded his head. "You got it."

"Except you didn't know about Kali's plan to use Noah as bait to lure Rina and Mom there."

He frowned now, producing three vertical lines between his eyebrows. "No, I didn't. I knew she had a vendetta against Rina, but I didn't know the plan had been to have Noah reach out to her. Of course, he wasn't under his own control, or he never would have."

Right. Kali had put a spell on run-of-the-mill stones from Earth to make them emulate a faerie stone. She'd developed the idea based on the stone Bree had given to Tristan and he had given to me—it created a connection between us so he could feel my emotions and keep his own in check. Kali's stones were a little different, though. She'd implanted one into Noah, Mom's twin, let it soak in his blood to absorb his genetic imprint, and then broke a chunk of the stone into pieces. She placed those shards into the hearts of Norman soldiers and linked them all to Noah.

My fingers absently rubbed at the cotton cloth covering Tristan's stone embedded into my skin. Bree had implanted it into my flesh over my heart so I'd never lose it to the Daemoni again. "So Kali had taken control of Noah, who in turn had control over a whole company of the British Army."

"Yes," Owen confirmed. "But Lucas had his own diabolical plan as far as those soldiers were concerned."

Lucas wanted more than control—he wanted the kind of undying loyalty a lykora gives to her master. So he'd sent Victor the vampire, Vanessa's twin and my half-brother, after Sasha the same night Kali had sent Owen after Dorian. Right after Owen and Dorian left and before Sasha could follow them, Victor had taken advantage of the chaos in the rest of the safe house and popped into the room. Sasha had put up a big fight, but the vampire had been able to clip her wing and collect enough blood for Lucas to carry out a most atrocious act of war. He'd used her blood to create superhuman soldiers with all of Sasha's qualities—the ability to grow to monster size, inhuman strength and speed, and unsurpassed loyalty. Combined with the bewitched stones, this gave Lucas the ultimate control over all of them. He had used Noah to create a new army that was better than the Daemoni, because in his eyes, Normans were expendable.

Tristan finally showed his beautiful self after we'd gone over the whole story and I'd taken another chance to throw the guilt on Owen for everything he'd put us through. Not just Tristan and me, but also poor Blossom, who'd really pushed her magic doing locator spells and trying to break through Owen's cloaks on Dorian.

"Are you done torturing Scarecrow for the tenth time?"

Tristan asked as he came in wearing Norman clothes of khaki shorts and a green V-neck Polo that couldn't have hugged his powerful build more perfectly. The gold in his hazel eyes sparkled with his teasing, and the corners of his mouth lifted in a sexy smirk. "You know that's not the real reason he's here."

I shrugged. It hadn't really been ten times. "We were waiting on you. What better way to pass the time?"

Tristan sat on the edge of the desk next to me and turned his attention to Owen. "So you were going to tell us about Noah and those soldiers."

Owen rose to his feet, walked a little circle around the chair, and leaned his arms on the back of it. "Yeah, that. It's not only about Noah. It's much, much bigger."

He explained how Lucas had teamed up with the U.S. Department of Defense—as well as other government entities around the world—to supposedly supply them with super-soldiers, but intending to keep them for his own plans. He told us how Lucas and Kali had kept the Summoned sons and some of their offspring locked up on DoD property, such as the building where we'd found Dorian the first time in Virginia. Like they'd done with Noah and his battery of soldiers, they'd been using the stones Kali had created on *all* of the sons and many of their descendants, then implanting chips from those stones into Norman soldiers around the world.

"So we could potentially have thousands, maybe tens of thousands of human soldiers under Lucas's control," Tristan surmised. "Some of them, if not all of them, enhanced with Sasha's blood and extremely dangerous."

"And of course, we can't kill them," Owen added. That was part of the Amadis creed—we couldn't kill norms unless absolutely and entirely necessary for the protection of others. Which it may come down to if this war really happened.

Charlotte, Owen's mother and our second-best warlock, rapped her knuckles on the doorframe before entering my office, her blond hair swishing over her shoulders as she crossed the room with long, purposeful strides. Like me, she gave the outward appearance of being okay, but the pain of losing her best friend, my mother, lingered just below the surface.

"If that's not bad enough," she said, "you need to turn on the TV."

Vanessa followed her in, slowing for a moment to brush her pale hand over Owen's arm before coming to my side and draping an arm across my shoulders. I leaned against her, feeling the silkiness of her white-blond hair against my cheek as I accepted her sisterly hug, while Tristan jabbed buttons on the remote to turn on the flat screen in the corner. Every channel showed the same scene: what looked like a riot at first glance, but it quickly became obvious we were witnessing a Daemoni attack. On the norms. In public.

"It's happening in several major metropolitan areas around the world," the reporter announced as vampires tore open the throats of humans nearby and a shifter changed on the fly.

Then Ian's ugly ogre face and dull red hair filled the screen, his crooked yellow teeth showing in a nefarious grin.

"Guess what, mates?" he said into the camera. "Vampires, werewolves, witches, and warlocks—we're all *real*. And we're coming for your blood . . . for your flesh . . . for your *souls*."

I gasped, and my hand flew to my mouth.

"They've come out to the humans," Sheree said from the doorway, her voice full of disbelief, and her brown eyes wide and round. She lifted a long finger to her mouth and gnawed on a fingernail.

Vanessa slapped her hands on her thighs. "It was only a matter of time. Lucas has been planning it for ages."

We remained glued to our spots throughout the morning and into the afternoon as we watched the carnage unfold around the world. Blossom and Jax had come into my office and watched with us, and then Ophelia and other household staff joined us, too. Everyone's minds churned over the same question: What were we going to do now?

Then Charlotte thought and began to voice exactly what Tristan and I had been thinking. "Looks like our reprieve is over. It's time to plan for war—"

Her words were stifled by the sound of a loud explosion and the ground quaking under our feet.

CHAPTER 2

I gripped the edge of the antique desk with one hand and reached out to hold onto Tristan's forearm with the other until the shaking stopped.

"That wasn't an earthquake." He barely spoke the words before another bang and subsequent tremors rocked the ground.

"Daemoni!" The thoughts came from all over the island, screaming into my head the moment I opened my mind to them.

"We're under attack," I announced before delving into a sentry's mind—a wizard keeping watch from the tower near the village.

Through his eyes, I shared with everyone in the room the vision he saw—Daemoni surrounding the island, uncloaked and in broad daylight. All mages hovering over the water, all shooting spell after spell at our shield.

"Owen and Char—" I started.

"Already on it," Owen said, his voice strained.

My mind left the wizard's, and my vision returned to my own, finding the two warlocks standing in the center of my office. Their hands lifted high above their heads, and their brows and lips set into hard lines as they concentrated on keeping the shield over the island as strong as possible. We took another hit, and both their faces turned various shades of red as the chords in their necks tensed and tightened.

Sweat beads popped out on Owen's forehead. "They have some powerful warlocks. Maybe a sorcerer."

"Go join the others," I ordered. "Do what you can."

Owen and Char disappeared from the room to join the mages who maintained the shield on the other end of the island. When they came together as a group, their power would multiply. Hopefully, it would be enough.

"We have to get to town," I said. "In case they make their way through."

"Change first." Vanessa pointed at Tristan and me before popping out of sight.

Right. We both still wore Norman clothes that provided no protection. We flashed to our suite and changed into our fighting leathers within a minute. After making sure Dorian was safe in his room with Sasha, we flashed to the Amadis village on the other end of the island. We appeared in front of the council hall at the top of a hill, looking down the main street of town that sloped toward the pier and the sea. Some panicked people ran amok in the streets, but many apparently hid in their homes and businesses.

The air crackled with powerful dark magic feeling thicker than it should have. The intensity of it meant our shield was failing, and if the Daemoni managed to pierce it, we'd be in deep trouble. Most of the Amadis who lived here on the island were among our weakest. My personal team contained some of our strongest fighters and other guards protected the mansion and council hall, but for the most part, everyone else lived here because they weren't warriors. This island was their place of refuge. If the Daemoni broke their way in, though, it would be far from a safe haven.

Tristan and I lifted our hands to aim our palms toward the

Daemoni to return fire, but the mages were too far away. By the time our powers reached the enemy, their potency had weakened too much to penetrate the shields and were easily deflected. Blossom and two other witches joined us, but their spells also bounced off the offenders' protection.

Owen, can't you blast them with something? I called out to him.

"*Not if you want me to hold this shield up,*" he answered from his position in the tower with Char and the other mages. "*There are too many, and they're too powerful. We're losing our hold as it is.*"

Real panic started to rise from the pit of my belly, sending my heart into a gallop. I needed to protect my people.

What if we made the shield smaller? I asked Owen. *Would it be easier to hold?*

"*Yeah, but how? We've already brought it in from the sea to the edges of the island, but we have to cover the entire thing.*"

No, you don't. Hang on. I used my telepathy to call to Ophelia and ordered her to clear everyone out of the mansion and to take cover in the village. *Tell the guards to come to the council hall.* Without waiting for a response, I switched to my son's mind. *Dorian, I need you to bring Sasha and come here to town. Now!*

He ignored me, but I could feel his mind signature, locating him where we'd left him in his room at the mansion.

Dorian! Now! We're under attack!

"*Ugh! Whatever. I'm coming. Geez.*"

The sulfuric stench of dark magic filled my nose. A red flash of light flew from the sea and slammed into the island. A building near the shore exploded into shards of wood and pieces of plaster.

"*They're getting through,*" Char said to me. No kidding.

Dorian dropped from the air to my side with Sasha in his arms, apparently having flown here. I reached my mind out to the mansion and found no signatures there.

"Get inside the council hall," I told my son, but he ignored me again, his gaze locked on the Daemoni in the distance.

I wanted to shove him away and prevent him from ever setting eyes on them again, but I didn't have time for the argument. My mind scanned the entire northern half of the island from the beach to the forest to the cliffs to be sure no one remained before I gave the orders. That part of the island was clear of any mind signatures. Perfect.

Tighten the shield to only surround the village, I ordered Owen.

"*But the mansion—*" He began to argue.

There's nobody there. Just protect the people. Another flash of light hit a second building. People poured out of the pub next to it, screaming with panic and running up the hill toward the council hall. *Do it, Owen, before it's too late!*

More spells soared through, one hitting an old cypress that exploded into slivers. Another hit the blacksmith's shop not too far below us, taking out one side of it. The people running up the hill dropped to the ground or scattered between the buildings, fleeing the main street. Tristan swept Dorian and me into his arms and plastered us to the ground, making us smaller targets as another spell headed straight for us. It soared over our prone bodies and took out what sounded like a tree behind us, but I couldn't get up to look.

The odor of Daemoni and dark magic faded, and the next round of spells ricocheted seemingly in midair. Owen and his mage team must have strengthened our magical armor. Sounds of explosions from the north side of the island meant they had, indeed, contracted the shield to protect the people. That was okay, as long as they were safe. Although millennia of history filled the halls of the matriarch's mansion, ultimately it consisted of only stones and material possessions. We could always rebuild it.

The attack on the northern side of the island lasted for several more minutes. Knowing we were safe here, though, Tristan and I sprang to our feet to check on our people. I reached my mind out for everyone on my team—Owen, Char, Blossom and Jax, Vanessa, and Sheree—and found them safe and sound. Blossom, Jax, and Sheree were already helping some of the Amadis in the lower part of town who'd been hurt from debris. Vanessa stood on the roof of the council hall, her fists on her hips and her ice-blue eyes staring hard at the Daemoni on the other side of the shield.

"They're all warlocks," she said after she jumped down to stand next to Sasha, who had already grown to her extra-large size, towering over all of us. "All of their best mages."

I reached my mind out to those on the other side of the shield, bracing myself for entering the Daemoni's putrid minds that filled me with the worst kind of dread. I pushed past the darkness and listened to their plans.

"They've sent their most powerful mages here while their vamps and shifters are attacking the norms."

I skipped to a new mind signature, and as soon as I tried to latch onto the thoughts, intense pain seared through my eyeball and into my brain as though a nail had been driven into it. I clutched at my head, doubling over. I squeezed my eyes closed and concentrated on pushing the pain out.

"Lex, what's wrong?" Tristan's large hand landed on my back and tried to soothe me.

My head tilted, and my jaw clenched until finally, the agony dulled.

"They have a . . . sorcerer . . . *and* a sorceress with them." I tried to breathe through the lingering pain and finally managed to open my eyes to find Tristan and Vanessa hovering over me. "Kali must have taught them how to block me from their minds. Shit, that hurt."

Tristan reached out and wiped his thumb over my upper lip. It came away bloody.

"They haven't been involved in the attack, though. Yet," I added.

"They're just wearing us down right now," Vanessa said.

Avoiding the sorcerers, I took my injured mind to one belonging to a warlock to study her thoughts further and nodded. They'd already figured out the north end of the island had been deserted, so they gave up on their attack up there, and the explosions stopped. But they weren't giving up for good. They were only regrouping.

"They're getting ready to hit us with their heavy guns," I confirmed, and I opened my mind to those of the entire island. *Everyone take cover! It's not over!*

People shrieked and ran into the streets before flashing away, hopefully gathering together under the protection of our weaker mages, which was protocol in the event of an attack. Many of the witches and wizards of the village may only be able to shield their homes or a single room, but that was better than nothing if our main defense collapsed.

"*Sorcerers?*" Owen asked me.

A sorcerer and a sorceress, I told him and Char. *Can you hold them?*

"*We will for as long as we can*," Char said. "*But Owen needs to get down there to protect you and Tristan.*"

Before I could argue, a succession of bright yellow and orange lights shot across the water and blasted into our shield, breaching it almost immediately. The next spell hit our watchtower right behind the council hall, blowing it into pieces. The very tower where our mages powered the shield. Owen appeared next to me at the same moment and immediately threw a bubble over Tristan, Dorian, and me.

"Come on," Tristan said, pulling Dorian back into his arms.

He flashed, and I followed his trail with Owen and Vanessa right on mine. We appeared inside the dungeons under the council hall, where they'd once jailed Tristan when he'd been accused of betraying the Amadis. I called the others to come join us, but Blossom, Jax, and Sheree refused to leave the injured behind.

"I have a shield on them," Blossom assured me. *"You just stay safe, Alexis."*

Char didn't answer me, and I couldn't locate her mind signature in the chaos, but she'd been in the tower with the other mages when the Daemoni had hit it. My heart wobbled, but I refused to believe she was dead. I couldn't handle another death so soon, especially hers. I glanced at Owen, and his face remained stoic. He refused to believe, too.

I sat against the cold, stone wall of one of the cells, closed my eyes, and used my mind to peek into others' heads until I found a vampire who peered outside from his window. Now that the main shield had collapsed, the sorcerer and sorceress seemed to have backed off. In fact, magic spells no longer rained down on the town. Only a few random shots came, as though they were double-checking that the shield had actually fallen.

I heard, *"It's a go,"* from one of them before they all disappeared, only to reappear several miles away, nearly out of my mind's reach.

"What are they doing?" I asked aloud, not about to give the all clear to the island yet. Something was up. Then I heard the planes in the distance, quickly approaching—with no mind signatures inside of them. Were they drones? The answer to my question came a moment later when the bombs began dropping. On Amadis Island.

"We can stop them," Tristan said after several bombs hit the town with loud explosions, shaking the ground beneath us. Dirt fell from the ceiling and walls.

Owen's sapphire-blue eyes squinted. "It'll take a minute to power up the shield."

"I meant *we*." Tristan looked at me, and I nodded.

"Stay here," I ordered Vanessa and Dorian.

Tristan, Owen, and I flashed outside, and we all raised our palms to the sky as more planes flew overhead and more bombs fell. We used our powers to stop three from slamming into the village and turned them toward the sea. But we'd barely rerouted them when more came. It took almost every ounce of energy I had to keep them from hitting the island. Then finally, they began to ricochet in midair like the spells had done earlier.

"*We can shield against those!*" Charlotte whooped into my mind, and I let out the air I'd held trapped in my lungs at the sound of her "voice."

Owen joined his mother and the other mages who'd survived, and they strengthened the shield over the town. Unable to hit us anymore, the jets banked away and flew off. Dozens of columns of black smoke rose into the air from the main street in town and more in the residential district. My stomach sank at the thought of Amadis lives lost. I felt the grief spreading from people's minds at the heartache right before them, but we still hadn't given them the all clear to come out from their shelters.

"Take cover, Alexis," Owen said. "We don't know if they're gone for good."

Tristan took my hand and flashed us back to the dungeons.

"Is it over?" Vanessa asked.

"Can I go back to my room?" Dorian demanded.

"We don't know yet," I said, and I gave Dorian the mom-eye for his rudeness. "And you can go back when we say you can go back."

He rolled his eyes and diverted his attention to Sasha, who had shrunk some, but remained alert.

We sat in the cold, dank cell for hours. The Daemoni mind signatures hadn't slipped completely out of range—they remained close enough for me to feel them, but not close enough to hear their thoughts and plans. I wouldn't give the green light to my people until I knew we were safe.

"*Alexis,*" Charlotte mind-spoke to me from where she and the other mages continued powering the shield from the main room above us. "*Chandra just called. She's been trying to reach you. One of her villages in India has been bombed, too.*"

My stomach sank. A little while later, another, similar report came in on Char's phone, this one from Jelani in Africa. One by one, Rina's council members checked in, delivering the same news over and over. The Daemoni, using the norms, had bombed dozens of our villages and colonies around the world.

And I couldn't do anything about it. I was stuck here in the dungeons, but even if I weren't, what could I have done? The attacks had stopped hours ago, so all I could do now was to tell them to stay undercover and keep safe.

"I feel like I'm telling everyone to just squat down like sitting ducks, when we should be fighting back. What kind of leader am I?"

"You've told them exactly what Rina would have," Tristan said, trying to assure me. But it only irked me.

I shook my head as I paced the cell. "No. We have to do more. We won't survive if we're always on the defensive. We're stronger than this. We have to fight back."

Finally, the Daemoni mind signatures retreated completely, and after having Owen return the shield to cover the entire island, I gave the all clear. We popped outside, and my heart dropped at the sight.

In contrast to the stunning sunset on the water, the destruction was heartrending.

The main street from the council hall to the pier at the other end housed the business district. Most of the village's suppliers of goods and services lined the cobblestone street, and those buildings closest to shore had been completely annihilated—the only supplier of mage reagents on the island, the Blood Bank where we donated blood for our vamps, and one of the three pubs. Other structures, like the blacksmith shop, had suffered major damage. Several homes had also, and two were destroyed altogether.

We had three fatalities on the island, and I supposed we were lucky with such a small number, but my heart shrank at more losses and more funerals. Dozens of people had been injured, several badly. Fortunately, most of them could heal themselves, and the mages who couldn't drank a healing potion made from vampire blood. It wasn't perfect and didn't completely eliminate their pain, but it helped speed the healing process.

Owen, Charlotte, and the rest of the mages did their best to put homes and businesses back together, but some parts had been completely disintegrated or burnt to ashes and others damaged beyond repair, returning none of the structures to how they'd been before the attack. We had to make the decision to destroy two more business buildings and three homes—one of them Char's—because they weren't safe for anyone to be near. She'd been able to retrieve some of her belongings, but most everything she'd owned had been destroyed by fire from the bombs.

As everyone came together to help each other, I fielded calls from around the world. The Amadis had lost hundreds of people. The Daemoni had flattened entire villages. Each casualty report felt like a punch to my stomach, leaving me breathless and my body trembling.

Not until the quiet hours between midnight and dawn were we able to return to the matriarch's mansion to assess the damage there. My stomach knotted itself once we decided our people were taken care of and we could go. I feared the extent of the destruction of the beautiful marble and stone structure that had been here for millennia. We didn't know its true age because it had already been standing when Cassandra found it over two thousand years ago, as if waiting for her discovery. If

Charlotte's house hadn't just been demolished, I would have suggested we stayed there for the night so we could see the bad news in the light of morning. Not that the darkness would affect our vision. It just seemed that the sight we would see would be more dreadful in the night.

My breath caught when we appeared in front of it.

CHAPTER 3

"Wow," I breathed. "It's completely fine."

At least, the matriarch's mansion *appeared* to be intact and unharmed from the outside. Several ancient cypress trees had been destroyed around the building, huge craters were left in the ground right next to the foundation, and bomb shrapnel was scattered over the earth. The nearby training gym had been obliterated to no more than a pile of broken stone. But the mansion itself stood in all its splendor, entirely unscathed.

"It's protected by the Angels," Ophelia said matter-of-factly. The centuries-old witch had just appeared right next to me, startling me. She gave me a smile, her face crinkling under the deep creases lining her skin, and then she bustled inside, ready to get back to work. If the children in the village hadn't needed her care and cooking so badly, she likely would have been here hours ago. Once she disappeared into the dark foyer, her voice carried out to us. "Oh, dear."

Since everyone on my team except Char had been staying at the mansion, they'd all come back with Tristan, Dorian, and me. Char did, too, needing a place to stay. We hurried inside after Ophelia, who continued moving throughout the first floor, sighing and repeating, "Oh dear, oh dear, oh dear."

Although the exterior hadn't so much as a scratch, the interior proved to be a bit of a different story. Shards of glass and various broken items littered the floors of every room— vases, lanterns, pictures, books, and antique knickknacks that had fallen from their places on shelves and the walls. A few pieces of smaller and lighter furniture lay on their sides. When Mom and I had lived in California many years ago, we'd survived a bad earthquake. The impact of the bombs right outside had caused similar damage inside the mansion.

"What a mess," Ophelia said as she traveled through the dining room where we all stood, waving her hand and putting things back right. "Easy enough to fix, though."

Blossom, Charlotte, and Owen helped her make the repairs while Tristan and I followed Dorian upstairs to his room. He was about to slam the door when Tristan caught it.

"Next time I say to do something, don't ignore me and don't argue with me," I said to Dorian as Tristan and I stood in his doorway. I'd waited to discipline him until we were in private, but he still scowled at us.

"I don't like you in my head like that," he answered, his tone not too kind as he watched his toe scuffing at the stone floor.

"Well, too bad. It works, and it's a lot faster than a cell phone."

"It's weird."

"Everything's weird about our life, but that's what it is —*our* life. Deal with it."

He looked up at me through his lashes and sneered. "Why are you on my case?"

"Because you need to listen to your mother when she calls you," Tristan said.

"You could have been killed," I added.

He rolled his eyes. "I came, didn't I?"

"Watch your tone, young man," Tristan warned.

"Don't talk to me like that," I said at the same time. "And don't roll your eyes at us!"

Gosh, we sounded like typical parents for once. A little taste of normalcy was always nice, except not when reprimanding our snotty teenager who wasn't really a teenager. Dorian lifted his head to look at each of us, and then let out a grunt and started to turn away.

Tristan took a step inside the room, right up to Dorian, crossed his arms over his chest, and glared down at our son. Dorian's eyes grew wide, and then he finally showed some kind of respect . . . and maybe fear, too, as he backed down, dropping his shoulders and his challenging glare.

"Sorry," he muttered as he stared at the floor.

Tristan clamped a hand on Dorian's shoulder. "Listen to your mother."

"Yes, sir. I promise."

We stood there in silence for another moment before Tristan and I left him for our own suite. We hadn't quite reached it at the end of the hall when Dorian's door slammed shut. I let out a sigh. Whether he stayed with us or went to the Daemoni, I was losing my baby.

"Good call on pulling the shield off the mansion," Tristan said as we picked up the few things that had fallen in our suite.

"If I'd known it would have survived like this, I would have done it much sooner." I stood on my toes, reaching above my head to rehang the curtain over the door to the balcony. "In fact, we shouldn't even waste the mages' energy in keeping it shielded now. What if the Daemoni attack again?"

"Exactly." Tristan came up behind me, easily set the curtain rod in its place, and then slid his arms around my waist. "Nobody will allow you to be unshielded."

"Or you. You're just as important as me," I reminded him.

"Not quite."

"You're my second."

"But I'm replaceable. You are not."

I turned in his arms and glared up at him as I lifted my hand to his ear and squeezed it. "Don't you ever say that again. You most certainly are *not* replaceable."

His eyes tightened as he suppressed a full-out wince. "Maybe not to you, but to the rest of the Amadis, I am."

"Don't underestimate your value, Mr. Knight." I lifted onto my toes to place my lips only an inch from his. "Without you, I'm useless, and they all know it."

He bent down to close that last bit of space and pressed his mouth to mine. The tingle that spread over my skin as our mouths moved together and our tongues met was most welcome, exciting yet calming after this terrible day. His hands caressing my back gave me a feeling of security, and I relaxed into his arms, ignoring the pull on my mind.

"*Alexis!*" Vanessa yelled into my head, her persistence breaking through.

I groaned as Tristan continued kissing me. *A little privacy, please?*

"*Um, sorry, but there's something you need to see on TV.*"

I sighed and pulled away. *Again? Can't it wait?*

"*Oh, I'm sure it'll be on in the morning, but you probably want to know about it now.*"

On our way down. I looked up at Tristan with a frown. "I guess there's more for us to see on the news."

Tristan and I went back downstairs and found everyone in the theater-style seats in the media room, their eyes glued to the multiple screens hanging on the wall. Apparently all but one television had survived the bombing. The TVs showed the same press conference being translated for the stations around the world we were tuned into. The English version's volume was turned up so we could hear some representative of the

United States government who stood behind a pedestal with an American flag on it. Across the bottom of the screen scrolled the words, "Are we on the verge of World War III? Leaders around the world believe so." The lady on the screen with the salt-and-pepper hair wasn't the president or vice president or anyone I recognized, but based on the lies she spewed, I'd bet she was Daemoni or in their back pocket. Tristan and I stood behind the occupied chairs and watched.

"It is true that there have been several airstrikes around the world," the woman spoke into the microphone as cameras flashed from the press. "These *creatures* need to be stopped. They have ravaged our streets and killed hundreds of thousands of people in every corner of the globe in less than a day."

I bit back a snicker at her choice of words—like globes had corners.

"They seemed to have been going for the shock factor, and they have definitely shocked us. But we didn't stand around and wait. We humans will not bow down to these *monsters* that shouldn't even exist." She leaned forward over the pedestal and glared directly into the camera. "We will fight back, and we have already started. As of this morning, we were able to locate the strongholds of the most dangerous faction of these creatures. They claim to be our ally and promise protection, but they are the most vicious of all, preying on the hopes and fears of innocent humans. They inhabit towns in nearly every country, and we struck every cluster we know about, including their main headquarters in the Aegean Sea, off the coast of Greece."

I slapped my hand over my mouth, but my gasp was still audible. My body began to tremble as the bitch continued, filling me with anger.

"We believe the bombs caused extensive damage, but we will not be complacent. These creatures are difficult, nearly impossible to kill, as many people have learned when they tried to protect themselves from attack today. We will continue seeking out members of this most dangerous faction, called the Amadis, as an end to them will likely end all of the attacks. Beware if any of these non-human entities approach you and offer protection. *None* of them are safe, especially those claiming to be good, because they tell only lies. They will try to deceive you into welcoming them into your homes so they can kill you when you least expect it. We are most especially interested in locating this pair."

The scene of the press conference disappeared from the screen, replaced by photos filling the entire space with two very familiar faces—Tristan's and mine. And I couldn't help it. The urge started in the pit of my belly and bubbled up my throat until it burst out of my mouth. I nearly doubled over with the giggles.

"She . . . can't be . . . serious," I gasped as I tried to regain control.

"They have assumed various aliases over the years," the woman's voice continued as our mugs remained on the screen, "but you will notice the woman is none other than A.K. Emerson, the internationally bestselling author who supposedly died two-and-a-half years ago while honeymooning with this man. They have both faked their deaths, proving their guilt. Emerson's books, read by millions around the world, are about these exact same creatures who have murdered so many people today, on her orders. She must be found, and she must be stopped."

"Looks to me like the shiela's pretty serious, princess," Jax said.

"I don't even . . ." I shook my head as the giggles over the ridiculousness of it all died away. I let out one last laugh. "What the *hell*?"

"Dude, Alexis," Owen said, turning in his seat to look at us, "you're like Harry Potter. They just made you Public Enemy Number One."

I rolled my eyes. My body still shook from the shock and absurdity, and a part of me still wanted to laugh. But another part of me wanted to fly into a rage. *Control. Maintain control. Do not lose your temper.* It took everything I had to hang on to it.

"She's obviously working for the Daemoni." Blossom gestured toward the woman on the screens. "She pronounced Amadis perfectly on her first try."

"They're using their best weapon," Tristan said from beside me.

I nodded. "Lies and deceit. The Daemoni have effectively turned all humans against us. They didn't have to transform the norms into vamps and shifters to build their army, after all."

"That's good for the norms' souls," Sheree piped up.

"True," I said, "but not good for us. How are we going to fight the norms when we're supposed to protect them?"

The question haunted me through what little remained of the night. I must have drifted off because when the nightmarish vision returned, the woman being shot by the Norman soldiers didn't just look like me, but *was* me. I'd replaced Mom as their target.

I didn't visit the cliffs the next morning. The bombing yesterday loosened my grip on the past and brought me fully into the present. I longed for guidance from Mom, Rina, and the rest of my ancestors more than ever, but enjoying my solitude on the side of a cliff while watching the sun rise felt like a luxury I couldn't afford.

"I suppose it's time to call my first council meeting," I said to Tristan as I sat at Rina's desk—my desk—sipping coffee and staring mindlessly at all of the newspapers spread out in front of me. Headlines screamed WAR and ATTACK and THEY'RE REAL! on the front pages. My face was plastered all over them, right next to Tristan's.

The talking heads on television droned on with words that

had been force-fed to them, speculating with each other about the ongoing supernatural attacks and the mysterious and very dangerous Amadis faction that had instigated it all.

"I'd say that's a good idea," Tristan replied from his seat on the couch by the fireplace. "You might want to wait until we get word from Solomon, though. He should be able to give us news straight from the U.N."

God bless Solomon. I wouldn't have blamed him if he'd been locked in his room, mourning Rina's death as her life-mate, but he'd said he needed a distraction, so he returned to his post at the United Nations a few days ago. We hadn't heard from him since everything went down yesterday, though.

"Good point. I suspect some of the council members need another day to help their areas recover, too."

Tristan looked over at me. "Don't expect them all to show up in person. A conference call will have to suffice."

"That's better anyway. I don't want anyone leaving their regions." I mentally called out to Char and asked her to give everyone a call and set it up, and then I stood and walked over to Tristan. My body purposely blocked his view of the television screen and CNN, which reported nothing new, but merely played scenes from yesterday on a continuous loop. He reached out to place his hands on my hips, but I didn't budge when he tried to pull me to him. "In the meantime, we need to make sure they can't attack us like that again."

His gaze jumped up to my face, and he lifted an eyebrow. "Retaliation?"

I widened my eyes with mock innocence and placed my hand on my chest. "Amadis wouldn't do such a thing!"

His eyes narrowed with skepticism. "But you would."

My lips turned slightly in a half-smile, and I cocked my head. "And so would you."

He didn't argue with me. "What's going on in that head of yours?"

"I think we can figure out where one of the Daemoni's

covens is. Several of their mind signatures went straight east when they left, and I saw this in one of their minds." I shared with him a visual of some kind of residential compound outside a city comprised of modern buildings mixed with old Middle Eastern architecture and a bridge somewhat resembling the Golden Gate in San Francisco.

"Based on that skyline, it looks like the outskirts of Istanbul."

I smiled. "I knew you'd know. If we get close enough, I can find their signatures again and pinpoint their location."

He pulled me harder this time, into his lap. His strong arms embraced me, and I leaned my head against his shoulder. "And what do you plan to do, *ma lykita*? Convert them?"

I shrugged, not having considered that possibility. "Of course, if they want to, but that's unlikely. Their minds were pure evil, and I want to get rid of them. Make sure they can never attack us like that again."

"So retaliation."

"Well, it's not really retaliation if our goal is to *defend* ourselves, right? To prevent more people from being harmed or killed?"

"Alexis—"

I sat up and turned to look him in the eye. "We're protecting our island and our people. We might be protecting norms, too, because if they're bombing villages and colonies, Tristan, then they could be killing nearby norms, also."

"*Ma lykita*—"

"If we can show our people that we can stop this coven, then they'll see how they can stop the others. We owe it to the families who lost loved ones yesterday. To those who fear for their lives now."

"Alexis, I'm not arguing with you. I agree."

I drew back and stared at him. "You do?"

"Yes. And I think the others will, too."

"Even if it's not the Amadis way?"

34

"Everything else in the world has changed. We must, too."

I nodded as Mom's, Rina's, and Cassandra's words from yesterday morning came back to me. "Exactly. And we don't have to kill them. We just need to flush them out and expose them for who *they* truly are. Including Lucas. We're going to fight fire with fire. He's not the only one who can use the media to sway the public."

Tristan smiled, catching on. "The world needs to know who the real Public Enemy Number One is."

I pressed my lips together and stared at my hands twisting in my lap. "Do you honestly think this is a good idea? Or am I just being hot-headed as usual?"

"I think it's a show of strength, which is necessary. Between the change in leadership, the attacks on the Normans, and the bombings of the Amadis, the Daemoni will think we're weak and disorganized, trying to rebuild. They won't be expecting this."

I mulled over this and finally nodded, but couldn't quite look up at him yet.

"You know I'm completely relying on you for this strategy stuff, right? Because I have absolutely no idea what I'm doing. Everything comes from my gut instinct, but that usually leads me to doing stupid things."

He lifted my chin, forcing me to look up at him. "I won't let you do anything stupid, my love. I'm here for you. I'm by your side, as I've promised I would be."

His eyes studied mine for a long moment, as though ensuring I understood and accepted.

"Thank you," I whispered.

His mouth spread into a lovely grin. "Do you really think I'd let my wife look bad? How would that reflect on me?"

I chuckled and rolled my eyes, and then mentally called my team to my office to formulate our plan.

"Good idea, but not the part where you go, Alexis,"

Charlotte said after we'd mapped it all out. "It's too dangerous."

My head jerked to the side to glare at her. "You know I'm not staying behind. You need my telepathy."

"I have to agree it's too dangerous," Blossom said as she combed her fingers through her long, dark blond hair. My gaze shot to her now. She knew me better than to think I'd cower from a fight just because I was the matriarch. "Those sorcerers do a number on your head. It can't be good for you."

My glare softened with her concern for the headaches the sorcerers gave me.

"Then your telepathy won't be any good anyway," Vanessa added. "And since they seem to like your electrical power so much, they'll drain your energy, too, making your whole self useless."

I suppressed a frustrated growl. The sorcerers, the Daemoni's most powerful mages, could pull energy from the world to boost their own magic. Kali had a special magnetism to my electrical powers, like vampires had to my blood, and she'd tried to drain me every chance she had. No doubt the other sorcerers would, too.

"I'm going," I insisted as I stood up to my full height— which wasn't much—and crossed my arms over my chest. "Stop ganging up on me."

"Chances are low the sorcerers will even be there," Tristan said. "They don't play well with others."

"Agreed," Owen piped up. "I seriously doubt they're shacking up with a coven of mages weaker than them. It's not like they need the protection."

Charlotte's mouth twisted as she considered this, but she had to know the guys were right. She, and Blossom and Vanessa, too, also had to know their argument was futile.

"We'd better be prepared," Char said as her way of giving in. "Vanessa, stay close to her. If someone gets a drain on her powers, you'll have to break the connection."

"Sure, I'll get my ass fried. Again," Vanessa grumbled, and I gave her a grateful smile.

"What if the island's attacked again while we're gone?" Sheree asked. "Char and Owen won't be here to help with the shield."

"Then that means we've failed," I muttered. "The whole point is to keep them from attacking again."

"Unless other mages come from somewhere else," Vanessa said. "There are covens all over."

I looked at Tristan. His eyes were already a little glazed as he considered the options to determine the best solution.

"We'll be facing some powerful mages, even if the sorcerers aren't with the coven," he said after a moment. "We need Char and Owen with us."

Owen gave a sharp nod. "Damn straight."

"Wouldn't miss it," Charlotte agreed, and I glared at her again. She shrugged. "This is my job."

"And mine, too," I countered. She opened her mouth to argue, but then snapped it shut.

"Stubborn like your mother," she groused, and for once, I accepted that remark.

"So we need to gather all the mages we can to the council hall and have them work together to keep Owen's shield up," Tristan said. "Blossom?"

She nodded. "I'll stay here."

Jax shifted his weight and rubbed his hand over his bald head as he stared at the floor. I didn't have to read his mind to know his dilemma.

"Stay here in case Blossom and the others need you, Jax," I said.

His eyes shot up to me with surprise, and I nodded. He gave me a grateful smile. He hadn't wanted to choose between protecting me and protecting Blossom, but I didn't see why he had to make that choice. Being near a city in the desert, this mission didn't necessarily require the kinds of advantages a were-croc from the Australian Outback provided.

"Better hope the council doesn't get a whiff of this plan," Charlotte said once we'd finished going over everything. "Especially your part."

"Times have changed," I said. "We have, too, and they need to get used to it. Besides, with them, it's better to ask forgiveness than permission."

"You don't need to ask anyone for permission or forgiveness," she replied. "You just need to be prepared for some backlash."

I snickered. The sass she'd just given to me was nothing compared to how the council, and probably many Amadis, would react, but that was okay. In fact, it was all part of my and Tristan's overall plan.

I placed my hands on my hips, jutting one to the side as I looked at the faces of my team members. "I'll say it right now, so it doesn't come as a surprise at tomorrow's meeting. *You* guys are my council members. There are some of Rina's who I will keep, like Solomon. But anyone who gives me backlash for doing what I'm supposed to do—for protecting the Amadis and the Normans—and doesn't like *how* I do it, well, then, I don't need them. This is war, and we are going to *fight*, not stand around like a bunch of pussycats." I paused as my gaze fell on the were-tiger, then quickly added, "No offense, Sheree."

"None taken," she said with a small smile.

"There may be casualties," I continued. "God forbid, but we might actually have to kill people, and maybe not just Daemoni. Not when they have the norms turned against us."

"This is no longer a gentleman's war," Tristan said from beside me, succinctly saying what I'd been trying to iterate. "The secrets are out. The norms are more involved in our war than they'd ever been before in the history of mankind. It's going to be bloody, and it's going to get very ugly."

"And whether we like it or not, we're going to get as bloody and ugly as we need to if it means stopping the Daemoni," I said. "We will *not* let them take over this world."

"Cheers to that." Char pretended to lift a glass to us.

"You know you're preaching to the choir?" Owen asked.

I nodded. "Yeah, well, tomorrow will be a different story, and we need to know our choir is going to back us up."

After they all left to prepare for tonight's covert mission, Tristan and I sat on the antique couch and stared at the fire in the hearth.

"Nice job today," he said as his hand gripped and kneaded my shoulder. "You sounded like a real matriarch."

I snorted. "Did I?"

He nodded. "You were good."

"I'm glad you think so. I'm still not so sure."

"Trust me. You were." He gave my neck a gentle squeeze. "It looks like they were right."

"Who?"

"Rina and Sophia. You *are* ready for this."

I blew out a sigh. "Not exactly. I guess I just know how to put on a good show."

"Fake it till you make it, if that's what you have to do."

I leaned into his arms, and my voice fell softly. "I don't even know how to fake it. I don't know what I'm doing at all."

He slid his hand down my arm and pulled me closer to him. "You need to trust yourself more . . . and me and the rest of your team. Your new council."

I rested my head against his chest. "I do trust you. And them. But not so much myself."

He brushed the hair away from my face and grasped my chin between his thumb and forefinger, lifting my head up to look at him. The gold in his eyes sparkled. "You're making smart decisions, my love. Trust me. If we thought this was a bad idea, we'd tell you. We'd give you other perspectives and ideas to consider, like Char did. That's our job more than ever now."

His eyes held mine for a long moment until I nodded with understanding. Then he leaned in and pressed his luscious lips to mine. My anxieties trickled away as his kiss continued to calm me.

CHAPTER 4

A little after midnight, after making sure Dorian was asleep and Sasha was planted at his door as his protector, Tristan and I prepared to head out to meet the others on the cliff. We'd hoped to have plenty of time to search the area around Istanbul until we found the coven, using the cover of darkness to hide from any norms who might be awake. Then we'd execute our plan right before sunrise, when most of the Daemoni would be hunkering down for the day, and be back here before anyone on the island missed us. In the meantime, Blossom would ensure the media received our news release in time to hit Europe's morning newscasts.

We ran into the first snag of our plan before we could even leave the mansion. Julia stood at the bottom of the stairs, her dark eyes narrowed with suspicion as Tristan and I descended. The vampire who'd loved my grandmother in more ways than one had made herself scarce since the funeral, staying away from the mansion and anything to do with leading the Amadis. I hadn't decided yet what to do about her, so I'd let her mourn in peace.

"You're planning something," she accused before we even

landed on the bottom step. "A covert mission you're keeping from the council."

"Which makes it none of your business," I said, lifting my chin. She stood more than half-a-foot taller than me, but I refused to let her intimidate me anymore. I hadn't liked her since the day we'd met, and the feeling was fairly mutual. We tolerated each other for Rina's sake, but I no longer had to.

"This is a disgrace." She glared at me as she tossed her raven-black hair over her shoulder.

My brows shot up. "Excuse me?"

"What you're doing. Ms. Katerina would have never been so secretive, doing things unbecoming of the Amadis."

"You don't even know what we're doing. And you're right. Rina never would have. She didn't *have* to. Things are different now. You of all people should understand why we need to act."

"I, of all people, know what your grandmother would have wanted, and *you* are disrespecting her memory."

My mouth fell open. Tristan stepped down, into Julia's personal space.

"And *you* are disrespecting your matriarch," he growled quietly.

Julia's hard gaze snapped to him, then back at me. "You shouldn't even be the matriarch."

My jaw dropped even lower, making the muscle pop. Then I snapped it shut, my teeth clacking audibly. Because I stood shorter than both of them, I stayed on the higher step to be closer to eye level, and I leaned toward her.

"I'm going to let that slide as a statement made out of inconsolable grief for the woman you mourn, and not made as an act of treason against *me*," I said. "Because *I* don't go around half-assedly accusing people of being traitors. However, I honestly don't think you knew Rina as well as you think you do, nor do you truly understand her and what she'd want me to do. She knew—still knows—that I am not her, and yet she entrusted me to fill her shoes. So think before you spout off with your advice for me."

The vampire's nostrils flared as we glared at each other. "She didn't think you'd be filling those shoes until you were educated properly. And do not worry. I have no advice for you. I don't know how to think at that level."

She meant it as an insult, but she simply reinforced what I'd told my team earlier.

"Then consider yourself dismissed." I pushed past her and strode for the front door. "No need to attend the meeting tomorrow. Spend your day preparing to leave the island, please. You can serve our people out on the frontlines, where you belong."

Tristan pushed the wooden door open, and we both passed through. It shut heavily in the stunned vampire's face.

"Well," I said, "she's off the council a lot easier than I expected."

Tristan took my hand. "Rina trusted her for a reason."

"She tried to banish you from the Amadis. I don't care about her excuse that Martin or Kali or whoever had any kind of influence over her. I could never bring myself to fully trust her on my council. And as we just saw, she's too old school and will never respect me."

"I'm not arguing with your decision. I'm glad to have her gone, too. Just don't get crazy and try to banish her from the Amadis."

"Don't worry. I won't stoop to her level."

We flashed then to the cliffs where the rest of my team waited. If not for our superior vision or the full moon striking their blond hair, we'd have barely been able to make out Owen, Vanessa, and Char, who were dressed in black fighting leathers. Sheree, however, sat in her tiger form, her black and orange tail swishing around her paws. Two others who joined us had already transformed, too, into their wolf alter-egos.

One of the silver linings of Owen spending time with Kali

was that he'd learned and perfected the magical art of creating portals from one place on Earth to another. Norms had learned how to block flashing's magical energy to ensnare us, such as when they had captured Vanessa and me in the middle of nowhere Georgia when we'd flashed from the destroyed Amadis jet last spring. So this new skill of Owen's proved to be quite convenient, allowing us to travel even faster and farther than flashing, using a different kind of magic the norms couldn't impede. He used the ability now to open an entry straight into the outskirts of Istanbul, and we stepped through the portal, leaving Amadis Island for a dark alley on the edges of the city in Turkey.

Charlotte and Owen cloaked and shielded us, and I reached my mind out, scanning the signatures, searching for the evil minds who'd attacked us yesterday. I came across a nest of vampires who'd just finished feeding—we'd arrived too late to help those poor norms—and werewolf packs and feline dens roamed the countryside under the full moon. Unfortunately, I couldn't locate the mages.

"They probably have a powerful shield up," Owen whispered.

"I sense dark magic in the air," Char added. She wrinkled her nose. "The stench is nauseating."

I pressed my lips together and went back to the vampires' minds, hoping to find any clues.

"I'm not getting anything," I said after a while.

"Then we search on foot," Tristan said.

Since flashing was too dangerous these days, we raced through the streets of the suburbs under our magical cloaks, searching for the compound I'd seen in the warlocks' minds after they attacked us. We split up, covering more area faster, and I kept us all connected through my mind. I tried to watch the scenery through everyone else's eyes, but after the third time of running into Tristan or Sheree because I couldn't see my own surroundings, I had to forego that idea.

"*Quarter mile ahead,*" Vanessa said. She and Owen had been running three blocks to our right. "*On your side, Char. The odor is coming from up there.*"

The tiger running beside me sneezed in agreement. I smelled something faint, but Tristan's and my senses weren't quite as strong as the vampire's and shifters'.

"*The wolves smell it, too,*" Charlotte said from three blocks to our left.

Tristan, Sheree, and I cut toward her and the werewolves as soon as we could. Vanessa and Owen merged in with us. We slowed down as we approached the dead end of the road, where the compound sat on the edge of town, looking dark and empty. Owen joined our cloaks so we could see each other as we stood a block away, studying the place. I reached my mind out, searching for the Daemoni mind signatures, but found none close by.

Are we muffled? I asked Owen, and he nodded, so I spoke aloud, though in a hushed whisper. "There's a wolf pack that lives on the opposite end of town, and I sense a vamp nest about four miles away, in the next town over, I think. They're all hunting and terrorizing."

Sheree dropped her big head, and a soft growl rumbled in her throat. She'd rather be helping the norms or trying to convert any newly turned. I lay my hand on the soft fur of her shoulder.

"Sorry, but we need to do this to protect us all," I told her. "Otherwise, there won't be an Amadis left to help anyone."

Her orange, black, and white head nodded in understanding, but I could feel her frustration and heartache for the norms whose lives couldn't be saved tonight. At least not by us. I felt the pain, too. War sucked.

"So no stragglers nearby?" Charlotte asked me. "No one's going to ambush us?"

I shook my head. "I don't sense anyone. Of course, I don't sense anyone inside there, either."

"Their shield is thick," Owen said. "What we see is probably a mirage. What they *want* everyone to see."

I gnawed on my lip as a thought occurred to me. "What if this isn't really the place? What if they only made it *look* like the place?"

"Then they know you saw it in their minds," Tristan said. "There's no reason to create a decoy unless there's somebody to trap."

"Which means they'd given the image to me on purpose." The fabric of this grand idea began to unravel around us. "They could be setting us up."

"Are there any other places shielded so heavily?" Tristan asked the warlocks. Both Char and Owen shook their heads in response.

"Vanessa's and the shifters' noses led here. It's the only place the Daemoni have secured," Owen said.

Tristan looked at me. "And you don't sense any other Daemoni mind signatures close?"

I checked again. "None. The vamps and the shifters have moved even farther away."

"So if it's a trap," he said, "they're all hiding inside, and our mission is to flush them out anyway, not invade or fight."

"Right," I said. "Create a scene, attract the norms' attention, and expose the Daemoni as the dangerous ones when their spells start flying everywhere."

Owen rocked back on his heels. "So we proceed with the plan."

All eyes landed on me for confirmation. I nodded. "Let's do this."

Everyone scattered, taking their places. Sheree and the werewolves would keep guard, Vanessa and Char hid in the shadows waiting on our signal, and Tristan, Owen, and I silently skirted around the base of the large home. I zapped electricity close to the ground to light up the coven's shield so Owen could possibly find a weak spot.

"There." He grabbed my wrist and stopped me. He pointed to a spot on the ground covered in tiny, white granules. "Huh. I don't think it's a trap. This is sloppy for their caliber, which means they're cocky. Too arrogant to realize they've made a mistake."

"That's a sorcerer for you," Tristan muttered.

"What is it?" I asked.

Owen swirled a finger in the white stuff, then held the tip to his tongue. He nodded. "Yep. Rock salt. One of them must have used it for a spell or incantation and didn't clean it all up. It's interfering with the integrity of their shield. Idiots."

"Will it interfere with your magic?"

"Salt can help or hinder my magic, and in this case, hinder. So we're going to blow it away. Our timing needs to be perfect. As soon as the salt's removed, their weak spot will strengthen."

The three of us knelt down and huddled near the small pile of salt. I held my palm close to the shield, near the ground, and let out a slow charge of electricity. Tiny cracks of blue light spread from my hand, lighting up a small area of the shield, but the charge didn't penetrate it. After several long moments, my heart racing the whole time, the edge that touched the salt began to crinkle and retract, like a piece of plastic held above a flame. Owen moved his hand right next to mine, while I continued melting a small gap into the shield.

"Ready, Tristan," he whispered.

From my other side, Tristan blew a huge gust of wind, scattering the salt. Immediately, the shield started reforming against my charge, reaching for the clean ground. As soon as the last granule cleared, Owen shot his own power at the shield. It increased the damage I did exponentially, opening a gap big enough for each of us to slip through.

"I'll hold the opening," Owen said. "You guys hurry."

Tristan and I gave the signal, and Vanessa and Char darted out of the shadows and under the shield. I jumped to the flat roof, Vanessa right behind me in case I needed backup. While we crept across the roof, Tristan and Char stayed on the ground, doing their part. Once Vanessa and I scoped out all of the conductive materials up here, we moved to the center, and I used them to create a web of electricity across the top of the building. The charge flowed into the structure, sizzling through wires and metal, causing appliances to pop and spark. At the same time, I used my other palm to push Amadis power down through the roof and into the building. Meanwhile, Tristan was lighting up the perimeter with fire, and Char followed right behind him, fueling the flames with magic. The sleeping mind signatures inside sprang awake and chaos erupted.

"*Now,*" Tristan said into my mind.

Let's go, I told Vanessa as I tried to run for the edge of the roof. Except I could barely move. My body felt suddenly weighed down, as though the gravity had shifted under my feet, and I would sink through the roof and into the house. All of my energy flowed like a river through my veins and drained out of my palm and into the building—it was being *drawn* out of my body rather than me pushing it. Then an ice pick shoved into my brain. Gasping from the pain, I pressed my hand to the side of my head. No, not a physical ice pick, but it sure as hell felt like one. The sorcerers were here.

They've got me! I managed to scream out to Vanessa, but I couldn't be sure she heard me through the block on my mind.

She was already on the edge of the roof, ready to jump, but caught herself when she looked over her shoulder at me. She spun and charged, slamming into my body.

"Oof." The sound came out of my mouth involuntarily as Vanessa knocked me down with her full strength. Damn, vampires were like freakin' boulders. But it worked.

"Are you good?" she asked as she helped me up.

I nodded, keeping my hand fisted to protect the sorcerer from reaching my power. We ran for the edge of the roof and jumped. I landed on the balls of my feet only inches from the flames that already reached two-thirds up the side of the building. We ran past Owen, and he followed us out into the street, where we turned and watched under the protection of his cloak.

Over a dozen mages poured out of the house, a couple of them running to douse the flames with magic, but Char's spell prevented them from extinguishing the fire easily. In fact, every time they tried, the flames only grew higher, casting a bright orange glow over the neighborhood. Good thing her spell would also keep them contained to only this building. The rest of the mages searched for us.

"Come out, come out wherever you are," a female warlock taunted, her gaze sweeping side to side as she tried to locate us.

The fire must have lit up the norms' windows or perhaps the loud roar of the blaze woke them. Several came out of their residences in nightclothes and wrapped in blankets. They only stared wide-eyed at first, taking in the scene of a massive fire, the flames casting dancing shadows on their faces. As we had hoped, some had their cell phones out, filming the scene. Then the mages started shooting spells that blasted into the street. The norms screamed and ran.

A spell shot toward a fleeing child, and I jumped behind the girl, blocking the hit. But although I was still under the cloak and shield, the ricochet showed the mages exactly where we stood.

"Go," Char ordered. "Get Alexis out of here."

Tristan, Owen, Vanessa, and I took off down the street, Owen keeping a cloak over us while Char protected Sheree and the wolves. They weren't far behind us, but needed to serve as a distraction to give us time for me to escape. I'd insisted on coming, but since the sorcerer had indeed been with the coven, I was in too much danger to stay. Vanessa had been right about my electrical power being a weakness. We hadn't come for an all-out fight anyway and didn't need to strengthen them with my power. Or put the norms' lives in any more danger. Our only choice was to run.

"*They've exposed me!*" Charlotte called out.

I glanced over my shoulder. She and the shifters were behind us, their shield and cloak gone. Spells shot at them, and the wolves spun around and took off running, snapping and growling, back toward the Daemoni. Sheree followed, letting out a loud roar.

No! I yelled at them. *Retreat. You're almost here!*

Char reached us just then, and Owen pulled her into our protection. The were-animals came sprinting down the road, spells shooting at their heels. People screamed from behind windows as they watched the beasts run by.

"Hurry, Owen," I muttered as he worked at creating the portal. He finished just in time to protect the shifters, and then we all scrambled through the hole in the air to safety.

We fell into the sea. Although Owen could create a portal to leave the island, he couldn't create one that entered the island within its shield. We swam for land and collapsed on the beach near the mansion.

"Nice job," I said, congratulating everyone as I pushed myself to my feet.

"I think our mission was accomplished," Char agreed. "That was cutting it close, though."

The sky began to lighten overhead, and a spectacular sunrise probably lit up the water on the other side of the island. But we didn't have time to watch it.

Owen jumped to his feet. "Let's go see if it paid off."

Except for the wolves, who'd already transformed and left for their homes in the village, the rest of us hauled ourselves to the mansion. Blossom and Jax greeted us inside the foyer.

"No problems here?" I asked.

She shook her head. "No. All's good."

We gathered in the media room just in time for the morning news to come on across Europe.

"We've received a red alert for another supernatural terrorist," an anchorwoman reported from behind a standard news desk. A picture of a man with white hair and a white goatee, but fairly young looking showed on the screen. Lucas. I almost squealed. "This man, Lucas Emerson, is reported to be the actual ringleader of the recent and continuing attacks on the human race. He is considered powerful and very dangerous. If you see him, please alert your local authorities immediately. Do *not* approach him yourself."

"Good thinking to keep the norms away from him, Blossom," I said. She gave me a proud grin.

We watched the news come on in every country, reporting the story Blossom had submitted. The Amadis had people in the media, and we knew a couple of executive-level contacts. Since the Daemoni obviously controlled the news, though, I hadn't been certain our people would be able to air the story. They'd come through for us.

We celebrated our victory for several hours, until the east coast of the U.S. finally began waking up. The morning news shows began with our story.

"Um . . . hold on for a moment, folks." The news anchor, in the middle of reporting about Lucas, pressed a finger to her ear and nodded before looking back at the camera. "I apologize. There's been some kind of mistake."

The channel cut to a commercial. When the news program returned, the scene had changed from the anchor at her desk to several people at the front of what appeared to be the White House pressroom. The podium displayed the president's seal, although he wasn't present. I recognized the vice president, however, as well as the woman who had held the conference the other day.

And I also recognized Lucas.

He wore a suit with a red, white, and blue tie, looking like a professional businessman rather than an evil warlord of demons. My stomach sank.

"Fuck me," I whispered under my breath. "He's in the *White House*?"

"We apologize for this last-minute calling of the press, especially at this early hour," the woman said into the microphone. "However, false news has already been spreading around the world, and we needed to put an immediate stop to it. Madam Vice President?"

The other woman with Lucas nodded and stepped up to the podium. "News stations around the world in earlier time zones than us have been reporting false information about a fine gentleman, Lucas Emerson, who is here with us now. The story proclaimed Mr. Emerson as leader of the supernatural terrorist group the Amadis—"

I shuddered at the thought. We most certainly had not said that in the news release we submitted.

"—which has been attacking, murdering, and terrorizing humans around the world. It is believed the news story was submitted by the Amadis themselves in a blatant attack of libel and scandal on Mr. Emerson, who is a well-respected defense contractor serving several countries, including the United States of America. I can personally vouch that Mr. Emerson is not associated with the Amadis in any way, and is, in fact, helping us build defense systems against the supernatural creatures."

Several snorts sounded around the room. My heart stopped as Lucas stepped up to the microphone.

"I have known about the Amadis group long before its blatant attacks and have spent much time, effort, and resources on trying to defeat them," he said. At least that wasn't a lie. "Now I am working with militaries around the world to train and prepare them to fight these abominable and unnatural creatures. With diligence and determination, we *can* defeat them, and they know it is only a matter of time. Therefore, they are grasping at straws by accusing me of their own atrocious acts. Consider the pen name of their leader—

A.K. Emerson. She has previously claimed that she is my daughter."

He looked directly into the camera now, as though he looked directly at me. Which was exactly what he intended.

"Rest assured that I would *never* produce such scum. She is deluded. You have seen her insanity on camera in the past during interviews. And this instability makes her more dangerous than any enemy man has ever faced. This footage proves that she must be stopped immediately."

Lucas's face faded out as a video played, showing a nighttime scene of a home on fire, people screaming in fear and running chaotically through the street. Lights flashed across the screen and blasted into homes. Two wolves and a tiger ran down the road, looking feral as they appeared to be chasing innocent humans. The scene cut to daytime with authorities investigating the sight. Four charred bodies, two the size of a child, lay in the street, the camera focusing in on the gruesome image. Then the scene changed once again.

"As you can see, she and her husband were directly involved in this sadistic attack on an innocent family in Istanbul, Turkey."

The new video showed footage of Tristan and me at the side of the house. A flame shot out of Tristan's hand and into a window. The video was bogus, but we couldn't exactly call the media and tell them what really happened.

"You know her as A.K. Emerson," Lucas said when his face returned to the screen, "but her real name is Alexis Ames Knight. *She* is the dangerous one you must be wary of. *She* is the one you must report to authorities if you see her. She is the one you should not approach on your own, but allow the authorities to do their job. If you're watching, Mrs. Knight, take heed: We will not back down until we have reclaimed this world as ours. We will make you *all* extinct. Souls like yours can never win."

I threw up a little in my mouth.

"Asshole liar," Vanessa muttered.

"Actually, he didn't state a single lie," Tristan corrected. "Excluding the video, anyway."

"No," I agreed, "except he has the norms convinced that he's one of them. When he says *we*, they have no idea he means the Daemoni. When he says souls like ours, they think he means the damned. He has them completely snowed, and the world is going to end because of him."

"I can't believe he turned that around on us," Blossom said.

"It's not terribly surprising," Char replied. "We don't think like him."

I stared at Lucas's face on the screen, and my skin crawled. "Well, maybe we need to start."

CHAPTER 5

I turned on my heel and strode out of the room before I totally lost my cool. Tristan followed me to my office.

"You didn't see this coming?" I asked him as soon as the door shut.

"I see solutions, not the future. I don't know all the facts on their side, so I can't see what their best decisions are. I didn't know just how far up the political ring Lucas had reached."

"Pretty high up, I'd say. The freaking vice president of the United States vouched for him. *Praised* him!" I blew out a breath pregnant with frustration and despair as I dropped into my chair behind the desk. I set my elbows on the desktop and rubbed my temples. "They may as well be worshipping Satan himself. How do we protect people like that? Why should we?"

"They don't know, my love. We have to believe in the goodness of humanity."

I looked up at him and tried to smile, but couldn't. I didn't see his face, but saw the video of the blackened bodies instead. Was there any way that could have been real? The fire was supposed to have been contained. What had the Daemoni done? Tears stung my eyes.

"I don't know how to fight this kind of darkness, Tristan. They murdered those poor, innocent children and made *us* look like the baby-killers."

He came around to my side of the desk, leaned against its edge, and crossed his legs at the ankles. "We can't underestimate them."

"I don't get how they did it. How did they see us? We were cloaked. How did they keep all of those norms quiet about what *they* did? There were dozens of witnesses and cameras."

"Powerful, dark magic. Mind control and memory erasure. Perhaps even possession." He lifted his hands, palms up. "They have all sorts of weapons at their disposal."

"So do we. But we can't use them."

"We *won't* use them. It's not worth it. Trust me, *ma lykita*. We will fight the right way."

"And we will lose," I said with a sigh.

He squatted next to me and placed a large, warm, comforting hand on my shoulder. "Council meeting starts in five. Let's figure out how we *can* win."

I forced myself to my feet and wrapped my arms around his neck. "I'm so glad you know what you're doing, because I haven't the slightest clue about war strategy. Or how to counter someone who's trying to take over the world."

"You know more than you think you do."

"Why? Because I have Lucas's blood in my veins?"

Thanks to the asshole sperm-donor, I had a darkness in me that my predecessors hadn't possessed. But I still didn't think I could ever know how to think like him. I wasn't sure I wanted to, but with all of humanity's souls at stake, I might not have a choice.

"No. Because you are the matriarch and leader of a powerful society and army, with the Angels behind you." He kissed my forehead, then added, "And because you have me."

"Thank the Angels." I tried to smile at the cocky grin he gave me, but couldn't. "I'm so scared," I whispered as I leaned my head on his shoulder. "So afraid of doing the wrong thing."

"There will always be that fear," he said, his voice low and serious. "Nobody who's ever been in war knows if any decision is absolutely right. At least, nobody with a conscience. I'm sorry, *ma lykita*, I wish I could tell you it would be easy, but always questioning yourself is part of being a leader."

And I thought simply being an adult sucked. Being a leader was like parenthood, except with thousands of children and a million times that many lives relying on me.

"*Alexis?*" Char called to me from the media room. "*There's more news on the telly.*"

Yay, I thought with a sigh as I reached for the remote control, wondering what was going to knock us down next.

"Breaking News" scrolled across the top of the screen, an anchorman sat at his desk, and video footage played in a corner box, showing people lowering various national flags from a long line of poles in front of a glass office building. "We have just received confirmation from the White House. With an overwhelming vote, unanimous by all of the major powers, the United Nations has ceased to exist. All treaties have been declared null and void." The video ended, and the camera zoomed into the anchorman. "Ladies and gentlemen, I do not know yet what this means, but we are closely monitoring this story and will find out for you."

A blue cartoon bear wiggling its butt against a tree replaced the anchor's panicked face as the network broke for a commercial.

"Shit," I muttered. "Do you think Solomon's okay? We haven't heard from him in days."

I considered for the first time that maybe he'd been discovered as a vampire when the Daemoni had made their existence known. In fact, they crawled all over the U.N. and likely would have outed him to the norms. Surely the news would have reported the "monster" at the U.N., while conveniently ignoring the real beasts. Unless they quietly killed him to avoid bringing attention to themselves. My imagination ran wild and worry pushed my brows together, but then I picked up on the new mind signature when it arrived in the mansion.

"I am fine, and I am here," a deep voice with a Haitian accent carried from the hall shortly before the vampire himself appeared in my doorway. Tall with a medium frame, the ashy skin of a pale vampire with black heritage, and cornrows that reached his shoulders, he most certainly was here. I jumped to my feet and rushed over to greet him with a hug. "I do bring news, but not what you want to hear."

Tristan strode behind me and clapped Solomon on the shoulder. "Let's get to the council meeting so we can discuss it."

We flashed to the council hall where Owen and Char already worked on setting up the ability to hold a conference call. Rina would have never fathomed such a thing when she ruled. If her entire council couldn't be physically present, they would wait and proceed when they had a majority. Tristan and I had sat in on meetings from our office in the Captiva safe house, but it had probably taken Mom's power of persuasion to convince Rina to allow it.

The thought of Mom and Rina made my heart squeeze.

First order of business involved swearing Owen, Vanessa, Blossom, Jax, and Sheree into the council. Second was finding out which existing members would stay. Julia's absence had already been noticed. Swearing in my team members and dismissing Julia were no-brainers, so this felt like my first official action . . . request? . . . no, my first official *order* as matriarch. It was time to get real. My throat suddenly dried up, and the speech I'd mentally prepared vanished from my memory.

Back in the day—about six or so years ago—when my books started becoming a big thing, I'd often felt like an imposter. Like a fraud pretending to be something amazing, while always fearing that eventually someone would figure out the truth. Apparently, I wasn't alone in that thinking. Creators of all types lived with constant doubt of their own talents and abilities, especially the more popular their works became.

But that feeling didn't compare to this.

I didn't belong here, in this seat. I'd only sat at this table a handful of times, and now I occupied the leader's chair. The matriarch's throne! Who was I trying to fool? Me as matriarch? Ha! I hadn't even had the chance to learn how to lead an army —had struggled to lead my miniscule team—so who would ever entrust me to rule an entire society? Certainly not everyone here in this room with me right now. They knew better.

"*We entrust you.*" Three words whispered into my mind. Cassandra's voice, although somehow layered with Mom's and Rina's, too. "*The Angels believe in you.*"

I glanced up at the statues of the angel-warriors that glared down on us from their perches near the ceiling. Their large wings were spread wide, and they held swords in each hand, fierce determination carved into their stone faces. During the abomination of Tristan's trial, I'd thought them angry with us. For some reason, I now felt as though their eyes pierced me through to my soul. As though *they* were the ones speaking to me, and at the same time, waiting for their orders. From me.

Tristan's hand slid over my thigh under the table and gave me a reassuring squeeze. *Fake it until you make it,* he'd said. That's exactly what I had to do.

With a deep breath, I stood, placed my hands on the edge of the round table, and leaned forward. I wanted to make sure those listening through the device set in the middle of the table heard me loud and clear. I just hoped my voice wouldn't crack like a preteen boy's and betray my lack of confidence. I cleared my throat to be sure.

"Many of you have served my grandmother and the Amadis for a very long time," I began. Unable to look at any of the faces sitting around the large, stone table for fear of losing my nerve, I stared hard at its center. "She brought the kind of leadership we needed during her era. I didn't always agree with her decisions on the surface, but I knew deep down she did what was right for the Amadis and humanity at the time."

Swallowing down my nervousness, I took the chance of looking up. Several people nodded in agreement. Someone on the phone let out a "hear, hear" and another agreed with an "aye."

I glanced at the angel statues again and then let my gaze travel around the table to all of the faces, different colors and nationalities and even species, watching me intently.

"However, this is not that time. The Angels have already warned me that everything has changed, and we have witnessed that with our own eyes. With our *lives*. The world is a different place than it was a century ago or even a month ago. And we must be different, too. The Amadis were started as the Angels' army on Earth. We've been fortunate over the last few centuries to behave as more of a society and culture, immersing ourselves in human civilization, rather than an army involved in constant war. We've had to fight small skirmishes, yes, but not like the battles we face now. It is time to rise up and be the warriors we are supposed to be."

I looked each of them in the eye as I continued, my confidence growing with each word of conviction I spoke.

"There will be blood. There will be carnage all around. I may not have a lot of experience with war, but I do know this much. We've already seen it. I also know this: We will be a part of it. We will *fight*. We will be the ones drawing blood if necessary. We will serve our purpose, whatever it takes."

"Absolutely," Charlotte said. Solomon and my new council members nodded in encouragement. Exactly what I needed.

"I will say it now, and I will say it clearly. I am *not* my grandmother," I declared. "I will not sit on the sidelines and watch, formulating complicated, covert plans that eventually bring results down the line. That may have worked in more peaceful times, but not in today's new world. We will *act*. And we will do so swiftly. We will take the offensive. When I say we will fight, I mean it. And I mean *we*. I will not ask anyone else to do what I will not do myself. So don't try to stop me. Rina entrusted me to lead our army, and I will continue doing just that as matriarch. I will not sit by in the comfort and safety of a palace while my people's lives are being sacrificed."

I paused for a breath and took a moment to scan everyone's minds. As expected, some were balking at my directness. I pushed on because this was important to me to address now so I wouldn't have to deal with the backstabbing later.

"If you are ready to plan and execute a true, physical war for humanity's souls, I invite you to remain on my council and join us in defeating the Daemoni." I looked at the few faces who had been involved in accusing Tristan of treason. "But if you cannot respect me as your matriarch and the decisions I make as such, then consider yourself dismissed. This is the very reason Julia is not here today. I appreciate advisement, but I will not tolerate disrespect of me or of Tristan as my second. If you have a problem with our style of leadership, you may leave now."

"You mean making rash decisions for ill-planned missions such as the one last night that has backfired in our faces?" Armand asked. The French vampire with the dark widow's peak had been one of Tristan's accusers, and I knew full well he had no confidence in me as a leader.

"The mission was well-planned," Charlotte corrected. "We initially achieved its primary purpose."

"Which, as Armand put, backfired in our faces," Robin, the were-falcon, said.

"We didn't know the full extent of Lucas's infiltration into the world's major powers, such as the United States," Tristan said. "Russia would be expected because the Daemoni's major cities are located in her borders. We knew Lucas had been dealing at some level with the U.S. and other militaries, but not so overtly with the executive branch. He used to lie low from them, working behind the scenes. Now we know that has changed, too. So we have more information than we did twenty-four hours ago, which is a benefit."

"Four humans were killed because of it," Armand said. "Including two children!"

"Which is terrible," Charlotte agreed, "but we don't know where those bodies came from. They may have already been dead. Or they could have been fake. The Daemoni mages may have been creating an illusion for the Normans."

"Or, they could have killed four innocents to make their point against us," Robin said, her dark, beady gaze bouncing among my team's faces.

"Yes, they could have," Tristan agreed. "But they would have anyway. Maybe not at that exact place at that exact time, but they will continue serving the media whatever Lucas fancies to make us look bad, no matter what we do."

"But your actions last night only helped them," Attair, a Middle Eastern warlock, said from his end of the phone line in Jordan. "How can we know you two aren't serving Lucas? That vampire, too."

Vanessa glared at the black device in the center of the table.

"Attair, you're dismissed from the council," I said without further ado. Such outright finger-pointing couldn't be tolerated. I looked at Owen to disconnect Attair's line into the conference call.

"He has a point, though," Armand said. "You're willing to

risk yourself, the only matriarch we have, and look at the results."

"You may go," I said.

He stood up. "Of course you want rid of anyone who disagrees with you. You only want sock puppets." He looked around at my core team. "You *all* have ties to the Daemoni, including that boy of yours!"

I jumped to my feet and glared at him. My words came out through a clenched jaw. "I said you may go."

"Behavior like this will be the downfall of the Amadis," he declared. He returned my glare, his eyes hard as marbles. "*You* will be the end of us all."

Now Tristan rose to his feet and leaned over the table toward the vampire. I couldn't see Tristan's face well or the look in his eyes, but I was pretty sure I wouldn't want to be on the receiving end. "Leave. Now."

"Gladly," Armand snapped. "I will not be a part of this fiasco."

He strode out of the council hall.

"Anyone else?" I knew full well there were more as thoughts screamed accusations at Tristan and me. I looked at Robin and waited with a lifted brow.

"I'm not accusing you of working with the Daemoni," she began, "but I do have to question your actions. You are the last of your kind. *Our* last hope. You should be kept safe at all times, concerning yourself with making a baby, not making war."

A few others agreed out loud.

"Here here," Marta, who had replaced Adolf when he'd died in battle, said through the speaker. "We need another daughter. A *true* second. Tristan should not be your second. If something happens to you, do you really expect him to lead the Amadis?"

I chuckled darkly and shook my head. My patience was waning.

"Are you people *serious*?" I demanded. "Have you seen what's going on in the world? Do you realize that if we don't act—if *I* don't serve my purpose—there won't be a need for the Amadis? The world as we know it will be over. Norman souls—the very ones we are here to protect—will cease to exist! And so will we. It won't matter who's next in line to lead if we're all gone anyway!"

"We can't just focus on the here-and-now," Savio, an Italian were-shark, argued from across the table. "We must look to the future, too."

"If we *don't* focus on the here and now, we won't have a future," Charlotte said. "Alexis is right. We're at true war here, fellas."

Solomon sat back in his chair and crossed his thick arms over his chest. "Agreed. Katerina saw this coming when she knew she'd be ascending. She knew the Amadis needed someone who could fight a full-on war, not quiet, covert tussles. She saw what could be our final battle on the horizon and knew she was not the right matriarch to lead it. Neither was Sophia. Alexis is."

Warmth flooded my heart with his support, spoken in his deep voice with the beautiful island accent. I hadn't felt such confidence in me from Solomon before, and this meant a lot.

"Of course you would say that," Marta said. "You don't see things the way some of us do. How convenient that Ms. Katerina *and* Ms. Sophia were fed right into Lucas's hands at the same time. How nice for him that his daughter instantly became leader of his enemy, and how fortunate that a Summoned son was allowed to return to the Amadis, which has never been possible for a son to do before."

"Dorian has not officially been summoned," Solomon said, but Marta ignored him, carrying on with her horrid accusations.

"How interesting that our leader is the enemy's daughter,

and her second had once served as the enemy's second. I could continue with those whom you just swore in as your counselors —the son, in some weird, twisted way, of a Daemoni sorceress who caused the murder of our matriarch, and who'd been serving the enemy that very night; the wife who supposedly didn't know her husband had been possessed by said sorceress for *decades*; a half-sister who's also the daughter of the enemy's leader and whose twin brother is that leader's new second . . ."

Her words felt like a knife to the gut. As much as she twisted everything around, enough truth remained that her accusations could be believable. Did others really believe such things?

"Enough!" Tristan barked, cutting them off. "You will not disrespect your matriarch and my wife like this."

He glared at them all. The room fell quiet, but with a tension blanketing us. After another peek into everyone's minds, I realized the futility of this conversation. Some of Rina's council would never trust me or anyone else as their leader. Their minds would never be changed, and they'd constantly be nitpicking at everything we did.

"You all are dismissed," I said. "We have more serious topics to discuss and worry about than petty accusations. I didn't *ask* for my grandmother and mother to be murdered before my very eyes. I didn't *want* for them to leave this world, to leave me and my family and all of you. I didn't have any desire to become matriarch so soon. But it is what it is. None of us can change what happened regardless of how much we hate it. What we can do is stop arguing amongst ourselves and start planning to battle the real enemy. If you can't see that, then I'm done with you."

I sat down and waited for the room to clear out and the callers to disconnect. After the first three left the room and a few calls dropped, several minutes passed as I studied those who still sat in their seats. I couldn't get a feel for the callers, but when Owen told me who remained connected, I felt like I could trust them.

"Okay, then," I finally said. "Now that that's over, let's get down to what's really important—discussing our strategy in this war."

"Do you want to replace any of the vacant seats?" Solomon asked.

Oh. I should have expected that question. Tristan and I had already discussed it.

"For now, I'd like to keep my council as it is," I said. "Those who have been dismissed can still command their regions, or their seconds-in-command can take that responsibility, but I don't want to add anyone to the council at this time. We have a war to plan, and the more nimble we are, the better. So let's get down to it."

"Should we get an update on where things stand with the Amadis and the rest of the world first?" Charlotte asked, another reminder of normal procedure.

"Of course," I said hurriedly, giving her a mental thank-you. Damn. I was doing a lousy job already, and we hadn't even started the strategy making part. "We all know the Daemoni have revealed themselves worldwide and have brought us into the fray in the worst way possible. We tried to counter them last night, but Lucas pulled out his trump card."

"Oh, that's not the worst of what he has," Vanessa muttered.

"No, it's not," I agreed, "but it certainly beat our first move. Those of you on the phone, any more news from your regions?"

"Nothing I haven't reported yet," Jelani, a wizard from Africa, said. None of the others had more news to report either.

"Many of our business interests have suffered," Tristan said, bringing up another topic I almost forgot to address.

"We've lost almost every business we own. As of yesterday, the millions in stocks we possessed were sold off at my direction."

"Just in time, Tristan," Jelani commented. "Even in Kenya we know the stock markets are crashing."

Tristan nodded. "We need to stockpile resources while we're able to so we can be prepared to support our people. The world is definitely changing and headed for war."

Taking that as my cue, I turned toward the large vampire sitting on the other side of Owen. "Solomon, can you tell us about the U.N.?"

He nodded and leaned closer to the phone device.

"For those who haven't seen it on the news right before this meeting, the United Nations has officially collapsed," he said. Someone on the phone must not have known because a gasp sounded through the line. "The vote was made and confirmed this morning. All treaties and alliances are officially null and void."

"This is the work of the Daemoni?" I clarified.

"Indeed," Solomon said. "They have been working on tearing down the U.N. for many months. The attacks and bombings the other day almost backfired on the Daemoni. The Normans started the meeting with a proposal to ban together against the supernaturals, and I thought for a moment the world might actually see complete unification among humans. But Lucas's people quickly interfered with their powerful influence, putting a stop to that kind of thinking. They convinced the delegates that all countries should have autonomy to handle this situation as each sees fit. Many are already prepared to go to war, blaming each other for harboring the monsters, as they called us."

"Which is exactly what the Daemoni need," Tristan said, resting his forearms on the table. "They need chaos, not any kind of unified fronts. They need Normans slaughtering other Normans, not making treaties with each other and playing nicely."

"But if they've turned the norms against us, and don't need their huge army to defeat us anymore, why are they bothering?" I asked, my naïveté about politics and strategies for taking over the world showing.

"They need the world to hit rock bottom so they can come to the rescue with promises of a new and improved society," Vanessa said.

Solomon nodded. "I agree that is exactly what they're doing."

"Very Hitler-esque," Sheree murmured.

Charlotte let out a quiet huff. "Who do you think was behind that movement?"

"Aren't most of the countries in the U.N. sided with the Daemoni?" I asked, ignoring her rhetorical question. Mom had mentioned this several months back. "Wouldn't the Daemoni just be fighting each other?"

"Yes. Unfortunately, we were unable to bring any more leaders to our side," Solomon replied. "I'm afraid Lucas's accusations have lost us any allies we already had."

"But it will be the *norms* who will be fighting each other," Vanessa clarified. "It's just a game to the Daemoni because they have nothing to lose and everything to gain. They'll have fun with their war, creating violence and chaos, and amusing themselves with the battles between norms. Their very favorite form of entertainment."

"And when he's bored and ready to end it all, Lucas will use his Norman super-soldiers to win, leading the world to the future he wants," I concluded, catching on.

The grim look on everyone's faces confirmed my conclusion.

"So we need to figure out how to disable the stones in the Norman soldiers," I said.

Tristan nodded his agreement. "Yes, that will be paramount to our strategy."

"Are the soldiers in one location?" Chandra, a were-leopard from India, asked.

"Not likely," Tristan answered. "I'm sure Lucas dispatched them around the world before the Daemoni came out to the Normans. The Summoned sons and their offspring are like the remote controls of the soldiers, and they may still be in one place. That would make it easier for Lucas to control them and orchestrate his war."

"Do you think they're still at the Defense buildings in Virginia?" Chandra asked.

"It's been a few weeks since we were there, but if Lucas is still set up in that building, it's possible."

"We need to go there immediately," I said hoping we could figure out how to break the curse on them while we were at it.

"We need to make finding the Summoned sons a priority," Tristan agreed.

"My core team here will take this mission," I told the others. Not surprisingly, many people had something to say about that, most of it protests. I made everyone quiet down. "You all have your own regions to worry about. You'll need to carry out your own plan of action where you are, and eventually, be ready to take down the Norman soldiers so you can extract their stones. But first, we need to cut them off from their controllers."

"We're already familiar with what they've done," Tristan added. "We have firsthand experience with what the stones can do, and we know how to locate and extract them. And *because* of the situation and the danger, Alexis should be there to monitor our enemies' thoughts, especially if she's able to reach Lucas. Learning his plans for all fronts of this war could be all we need to succeed."

Nobody could argue with him about that. Yet, a tingling came in the back of my mind. When I checked those around me, though, their thoughts showed agreement.

"I suggest you gather as much intelligence about Lucas's whereabouts as possible first," Solomon said.

"He was at the White House this morning," I reminded him.

"And since we and the rest of the world know that, he may be on his way out of the area," Tristan countered. "There's a good chance he'll go into hiding from everyone since he'll be pitting them all against each other. And he can move quickly."

"If we go to Virginia when he could already be in Hades, taking the Summoned with him, we'd be wasting our time," Vanessa said.

Tristan nodded. "Exactly. Also, the Daemoni had obviously been expecting us last night, so we need to revise our strategy and make it look like we're retreating for now so we can surprise him later."

I didn't like the idea of waiting—which could also be a waste of time—but everyone else agreed with this proposal, and they had much more experience than I did, so I went along with the plan.

"As soon as it makes sense, we're moving," I said. "I'd rather have to chase after Lucas and the Summoned than be sitting here doing nothing when he lets those soldiers loose."

"What about the people here on the island when we go?" Blossom asked. "Without Owen and Charlotte here to give the shield the most power, the island will be left quite vulnerable."

"We need every single body who can fight to leave the island and do just that," Tristan replied. "The elderly and the young can and probably should be moved to safer locations. I expect the Daemoni will continue targeting the island, and if not them, the Normans will, based on the information they're being fed."

"There are a few villages that remain untouched," Minh, an Asian witch, said from the phone. I couldn't help but picture her wearing the ridiculous green hat she'd worn the first time I'd met her. "The Daemoni apparently don't know they're there."

"Dingo Bend?" Jax asked.

"Yes, that's one," Minh confirmed. "Kuckaroo was hit, but not too badly. Dingo Bend, though, remains a good place for our weak to hide. It's shielded and cloaked well in the middle of the Outback."

Another, stronger prod in my mind. My first thought was my instinct or even Mom or Cassandra or the Angels trying to tell me something. But then I latched onto it . . .

"If we can get people to go, we probably should," Tristan said. "I don't know how much longer this island will continue to be safe."

At the same time, Dorian screamed into my mind: "*MOM!*"

CHAPTER 6

*D*orian, I called back, the hair on the nape of my neck rising. *What's wrong? Are you okay?*

"They're coming back."

The unmistakable fear in his voice sent a shiver down my spine, and then I picked up on the mind signatures. I jumped to my feet. "The Daemoni."

Without further explanation, I flashed to the mansion on the other side of the island and sprinted inside and up the steps.

"Dorian!" I screamed all the way up, my heart and my thoughts racing even faster than my body.

Had they really come back for him? Lucas had made it sound like he'd wait for Dorian to make his choice. Were these rogues? Or had Lucas only been telling his usual lies?

I barely reached our wing and his door when Dorian plowed into me.

"Mom! I was trying to get your attention," he accused. "They're coming."

As if to punctuate his statement, the ground and the walls of the mansion shook.

"Get down!" I threw myself on top of him, flattening both

of us to the floor as the building continued to tremble. Dresser drawers shook open, and long forgotten toys fell off the shelf. Sasha stood over us, the size of a horse, growling.

"*Alexis, they're already in,*" Owen said. "*It's not good here. Not good at all.*"

We're coming. I wrapped my arms around Dorian. "We need to get to the council hall again."

"I can fly us there."

I shook my head. "My way's faster."

After a quick mental check to make sure everyone had vacated this end of the island, as we'd instructed them after last time, I flashed to the main room of the council hall, taking Dorian and Sasha with me.

Pull the shield in again, I told Owen the moment we appeared.

"*I can't.*"

What do you mean, you can't?

"*I don't know. All I can figure is the bombs the other day weren't your everyday explosives. They must have left some kind of magical trace that's interfering with our shield. We have no control over it, and they're blasting right through it.*"

I looked through his eyes to see what he saw from his vantage point on the council hall's roof: Smoke and fire throughout the village. Buildings seeming to spontaneously combust.

"*They've cloaked the bombs this time,*" Charlotte explained. "*So we can't see them to reroute them.*"

I pressed my lips together before the scream of frustration building in my chest could fly out.

You all need to take cover then. I hoped they couldn't hear the defeat in my thoughts as they would have in my normal voice.

My eyes scanned over the hundreds of people stuffed into the council hall—at least a quarter of the village had sought shelter here in the time it had taken me to retrieve Dorian.

They looked at me expectantly, their faces full of fear and confusion. I glanced around the top of the room, pausing briefly to eye the angel statues, who looked more determined than ever. Would they protect the council hall like they did the matriarch's mansion?

Maybe we should all go to the mansion instead, I said to Tristan. When he didn't answer, I looked around the room again. Neither he nor Dorian were in here. *Tristan? Dorian!*

My thoughts were drowned out as an explosion cracked directly overhead, and the ceiling of the council hall fell. Boulder-sized blocks of marble dropped into the room. Several vampires jumped up and let their bodies break the stones' falls. Two blurred to cover me, one of them taking me to the floor as smaller marble chunks and dust rained down around us. Magic sizzled and popped in the air as mages rerouted the biggest pieces before they crushed bodies underneath them. But still screams and wails tore through the room.

I squirmed under the heavy body pinning me to the ground, needing to help those in pain.

"Are they gone?" Vanessa hissed into my ear.

"The Daemoni are. Not like drones have minds to read, though."

"We are not letting you up until we know for sure," Solomon said from right next to us. They'd been the vampires who'd rushed over to protect me.

Tristan, I yelled out. *Dorian!*

"We're fine," Tristan answered me. I found his and Dorian's mind signatures in the hallway off the main room. *"We're blocked in, but I can get us out when it's safe."*

More explosions sounded nearby, each one hurting my heart as I thought about my people suffering or dying. The minutes passed like hours. Sobs and sniffles and wails of pain continued from all around me. And I was stuck, unable to do anything to help them, to relieve their pain, to protect them. After all had been quiet for at least an hour, Vanessa and

Solomon finally let me up, and I gave everyone else a mental all clear.

Piles of marble and stone filled what had once been the council hall's main room. Hands and feet showed first, then arms and finally faces followed, all covered in white dust. People coughed and choked as they dug their way out. After ordering my team to assist the others, I flashed to the hallway and began throwing marble boulders behind me as I searched for my husband and my son.

"*Watch out*," Tristan said as a particularly large chunk, wedged under several others, gave me trouble. I jumped to the side at the same time the boulder shattered into pieces, Tristan's fist punching through.

I grabbed at his hand and pulled. A slightly smaller hand pushed through a hole, too, and I wrapped my other palm around Dorian's wrist. Using all of my strength, and with their help, I yanked them out of the pile of rubble, then pulled them into my arms.

"Oh, thank the Angels," I breathed as I held them. Their arms wrapped around me and each other, and we stood in a family hug, relief washing over us.

They weren't my only family, and unfortunately, not everyone fared so well. After a quick squeeze of my dust-covered men, I broke away so we could help our people and then assess the damage.

"Fourteen deaths, hundreds injured." Sheree reported the final count a few hours later, her voice thick as she held back a sob. I stood along with the rest of my team at the top of the hill where the council hall had once been. Now only jagged pieces of the four outer walls remained. And the angel statues. Amazingly, all four of them were still in perfect condition, lined up against what remained of the marble front steps.

"We've run out of the potion with vampire blood in it," Blossom said. "The vampires are helping the injured shifters and mages, though."

"I can give more blood," Tristan said.

"I can, too," I offered. "We need to strengthen everyone before forcing them to evacuate."

I looked to Owen and Char, who'd been assessing the physical damage to the island.

"Not a single structure left undamaged," Owen said. "Most are completely destroyed."

"Except the matriarch's mansion," Char added. "Damage to the contents again, but the building itself is fine."

"I should have ordered everyone there," I said miserably as I pushed a hand through my gritty hair. A cloud of dust poofed out around my face. "I was about to, but I was too slow."

"You couldn't fit the entire village in the mansion, *ma lykita*."

"No, but we could have saved a lot of them."

"And how would you have chosen who would be saved?" Blossom asked, and I gave her a blank look, having no answer.

"Don't blame yourself for this," Sheree said, covering my shoulder with a warm hand. "This is the work of evil. We will fight back, but as you said only hours ago, there are going to be casualties."

I turned to stare at her in shock. Sheree was usually the pacifist. Even she'd been pushed to her limits.

I blew out a breath. "Those of us who can need to give blood. Then we need to get all of these people out of here. This island isn't safe anymore."

It didn't take much to convince some people to leave the island, but others stood their ground.

"This has been my home for centuries," a stubborn old wizard complained. He eyed me with cloudy gray eyes barely visible through the wrinkles in his skin. "I'm not leaving it!"

"You're not safe here," I said. "I can't allow you to stay."

"It should be my choice. I'd rather die here in my home

than be forced to go to some strange land and die there anyway."

I let out a sigh. The crotchety old man had a point. I couldn't guarantee that Dingo Bend or anywhere else would be much safer than here in the long run. But I sure wished I had my mom's power of persuasion.

"I'll take care of this," Sheree said, and she nodded toward the pier. "Blossom, Jax, and Owen are back."

I gave her an appreciative smile before running over to the trio. Owen had created a portal to Dingo Bend, and they'd gone through to make sure it was indeed safe for our people.

"They're fine there, but looking forward to having more strength in numbers," Blossom said.

So we began ushering people through the portal, where they'd come out halfway across the world in the middle of the Australian wilderness. I didn't envy them. That place hadn't exactly been kind to me.

"I don't like leaving you," Ophelia said to me when her time came. "Someone needs to keep the house. I don't like leaving my post."

"You know the mansion will be fine, and there will be nobody here for you to take care of," I told her as I wrapped my arms around the old witch's plump body. "The kids in Dingo Bend need you and your kitchen skills."

"You know I'd take Dorian if they'd let me."

"I know." I gave her a smile and a shrug. They wouldn't let her because nobody wanted the risk of danger he'd bring. "That's okay. Tristan and I will take care of him, as we should. We *do* want him around."

"You keep safe, my dear." She returned my hug, planted a kiss on my cheek, and sucked in a deep breath, lifting her droopy bosom, before stepping through the portal. A second later, she was gone.

After the elderly and the young were evacuated, we divvied up the remaining Amadis who would go on to fight among the regions, and Owen created portals for them. I stayed to thank each and every one of them—and to say a prayer for their safety. Maybe someday we'd all be able to return here.

My gaze swept over what had once been a lovely village with a main street and an eclectic collection of homes. I remembered the awe and excitement I'd felt the first time I'd been here, seeing real-life creatures that only days before I'd believed to be fiction. They'd been going along on their normal, daily business with barely a care in the world. Watching everyone shop, kids play in the streets, and adults enjoying a pint together, whether some kind of special brew or blood, had been a highlight of my life. And now, their homes had been reduced to smoking wood and stone, and their businesses and livelihoods were nothing more than piles of litter. Too many lives who'd once been bustling along that day were now gone.

What would Rina think if she could see this?

Tears slipped over the rims of my eyes as I stared at the scene before me, darkening with twilight as the sun set over the sea in the distance. She probably could see this through the veil. All of the matriarchs who had once called this place home were probably watching, their souls filled with disappointment and grief.

Tristan sidled up next to me and slid an arm over my shoulder.

"Everybody's gone," he murmured.

I scrubbed my hands over my gritty cheeks and nodded. "I'm going to get cleaned up then."

I flashed to the mansion and trudged up the stairs to our suite. As soon as I was inside, I shed my leathers—white from dust now instead of black—while making my way to the bathroom. After letting the shower heat up to steaming, I stepped inside, sat on the floor, curled my knees under my chin, and let the sobs out.

They came from so deep within, my body physically hurt

as they wracked their way out. My heart broke over and over again as the images of my people's faces and their homes flashed in my mind. My stomach clutched and heaved at the same time. Not even a month had passed since Mom and Rina died, and there had been so much more death and destruction since then. Way too much grief for one person to handle.

And there would still be more. I knew this as much as I knew my own name. No matter how you tried to dress it up—soldiers in fancy white and gold uniforms of centuries past pretending like they were gentlemen as they slayed their enemies, guerilla warriors ambushing their unsuspecting rivals, or privileged politicians using drones to do their dirty work—war was ugly. Despicable. Not for the tenderhearted.

Lucas had put me in this position because he believed I had a dark side—as dark as him, maybe. He slayed Mom so he could watch me shed any Amadis pretenses and show him and everyone in the world that darkness within me. I'd thought at first the Angels had set me up like this for a similar reason—because I had more of that ruthlessness needed for war than Rina or Mom did. My stomach was strong enough, my heart hard enough, and my soul cold enough to do what would need to be done to bring us to victory.

What had I been thinking? What had the *Angels* been thinking by saying I was ready for this? Even seeing troops fighting each other around the world in Norman wars . . . even witnessing skirmishes like Kuckaroo where people died in front of me . . . war had remained more of an abstract concept to me than a daily reality. I didn't have enough experience with true destruction and defeat until now. I'd thought battles would fuel me—feed my anger and need for vengeance, keep me focused on the end goal. I hadn't known how it would truly affect me until it became real. So very real.

The violence and destruction of it all tore me apart. Ravaged me from the inside. I still felt anger and vengeance. I still focused on the goal of ending Lucas and the Daemoni.

But I felt hollow now. Empty and hopeless. Unable to see how there could ever be light again.

Tristan found me a little while later in the same fetal position as he stepped into the shower with me. He picked me up, sat down on the built-in bench with me in his lap, and held me as the water rained down on us, my tears still coming just as fast.

"What have I done?" My voice came thick and rough as I asked the question out loud.

"You've done everything you could," he answered. "You'll continue doing all you can. You were right before. Sheree was right when she said it. War brings casualties."

"It's one thing to say it, and another to have it thrown in your face." I wrapped my arms around him and leaned my cheek against his bare chest. "I hate war. Why is this happening now? Why the war of all wars when I'm in charge?"

He pushed my sopping wet hair away from my face and stroked my cheek with his thumb. "You know the answer to that."

"Because Lucas gets a kick out of tormenting his own daughter. It's all part of his game."

"You are the biggest challenge he'll ever face, and he knows it. He probably gets a sick hard-on over it. That much is true." He leaned in and brushed his lips over my forehead. "But that's not really why this is happening now. He's not really the one in control."

"Then why, Tristan? Why are the Angels doing this to us? Why is God allowing all of this?"

"I don't know, Lex. I can't begin to know what God has planned or what the Angels are thinking. But I do know they believe in you and your ability to handle this."

"Well, they're wrong."

He pulled back and looked at me with a lifted brow. "You're calling God and the Angels wrong?"

I shrugged. "I don't know who it is, but someone up there, in the Otherworld, has made a really bad call."

When he tried to argue with me, tried to convince me how wrong *I* was, I shut him up the one way I knew how: I covered his mouth with mine. I didn't need more arguing and tension tonight. I needed his body wrapped around mine. I needed love like a dying man in the desert needs water. I needed *his* love to fill me back up with everything today's attack had sucked dry.

Unfortunately, too many minds occupied this mansion—the only safe place on the island—who could hear me if I really let go of my inhibitions, so I didn't get everything I needed. But at least I got some time alone with my man.

Later, when the mansion was quiet, I lay in our bed next to Tristan and stared at the sheer canopy above us. Whenever I closed my eyes, not only did I witness Mom's death over and over, but now I also watched the Amadis village exploding with unseen bombs, the scene looping on repeat. The Daemoni and the norms had found a way to breach Owen's shield. How? It had to have been the work of the sorcerers, of course, but what exactly had they done to those first bombs that we hadn't noticed? That allowed them to sit back and wait until they could catch us by surprise again? Lucas and his Daemoni always remained several steps ahead of us, even Tristan. How would we ever win this war at this rate?

Unable to lay in bed pretending to rest and regenerate a moment longer, I slid out of the blankets and made my way down to the Sacred Archives. I hadn't been in there yet since becoming matriarch. I'd been curious to know if I'd suddenly be able to read all of the books lining the walls, but not enough to overcome all of the other emotions I'd been dealing with since Mom's and Rina's deaths. The time had come, though. I could only hope somewhere in there answers could be found.

Because right now, I had none.

As always, crossing the threshold felt like entering a different world—or a different realm. An unearthly glow lit the room and all of the books on the shelves lining every wall. The air itself felt heavier yet also lighter and smelled clean and pure, like sunshine. It left a sweet flavor on my tongue and the back of my throat when I inhaled. Except . . .

I licked my lips and drew in a breath. There was something different this time—a tinge of bitterness in the air. Was this new or something only matriarchs could distinguish?

I hadn't known why I'd expected the Sacred Archives to be different for the matriarch than it would be for the daughters after her. I couldn't recall Mom or Rina ever telling me this. I'd created the theory on my own after my first visit here, when I discovered I could barely read anything in any of the books contained within. The pages of most of them were filled with swirls and lines, some heavy and others light, that presumably meant something, but I hadn't been able to decipher them then. So I'd concluded it was the language of the Angels and only the matriarch could interpret it.

With high expectations, I reached for a random book on the shelf in front of me. My fingers caressed the smooth, soft pearlescent cover before lifting it away. The strange symbols marked the inside of the book, but I could decipher them no more easily than I could during my first visit here over two years ago, right after my *Ang'dora*.

My assumption had been wrong.

I blew out a breath as I replaced the book on its shelf and turned in a circle. My hopes for what I'd find in this room had soared even higher than I realized, and as disappointment came crashing down, the feeling of abandonment overwhelmed me.

"Isn't there anything I should know? Isn't there *anything* you can tell me?" I asked aloud, pleading with the Angels or my ancestors or whomever might be listening to me. "I'm weak, and inexperienced, and ignorant about way too much.

You've chosen the wrong person. I'm not equipped or prepared to serve in this way. Please . . ."

I turned in another circle, my gaze sweeping over the hundreds of book spines. And then, finally. A book slid out of its spot completely on its own. It lifted into the air and floated over to my outstretched hands. I opened it hurriedly, turning the pages greedily. But they were all blank.

The urge to throw the book on the ground and stomp on it like a two-year-old nearly overpowered me. If I didn't have a special soft spot in my heart for all books in general, I just might have done so. But right when I was about to send the worthless thing back to its spot on the shelf, black marks started appearing on the first page. Swirls and lines, some heavy and some thin, that looked a little tribal and a little Celtic at the same time.

"What good is this if I can't understand it?" I demanded aloud. My inner tantrum-throwing child pushed harder against the surface. I stared at the drawing, beautiful in its own way, and as I did, the meaning began to clarify in my mind. The swirls and lines represented my name: Alexis.

More marks started showing, as though bleeding through the page, and I plopped to my butt on the floor while watching them appear. I didn't know how long I sat there, possibly hours, but the symbols themselves taught me how to read them. And I learned this language was personally for me. Every matriarch had her own, and the books in the Sacred Archives were filled with messages they'd received from the Angels. Nobody could read them, not even other matriarchs . . . unless the Angels deemed it necessary.

Some books contained their histories, just like my own book Rina had shown me when I'd first arrived on the island. It floated down to me, and now, I saw, was filled with much more than it had been originally—all of my personal thoughts on my experiences had been added in this language only I could read. And, of course, all of the events since I'd first seen the beautiful book. I stared at the last page that had filled in my history book, hoping to see a glimpse of what would come next, but nothing more appeared. I sent it back to its place.

The other book lay open on my lap. The symbols in it had also stopped coming. I placed my elbows on my knees and dropped my head into my hands.

"I know nothing more than I did before," I muttered. Nothing useful, anyway. I still felt as lost as ever. "I have no answers. No preparation. Nothing to equip me for this awful task you've put in front of me. How could you choose me without preparing me?"

"*Oh, He has been preparing you, child. But know that He does not choose the prepared and the equipped. He prepares and equips the ones He has chosen. And you have been chosen.*" Cassandra's voice, I was sure. It sounded clearer than it had the other times, when it seemed like Rina and Mom were in the background.

"What does that mean? How does that help me now? We're at war, and I don't have the slightest inkling of what to do." I lifted the book—my new book with the messages from the Angels—up in the air. "Please tell me!"

"*The Angels only send messages when you need them. They only interfere when necessary.*"

I groaned with frustration. Rina had told me this numerous times, but I certainly felt like there had never been a more appropriate need for them to talk to me. To give me direction. To interfere and set us on the right course of action.

But since they didn't . . .

Realization dawned on me. The Angels interfered when I, and my people, would not be making the right decision. When we would act when we shouldn't, or not act when we should. So if they didn't have anything to tell me, any new direction to give me, that could only mean one thing.

Our plans were on the right track. We'd been making the best decisions so far. And now, my team needed to leave the island and pursue our mission of finding the Summoned and their offspring so we could begin to end this war. And possibly end the Daemoni—or at least Lucas.

As I finished accepting this epiphany, new lines scrolled on the page: "We are always here with you."

And with that, the book began shrinking in my hand until it became the size of a pearl, a little glowing ball sitting in my palm. Then it disappeared completely, as though dissolving into my skin. I could only hope that meant that wherever I went, I had access to the book and the Angels' messages.

Because it was time to leave the island and go to war.

CHAPTER 7

"*A*re you sure you want to take this risk?" Galina asked through the teleconference device sitting on my desk.

The core of my team who had been with us throughout the search for Dorian were the only souls, besides Solomon, who remained on Amadis Island, all of us confined to the shelter of the protected mansion. We gathered in my office now, huddled around my desk with the other council members on a conference call. We were back to planning our war strategy after being interrupted the other day.

I glanced over at Tristan, who sat next to me and gave me a slight nod. He and I had already discussed our thoughts and ideas several times and, to some extent, with those in the room, and we were all together on this. I had to be the one to give the directives to the rest of the council, though. We would show Tristan had worked with me in the formulation of the plans because they would trust him, his experience, and his ability for strategic thinking, but they had to see that *I* gave the orders. I bit my lip at the irony of this compared to the orders about to come out of my mouth.

With my fingers tightly woven together, I pressed my palms into my stomach, as though I could calm the butterflies within. It had been one thing to discuss these plans with Tristan and my closest friends. Giving orders to the council felt entirely different. More real. When this meeting came to a close, people would be following my commands that could possibly cause them to kill others and to be killed.

At the same time, the orders I'd be giving would be empowering them to make these same kinds of decisions themselves. They would have the same responsibilities and burdens. But I would ultimately be held accountable, and I was all right with that. I just had to trust my people. That was the hard part.

But the only way we could win.

"Yes, we *must* take the risk," I finally said in answer to Galina's question. "Lucas expects one of two things from us. He thinks we'll either fall apart with the loss of our matriarch, or we'll run into a head-on fight. He believes and hopes for the latter. He *wants* me to fight him. That's what he's wanted from me since the beginning. That's why he killed my mother—" I paused to swallow, my throat dry and thick, before I could go on. "—to spark a desire for vengeance. He expects me to lead you straight into a war he's sure we can't win. He expects to annihilate the Amadis right away, and if we survive, he thinks Tristan and I will give in and bow down to him. That's his plan. Or to kill us all, including Tristan and me. Either way, he wins."

Tristan nodded as he gave my thigh a squeeze. "Jumping right into war is our most dangerous option. We are not in a situation to defeat the Daemoni right now, when they have the norms turned against us. Until we can take the norms out of the equation, going to war now is like taking on a two-headed snake."

"We won't fight the norms," Sheree pointed out.

"Of course not," Tristan said. "Which means we'd be battling only one head although both would be striking at us."

"And their heads are about a hundred times bigger than ours," Charlotte said.

"That's a setup for defeat if I ever saw one," Tristan agreed, "and we all know charging headfirst into a war we cannot win is stupid at best and deadly at worst."

"So we're going to be *smart* by letting Lucas have his way with the Normans?" Minh asked, doubt clearly lacing her tone.

"We're going to let him *think* he's having his way," I corrected.

"We want Lucas to think the Amadis has self-destructed," Tristan said. "We want him—and the Normans in his pocket —to believe they've already defeated us with their bombings. He knows there's been some internal rumblings thanks to Kali, who planted plenty of seeds of doubt within the Amadis."

"He thinks we're weak," Owen chimed in. "Kali did everything she could to disrupt the Amadis from the inside, and Lucas knows this."

"Exactly," Tristan said. "He already knows there's a lack of trust in my character, in Alexis's leadership abilities, and in many of our loyalties among the Amadis."

"He's pushed every single button of mine he can think of," I said, "because he wants to see what I will do as matriarch. He wants to see how I'll react, because he thinks I'll either fail by getting everyone killed or by leading you right into his darkness. He pretty much said so that night at Whitby Abbey."

"He wanted you to react that night," Vanessa said. "The hope was written all over his face."

"Yes, he did," I said quietly. "Which was exactly why I didn't."

I knew why I hadn't reacted to Lucas's abhorrent actions that night—why I'd run to my mother's side instead of after him. What kept me up at night was the part right before then, when I remained frozen to the ground while the bullets slammed into her body. I'd never be able to overcome the guilt for not using my powers to stop them in midair. Of course, it had happened so fast, and both Char and Owen had been down, meaning the shield around Mom had fallen, too, but I hadn't realized that. I hadn't known how vulnerable she'd been. Those felt like flimsy excuses, but they were the truth.

"That may be the same reason he set the Daemoni loose on the Normans," Minh said. "To force you into a reaction. Into war."

My heart grew even heavier than it had already been. "Possibly."

"No, not possibly," Vanessa said. "He would have done it anyway. You heard him—his plans have been in motion with the norms for years. He didn't know things would go down the way they did at the abbey. Only Kali knew Katerina and Sophia would show up, and only Owen knew you, Tristan, and the rest of us were coming. Lucas has had wet dreams about that kind of perfect storm, so when he saw the opportunity that night, he took it. But the rest of this, with the norms? It would have happened even if that night hadn't gone down the way it did. Maybe not so soon, but it wouldn't have been long. He's been planning it forever and put the wheels in motion long ago."

"And that's exactly why I won't react now either," I said. "He's had time to pull all of this together. We're not going to go off willy-nilly into his fight. We're going to war, but not in the way Lucas expects."

"Explain what that means," Minh said.

I looked at Tristan, who'd masterminded this plan, and he nodded.

"He knows Alexis has me and some of you others who have experience, but he thinks she'll be impatient and too worried about the Normans. He expects her to be emotional and impulsive, throwing us all into his war. He doesn't think she'll be able to hang on to control for long, though, and believes that Alexis will fail as matriarch. So we're going to make him think she already has. That she and I have already lost control and that the Amadis have disbanded."

"And you ousted those others from the council the other day as part of the plan," Jelani said. It wasn't a question. He was catching on.

"Yes," Tristan and I said at the same time.

"There's already been a few small waves of blowback, but we have people making it sound much worse than it is," Owen said.

"Why not stage a coup?" Galina asked. "We could make it look like you've been ousted."

Tristan answered with the same reply he'd given me when I'd suggested the idea days ago. "We don't want to show any unification among the Amadis. A coup would mean everyone would split into two factions, but they would still have allegiance to the overall Amadis creed. We want Lucas to believe that all but a few so-called fanatics have given up on our cause."

"That's why you had some of our soldiers go out into the Norman world when our weakest left for refuge," Minh said. "So it looks like they're all abandoning the Amadis and scattering."

"Exactly," I said. "And we need to keep up this appearance. Everything we'll be doing is with purpose, but it can't look that way. It has to look the opposite. We have to convince Lucas, his Normans, and everyone else that the Amadis has fallen apart and we're no longer a threat."

"Our intelligence teams will need to do exactly opposite of what they've been doing," Tristan said. "We need spies in the Daemoni, so our people need to come out and show that they're switching sides."

"The Daemoni will kill them," Chandra protested.

"Not if they go to the right people in the right way," Vanessa said. "They're supernaturals, and the norms are turned against them. Converting to the Daemoni appears to be their only choice if they want to be protected. That's how the Daemoni will see it, and the right people will see the advantage of having Amadis in their ranks."

"Meaning, our people will need to give up some goods on the Amadis to prove they've switched their loyalty," Charlotte added. "Information that looks important, but isn't crucial to our plans."

"We can come up with some good stuff," Owen said.

"What about those super-soldiers you spoke of?" Minh asked.

"We'll be working on that in the meantime," Tristan replied. "While the rest of the Amadis looks like it's disintegrated, we need you and your top people to be prepared for action with those soldiers when we give the go. Removing those stones and breaking the connections between Lucas and the Summoned, and between the Summoned and the Norman soldiers is still a top priority."

We spent several more hours going over specific plans for how each council member would lead their region and our people within it. Many of those plans made my heart ache. Some of my own people would think Tristan and I had abandoned them. Others would be asked to leave the Amadis protection on a volunteer basis, although nobody would be truly unprotected as far as we could help it.

"There sure is a lot of deception going on," Sheree said at one point.

Tristan nodded. "Deception is necessary in a war."

"There are tens of thousands of Amadis," Vanessa said. "If they all knew the truth, someone would be bound to slip to the Daemoni or to the wrong Norman."

"We've all kept our secrets about our very existences for this long," Chandra pointed out.

"Because doing so protected their lives," Tristan said. "Now, if the Daemoni get a hold of them, self-preservation will come from *divulging*. The Daemoni invented torture, so the less our people know about our plans, the better for them and for us."

Once we finally finished with the council members scattered around the world, my core team developed our own plans for hunting down the Summoned and their offspring, destroying the stones, and severing Lucas's control of them. Then we could worry about how to bring the humans to our side before taking on Lucas himself. Of course, like the rest of the Amadis, we'd be converting along the way. Regardless of how discombobulated we appeared to be on the surface, we'd always be connected by our prime directive: protect souls.

We couldn't act yet, though. We needed to give our people time to stage our show and for Lucas to let down his guard. In the meantime, others began gathering intelligence, and Solomon tried to track down any prominent Normans who remained on our side and could possibly use their influence to sway others. I spent time in the Sacred Archives looking for more answers, reading the books and messages the Angels allowed me to decipher. Mostly just history, with a few lessons to gain here and there. What I did come to learn was no matriarch before me had faced war on this scale.

"Why me?" I muttered under my breath as I headed for the stairs and my suite where my husband waited for me.

"Alexis," Blossom said softly as I rounded the corner between my office and the kitchen. She held a large mug in her hands as she fell into step next to me, and I cringed at the smell.

"Aren't you out of those herbs yet?" I complained as we continued toward the foyer.

"Nope. Don't you worry. We have plenty." She held the mug out to me, and I pulled back, wrinkling my nose. "Drink up."

I reluctantly took the cup from her and tried not to gag from the gasoline smell wafting up from what looked like innocent green tea. "I don't know why anyone thinks bringing a baby into the world right now is a good idea."

"*You* bringing a baby into the world is an excellent idea. Exactly what we need more than anything."

"Her very existence would destroy our plans."

"Well, yes, I imagine the Amadis will rally together at the news, despite orders." Blossom put a hand on my arm, stopping me at the bottom of the steps. She looked directly into my eyes, her brow lifted. "But then we'll make new plans. Drink, Alexis."

I almost made a comment about her sounding like my mother, but the thought hurt too much. In fact, the ache in my heart exploded, and the only way I knew how to rein it in again was by distracting myself with other, different pain. So I held the mug to my lips and tilted my head back.

"Blech. That shit is nasty," I said with a full body shudder before I gave the cup back to her.

"Good." She gave me a smile, and I returned it with a glare. "The more potent it is, the better. Good night, Alexis."

She turned and headed back toward the kitchen. I blurred my way up the steps, trying to outrun the disgusting taste in my mouth. I flew into our suite, right past Tristan, who lay on the bed reading, and into the bathroom to brush my teeth while the liquid settled in my belly and the warmth spread. I wondered if that meant the potion was working. Part of me hoped it wasn't—that my ovaries and other girl parts couldn't be primed for conception by magic or anything else. I meant what I'd said to Blossom: nobody should be bringing a baby into this world right now, especially not me. Not when we couldn't promise a future for anyone, including the Amadis.

Minutes had gone by while I brushed my teeth and tongue, eradicating the gross flavor of the potion from every taste bud, and only now did I notice a bath had been drawn in the pool-sized tub. Candle flames bobbed and weaved around the bathroom. I stepped toward the door and leaned back to see Tristan sprawled out on the bed, wearing only black boxer briefs. He gave me a smile that made my bones melt and my thighs quiver.

"What's going on?" I asked hesitantly, returning his smile because I had no choice. He made my body react in all kinds of ways I had no control over.

In a flash, he stood in front of me, and his hands cupped my jaw. He tilted my head back and leaned in, close enough for me to feel his breath on my lips. Thank goodness I'd just brushed my teeth. Otherwise, I'd be assaulting him with horrible potion-breath.

"I thought you could use a relaxing soak," he murmured before brushing his mouth across mine.

I slid my hands around his neck and up into his hair. "Oh. Is that all? I get to sit in a bath by myself?"

I pretended to pout, and he sucked my protruding bottom lip in between his. My knees nearly buckled.

"Most definitely not," he said as his fingers flew through the tie of my leather corset and down the laces to loosen it. "I'll be joining you. And there will certainly be more than sitting involved."

"If only." I let out a sigh as I closed my eyes while he pulled the corset away from my body, freeing my breasts. My fighting leathers, worn pretty much at all times now, felt like a second skin—until the moment my boobs were freed from the bustier. Only then did I realize just how confining the corsets were. And normal women complained about bras . . .

"Open your mind and tell me what you hear," Tristan murmured before his lips explored my collarbone.

I didn't need to count the mind signatures to know too many people were way too close for me to truly enjoy making love with him, and I couldn't have counted even if I wanted to. Because now his tongue swiped over my breast and around my nipple and his hands gripped my hips, his fingers digging into my pants as he pulled me closer. Pleasure jolted in every direction across my body. I opened my eyes just enough to see him on his knees in front of me, his lips now skating over my chest to my other breast.

"You don't hear anything do you?" he asked before rolling his tongue over the dark pink tip, his hazel eyes trained on my face, an eyebrow lifted.

What? He'd asked me a question, but I was already so turned on, I couldn't focus. *Mind signatures.* That's what he was talking about. Right. But I found none. I leaned back, pulling my breast away from his reach and missing the warmth already, but panic tried to slide its way into my peaceful and lovely moment.

"Where is everyone?" I demanded.

"Relax, my love," he murmured as his arms snaked around my back and he pulled me to him. "There's a super-duty muffling spell on our suite. And just in case, they all went to the village to search for any supplies they could find."

"In the middle of the night? And Dorian, too?"

"It's the best time to hide from any norms who may be watching the island, but Owen and Char have cloaked everyone anyway. Don't worry. Please relax, Lexi, and let us have this night together. It might be our last good one in a long time."

The idea of Owen muffling our suite so we could have uninhibited sex made my stomach twist with embarrassment, but I couldn't resist the beautiful man in front of me or the thought of a blissful night of making mad love to him. It had been way too long since I'd really been able to enjoy our time together. My whole body suddenly flushed with excitement.

"Make it count," I said, my voice already husky.

"Oh, I plan on it."

His mouth clamped down on my breast again, and his tongue swirled around the hard tip of my nipple. He easily undid the button of my pants, and in a moment, they lay on the floor in a heap. His hands traveled all over my body, leaving a trail of electric sparks, as his mouth continued to work on my breast, sucking and biting, pulling a direct line of pleasure all the way from my core. By the time his fingers slid up the insides of my calves, then my thighs, to the pulsing junction in between, I was soaking wet and trembling with need. But he only gave me two teasing strokes of his fingers before he rose to his feet and took a step back to gaze appreciatively at me. His eyes may as well have been hands touching me everywhere with the way my body reacted.

"You look as though you've never seen me naked before," I said, practically panting. *Can he just touch me already?*

"Your beauty astounds me every time, as if it is the first," he murmured. "I still always have to wonder how you can be mine."

He still didn't move. Only his eyes, the gold sparkling as they swept over me and then lingered down low, and his tongue, as it slid tauntingly over his bottom lip. Intense need jolted through me.

"If you don't come here and kiss me and touch me and make love to me fast, I will only be my own," I growled, one of my hands reaching out for him as the other slid down my belly, ready to take care of things if he didn't.

He chuckled as he came back in, and then crushed his mouth to mine. His lips moved hungrily with mine, our tongues licking and twisting together, tasting and consuming each other as though we were the other's last meal. And then his mouth was gone again, traveling downward, over my chin, down my throat, to my chest. His hands slid down my sides to grip my waist, and he easily lifted me, setting me on the counter. I leaned back on my elbows, and he dove down.

Warm wetness engulfed each hardened nipple, one at a time, as his palms skated over my hips and thighs and to the backs of my knees. He pushed my legs up and out, opening me for him as he lowered himself to his knees again. His head dipped down, and mine fell backwards. I already hovered on the edge of an orgasm before his tongue made its first swipe. My body quaked uncontrollably with the second one. And I danced on the edge, shaking and gripping the counter, as his tongue did magnificent things to me.

"Let go, Lexi," he murmured against me. "Be mine."

He sucked then, and his fingers slid in deeper and curled upward. And I more than let go. I exploded, screaming his name over and over as his lips and tongue and fingers continued to lift me up, up, up until I burst again and again, lights popping before my eyes and my muscles seizing. His mouth pulled away, and all at once, I was grateful for the relief yet still wanting more, more, more. He kissed the inside of one thigh, his tongue swirling against my skin, and I almost came again.

He stood, and I reached out for him, but he wouldn't let me touch him. He lifted me by the waist again and carried me over to the tub, where he set me down. My legs gave in, too weak to hold me, and I slid into the warm water. My eyes never left his perfectly sculpted body as he pushed off his boxer briefs and stepped into the tub with me. I took hold of him before he could immerse himself completely in the water, and he groaned as I stroked the thick length a few times and then took him the way he'd just taken me.

"Lex . . . I can't . . ." He moaned again, and his hooded eyes slid all the way closed.

"Don't," I said.

"Not yet. I want inside you."

Before I could stop him, he sank all the way into the water. I glared at him, but he returned it with a smirk.

"Turn around," he whispered, leaving me no choice but to obey as his hands again gripped me and turned me so my back faced him.

He pulled me in between his legs, then slid his wet, bubbly hands up my spine and pushed my hair over my shoulder. His mouth and tongue tickled the nape of my neck as he scooped warm water over my skin. His erection pressed against my butt and up the small of my back. I curled my legs underneath me and rocked forward slightly onto my knees, teasing his tip as his hands and mouth continued to caress my shoulders and back. Anticipation built again, pulling my breasts tight and pulsing between my legs. I leaned forward further and lifted up. His hands grasped my butt and squeezed right before I moved down and over him, pulling him inside me. We both let out a quiet cry.

His hands gripped my hips as I slid up and down, both of us moaning and groaning as the friction sent spikes of pleasure up through my belly and out across my body. Then his palm slid forward and up over my breast, while the other slid down my front, causing chills to sweep over my skin. I leaned back against him, arching my head over his shoulder as his fingers stroked and my hips rocked and his breaths came hot on my ear, sending wave after wave of pleasure until my insides exploded again. I screamed his name, and he yelled out mine as we both came together, quaking and convulsing and losing ourselves into the other, becoming one soul, one body, one entity of love.

I'd nearly forgotten how beautiful and primal we could be together when I didn't have to hold back. The sense of freedom overcame my mind, body, and soul now that the mental wall had fallen, and our lovemaking became so much more through the night as we slammed our bodies against walls and into the ceiling, doing all those things we couldn't do when others were around.

And I no longer cared that everyone knew what we were doing even if they couldn't hear us. Because Tristan was right —we needed this night together. It would be our last for a long time. Maybe forever.

CHAPTER 8

*T*he time to move out arrived quickly. News on the television and the web became unreliable as governments and the Daemoni censored the media. We couldn't even access any networks in some countries, and others contradicted each other's reports. The world was quickly descending into Lucas's orchestrated chaos.

We spent a few days consulting with our generals, so to speak, ensuring they were capable of handling the Daemoni and the humans on their own within their regions. Our intelligence teams began to report back that the Daemoni believed the Amadis was falling apart. As soon as rumors began that I was no longer in control, we started packing up and making plans. Solomon had a few places for us to visit in Europe to try to secretly align with some Normans, although he warned us that he couldn't guarantee anyone would come through.

"We're leaving in eight hours," I called through Dorian's door while knocking on it at the same time. "Are you packed?"

The door flew open, and my son stood there with wide eyes, taller than me but looking like a frightened child.

"You're not making me go with the others, are you?" he

asked, panic lacing his voice. Sasha stood next to him, the size of a Husky instead of a toy dog. Her stripes vaguely showed through her thick white coat. Dorian's anxiety had her on edge.

"No, little—" I paused. He wasn't exactly a little man any more. "No, Dorian. Of course not. You'll be with Dad and me."

He looked away, at some point over my shoulder, and nodded, but I couldn't help but notice how his bottom lip trembled in the most minute way.

"Dorian." I stepped closer to him and put a hand on his upper arm. Sheesh. It was thicker with muscle than it should have been at his age. "What's wrong?"

"I . . . I just don't want you guys to leave me," he said. He averted his eyes for a moment, and then threw himself at me, like the little boy he should have been. "Don't leave me again, Mom. *Please.*"

I kicked the door closed, wrapped my arms around him, and held him tightly. "No, never, Dorian. I could never leave you. They *took* you, remember?"

"Because you left! What if they come back again?" His body shook in my arms, and fear weighed heavily in his words as he sobbed against me.

I gripped his shoulders and gently pushed him away from me, then walked him over to his bed. We both sat down, and I held him again.

"Dad and I will keep you safe," I promised.

"You can't forever, though." He drew in a jagged breath, then pulled away and scrubbed his eyes as if I didn't already know he'd been crying. He scooted away on the bed until his back pressed against the wall, then he tucked his legs up with his knees under his chin. He stared at the wall across the room, but his mind was elsewhere, and I looked to see where. *There.* At the DoD building, where Kali and Lucas had been holding him. Threads of panic ran through this mind, although I could grasp no coherent thoughts.

"Dorian, what did they do to you?" I asked, not for the first time. He'd never given me an answer before, but he'd never been as open as this either. Maybe he'd tell me this time.

"Nothing," he muttered, his voice rough.

And maybe he wouldn't.

I scooched my way back to sit next to him and placed my hand on his leg. "I think they did. You know you can tell me."

He shifted away from me. "They didn't *do* anything. Just told me stuff."

"Like what?"

When several moments passed and no answer came, I looked into his mind again while watching his face. His jaw muscle popped.

"Get out of my head," he growled. Well, that was new. He could sense me in his mind now. "How come when you want to, you can just let yourself into my head, but when I needed you, when I tried to warn you about them coming, you ignored me?"

I sighed at his accusatory tone. "I'm sorry. The way it works is weird. I was focused on the meeting, and I felt you, but didn't realize it was you or what you were saying until it was too late. I have to have my mind open to you all the time to be able to hear you whenever."

"And it's not?" he sneered.

"No, Dorian, it's not. I try to give you privacy."

"Except just now."

"Except when you have me freaking out about how you're doing and you won't talk to me, yes." I cocked my head to the side to look at him. "I'm so worried about you. And I don't know how to help you if you won't talk to me."

"I'm fine," he mumbled.

"No, you're not. And how could you be? They're horrible, evil people who kidnapped you!"

He rolled his eyes. "Uncle Owen kidnapped me, and he took care of me. He made sure nobody hurt me."

"Just being away from us had to have been traumatic." I placed my hand on his shoulder and squeezed.

"Yeah. It sucked. But I'm fine. Don't worry about me, Mom."

"I can't help it. You're still my baby."

He snorted. "Right."

I watched him for a long moment, feeling the sadness emanating from his body as though it leaked out of his soul.

"What did they do to you?" I asked again. "And don't tell me nothing because you came back half-a-foot taller and half grown up."

He shrugged. "That pretty redhead asked what I wanted more than anything in the world. When I said to go home, she said it had to be something else, so I said to be big and strong like my dad. And she said okay."

Bile rose in my throat. That "pretty redhead" had been Kali, possessing a young witch's body. And of course she'd put a spell on him to make him grow—the sooner Dorian went through puberty and gained his powers, the sooner the Daemoni would have him. That was their plan anyway. I'd do anything in my power to stop that plan.

"What else?" I asked.

"Nothing."

"Dorian . . ."

"Seriously, Mom. Nothing. Just told me stuff, but it was stupid. I don't believe it. A lot of it, anyway."

I studied him again and peeked into his mind, but he concentrated on the ranks of characters in his favorite video game so he wouldn't think about the stuff they told him. He'd already figured out how to keep me from accessing his memories and thoughts.

"Well, don't believe any of it," I finally said. "They lie. They don't know how to tell the truth."

"Right," he said. "Except it's true that Dad used to be one of them, and your own father leads them? The dickwad who *murdered* my mimi?"

"Watch your mouth," I said automatically.

His eyes cut sideways at me. The look in them caused me to pull back. He had the same hazel irises as Tristan, and I swore I could almost see flames around the pupils.

"Yes, that's true," I admitted quietly.

"So not *everything* they said is a lie."

"Tell me what they told you, and I can tell you which ones aren't true."

He blew out an angry breath, and then sprang across the bed and to his feet, as if a switch had been flipped, making him suddenly irate. "Just forget it, Mom! I don't want to talk about it."

"Dorian—"

"Leave me alone!" he shouted so loudly, I felt the vibration in my bones. He flicked his hand, and the door flew open—another newly acquired power.

I narrowed my eyes and walked right up to him. "Don't you talk to me that way. I am still your mother."

"And if you care about me at all, you'll just let me be. Don't make me say the things they told me!"

Realization dawned on me then, and I could easily conclude what "stuff" they'd told him. The same things they'd told every Amadis son—the Amadis didn't care about him, he'd always be treated like dirt here, the Daemoni would become his new family, and they'd worship him like a king. That the Amadis would kick him out and want nothing to do with him. No wonder he'd been so scared that Tristan and I would leave him. They'd already planted the seeds in his mind of what they thought his future would grow into if he stayed with us. This explained his mood swings, too.

"Dorian, don't believe them. Nothing has to be the way they said."

"No, but it will be," he said under his breath, but I heard him loud and clear.

"Dorian," I gasped.

"Just leave me alone, Mom." He sounded weary now. "I'm not going anywhere, except with you. Just let me pack."

I stared at him for a long moment, but finally nodded. "You can only take a backpack."

I strode for the door, vowing to myself to make sure he knew he was always wanted here with Tristan and me.

"The Daemoni have already dug their dirty, disgusting claws into our son," I told Tristan a little while later while we checked our weapons in our suite. I only had my trusty dagger, inherited from Cassandra herself, and a knife I kept in my boot, but Tristan had all kinds of things hidden here and there among his leather fighting gear. Not that he ever used them. He mostly relied on his supernatural powers.

"Did you really expect anything different?" he asked.

I frowned as I looked at him. "I expected them to tell him lies, which I guess they did, but they also told him the truth about you and Lucas. And they already started their whole spiel about how he belongs to them."

"I know, Lex. He told me."

My brows rose. "Really? He talked to you about it? And you didn't tell me?"

A feeling of betrayal niggled at me under my skin. I couldn't decide whom I felt more betrayed by, though—my son or my husband.

He chuckled quietly. "Yeah, he came to talk to me. I figured he'd tell you when he was ready."

I grimaced. "Well, then. He wasn't exactly ready to tell me anything at all. I was happy to get out of him what I could. Why would he tell you everything and not me?"

Tristan set the silver throwing star he'd been polishing on the bed and strode over to me. He wrapped his arms around me and planted a kiss on the top of my head. "Because you are his mother, and he doesn't want to disappoint you."

"And you are his idol."

"I'm also a guy, and he knows I'm not perfect. Especially now that he does know about my past with them."

"But why would he disappoint me? It's not like he's done anything wrong."

"Because he thinks it's inevitable that he *will* do something wrong. That he'll leave us. He's already feeling guilty about it."

"Oh." I pressed my cheek against Tristan's solid chest and considered this for a moment. "Well, he has nothing to feel guilty about now, and all he has to do when the time comes is say no."

"*Ma lykita*, it's not so cut and dry. He will have a decision to make, and only he can make it. Our boy is carrying a heavy load on his shoulders."

"He doesn't have to. He just has to know this is where he belongs."

"Yes, my love, but be prepared that no matter what we do, we might not be able to change anything. Or maybe we do by pushing him the wrong way. He needs space to learn and grow and be able to make the decision for himself. And he needs love and trust to do the right thing."

I made a face, but eventually nodded. "Okay, fine. I won't pressure him. But do you really think he'll be okay?"

Tristan blew out a heavy breath. "Honestly? I don't think you want to know my answer to that."

My heart squeezed. I knew he was right. My son would never be okay again.

But really, I didn't know if anyone in this world would be right again. Once we left the confines of the mansion and the Amadis Island in the wee hours of the next morning, I learned just how right I was about that.

The world would never be the same again.

CHAPTER 9

$\mathcal{S}$ ince flashing was no longer an option unless we wanted to be trapped by the norms, or worse, the Daemoni, Owen created a portal for our entire group to pass through, taking us into the Italian countryside. We needed to arrive somewhere secluded, but our target was Rome. Well, Vatican City, more specifically. Solomon thought the Pope would still be on our side, and therefore, his millions of followers. The problem was getting to him.

We arrived in some overgrown vineyards on the side of a hill, a place Savio had told Charlotte about shortly before I kicked him off the council. He'd said the owner of the small winery had let the place go for years after her husband passed away, and then she died, too. If she'd had any heirs, they hadn't claimed the land. With no reason for the Daemoni to expect our appearance here and no norms around to witness, it provided the perfect place for us to suddenly appear.

From what I could see in the pitch darkness of night, the buildings at the bottom of the hill appeared to be in poor shape and weeds had devoured the vineyards, but the place must have been beautiful at one time. Did the owner truly not have any heirs, or were they for some reason not interested in the family business? Why hadn't someone else bought the place? Maybe in a simpler time, owning a winery could have been fun for Tristan and me, part of that normal life I'd always dreamt about as a kid. But our lives weren't normal and they never would be, I thought with a sigh as I scanned for nearby mind signatures.

"We're good for at least ten miles," I said quietly when I found nobody around.

We'd picked the dead of night for traveling because most Normans would be sleeping, decreasing the threat of them coming after us. The Daemoni were more likely to be out, but we didn't worry about having to fight them. At least, not until we reached the city. Considering their food source seemed to be scarce out here in the boonies, any Daemoni nearby were weak and at ankle level of the totem pole. Once we made our way into the city, we'd be facing a bigger threat, but we didn't plan on anyone noticing our presence. Our large group didn't allow us to travel with any speed under a cloak without running into each other, but when we came close enough to the city, Owen would hide us.

Blossom had concocted a velocity potion to make the mages, shifters, and Dorian able to run as fast as the vampires, Tristan, and me, and they all swallowed it down. Then we raced toward the city, our bodies nothing but blurs to the Norman eye. Vanessa and Sheree in her tiger form bounded ahead of us, and Solomon and Jax brought up the rear. Even with the magical enhancement, Jax wouldn't have been able to keep up with us in his crocodile form for the long distance we had to travel, but when I glanced over my shoulder, I saw that he didn't run unprepared. His eyes glowed in the dark, his teeth extended several inches beyond his lips, and although crocs weren't known for long and sharp claws, they were certainly frightening enough on his human hands that had become webbed and partially scaled.

My mental antenna constantly probed for mind

signatures, but found none, even as we approached the suburbs. A feeling of trepidation slid down my spine at this, strengthened by the realization of just how dark and still our surroundings were. No streetlights. No cars on the roads. Even in the middle of the night, there should have been some sign of life.

But there was none.

Only dark homes and dark businesses. Even a gas station we passed appeared to be abandoned, a car sitting at the pump with the driver's side door still open.

"*Something's wrong*," Vanessa thought into my head. I kept my mind open to all of them as a gateway that allowed a silent conversation.

"*It's an old-fashioned ghost town*," Owen agreed.

"*Because of the Daemoni attacks?*" Blossom asked.

"*Had to have been*," Charlotte said. "*It looks like they all ran when the Daemoni came out and never returned.*"

"*Maybe the norms bugged out to a safer place*," Owen suggested.

Except there was nobody in the country, either, which is where they would have gone during the attacks, right? I said.

"*That or they holed up somewhere protected*," Tristan offered.

"*Or they've all been eaten or turned*," Solomon countered, stating in his normal matter-of-fact tone the conclusion we'd all been thinking but not saying out loud. Or thinking out loud. Whatever.

"*This place is downright creepy*," Blossom said.

Although Sheree's thoughts weren't clearly human, we could feel her agreement. The fur along her spine lifted, and her ears twitched as she listened in every direction. We all ran a tad slower, on higher alert. Dorian moved closer between Tristan and me. Barely more than a minute later, I picked up on the brain waves—mind signatures of a whole slew of norms, clustered in an apartment building a few miles ahead. Just as I was about to signal to my group to turn and order

Owen to cloak us, my mind translated an Italian thought: "*Almost . . . now!*"

Flood lights lit up the entire block, bright as day. Generators kicked on somewhere in the distance, but we still heard the clicks of weapons being cocked.

Run! I screamed at my team, but we weren't fast enough.

A warning arrow flew in front of me, and Vanessa suddenly stopped, swearing up a storm. Damn. Even with our supernatural speed, they'd managed to catch us. We halted and threw our hands in the air—except Vanessa, who yanked the arrow out of her thigh and snapped it in half before throwing it on the ground. Several people stepped out of the shadows of the storefronts with guns pointed at us. At least they hadn't used those for a warning.

Tristan shouted something in Italian, and Vanessa did, too, probably cussing them out for shooting her. At least she didn't immediately attack in retribution. I picked up on a few thoughts as they spoke, figuring out the conversation. Tristan tried to convince the Normans that we were like them, harmless and simply headed into the city. A woman said something about the city being swarmed and dangerous. A man pointed out our unnatural speed and asked with sarcasm if the tiger was a pet.

And then a younger woman yelled in English, "It's her! A.K. Emerson!"

The norms didn't even hesitate. Gunshots cracked through the night. The racket instantly brought me to the horrible night of watching my mom die, but the noise sounded different. The shots came slower, not from automatic, military-grade weapons, but from civilian handguns. By the tangy smell of burnt gunpowder, old handguns at that. And I wasn't as surprised by this as I had been that night. I didn't just stand there stupidly in shock, but instead lifted my hand and flicked my finger to suspend the bullets in the air. With Tristan, Blossom, and Char's help, it was easy to do long enough for

Owen to put up a shield. Singing above the gunshots came the high-pitched sound of a warning siren.

But they weren't warning anyone—there was no one around to warn. They were calling for help.

Seconds later, newcomers dropped onto the scene: Daemoni. Several vampires, a few witches and wizards, and someone with magic powerful enough to cause the air to whoosh around us as our shield disappeared. Had to have been a sorcerer, although he hung back. My mind felt him two blocks away, but only for the briefest of moments before sharp pain fired into my brain, blocking him out.

The vampires—a dozen of them—swarmed in on us, their hungry grins displaying their long, glistening fangs. The thrill of the kill sparked in their glowing, red eyes. Holding one hand to my head, I shot electricity at them. The mages shot spells back at us, and the battle began.

"Run!" I yelled at the norms as Blossom blocked an errant spell headed for the building to our left. "Take cover and stay there!"

The norms who'd been shooting at us only moments ago scattered, thankfully leaving the fight to us. They did it to help the Daemoni—obvious since they'd called them here—but I didn't care. At least they'd moved out of the way, and we didn't have to worry about unintentionally hurting one of them. We needed to focus on the evil creatures moving in on us.

A dark-haired vampire who strode toward me, moving slowly as he planned his attack, looked very familiar. I felt sure I'd seen him at Mom and Rina's funeral. I'd been a little distraught that day, okay, a lot, but I remembered the curling lines of ink crawling up his neck from under the collar of his shirt. I still couldn't see the tattoo underneath, but the tendrils were definitely the same. I tilted my head a notch. He narrowed his eyes slightly. I opened my mind to him.

"The Pope is dead, if that's what you're here for. You need to get out of here."

One of our own, performing as instructed. And doing a good job at it when he flew at me, his mouth wide open, his fangs directed for my throat.

"*GO!*" he yelled in my mind as I threw my powers at him, flinging him several yards away.

More Daemoni began landing in the road, popping out of nowhere. Which meant they could flash here. Tristan noticed, too. He threw his hand up and froze everyone except for us. A vampire hissed and snarled.

"If you don't want to fight, maybe you want to come with us," he offered, barely able to move his lips. "We all know you abandoned your own people. Left them to fend for themselves. Don't worry. We'll take care of them."

A witch snickered. "Who knows why Lucas still wants you, but if you begged hard enough, he'd probably take you in."

"*We can flash out of here,*" Tristan said to us, ignoring the Daemoni's taunts.

"*Maybe it's safe to flash here but not where we're going,*" Charlotte pointed out.

The Pope's dead, I said. *We need to get out of the area before we're overwhelmed.*

"*Let's try Köln then,*" Solomon suggested, and I remembered him saying something about an archbishop who worked closely with the European Union's leadership.

"*I'll make a portal,*" Owen said while already moving his hands together. He closed his eyes to focus for a moment, then he spread his hands apart, opening a hole in the very air in front of us. At the same time, several Daemoni appeared, one with an extremely loud pop very close to us. Tristan grunted as the Daemoni he'd paralyzed began breaking through his power.

"*There's snow in Germany already?*" Jax asked.

"*That doesn't look like Köln,*" Vanessa said.

"*Just go!*" Tristan ordered, his voice strained.

The sorcerer whose mind signature I'd noticed before had appeared directly behind us, and I couldn't read his mind, but I could feel his intense darkness. His magic focused on Tristan's paralyzing power, gradually lifting it from the other Daemoni, while also pulling on my energy to feed himself. Before he could sap me completely, I grabbed Dorian's hand and leapt us through the portal. We landed in about six inches of white powder, and then fell when the others plowed into us. The sun glaring on the freshly fallen snow nearly blinded me as I jumped to my feet and counted heads.

"Close the portal, Owen," I yelled when I confirmed we'd all made it through. The intensity of the sorcerer's dark magic tried to swallow me whole. He must have been attempting to come after us.

"It's closed, Alexis," Owen said.

"Where's the dark magic coming from?" Blossom asked, wrapping her arms over her ample chest and huddling close to Jax.

"This definitely isn't Köln." Charlotte turned in a circle, hands out, ready to fight.

"Hades," Tristan, Vanessa, and Solomon said at the same time.

I spun around, my eyes wide. An encampment of canvas tents stood on the snowy field about three hundred yards away.

Tristan tilted his head toward it. "That's the Shaman village by the entrance."

"We need to get the hell out of here," Vanessa said. "Before they notice us."

"Owen—" I started.

"Already on it," he snarled through a clenched jaw. He opened another portal, and we all ran through it, not even pausing to see where we headed.

As I ran into the new place, I watched the backs of Sheree and Solomon bring up the last of our group through another hole. We'd come through only six feet away from where we'd left.

"What the hell?" Charlotte declared.

"I don't know," Owen said. "Let me try again. Somewhere else. Where else besides Germany, Solomon?"

"Praha."

Owen nodded and created a new portal. We all ran through, only to end up even closer to the Shaman village.

"Someone's blocking my portals."

"Then they already know we're here," Vanessa said. At the same time, a wave of dark magic crashed into us, flattening us to the ground.

"Run!" Tristan barked as he jumped to his feet. He grabbed Dorian, threw him on his back like a rag doll, and sprinted away from the Shamans.

The flatlands of northern Siberia stretched in front of us with mountains rising in the far distance. We ran as fast and as far as we could across the plains, our speed allowing us to glide over the top of the snow that must have been the first blanket of the year. Thank the Angels it wasn't January. We ran until we hit the base of a mountain, when the others could no longer keep up with Tristan, Solomon, Vanessa, and me because the velocity potion had worn off.

"Maybe . . . we can . . . flash here," Blossom suggested, panting as she leaned over and braced her hands on her thighs. "We're in the middle of nowhere Siberia. Who even lives here? Do you really think there are traps?"

"We're way too close to Hades to risk it," Vanessa said, and by the way she rounded her shoulders, I could tell she suppressed a shudder. "No way are we getting trapped there."

"We could try a portal again," I said, although I wasn't sure that was such a great idea.

"What if we end up back at Hades?" Jax asked. "I'm not running all that way again. It might be easy for you, princess, but not for this lumbering croc."

"Especially because I'm out of potion," Blossom said. "We'll be too slow."

Dorian, standing off to the side, suggested quietly, "I could fly us out of here."

"No," Tristan and I answered at the same time.

"You can't carry all of us at once," Charlotte said, more kindly.

"No, but I can probably take two at a time. And Sasha could help." At the mention of her name, the lykora's little, white dog's snout poked out of the top of Dorian's jacket.

"It's too dangerous," I said.

"Uncle Owen can shield me, right?"

Owen shook his head. "Not if you get too far away from me."

"Then you stay with me."

"Absolutely not," I said. "I don't care if Owen shields you. It's too dangerous!"

"But—"

"No, Dorian," Tristan said firmly. "It's not a viable option. It will take too long, and there are too many risks involved."

"I was just trying to help," he muttered as he kicked at the snow and sent a rock underneath flying.

"And we appreciate it," Blossom said. "Very much. But your dad knows the best solution."

"And that's not it." I turned to look at Tristan, who gazed off into the distance. "So what is our solution?"

"There's nothing around here for hundreds of miles. Trust me, I know. Only a few villages of indigenous people, most of them Shamans."

"Great," I muttered.

"They're mages," Blossom said. "Not all are dark."

"No, but most around here are Daemoni," Vanessa said. "Any Amadis would be in hiding."

"So what should we do, Tristan?" I asked, starting to feel the hopelessness of our situation.

"I think we can flash," he answered, surprising all of us. He turned back to face our group. "This is the Daemoni's kingdom. Why would they prevent flashing here? They need to get in and out, close to Hades. We have about six hundred miles between here and any resemblance of civilization, eight hundred to decent transportation. Our only other option is to hike it, and I don't think we'll all last."

He nodded toward Dorian, whose lips were already turning blue. His whole body shook from the below freezing temperature. We hadn't expected to find ourselves in winter conditions in the beginning of October, so he wore only a light coat over a t-shirt and jeans on his legs.

"Owen," I hissed. "Can't you do something?"

"I'm so sorry, Dorian!" Blossom squealed, and she waved her hand toward the man-boy. He immediately stopped shivering. "The spell won't last forever in this cold, though. I've already had to redo my own since we've been standing here."

"Looks like flashing is our only option," Char said.

Nobody liked the idea or the risks that came with it, but we couldn't argue with Tristan. He knew this place better than any of us, except maybe Vanessa. She hadn't come up with any other solutions, though, so apparently flashing was it.

"We're going to a small village outside of Vorkuta," Tristan said. "I don't think it'll be safe to flash once we get there. We'll make our way to Vorkuta's train station, which will take us to Moscow and the rest of civilized society so we can get back on track. If we get trapped and separated anywhere along the way, we meet in Prague."

"There's an old hotel two blocks from the safe house in old town Praha." Solomon's eyes cut to me when my brow furrowed with confusion. "Praha is Czech for Prague," he clarified. "The hotel looks abandoned from the outside. Meet there."

"You vamps are charged up with mage blood?" Charlotte asked, and both Solomon and Vanessa nodded, meaning they'd be able to flash. "I'll help Sheree. Blossom, you can help Jax?"

"Of course." She moved closer against him—if that were possible. I noticed her lips beginning to pale. The cold was becoming too much for her.

"I'll take Dorian and lead Alexis," Tristan said. "Owen and Vanessa, follow our trail, and the rest of you follow in suit. We're good?"

Everyone nodded, but only after a moment of hesitation. Blossom's eyes grew round and huge, and she gnawed on her lip.

Solomon, I said, only to him. His dark gaze darted over to me. *Lead Blossom and Jax. If we get separated, I don't know what they'd do on their own.*

Except for a night on Amadis Island when Rina gave her blessing to search for Dorian last March, Blossom had never been out of the United States until a month ago, when we traveled through a portal from Virginia to England. Jax wasn't much the world traveler himself, having spent several decades isolated in the Australian Outback.

Solomon nodded and stepped over to Blossom's side. "*I'll take care of them.*"

Tristan blew out a hard breath, gripped Dorian's forearm, and slid his other hand into mine. "Let's do this."

He gave my hand a squeeze before flashing and taking me with him. We arrived on the side of a mountain in the middle of a blizzard. As soon as everyone else appeared, he flashed again. After the first couple of times, we had to take breaks for the less magical among us. The pauses lasted only about five to ten minutes at first, but then we came close to the only civilization we'd seen so far—a drab city of featureless buildings that all looked the same except for their paint colors of dulled blue, orange, green, and yellow. A greenish smog hung over the city, and even the freshly fallen snow wasn't quite white, but more of a pale pink. Tristan called the city Norilsk, a mining town, evidenced by the plumes of smoke rising from stacks on the other side of the city. Also a Daemoni-controlled area that we needed to vacate immediately. After the back-to-back flash, our breaks grew longer, becoming twenty and thirty minutes each. Even the vampires were languishing, using all of this power in the daytime.

"One more flash to go," Tristan said after our current break had stretched into nearly an hour.

We stood on the edge of a lake or bay, and although we followed the sun, daylight was quickly disappearing—the days were short this far north. In a few weeks, there would be an endless stretch of nothing but night. At least, it would feel endless to me. I didn't know how people could stand living this far north, with no sun for weeks on end. And even though the cold didn't really bother me, I still preferred the warmth of the sun and the feeling of sand between my toes, not snow clumping to my boots.

"We've made it this far," Charlotte said.

Yes, we'd made it this far, but each flash had been a heart-stopping, breath-holding moment of fear and uncertainty. Not until we all popped into sight could I feel the slightest bit of relief. Then we'd have to do it all over again, the bottom of my stomach falling out each time. *Would this be the time we got caught?* The question echoed in everyone's minds right before a flash.

"One more time," Blossom muttered, her arms looped around Jax's and Solomon's, holding tightly to both. "We can do this."

She didn't sound as confident as she probably wished she did, making it apparent she tried to convince herself more than anyone.

"You're doing great, Blossom," I said. "Soon we'll be in more interesting areas with much better scenery."

She gave a weak laugh. "Yeah, this hasn't exactly been the kind of international getaway I'd always dreamed about."

Well, that wasn't going to change. We weren't exactly on vacation, after all. But moving farther west meant we'd be closer to civilization and farther away from Hades. Although, I didn't know if that really meant we'd be much safer, with the way the world was quickly going to hell. It was up to us to stop it from getting there, though, so regardless of scenery and the hell we headed toward, we had to keep moving.

"Okay, one more time," I said. "And then we can rest."

CHAPTER 10

"Yes," Tristan said. "We'll take a long break until the middle of the night. I promise."

We flashed to the side of another mountain, with what looked like a city in the far distance. Thick, dark clouds hung overhead, threatening a snowstorm that could begin any minute, and giving an earlier than usual twilight. Even as we stood there, taking in our surroundings, the lights of the city began to blink on.

Tristan tilted his head downward. "We'll find shelter down there."

I followed his gaze to the bottom of the mountain and focused on what looked like a tiny village directly below us.

"You want to go into a town?" I fixed in on the mind signatures below. Only a couple dozen, from what I could tell from here. "With Normans?"

"Just because they're Normans doesn't mean it's safe," Charlotte pointed out.

"They'll just call the Daemoni like the ones in Italy," Blossom said.

"We need to rest, right?" Tristan asked. "I was here two years ago, and half the town was empty then. I doubt there's

119

been a surge of population, meaning there are vacant buildings to hide in for a few hours."

Big, fat snowflakes began to fall while the darkness of night quickly slithered over us. Dorian started shivering again, and I pulled him close to me, wrapping my arms around him and trying to share my body heat.

"I'll keep us shielded and cloaked," Owen said. "We need to take cover. This storm looks ugly."

About a mile outside of town, we crept into an old barn to hide out for the night while we scoped the area for any danger. As soon as all of us had gathered inside, though, the horses began neighing loudly, the cows mooed, the pigs snorted and chuffed, and some chickens squawked, creating quite the ruckus.

"Sheree, change," I whispered to the tiger, who immediately morphed into her human self, albeit naked. Blossom dug a set of clothes out of her bottomless bag, but even as Sheree dressed, the animals only grew louder. I checked on the owner's mind, and he hadn't heard them yet, but he would soon, and he'd be out here any minute.

"Do you think it's Sasha?" I asked.

Jax shook his bald head. "Half of us here are their predators, and they sense the danger. Even if we all look human, they know."

"Stupid animals," Vanessa muttered as she strode over to the barn door to leave.

"Don't take it personally," I said as I followed her out. "I like bacon and steak."

"That's why they're stupid. Those norms are more dangerous to them than Solomon or me. And any self-respecting shifter wouldn't eat a caged, domesticated pet."

"Nope. No challenge, no eat," Sheree said from my other side as we strode down the lane and closer to town. My head snapped toward her at the uncharacteristic statement. I hadn't known Sheree hunted at all. "What? A girl's gotta eat, and I can't always wait until I'm human to grab something out of the fridge. Especially now."

"So Bambi and Thumper?" I asked with surprise.

"Alexis! No!" she protested, but then said with an edge of guilt, "Well, maybe their dads. I like turkeys, fish, and . . . well, don't tell Jax, but gator's good, too."

I laughed. "Sheree!"

She gave me a grin. "My favorite's wild boar, though. *Wild* boar. Not Babe or Wilbur back in that barn." She shuddered. "I couldn't imagine . . ."

"I hate to break it to you," Vanessa said, "but Babe and Wilbur are what you get from the fridge."

I stared at her now, surprised she even knew who Babe and Wilbur were. She shrugged. "I like animal movies. So sue me."

"Opening a package from the store is not the same as eating it fresh," Sheree said.

I wrinkled my nose at that thought. No, definitely not the same, thank the Angels. "So you're saying that you prefer Pumba?"

Vanessa laughed, and Sheree groaned. "Stop it. Like I don't feel guilty enough as it is, you're going to make me starve to death before I'll eat another animal."

I bumped my shoulder against her, hitting her upper arm because she stood so much taller than me. "I'm just giving you a hard time, and I won't let you starve to death."

"That looks promising." Vanessa lifted her chin toward a small structure about a mile down the road. She disappeared in a blur, and then returned a few seconds later. "It's an abandoned cabin. No furniture and no heat, but it's shelter from this storm. And no people or Daemoni, so that's a bonus."

The wind whipped and howled around us, blowing snow in our faces as we moved toward the cabin. The weaker of our group, including Dorian and Blossom, pushed against the harsh gusts with their heads down and their arms held closely to their chests. With their Warlock bodies built a little tougher, Owen and Charlotte weren't hunched over, but they weren't a whole lot better off, either. As soon as we gathered inside the one-room cabin, Tristan pulled a cabinet off the wall and lit it on fire, providing some much needed heat and light. Everyone but Solomon and Vanessa gathered around it.

We hadn't expected to be so far removed from civilization when we left, so we didn't have much food with us. Dorian had the biggest stash of packaged crackers and snacks that we all shared. Except Solomon and Vanessa, of course.

"The things I do for you," Owen said as he gritted his teeth while dragging the edge of one of Tristan's knives over his forearm.

"You know it's better for us both when I do it." Vanessa licked the tip of her fang. Owen glared at her with a brow lifted. The rest of us suppressed a knowing laugh. A vampire's bite only hurt at first pierce, and then it became bliss . . . nearly orgasmic. Owen's face flushed a deep red, and his jaw muscle twitched as he held his arm over a brown plastic cup that had held potato chips a few minutes ago.

"You get the cup," he said with a half-snarl.

Charlotte used another container to supply Solomon with his own meal. Between the blood and the darkness outside, he and Vanessa quickly became hyped up. Sheree and Jax seemed pretty energetic, too. So those four took turns guarding the perimeter of the cabin while the rest of us grabbed some rest.

After a few hours on the hard, wooden floor with Tristan's arm as a pillow, my body felt as regenerated as it would get. I could hardly sleep in the lush, comfy bed back at the mansion, so enjoying much shut-eye here was out of the question. As soon as I sat up, Tristan did, too. He apparently couldn't sleep, either. We snuck outside, so we wouldn't disturb the others. Another few inches of snow had fallen, and the wind blew the frozen stuff into my face.

"Did you scope the town out?" Tristan asked Vanessa and

Solomon once we stepped off the front porch. He spoke quietly, barely more than a whisper, although the vampires stood thirty yards away, in opposite directions. Neither turned toward us, but kept their alert gazes outward, surveying the fields and the town.

"Couldn't leave you and Alexis without a watch guard," Vanessa said.

"There's a shield over the whole cabin," I reminded them.

"And we've already seen more than once that a sorcerer can break Owen's shields," Solomon responded. "We're barely more than fifty miles from a decent-sized town in Russia and still uncomfortably close to Hades. The possibility for such a sorcerer being nearby is quite great."

"Go check it out," Tristan said. "Alexis and I will keep guard."

Solomon let out a displeased grunt before they both blurred out of sight.

"What does he think will happen in the short time they'll be gone?" I asked rhetorically.

Less than a minute later, he and Vanessa returned.

"A lot can happen in the snap of a finger." Solomon clicked his finger and thumb together.

As if in response, gunfire ripped through the silent night. The tat-tat-tat-tat of an automatic weapon. Visions of my mom's body jerking with each hit tried to obliterate the snowy scene in front of me. I might have called out her name, but the memory disappeared when someone slammed me to the ground, driving my face into the snow.

"See?" Solomon hissed from above me.

I could barely move enough under his boulder-like weight to twist my head so I could breathe and see. Vanessa had already crossed the field and attacked the gunman, knocking the gun away, but he fought her off expertly. Another man joined the fight, and Tristan blurred over and paralyzed them both. He swept his hand out, and the two men flew closer to

Solomon and me, and Tristan and Vanessa appeared right behind them.

"Solomon?" the one on our right asked, his voice thick with a Russian accent.

"Evgeny?" Solomon responded as he slowly moved to his feet, allowing me up, too.

Both Norman men were dressed for the weather in thick snow pants and billowy, grungy coats. Dark, bushy beards covered their faces. Solomon strode over to them, and they exchanged some kind of familiar but hesitant greeting, a slew of Russian words running between them.

My weird mind had a way of translating people's thoughts easily, probably because people didn't really think in words. At least, not words by themselves, and definitely not coherent sentences. Their thoughts came as . . . well, *thoughts*. With images, feelings, sometimes all the senses kind of rolled together into one. My brain morphed those many layered thoughts into my own words, but unless someone mind-talked to me, that's not really how I received the messages. So I could interpret their thoughts enough to understand, even when any words were in foreign languages. However, translating actual vocalization in a tongue I wasn't quite familiar with, like Russian, didn't come so easily.

Tristan appeared by my side and paraphrased their conversation.

"They go back a few years," he whispered. "Evgeny had been a student protesting in Moscow when Solomon was there to help bring the iron wall down."

"Really?" I asked with surprise. "Solomon was involved with defeating communism?"

"Apparently. He'd served as Rina's foreign relations diplomat for quite some time, so it makes sense." He paused as he listened to the conversation, and then his head tilted and his brows pushed together.

"What's wrong? Tristan?"

He didn't answer me, but strode away, over to Solomon and the strange men. He spat Russian words out angrily, and Solomon's voice grew harsh, too.

"*They're saying they're hunters,*" Vanessa said. I glanced at her, not understanding. So what if they were hunters? "*Supernatural hunters.*"

My brow shot up with surprise.

"*Yeah,*" she confirmed. "*That Evgeny dude is saying he found out we existed years ago, and he's been hunting ever since. Finding vampires and shifters who attack humans and killing them. They're not the only ones. He says there are hunters throughout the world. Now these two want to kill us. Tristan and Solomon are trying to convince them that we're the good guys. It's not going so well.*"

We need to get out of here.

She gave me a slight nod, then blurred out of sight. She'd gone inside, silently waking everyone up and evacuating our group out the back of the cabin. All of them made their way into town except Owen, who joined me in front of the cabin. I mentally followed the group, and when they stopped, I glanced through Vanessa's eyes at a metal warehouse with a junk pile outside of it, including a bunch of old, broken down snowmobiles half-buried in snow. Charlotte and Blossom waved their hands over them, and three lifted away from the white blanket and their engines started up.

Owen threw a shield and cloak over me.

We're good to go, I called out to Tristan as we ran toward the others.

Not five seconds after Tristan's paralyzing power lifted from the hunters, more gunfire broke out, blowing snow at our legs as the bullets missed. Some kind of knife whizzed through the air not too far from Solomon's ear. As fast and as good as these hunters seemed to be, I had to wonder if they were entirely Norman. Could they have been two of Lucas's super-Normans? They hadn't had that glassy-eyed look the soldiers had had that night when Lucas took over their minds.

Owen, help Dorian, I ordered as we approached the junkyard and I saw Dorian climbing onto a snowmobile by himself. The warlock disappeared from my side and hopped onto the front of the two-seater before Dorian could scoot up.

Charlotte and Sheree already sat on another of the running snowmobiles, and Blossom and Jax waited on the third. They took off, headed for the small city in the distance, and the rest of us blurred after them. We dropped the snowmobiles near the train station and snuck through a hole in the fence that surrounded the train yard.

"How do we know which one to get on?" Dorian asked quietly as we sidled along parked trains, crossing over when possible to other tracks.

"The first one that starts moving toward the west," Tristan said.

"Like the one leaving the station this very second?" Vanessa pointed to a cargo train about two hundred yards ahead of us, pulling away from the loading platforms.

"If we can make it," Tristan said. "Is everyone good for one last run?"

We didn't have time to debate. For all we knew, it could have been the last train of the night, and we could be waiting for hours for another one to head west. Sitting still in one place was dangerous, especially this place so close to Hades. So Char and Owen zapped some energy into those who needed it, and we all took off in a sprint. Tristan reached a car with an open door before the rest of us and jumped up, grabbing onto the door handle to swing his body in. Then he helped the others who needed it. If any norms had seen Dorian make the jump, they probably would have claimed he flew. Luckily, no norms had seen it.

The train car was empty and loud, echoing the clanging metal of wheels on the tracks below. Tristan slammed the door shut, enclosing us in a pitch black so dark, even my excellent vision could barely see through it. He, Dorian, and I huddled together in a corner. Sasha grew to the size of a pony and curled in front of us, providing extra warmth. Blossom cuddled between her and Jax. The others found places, too, and finally, my team could truly rest.

At least until we pulled into a station and our car didn't move for several hours. We'd stopped at other stations along the way, and the sounds of people working outside hadn't bothered us before, but after listening to the thoughts of the ones nearby now, I told the others we had to get out of there. They'd be loading up the five empty cars, including ours.

The dark of night surrounded us when we slid out, and we had no idea where we'd arrived except in a big depot somewhere between Vorkuta and Moscow. We weren't even positive how many days we'd been traveling since daylight was so short and we'd only seen what little had leaked through the cracks in the door. Our phones had all died a while ago, and I'd yet to figure out how to charge them without destroying them. Our guess had been two days had passed, at least, but a few of us thought three.

Tristan led us away from the workers to a tight alley between train tracks.

"We just need to keep heading west," he said. "Straight west, northwest, southwest . . . it doesn't matter. Let's find another train."

We didn't have to wait long. After identifying the Norman who served as supervisor, I followed his thoughts until he revealed what we sought. There were no empty cars on this train, so we climbed into one stacked with boxes, but with just enough room to fit us all.

"We must be getting close to Moscow, based on the load," Solomon said while we waited for the train to leave. "Only another day or two."

"I'm hungry," Dorian said, not as a whine but as a

statement of fact, punctuated by a growl from his stomach. We'd eaten all of the food we'd brought, and we were all starving, even the vampires. The mages couldn't feed them because their own energies were sapped.

Sheree sniffed the air. Vanessa cocked her head and sniffed, too, then nodded.

"Food two cars up," Sheree said. "Doesn't smell like American food, but it's edible."

Tristan edged the door open and peeked out, looked both ways, and then over his shoulder at us. "Back in a minute."

A few minutes later—during which I couldn't breathe out of fear he'd be caught—he returned with his arms full of canned goods. Owen and Charlotte used magic to open what we discovered to be some of the nastiest meat I'd ever tasted. The picture on the cans made them look like Vienna sausages, but they tasted like—

"These taste like ass." Dorian made a face as he chewed the rubbery pieces.

"And smell like farts," Owen added, and I couldn't argue.

The gross factor was so high, it made it difficult to swallow even the bare minimum to supply us with energy. After the train had been moving for several minutes, Tristan cracked the door open and threw all the cans outside. We drained the last of the bottled water we had brought, trying to wash the taste out of our mouths.

"Doesn't Moscow have McDonald's?" Dorian asked.

"They do," Owen said, "and we're definitely making a stop."

"If it's safe," Tristan warned.

"We'll make it safe," Owen said. "Ever fought a starving bear? That'll be Dorian and me by the time we get there."

We talked about all the food we wanted to eat when we finally reached familiar choices, making ourselves even hungrier, but also distracting our minds from the long, uncomfortable trip. The distraction only lasted for so long, though. As each hour and then each day passed, we grew hungrier, thirstier, and grumpier. And I grew more pissed off at the Normans for their stupid traps and their refusal to trust us. We could have been fighting off the Daemoni by now, protecting their human butts, instead of taking all of this time just to travel halfway across Russia. Of course, the Daemoni put us in the middle of nowhere to start with, but I expected them to be conniving assholes. Not the Normans. By the time we reached Moscow an entire week since leaving the Amadis Island, I half-wondered why we should even fight for the Normans who'd been so easily swayed by evil.

When we reached the outskirts of the city, though, I knew we had no choice. Somebody had to.

"What's that smell?" Dorian asked, gagging worse than he had with the ass-meat. He covered his nose and mouth with his hand, trying to hold back vomit. I couldn't blame him. The horrific stench made my own stomach lurch, raising bile into the back of my throat.

"That, child, is the smell of rotting human flesh," Solomon answered.

CHAPTER 11

*W*hen the train began to slow, we stood and gathered around the door, waiting for a moment to bail before we pulled into what we expected to be a large and crowded train station. Tristan held the door open just enough for us to watch the land pass through a small crack. We'd barely rolled into the suburbs when the metal wheels ground against the tracks, slowing the train to a screeching halt.

"Why did we stop?" Dorian asked. "We're not at a station."

Tristan shook his head. "Can you tell what's going on, Alexis?"

I searched for mind signatures, and only found one adult Norman. "A guy's disconnecting part of the train two cars down."

A few seconds later, as I continued searching the area, a man in white protective gear ran toward our car, and we all jerked back, out of sight. He continued on past us.

"Something's wrong," Sheree murmured.

"As long as they don't suspect us, I'm sure it's fine," Char said.

"Was he really wearing a hazmat suit?" Blossom asked. I thought he had been, too.

"Maybe something toxic's in one of the cars," Jax suggested.

"There's definitely something wrong," I said, frowning as I searched the other mind signatures that had been with us all along, but for some reason I hadn't really thought about. Probably because their thoughts weren't clear, but jumbled. Incoherent. But not because they were drunk.

Before I could speak up about them, we began moving again. Back the way we'd come.

"What the hell?" Tristan muttered.

"We're *leaving*?" Sheree asked.

"There are two cars full of young children back there," I blurted, perplexed and now slightly panicked. Were those really child mind signatures? Like nearly infants? They sure felt like it, but I couldn't find a single adult around, except for the engineer . . . who seemed to be abandoning them. *Why?* And why did we already head back when we'd never reached the destination?

"Well, we're not going back east. Better jump while we can," Vanessa said.

Tristan nodded his agreement and threw the door open. The train picked up speed quickly, so we all sprang without another thought and landed on a grassy embankment. I ran down the hill for the cars of babies. At least they sat in passenger cars and hadn't been piled into cargo boxes. And when I arrived, I saw they weren't babies. Children, yes, but not infants. Their mind signatures had confused me.

"What's wrong with them?" Dorian asked as the others caught up to me outside one of the parked cars full of children.

Several faces looked out at us, many tear-stained. Why were they here alone? Why were we all being left here, several miles from the city limits and the train station? I searched outward, but found no mind signatures for miles. No, wait. A couple lingered here and there. But with the city landscape rising before us, there should have been hundreds of thousands in my reach. What happened to the people?

"These kids are disabled," Charlotte said, answering Dorian's question, not mine. "Either mentally or physically."

The truth was evident in the disfigured faces and vacant eyes.

"That's why they were abandoned?" I demanded, anger rising.

"This doesn't make sense," Tristan said.

He pushed open a door and entered the car, then spoke to the kids in Russian. A minute later, he came down, closing the door behind him.

"Son of a bitch," he growled as he kicked at a rock before returning to us. "Only one kid in there's capable of speaking and has a basic understanding of what's going on. They were sent away from their parents when the monsters attacked. The engineer told them their parents would come find them when it was safe. To sit here and wait."

"*What?*" I asked.

"It's common in wartime for parents to send their children to safety. It happened a lot in World War II," Charlotte said.

"But didn't they send them *out* of the cities?" Blossom asked. "To relatives in the country, where it was safer?"

"Usually," Char confirmed.

My anger began to boil. "So why the hell are these children—more defenseless than anyone—sent to the biggest city in Russia, by themselves, where there are probably more *monsters* than anywhere? And then *abandoned?*"

"Was there something wrong with the train?" Tristan asked me. "Is that why he uncoupled these cars?"

I threw my hands up. "I don't know. The guy didn't think anything about it. And apparently not, since he took off with the rest of it. Can you even do that with trains?"

"If there are engines at both ends, yeah," Owen said.

"Which means there's an engine at the other end," I said.

Tristan glanced at me and nodded. "We can at least get these kids to the station."

We ran down the length of a dozen cars to the engine. Tristan and Owen managed to fire it up, and the rest of us jumped into the car right behind it. It was stocked full of medical supplies. Why would the engineer leave this stuff out in the middle of nowhere, too? Surely somebody with a high-dollar contract on the delivery waited for these supplies. The situation grew more and more bizarre. More and more disconcerting.

We stood at the door, watching the landscape go by as it became more urban. We began to slow and missed the platform by a good thirty yards by the time we stopped, but at least we'd brought the kids this far. A small crowd of people wearing dingy clothes, many ripped and raggedy, poured through the station's doors, pushing each other out of the way as they swarmed toward the train.

"Must be their parents," Tristan said as he and Owen ran up to us. "Let's get out of here before someone recognizes us."

We jumped from the car and hurried down the tracks, away from the station and the crowd.

"Why would you bring them here?" A man with a thick Russian accent yelled from the roof of a building on the far side of the dozens of tracks. His voice sounded a lot like Solomon's old buddy Evgeny, and his mind signature confirmed it. Bullets started hitting the ground at our feet, spraying gravel at our legs and erasing any doubt. We took off in a sprint. "Yeah, you run, you sick fucks!"

We dashed across several lines of tracks and then up the hill that led away from the station and into the city. As we crested the embankment, I glanced over my shoulder to make sure the children were okay. Something felt off with the crowd, but I couldn't figure it out. Well, besides the facts that bruises and cuts covered many of them and dry blood stained their clothes and crusted on their skin. They must have been through hell and back with the Daemoni attacks.

Tristan and Dorian tugged at my hands, and I ran off with them, out of the train depot, down the street, and into the heart of a bad section of the city. Graffiti covered the dingy gray buildings. Homeless people loitered everywhere on the sidewalks—leaning against grime-covered buildings, sleeping half on the curbs and half in the gutters, wandering aimlessly with slow, bored gaits. The putrid sweet-and-sour smell of death, urine, and feces hung in the air, stronger here than it'd been before.

"I think we should go back to the train station," Blossom said, anxiety filling her tone. She held the collar of her shirt over her nose and mouth. "Find another train headed out the way we want to go."

Jax snorted. "You mean, where the bloody hunter is?"

"I have a guy here who can get us out on a plane," Tristan said. "He's on the other side of the city, though."

He began moving quickly down the sidewalk, and we followed closely behind, keeping our group tight. Tristan and his guys—he had them all over the world, able to serve in all sorts of not-quite-legal ways, from creating false identifications to stowing us away on trains and planes.

"Something's seriously wrong here," Vanessa said, her silver-coated brass knuckles already on her fists as her eyes darted around. How many times would we say it before we really believed it? "These aren't people. They don't smell right."

I grabbed the hilt of my dagger on my hip and thumbed the amethyst to make it appear as we passed a homeless woman who sat listlessly against the building, her head lolled to the side. Her skin shone a sickly greenish-gray, making her look dead. A newborn vampire in transition? Sheree's claws came out, and so did everyone's fangs. Then the bag lady's eyes opened, blood seeping out of them and her ears. Her pupils were cloudy, as though she had the worst case of cataracts I'd ever seen. Her mouth dropped open, and then she snapped it closed. Broken bits of teeth fell through her lips.

"She smells dead," Solomon said even as the woman slowly pushed herself to her feet and snapped her jaw again.

Another body that had been lying by the curb began to move, looking up at us. Blood leaked from his cloudy eyes, too. All the other homeless became more animated. All of them turned toward us, all with blood leaking from their orifices.

"Ebola?" Char asked, and she twisted her fingers in the air. Something invisible clamped against my face, like a mask. "Don't touch any of them. Tristan, we need to get out of here. *Fast.*"

Her voice sounded muffled, and although I couldn't see them, she must have put masks on all of us.

"*They* sure want to touch *us,*" Blossom squealed as one moved closer to her and lifted its arm up, reaching for her face.

Panic overcame me as realization hit.

"They don't have mind signatures," I whispered. "Neither did the crowd at the station."

"None?" Solomon asked, narrowing his eyes at me.

I shook my head. "I didn't sense them when the train stopped the first time, and I don't sense them now."

My heart picked up speed at the thought of what this could possibly mean.

Vanessa let out a list of profanities. "We gotta get the fuck out of here!"

"*Run!*" I shoved on Tristan's back while grabbing Dorian's hand. We sprinted down the block, jumping over motionless bodies, snaking around standing ones, all of them seemingly asleep, or even dead, but coming to consciousness as we passed. We rounded a corner to find a large crowd two blocks down.

Someone yelled something in Russian, a man's voice coming from our right—one of the few mind signatures I'd picked up on earlier. Not the hunter, thank the Angels. Tristan stopped in his tracks, and the rest of us plowed into him.

"He said they're all sick down there," Tristan said. The man, sitting at a second story window over the shop next to us, continued talking, his voice rising with panic. "He says we need to get out of the streets. Everyone's sick. This entire part of the city came ill within days, and it's been quarantined. No, wait. He says . . ." He paused and looked back at me with his brow furrowed. "He says they're dead, not just sick."

My heart went from racing to a full stop. My eyes felt like they'd popped out of my face. That explained the lack of mind signatures. "Zombies, Tristan? He's saying they're freaking *zombies*?"

"The psychopath actually did it," Vanessa muttered under her breath, but I was still stuck on what Tristan said to ask what she meant.

"You said there was no such thing as zombies!" I accused my husband. I'd actually asked him once.

"I said there's no such thing unless the Daemoni decide to create them," he corrected.

"And Lucas did it." Vanessa's voice filled with a mixture of disbelief and . . . awe? I spun around to stare at her. "He'd had mages working on special strains of super-contagious viruses, like Ebola, adding necromancy magic to the mix. I never thought he'd use it. Looks like he actually released something here, though."

The man in the window said something.

"He says it started down there," Solomon said, and our eyes followed to where the man pointed, toward the crowd. Beyond them rose a large, non-descript gray building. "Russia's equivalent of the CDC."

We didn't have time to figure out what this meant. As though it possessed a hive mind, the crowd down the street began moving toward us all at once. The ones we'd passed moments ago came around the corner, joined by many more. And once these zombies, or whatever they were, got moving, they didn't lurch along, slow and klutzy. They moved nimbly —and with speed.

"The children," I shrieked. "We left them!"

"Flash," Charlotte said, and I thought for the first time ever, I heard panic in her voice. "We *have* to flash out of here."

"We'll get trapped, though!" Blossom screeched.

The zombies charged at us from all directions, their stinking, rotting flesh right in our faces now. My stomach heaved, and my heart flew into a gallop at the same time. We were already trapped, I thought as I slammed my dagger into one's skull, and the body dropped, only to be replaced by another animated corpse. My blade slid into this one's eye socket, but again, when it fell, another began climbing on top of it to get to me. Their breaths smelled of days-old death. Air rattled in their rotting throats and lungs. I sliced and jabbed, killing them once and for all, but too many had amassed for us to keep up with. We twisted and waved our hands, and several flew away, but there were always more sprinting down the roads at us. Tristan's paralysis power didn't work on them, and the mages' spells had no effect, either. The dark necromancy magic made them immune.

"No choice," Tristan said as he grabbed my free hand while looping his arm around Dorian. "Follow my trail."

"Wait!" I tugged on his hand. "What about those children?"

He flashed without answering me, taking Dorian with him and leading me. We appeared back at the train station. The passenger cars where the children had been sat empty. A crowd of zombies kneeled on the ground now, tearing bloody chunks of flesh from bone. My brain tried to make sense of the scene, noticing the bones seemed too long to belong to those children, but my stomach didn't care. It churned, and I had to break away from our group to throw up.

"Something's not right," Owen said as he surveyed the train cars with those three lines between his brows.

I wiped my mouth. "You think?"

"I mean—"

The rumble of a jet sounded in the distance, quickly approaching. We all looked up as several planes descended, barely missing the tops of the tall buildings. Rivers of fire streamed from their tail ends, shooting into the city around us, and the sounds of inhuman screeching filled the air.

"Can we get the hell out of here?" Vanessa demanded.

Still holding Dorian in his arm, Tristan took my hand again and led me for the flash. I didn't argue this time. There was nothing to stay for. Nobody to save. I followed Tristan mindlessly, and felt Owen right on my trail, and someone after him. The others were following.

We appeared in a forest, and I immediately fell to my knees and covered my face with my hands. And sobbed.

"We brought those children straight to their deaths," I cried.

"We didn't know what we were doing, *ma lykita*," Tristan tried to soothe, rubbing his hand down my back. "And we don't know what happened to them."

"We saw it!"

"I saw animal flesh and bones," Tristan said. "If those children had been attacked, don't you think we would have heard their screams?"

I sniffled as I considered this. Surely we would have . . .

"And the scene didn't look right for an attack," Tristan continued. "No blood on the train cars or trailed on the ground."

I wiped my hands over my cheeks. "Where did the children go then?"

He gave me a small shrug. "I don't know. Maybe Evgeny saved them. He claims to protect humans, after all."

I sucked another ragged breath, followed by several more. We'd only been there for a minute, at the most, but what I recalled in my mind backed up what Tristan said.

"Okay," I finally agreed, relief flooding through me.

"Where is everyone?" Owen asked.

I glanced up at the concern in his voice. Only he, Vanessa, Tristan, and Dorian stood in front of me. They all glanced around. I stood up and turned in a circle, too, reaching my mind out. I sensed some signatures half a mile away, but they were Norman and not familiar. My hand went to my throat. My relief fled as quickly as it had come.

"Shit," I breathed as I sank to my butt again. "They got caught in a trap."

"We don't know that for sure," Owen said, but anxiety came clear in his voice. "Maybe we just got separated."

"Is there any water anywhere?" Dorian asked. "I'm dying of thirst here."

"Yeah, me, too," Vanessa muttered, but her thirst held a different meaning. She hadn't fed for days. We'd been too weak and dehydrated to feed her or Solomon. "I can't flash again—or do much of anything—until I feed."

"I think there's a town not too far away," I said. "There are a bunch of Norman mind signatures, anyway."

"I'll go and see if I can grab something," Tristan said. "Stay here in case the others come into your range, Alexis."

He blurred away before we could stop him or I could even tell him to be careful. Ten minutes later, he returned with paper sacks full of water and food. I didn't think I could stomach food yet after what we'd just seen, but when it came out of the packages and the delicious smells pushed away the disgusting ones, I couldn't help myself. It'd been too long since we'd had food or water. My body's needs overcame the images forever burned in my mind and the heavy feelings weighing down my heart. We tried to be considerate and save some for the others. We really did. But when they didn't show after an hour, we devoured it all. Then Vanessa could finally feed, too.

"I grabbed this while I was there." Tristan held up a Russian newspaper. He skimmed over the front page. "Yesterday's paper. It says the military was coming in to decontaminate that part of the city today."

"Oh, really?" Owen asked. "Then where the hell are they?"

"The planes," I said. "They burned the city."

Tristan nodded. "At least that part of it. This paper says the disease has been fully contained to a few square miles of Moscow, and that it came from the health department. An accident in a lab."

"Bullshit," Vanessa muttered.

"Are you sure?" Owen asked her, and she glared at him with her icy blues.

"I'll take Vanessa's word over the media," Tristan said.

"Can we get sick?" Dorian asked, fear lacing his tone.

Vanessa shook her head. "Supernaturals are protected. Part of his plan."

"Except Dorian's not entirely changed," I said. "He's still very human."

"He can fly, Alexis," Vanessa quipped. "I'm pretty sure that means he's not Norman. Besides, I'd be able to smell it in his blood. Another part of the plan."

"What plan?" Tristan asked.

Vanessa rose to her feet, paced a few times, and then stopped, standing over us with her hip jutted to the side. "One of the few I knew about. When planning for the Daemoni to come out and take over the humans, Lucas wanted a way to rid the world of the weakest. The disabled. The sick and the elderly. Some of the youth who didn't seem 'viable.' They couldn't be turned, and they couldn't serve as food producers, so why keep them alive? His words, not mine," she said quickly, holding her hands up when I lifted my brow.

"So genocide?" Tristan asked.

"Yep," Vanessa replied.

"By making them into *zombies*?" I asked with disbelief.

"Well, that's different. Sort of. That's been an ongoing experiment. This was probably a test, since it's been isolated to one part of Moscow, his way of killing two birds with one stone. He probably does have the disease completely contained. For now. He wouldn't want it to get out of control and ruin his people's food sources, now would he?"

"Says here there were outbreaks in major cities in the Middle East and Asia," Tristan said as his eyes skimmed over the front-page articles.

"Doesn't mean it's not contained," Vanessa said. "More purposeful releases. More tests."

Tristan read on. "All contained. All cities decontaminated. No certain numbers of deaths, but an estimated quarter-million."

Owen whistled lowly. "Anything else happen while we were out of touch with the rest of the world?"

Tristan turned the page and scanned. "Looks like World War III. Several countries have fired on others. Those who haven't are maneuvering into place." He turned another page. "The largest tsunami ever recorded hit the coast of India, with an estimated half-million killed or missing."

"Chandra's in India," I whispered. "I hope she and our people are okay."

Tristan continued with the laundry list of horrors. "The worst snowstorms on record for the month of October across the northern hemisphere. Riots. Record number of murders, including assassinations of high-ranking politicians throughout the world." He flipped the page again. "Pretty much every economy in existence is tanking or already crashed. In short, the world's basically gone to hell."

"Oh my god," I breathed. "All in a week? All works of the Daemoni?"

"Most of it," Vanessa said. "The so-called natural disasters, for sure. But the norms are pretty damn good at wreaking their own havoc."

I couldn't argue with her there.

"I'm sure they're having plenty of help," Owen said.

"What about Daemoni attacks?" I asked.

Tristan skimmed over more pages. "There have been some, but they're calling them Amadis, or simply supernatural, attacks."

I groaned and massaged my temples with my forefingers. "So according to the norms, it's us versus them. How does that help Lucas and the Daemoni in taking over the world? How does it make a name for them if all supernaturals are bad?"

"He has to cut down the Norman population before he can come in and save the day," Tristan said.

"The whole reason for World War III, tsunamis, and zombie diseases," Vanessa added. "And if the Amadis are decimated in the meantime, all the better for him."

"So then he'll come forward and say something about how some supernaturals are good for mankind—*his* supernaturals," I assumed.

"Maybe at first," Vanessa said. "But he's already pulling a Hitler by charming everyone, so when the time comes, he'll simply take over and let his creatures rule with fear. That will be his way of *saving* humans from all the hell they've been through."

Owen rubbed his chin and squinted his sapphire eyes. "So right now they're just making sure the Norman numbers are more manageable."

"Exactly," Vanessa said.

A frustrated growl rumbled in my chest, and I rose to my feet. "Well then, time to get off our asses and do something about it." I checked one more time for familiar mind signatures and blew out a sad breath. "They're not coming."

Owen stood, too. "Then it looks like we're going to Prague."

"And if they don't show up? What if they're locked up here?"

"Then we'll come back for them," Owen snapped.

I threw my hands in the air in surrender. "Okay. Sheesh. So how are we getting to Prague?"

"Good question," Tristan said, and when that phrase came from him, knower of best solutions, it was extra depressing.

CHAPTER 12

"We may as well start in that town," Tristan said. "There's a coffee shop where we can charge our phones and get back in touch with the rest of the world. The Amadis might have someone nearby who can help us."

"Except they're not supposed to," I reminded him as we set off through the forest in the direction of the small town Tristan had been to earlier. "They're not supposed to have anything to do with us."

"We just need to be smart about it." Tristan took my hand. "Trust me, my love. We'll get out of here and join the war as soon as I can possibly make it happen. That's how much I love you. Just keep your head down so nobody recognizes you."

I did just that, letting my hair down to curtain my face, as we walked into town and to the small coffee shop on the main, gravel road. No cars crunched over the snow or sat parked on the sides of the street, and the rest of the town seemed quiet, so the size of the small crowd inside the dingy little café surprised me. All were men, with dark hair and bearded faces wearing plaid flannel shirts, jeans, and work boots that left clumps of slush and dirt all over the linoleum floor. They talked to each other while gesturing animatedly at the newspapers in front of them on the vinyl-laminate tables. The walls were a light blue that might have been nice many years ago, but was now speckled with grease stains. Although the sounds of cooking filtered forward from the kitchen, no delicious smells made my mouth water—whatever they cooked back there smelled like dirt, and I was glad Tristan had already brought us snacks. Not that we had any Russian Rubles to buy anything.

We sat in the only available booth, and thankfully, nobody paid us much attention, not even a waitress to insist we buy coffee if we wanted to use the table. We took turns charging our phones in the single outlet by our table, and monitoring the web for more news. A bogus story had gone global a week ago, the morning after we'd stopped in Italy before we'd been rerouted to Hades, saying we'd attacked innocent civilians in the Rome suburbs.

"Besides this, there's nothing about us specifically," I said. "We're the top names on the list of supernatural terrorists, but nothing here. Why wouldn't Lucas fabricate more stories about us to keep the deceit going?"

"Because if someone spotted us on the other side of the world, he'd be caught in a lie." Tristan swiped through some screens on his phone. "The media would be anyway, meaning he'd have to fix the problem."

"I'm sure he could concoct some evil story to explain it away," I muttered.

"Yeah, but why risk it? Lies are more believable when they have some basis of truth."

I thought about the stories Lucas had delivered about us so far, and indeed, each one was grounded in some basis of truth about Tristan and me. Leaders of a secret faction of supernaturals? Check. Faking our own deaths? Check. Being in Istanbul and setting fire to a home? Check. Fighting in Rome? Check. To add insult to injury, every truth he used to twist the story around were choices *we'd* made, either because of who we were or because of what he'd done, making the lies all the more infuriating.

And showing once again that Lucas was a diabolical genius intent on tormenting me . . . and humanity. How would I ever measure up to that?

"Well, at least this means Lucas must have lost track of us after we ran from Hades," Owen said.

I nodded. "Yeah, there's that. He doesn't know where we are right now, so we can get back on track for our plan. So how do we get to Prague?"

Nobody answered me as they stared at their phone screens. Dorian obviously played a game, but I hoped the rest searched for solutions.

"I just linked through to check with the council members," Tristan said. "They'd been concerned about our lack of contact and are glad to know we're okay. I guess Galina had tried to warn us about Moscow, and Minh said she's been dealing with the necromancy in Shanghai. No word from Chandra, who'd been visiting our colony in Mumbai, where the tsunami hit."

Tears pricked at the back of my eyes as Tristan scrolled down through the highly encrypted forum—the best way we could keep in touch with my leaders out in the field without anyone knowing.

"They're proceeding as best as they can with keeping Daemoni damage to a minimum in their regions, but they're struggling with the Normans. Every region is reporting outbreaks of war or preparations for it. Borders are being tightened, and airports, highways, and pretty much every other source of transportation has been restricted or closed completely. No fly zones have expanded almost everywhere." He paused in his scrolling to read something more closely. "Looks like some of our people have found the super-sized Normans in their regions, but nobody knows where their controllers are. They're keeping a close eye on the battalions."

I rested my chin in my hand and tapped my cheek with my fingertips. "So we still have no idea if the Summoned and their offspring are being sequestered together or if they're spread out with their troops."

"Nope."

"So until then, we continue as we were. Prague, then wherever else Solomon thinks we should go," Owen said.

"Any ideas how we travel?" Vanessa asked.

Tristan shook his head. "I can't find evidence of any Amadis nearby, so they've either scattered or they're hiding like they're supposed to be. I can try to contact my guy, but I doubt he's in Moscow anymore."

"We could steal a car or truck," Vanessa suggested nonchalantly. "Although by the looks of this rundown town, I don't know how far any here will get us."

"We'll get stopped at the borders anyway," Owen said.

"Which is why we need papers first," Tristan said.

As they spoke, a sharp itch started in my palm, and no matter how hard I scratched at it, the tingling wouldn't stop. The thought of the virus we'd just been in contact with caused me to spring to my feet.

"I'll be right back." I barely spit out the words before running for the bathroom, trying my best to maintain normal human speed, although I was already freaking out.

I sensed Vanessa right behind me, but it was a one-person bathroom, so she had to guard me from the outside. A look around caused my nose to wrinkle. The germs here couldn't have been worse than the one possibly on my hand, though. I turned the hot water on and scrubbed the weird-looking soap bar on my hands, lathering up as best as possible. When I stuck my hands under the water, the temperature felt far from hot. *Shit.* I repeated the lather and scrubbed extra hard, practically taking the skin off, but the tingling wouldn't stop. With no paper towels, I had to shake the water off my hands while thinking about what I was going to do. What if I'd just infected everyone in this coffee shop?

I lifted my hands in front of me and stared at my palms as if they'd been the criminals acting on their own. A little rock suddenly appeared in my right hand. No, not a rock—a pearl. It began growing and transforming into a book with a pearlescent cover.

"Oh!" I said aloud.

"You okay?" Vanessa called from the other side of the door.

"Yeah. Fine."

I pushed the cover open and paged through to the messages I'd received from the Angels. New lines and curls appeared on the page as I watched with awe. My brows tightened as I tried to interpret the message. I *thought* I could make out "know" or "knowledge," "power," "possess" or "control," and "journey" or maybe "travels," but I wasn't positive. I studied the lines harder and tossed the words I'd interpreted around in my mind. What did they mean?

Vanessa knocked on the door. "Are you sure you're okay? You've been in there a while."

"Yes," I snapped, frowning. "Just hold on a sec."

So. Close. I felt so close to figuring out the cryptic message. And then my aha moment came. The book dissolved into my hand. I threw open the door, pushed past Vanessa, and strode over to the table.

"Let's go," I ordered. All three guys looked up at me. Dorian scowled.

"What's wrong?" Tristan asked.

"Nothing. The opposite. I know how to get out of here."

Before we attracted any more attention, I walked out of the coffee shop with Vanessa right on my heels. We headed down the road we'd come from as I led them out of town. We'd been keeping our voices low enough so most people didn't even know we'd been speaking, let alone able to hear us, but nobody could know what we were about to do. I didn't stop until we'd returned to our little spot in the forest.

"What's up?" Owen asked.

"Question for you," I said. "How are portals powered?"

"Extremely strong magic," he answered easily.

"Who has that kind of power?"

"Mostly only sorcerers. I'm probably the only warlock who can create them."

I nodded, knowing I was onto something. "So who could possibly block them or change the destination?"

Owen scratched his head, ruffling his straw-colored hair. "Only sorcerers, of course. Why?"

I leveled a look at him. Was it not obvious?

"A sorcerer had been in Rome," I said. "There's obviously at least one in or around Hades. I had those same blinding headaches I used to get when trying to get into Kali's head." I looked around for Blossom, who could confirm this, but, of course, she wasn't with us anymore. "I don't have one now. I've checked several times, and there are no sorcerers anywhere close. I mean, how many are there in existence anyway? They can't be everywhere."

Owen lifted his head in a slow nod. "Maybe a dozen or two in the world."

"What if there happens to be one where we're headed, though?" Vanessa asked. "Couldn't they block the portal from the other side?"

"How would they know we're coming?" I countered.

"They could sense the magic, if they're close enough," Owen said, "but we would be through before they figured it out."

"So we could be walking straight into their lair," Vanessa muttered.

"The chances are slim," Tristan said. "But it's still pretty risky."

"You think?" Vanessa snorted. "I don't think we should

chance it. What if we end up back at Hades again? We'd lose another week—if not our lives this time."

"What happened has been driving me crazy," Owen admitted. "I couldn't figure out why and how they were able to mess with my portal in Rome, after they'd let us get away in Istanbul."

"Good point," Vanessa said. "We know sorcerers had been in Istanbul, and they didn't do anything then. So it's not necessarily a sorcerer who blocks the portal."

"Unless they didn't know I could create portals until we escaped that night," Owen said, finishing his earlier train of thought. "They assumed Kali had made them all before. They must have figured it out and decided to reroute us in Rome. And trust me, that kind of magic—to counter a spell as powerful as a portal?—requires proximity. I think Alexis is on to something."

"I think you like the idea of having an explanation for what broke you," Vanessa said, "even if it's wrong."

Owen glared at her so hard, I thought beams might shoot out of his eyes and level her to the ground. "What's your problem?"

She threw her hands in the air. "I don't know. Maybe the fact that we just escaped Hades, suffered through starvation and dehydration, faced off with Lucas's pet zombies, and barely made it here alive? Or maybe that your mother and the rest of our crew are missing?"

"Exactly why we need to get to Prague as fast as possible. So we can find them!"

"Unless we end up back at Hades," Vanessa practically yelled.

I stepped between them and held my hands out against both of them. "Enough. We have to give it a try. The Angels said so."

Both Vanessa and Owen stopped snarling and glaring at each other over my head and dropped their gazes to me. Tristan looked at me, too, with a brow raised. I shrugged.

"Yeah, the Angels gave me a message. This is how I interpreted it. Since they only intervene if we're on the wrong track, then I'm assuming our other ideas of stealing a truck and finding Tristan's guy were wrong tracks. And they would have brought serious consequences if the Angels thought it so necessary to stop us that they actually sent me my first message." I paused for a breath, and nobody so much as tried to argue with me. "So using Owen's power to create a portal is what we're supposed to do. If we end up back at Hades, then that's where they want us to go, whether we like it or not."

They all stared at me with open mouths. Even Dorian, who might not have known about the whole message thing with the Angels, but also hadn't cared much about any of our conversations since the moment his cell phone was powered up. Their jaws snapped shut at the same time, and Owen and Vanessa backed away from each other.

"So. That's settled?" I asked.

Vanessa muttered something under her breath that I was pretty sure she wouldn't want the Angels to hear, but she nodded. Everyone else gave in right away. I just hoped I'd interpreted the message correctly and wasn't sending us headfirst in the wrong direction.

"We need to wait until it's dark here *and* there," Owen said. "No reason to risk anyone seeing us."

"Agreed," Tristan said, "but I think we need to stay on the move. I flashed as far south and west as I could get us from Moscow. Maybe the others hit the distance wall but appeared farther north. We could head that way, and Alexis could listen for them. Just in case there's any chance they're still here, and we can find them."

The suggestion was something potentially productive to do for the next three hours before dark, when we'd be gone from this area hopefully forever, so we began trekking through the forest northward. We ran for a while, letting Dorian fly with us, although he kept low, below the trees, but it allowed him to practice maneuvering around the branches. When I noticed a boulder by the stream that looked awfully familiar, I slowed down. The others did, too.

"You know, there's been something bothering me for a while," Vanessa said.

"What is it?" Owen asked.

"The streets and residences were all empty in Rome. The businesses were closed. No cars driving around. No *people*, except the small group that ambushed us. Same thing when we came into Moscow. Nobody in the suburbs. Alexis couldn't sense any human or supernatural minds in her range. Right?"

"Pretty much," I confirmed. "But they'd all been turned into the walking dead."

"I know. And the newspaper said most people fled the city. So what's been bothering me is that little town we were in earlier. This close to a city infested with what we can only call zombies. In a time when the world is falling apart. Everywhere else has been like a ghost town but there."

"They're probably the refugees from Moscow," Owen said.

"And they were just having coffee and croissants at a coffee shop like it was any normal day? Didn't that seem odd to you? Especially here in Russia. That's not normal in normal times."

My brow furrowed as my mind recalled the town and the people, and I realized Vanessa was right. Not only did the people not behave as though the world was crumbling around them, but they also seemed very American. Their fashion, their attitudes, even the way they held themselves, all slouchy and relaxed, didn't match up to the image I had in my head of Russians. Granted, my expectations were probably distorted by our American media, but the little bit I'd seen of the country and the people here clashed with those in the coffee shop. How could that be?

And what about the fact that all the other tables had coffee cups and dirty plates on them, but I never saw anyone actually eating? Nobody ever came to wait on us. I'd even noted how the place smelled wrong for a café. Then there was the bit about Chandra, who wouldn't have been in Mumbai, but should have been in Bangladesh.

Befuddled, I glanced around the forest we traipsed through, studying the trees, the snow-covered ground, the stream running to our right. Something felt off with it, too. It was October, which meant autumn, but an early, record-breaking snowstorm had hit the entire country, Tristan had said, along with freezing temperatures for over a week now. So why didn't I see our breaths puffing out in front of our faces? Why did the stream run so easily instead of being at least partially frozen? Why did the trees look like they grew tiny leaf buds when they should have been losing leaves or been completely bare?

And then my eye caught it: a wrinkle in the air.

Just a little waver, like when heat rises from the pavement in the middle of summer. I'd seen it before. This place wasn't real.

"Ah, there we are, poppet," a strange female voice said, booming from all around us. Wait. No, from within my head. Followed by the stabbing pain of an ice pick in my brain.

Our whole environment suddenly changed. We no longer traveled through a forest alongside a stream in daylight, but were inside, in a dark place. My vision came in and out as my head throbbed, and I couldn't make out any shapes in front of me. Only blurred blotches of light colors against the darkness. My whole body, inside and out, ached. My hands were pulled high above my head, and they must have been like that for some time because my legs felt too weak and exhausted to hold me up, causing the metal cuffs to dig into my wrists as my full weight hung from them.

I tried blinking away the blurriness, but the movement made my entire face hurt. My skin felt sore and tight—

swollen and bruised. Since I hadn't healed, I'd either just been given some kind of bad beating and didn't know it, or I'd been given lots of beatings and didn't know it.

What the *hell*?

Unable to see much in front of me anyway, I closed my eyes, which felt much better. I tried to reach out for mind signatures to find out what was going on, but I found none and doing so only made my head throb harder, causing me to whimper.

"Wake up, poppet," the female voice said again. Not in my head now. Right in front of me.

I tried to force my eyelids open and to focus on the pinkish-tan blob directly in front of my face, but I couldn't. They drifted back shut, the pain disappeared, and I found myself in the forest again.

"How are they doing it?" Tristan asked from my side.

I turned to him and ran into his arms, grateful to be with him again.

"How did they do it?" Vanessa asked this time, but the voice didn't really belong to her.

Red-hot pain racked through my cheek as the bone shattered. I jerked back awake, in the dark room again.

"Tell me how they did it, and we can stop wasting all this time," the voice said.

I didn't know what she was talking about. *How who did what?* I didn't understand anything going on. My entire body felt sapped of energy, and my brain was all muddled.

"Jeana, darling, don't be so impatient. You've sucked out all her energy. Give her a chance to wake up, you evil little wench," a male voice chastised lovingly. He didn't sound close, though, but more like his words came through a speakerphone or a computer.

The woman in the room, presumably Jeana, grunted, and the peach blob, which I assumed was her face, moved away, attached to the larger gray blob of her body below it. She disappeared into the darkness with the clack-clack-clack of a woman's heels on a cement floor, but I could still feel her presence nearby. The sound of running water carried over to me from somewhere close, but not too close. A moment later, footsteps approached, and then ice-cold water crashed over my head and face, sliding down my neck and into my leather bustier.

This woke me up.

The cold also helped numb the pain in my face, so when I blinked it out of my eyes, the movement didn't hurt so much. It still took a moment for me to focus on my surroundings, but they eventually came into view.

And I so wished they hadn't.

I wanted to run back to the forest, even if it wasn't real. Because I really didn't want to be here, chained to the wall by my wrists and ankles, too drained of energy to be able to do anything about it. The room was dark and cool, and I couldn't see more than ten yards in front of me as it faded into darkness, but it felt large and cavernous. A few feet away stood a metal table displaying what my imagination took to be torture tools, and I was pretty sure they weren't your run-of-the-mill Norman torture tools, but were cursed with magical spells. The kinds of spells that left dark magic in your scars, like what marred Tristan when he returned from his incarceration with the Daemoni. Off to the right and several yards away stood a desk with a computer screen and a bunch of papers on it. And immediately to my right, a body hung next to me.

The scream started in the pit of my stomach and exploded from my throat, but only came out as a choking gasp. I fought against the constraints, trying to wriggle free, but I couldn't move enough to even make the chains rattle. *Oh, no. God, please, no.* Tears stung the backs of my eyes. He hung there so lifelessly, and I could do nothing to help him. Nothing! I'd never felt so helpless in my life. I could barely recognize him through the blood matted in his blond hair and the streaks of sweat and grime on his swollen face.

"Owen," I tried to whisper, but my voice hardly made a croak, and my throat felt like a cat clawed at the inside. My breath became trapped in my lungs when he didn't answer. "*Owen . . .*"

The salty wetness burned my injured cheeks as tears streamed uncontrollably.

"He's not dead," Jeana said. She seemed to be the only other person in the room, although I couldn't be sure because I couldn't see . . . and because my damn telepathy refused to work. She was close, but in the shadows, and my eyes found her general shape, but couldn't quite focus on her. "Not yet, anyway. But he will be soon if you two don't cooperate."

"*Tristan!*" I tried to yell his name, praying he was looking for us, trying to rescue us, but again only a croak came out. The next name was more like a sad hiccup. "Dorian?"

"The boy's okay." Footsteps came closer again. "The other two, though—the traitors? They're being dealt with. The rest got away."

The traitors? She must have meant Tristan and Vanessa. Who did she mean by the rest? Char, Solomon, and the others?

"Unfortunately, we caught your flash a little too soon, and the rest of your group managed to escape. They're insignificant little cockroaches anyway and will be stomped out soon enough."

Yes, she spoke of my team. So hopefully she wasn't lying, and they were really okay. But we—Tristan, Vanessa, Owen, Dorian, and I—were not. Understanding began to creep into my murky mind.

We'd been worried the others had been caught by the magic traps when we'd flashed out of Moscow, but *we'd* been the ones ensnared, like flies in a spider's web.

CHAPTER 13

*a*s this truth settled into my bones, a spark of adrenaline shot through my veins, enough to clear my mind, but not to give me any strength. This Jeana-bitch-sorceress must have been draining me of all of my power while feeding me some stupid vision of a pretty forest and quaint little town. Panic rose like bile in my throat as I considered what she might have seen and heard. Had she been sharing the vision with me? If so, then she'd know the Amadis dissolution was a sham. What else had she found out? Did any of it matter anymore?

"Why haven't you killed us yet?" I asked, my voice scratchy, but no longer garbled. I didn't think Lucas cared any longer whether Tristan and I lived or died, but I could hope he still held out for us to run to his side, because at least that gave us a chance.

"Because I'm not quite done with you," Jeana said, tucking her shoulder-length, raven hair behind her ears as she came into view.

I expected her to look older, but her skin was as clear as her dark, sparkling eyes that told volumes of the darkness inside. She wore a see-through, button-down white top with enough buttons undone to show her voluptuous cleavage pushing out of her black lace bra, and a tight, black leather skirt that ended before her knees. With thigh-high, black boots, she looked like some kind of sexual dominatrix. The clack of her six-inch heels fell silent when she stopped at the cart holding the terrifying instruments. I half-expected her to pick up a leather whip, but instead she chose a shining silver tool with a crescent shaped blade. She wiggled her red-tipped fingers over the point, and then stepped right up to me, grabbed my face with her free hand, and squeezed my jaw.

"I'm tired of this game," she snarled in my face, gagging me with her breath that smelled like she'd been eating zombie flesh . . . and cherries. "Tell me how they did it. *NOW!*"

My brows scrunched together. Why did she keep asking me that? "How who did what?"

She growled and tightened her grip on my face.

"The soldiers, *poppet*." She lifted the blade to point to the corner where I could now see the shape of another person. A very large person holding a very large gun. "What did Lucas and Kali do to control them?"

I blinked and suppressed a ridiculous chuckle. "How the hell would I know?"

Something sharp poked into my side, right above my hip. "You wouldn't, but *he* would. Read his mind!"

And the pieces tumbled together. She'd been torturing Owen all of this time, but he hadn't given her what she wanted. I was her Plan B, a way to dig out of his memories how Kali had created the stones. Of course, Lucas had told me how he'd used Sasha's blood to "improve" the super-soldiers and force their loyalty, but Jeana obviously didn't know that. Why did she care what they did? To create her own soldiers, no doubt. Another sorceress making a power play for Lucas's position. The Daemoni thought *we* experienced organizational and leadership problems, but their greed for power over each other just might be their biggest downfall.

"Do it," she snapped, clutching my jaw harder and jabbing the knife into my skin.

"He's unconscious, possibly dead. I *can't* read his mind," I hissed through gritted teeth as a line of searing pain drew across my lower abdomen.

"These ovaries of yours are quite precious, aren't they? How badly do you want to keep them?" She dug the blade in deeper, causing me to yelp.

But my skin and even my leathers closed up right behind the knife. I forced a smile through the lingering burn. She lifted her upper lip in a snarl.

"She heals right away, Merrick," she said. Who was Merrick? The soldier in the corner?

"What *can* we hurt?" the man's voice from before asked, and I was pretty sure the voice didn't belong to the soldier. It still sounded distorted and came from the direction of the desk. I glanced over there. Oh, how lovely. She had us on video-chat. "Or should I say *who*?"

Jeana lifted her red painted lips into a grin and held her hand in the air as she took a step back from me. She snapped her fingers, and she suddenly held a body in a chokehold, the knife against his cheekbone.

"Dorian!" I cried. Would she really kill him for this? Did she not care about him and his potential role with the Daemoni as much as Lucas did? Or was this a ruse?

"Mom," Dorian said, and his lips moved with more words, but the crash of glass and metal and the loudest roar I'd ever heard drowned him out.

A winged wolf the size of an elephant dropped from the ceiling and landed on her paws next to Jeana and Dorian, her foot-long fangs bared and the fur along her back raised on end. Her black tiger stripes, normally hidden, stood out in stark contrast against her thick white fur. She leaned forward and growled, but she didn't immediately attack the sorceress holding her master.

Jeana smirked. "That's right. You just stay back, you oversized mutt."

Sasha snarled and snapped, but not close to enough to hurt the sorceress. Jeana's taunting grin grew. She thought the lykora obeyed her, but Sasha knew her intentions, and apparently Jeana didn't intend to truly hurt Dorian. At least, not for the time being. That could quickly change, so I played along anyway.

"Okay, okay," I said pleadingly. "I need him conscious, though. And I can't do anything with this mental block you have on my head."

Her eyes narrowed, and she tightened her hold on Dorian. "Do you really think I'm stupid enough to fall for that? I'm not letting you in my head."

"I can't read anyone's mind right now. I can't even *feel* them. I didn't know you had that soldier over there until you pointed him out. Your block is keeping me from getting into anyone's mind, including Owen's."

Jeana cocked her head. "You're lying."

I tried to shift, and the screaming aches through my arms and the rest of my body brought back the exhaustion. I slumped in the cuffs, and my hair fell into my face. I rolled my eyes to look up at her through the strands. "I guess you don't want to know badly enough."

Jeana's dark eyes studied my face for a long moment, and then suddenly the stabbing pain in my brain disappeared. Without letting go of Dorian, she kicked Owen's shin with her pointy boot, jostling him awake. Or to some level of consciousness anyway. He let out a groan. I let out a mental yell.

Tristan! Where are you? I screamed for him, searching for his and Vanessa's mind signatures as far as my feeble mind could reach, while also trying to pull thoughts from Jeana's mind. My brain felt so meager, though, along with the rest of me. All I could catch was something about Sasha, and then she slammed me out, making me gasp and squeeze my eyes shut from the pain.

"*Alexis, here,*" Owen whispered into my mind. He shared a thought, what I could only assume was a spell.

Owen, no.

"*Trust me.*"

I tried to glance sideways at him, but my eyes were too swollen to see him. I could feel a certain sureness from him, though, as weak as he was.

My eyes peeled open, and I glared at the bitch holding my son at knifepoint. "I was trying to show you something, you stupid bitch."

Her eyes narrowed to slits, and then she released the block again. Hoping like hell he knew what he was doing in his semi-conscious state, I shared Owen's thoughts with her. Her eyes began to widen. Her mind opened further, and she drank it all up. I could practically hear her purring.

"Got it, Merrick," she said, and her breath puffed out in white tendrils in front of her. She pulled back in shock. The air around us grew chilled, and frost spread across her skin, starting at her hands . . . where they touched Dorian. Was *he* doing that? Jeana murmured some kind of incantation, but it failed to stop the growing frost.

I lifted my head and gazed in awe at my son. His face was full of concentration, his brows drawn tight, his lips puckered. The frost spread from his body and thickened into ice as it grew over Jeana. What a powerful ability he'd developed, and I hadn't even known! When her arms became frozen into place, he slipped out of her grip and flew upward, through the hole in the roof Sasha had created. I sensed him land close by and wished he'd go farther . . . far, far away from this bitch. And I wished Sasha would go with him, but she stayed planted in front of Owen and me.

"Jeana?" Merrick called through the laptop. "What's going on, darling?"

The sheet of ice encasing the figure in front of me snapped and cracked as the sorceress broke out of her frozen cage.

"Nothing," she snapped as she shook off the last pieces of ice. "I'm on my way. But wait for me before you release the kraken. I want to watch."

She turned on her heel and jerked her head to the side. The pick jammed into my mind again, blocking everything out and making me scream with its forcefulness. My knees gave out, and my body sagged, causing the cuffs to dig against my already raw wrists. Jeana clapped her hands, and a door opened. Footsteps sounded across the floor on the far end of the warehouse as I watched her open a portal, step through it, and disappear. The soldier in the corner stepped out of the shadows at the same time two of his comrades strode up, all of them dressed in gray camo and combat boots. The three of them marched in proper form for the last ten yards. Their glassy eyes stared straight ahead, but really seemed to see beyond our heads, even as they lifted their military-issued guns to point at our chests.

Sasha growled as she moved over to stand protectively in front of Owen and me. The soldiers blinked in unison and furrowed their brows.

"We said to shoot!" Merrick yelled from the screen in the corner.

As one, the soldiers moved forward and looked as though they were going to fire. Sasha growled again and took one step toward them. They stopped and looked at her.

"Fire, you imbeciles!" Jeana shouted, now also from the computer. She came on screen, but her body was turned away from the camera. They must have had the controller wherever they were, a Summoned son or descendent issuing the orders. Which meant Lucas had handed the controller over to the two mages. I wondered if he knew about their plot against him, or if he was too arrogant to believe they'd try.

Owen's hands flicked above his head. I tried to swing my

head over to look at him, to see if he was giving me some kind of signal. I couldn't hear his thoughts, couldn't sense anyone's mind signatures anymore, and the pain in my brain and the rest of my body prevented me from turning enough to see him well. His hands twitched harder, though, and a gun flew out of one of the soldier's hands . . . and straight at mine. I grabbed for it, fumbling as I tried to get a grip on it. The soldiers stepped forward again, even the unarmed one. My fingers finally took ahold, one of them unintentionally on the trigger. Shots sprayed at the ceiling and then at the floor, and the soldiers all dropped then sprang upwards like cats to avoid the stray bullets as I awkwardly tried to maneuver the deadly weapon. If I hadn't already been trembling from pain and exhaustion, my hands positively quaked now. I was almost glad when the thing fell and clamored to the floor.

The mages on the screen yelled all kinds of obscenities, and the soldiers made another attempt to shoot us, but Sasha stopped them again. They wouldn't hurt her. They *couldn't* hurt her—her blood ran through their veins and they'd always be more loyal to her than to any controller. And they had to get through her to get to us.

I tried gathering all of my strength to break out of the cuffs or even to break the chains away from the wall, but I still had no power, no energy, no strength. I yelled for help, and the sorcerer laughed in response. Owen barely moved next to me, apparently having used his only bit of energy to summon the gun. And I'd gone and messed that up.

"Help!" I screamed again, ignoring the burning in my throat, at the same time a body dropped through the roof.

Dorian landed right next to me and held his hands on the cuffs above my head. Almost immediately, the cold seeped into my skin, refreshing on the raw cuts encircling my wrists. The cuffs grew colder, frozen, and then began to crack. As soon as I broke out of them, I fell over. Dorian squatted and froze off the cuffs on my legs.

"Get Owen," I gasped as I crawled for the lost gun, then pushed myself to my feet. I stumbled toward the soldiers. "Drop your weapons."

I sounded and probably looked very far from threatening, so when they didn't obey, I didn't blame them, and wouldn't have even if they were in their right minds. Sasha let out a low rumble. They dropped their guns and fell to their knees, their hands on the backs of their heads. I looked sideways at Sasha. Had she ordered them to do that?

I lowered my gun and freed my dagger from my hip, rubbing my thumb over the stone to make it appear. "Sasha, I have to get the stones out. It's for their own good. Hold them there or whatever you do, okay?"

"I got them, Mom," Dorian said from my side.

I looked over my shoulder, wavering on my weak legs as I did so. Owen, barely conscious, was freed and propped up against the wall, which he slowly slid down in a slouch. Dorian held his palm out and blasted what looked like snow at the norms. They froze. Literally. Dorian took their guns, and I lurched over to the first soldier. With what felt like my last bit of strength, I jabbed my dagger into his chest and dug the chip of stone out. I let it fall to the floor as I shuffled to the next one, while the first guy began what sounded like a confused string of Russian profanity. When I dug the second stone out, that Norman stared at me with confusion and relief.

"I . . . very sorry," he said in broken English.

I moved to the next, barely able to hold myself up anymore. When my knife pierced his skin, doors burst open from everywhere around us. More soldiers poured in, guns up, shouting at the three in front of me. A new guy held the barrel of his gun at the first soldier's temple. He dropped and scurried on his hands and knees until he found the stone chip I'd just taken from him. He pressed it back into his bleeding wound.

"No," I tried to shout but only whispered.

Another "NO!" tore through the room, though, as the second guy jumped to his feet. Shouting *no, no, no,* he dashed across the room for the nearest door. Another super-soldier gunned him down.

"No," I tried again. I watched him fall, then my mother, then him, then my mom, the images flashing back and forth until he hit the ground, lifeless.

I wanted to scream. Instead, I nearly passed out.

Dorian caught me from behind as I went down, and the dozen or so new Normans pointed their guns at us. Someone shot off a blast. Sasha whimpered, and at the same time, every single Norman's left shoulder twitched and dropped. Apparently not severely injured, Sasha grabbed Owen in her mouth and flew for the hole in the ceiling. All the soldiers began firing.

Not at Sasha, of course. At me.

Dorian tightened his hold around me, and lifted me up, up, up as I fired down, barely able to see where I shot through the gray creeping in on the edges of my vision, but nonetheless seeing clearly the men who dropped when my bullets hit them. My sight blurred and wavered as my mind tried to black out, but I couldn't unsee the scene below. Norms dead. Human blood spilled.

What had I done?

Dorian flew us out of the warehouse, and the cold air blasted in my face, the only thing keeping me conscious. We soared several dozen feet in the air across a snowy field lit by moonlight, to where I didn't know and didn't have the energy to ask.

"Alexis?" The beautiful, familiar voice called from far away.

"Tristan?" I murmured.

"Dad?" Dorian asked.

I tried to pinpoint where the sound came from.

"Dorian!" Tristan had spotted us. Dorian turned to our

right, and I caught a glimpse of Sasha following with Owen still in her mouth.

We landed on the snow, and I fell from my son's grip into my husband's arms. And finally, I allowed myself to pass out.

"He needs more to heal."

"You need to drink before you give him any more blood."

"How am I going to do that? Are you offering up?"

"You can have some of my blood, Aunt Vanessa."

I pushed away the cobwebs in my head, trying to make sense of this strange conversation going on in hushed tones, not close, but not far away either. My head ached. My tongue felt five times its normal size and my mouth way too small for it. And I swore it must have soaked up every drop of moisture it could to grow so big, because I felt as though I could spit sand. My eyelids slowly peeled open, feeling gritty over my eyeballs, and when filtered sunlight greeted me, they snapped back closed. I groaned from the pain in my head.

"Lex?" A breeze of air whizzed over me, and a large body dropped next to me—I sensed his presence but refused to open my eyes again to see, even though my husband's beautiful face waited on the other side. "Are you awake, my love?"

"Mmm," I managed to moan. "Thirsty."

Something hard immediately pressed against my lips, and I parted them. Wetness poured in. I could barely swallow, my throat so sticky at first, but I thought my mouth would simply soak up the water anyway like a dried-up sponge. Eventually, my tongue shrank to normal size, my throat worked properly, and I gulped down as much as he would give me. When he pulled the glass away, I whimpered.

"Too much at once will make you sick." He wrapped his arms around me and held me. I leaned against him, my neck barely able to hold up my throbbing head. "Are you healed up? Besides the dehydration?"

I mentally scanned my body. I seemed to be okay. Physically, anyway. "All but my head. How's Owen?"

"He'll be fine. Your ears were bleeding before."

I could only respond with a soft grunt. If Owen was okay, I didn't care about anything else at the moment. "Just want to sleep."

I snuggled closer against his body, inhaling his glorious scent that made everything feel better. Well, everything but my head. And my heart.

"You've been sleeping for two days."

That should have raised some kind of alarm, but I ignored it. I didn't want to know. I didn't want to be in this world.

"I killed them."

One of Tristan's arms tightened around me, and a hand stroked down my hair and back. "I know, my love. Dorian said you had to."

I shook my head, even though it hurt. "Didn't mean to. Didn't want to."

I pressed my face into his shoulder and cried.

"You did what was necessary to protect yourself and your son."

"If I'd had any power, I could have—"

"But you didn't. You did what you had to do."

I allowed myself more tears for the men I had killed, because they deserved more than I could ever give. They had families, parents, and maybe spouses, their own children even. The only thing I could do for them now was to ensure their families didn't die unnecessarily. To protect the Normans from the Daemoni.

But they weren't the only souls I cried for. "Those poor children."

"The children on the train?"

"We killed them. Brought them to their deaths."

KRISTIE COOK

"We don't know that for sure. They could have been rescued."

I finally pulled away and peeked open my eyes to stare at my favorite face in the world as though he were on drugs. "We saw the zombies at the train station . . . eating . . ."

He pushed his brows together and shook his head. "No. We didn't get there. We were caught in the flash, remember?"

My lids opened wider. "You mean the zombies were real, but we never made it back to the train station?"

He nodded. "When the zombies overwhelmed us, I tried to flash us back to the train station, but no, we didn't make it. That's when the Daemoni grabbed us."

"That doesn't mean the children aren't dead, though." I dropped my head and stared at my hands in my lap. We sat on a thin mattress on the floor in an otherwise empty room with white, sheer curtains on the window, where gray light of an overcast day poured in. "And it's our fault. We took them all the way there when the train engineer abandoned them."

"Vanessa thinks the Norman engineer had been under Daemoni control, somehow or another, and was forced to take the children there. To feed them to the zombies. We thought we were helping them."

"The hunter knew."

"But *we* didn't. How could we expect such barbarity? We can't take that blame, Alexis."

I forced my lungs to draw in a long, slow breath to settle the sobs, and then scrubbed the tears from my face.

"We have to stop the Daemoni. I'm failing them, Tristan. The Amadis and the Normans."

"We'll stop them, *ma lykita*. One way or another."

I nodded, but I didn't see how. I'd barely survived one stupid sorceress.

"Our son was freakin' awesome," I said. "If not for him and Sasha . . . Owen and I probably wouldn't have made it. He can *freeze* stuff, Tristan. And people too. It was so crazy."

168

"I think he can do more than that, but yeah, he's pretty awesome."

I sighed. "It just means he's that much closer . . ." I didn't want to think about what the future held for Dorian. I hadn't abandoned my mission of breaking the curse that led all the sons to the Daemoni. "Where were you and Vanessa? Where are the others? Have you talked to them?"

"Vanessa and I woke up chained up in an abandoned factory right outside of Moscow, about seventy miles from where we found you. We broke free, figured out where they had you—"

"How'd you do that?"

"From the Norman soldiers, the few minutes they were lucid in between the time we cut out their stones to when they were forced to put them back in."

I blew out another frustrated breath. "That happened to us, too. One of them refused to put it back in, and the others killed him. We have to find the controllers and remove their stones before we can do anything for the Norman soldiers. We can't let them kill each other like that."

"They don't know what they're doing. They didn't know what they were doing when they shot at you."

"I know. Why do you think I feel so horrible about what I did?" I'd never be able to erase from my mind the image of those soldiers lying in pools of blood because of me. I could try folding it up and tucking it away, but I had a feeling memories like that didn't like to stay in storage. They'd haunt me forever, which I deserved. "Did you find out where Char and everyone else are, too?"

He shook his head. "The norms didn't know. Vanessa and I had to focus on getting to you as fast as we could. We've been hiding out here since with Baby Cakes until you and Scarecrow recovered. We haven't been able to get a hold of them and haven't heard from them, either. I'm hoping they're still waiting for us in Prague."

"*Baby Cakes*? Is that a name?"

A petite female suddenly appeared in the room with us, tossing her straight brown hair over her shoulder and jutting out a narrow, jean-clad hip.

"Did you call?" she asked as she unzipped her leather jacket.

I looked at Tristan and back at her.

"This is Baby Cakes," Tristan introduced. "A faerie who's been . . . *kind* enough to help us." He sounded like the word 'kind' had been hard for him to spit out. "This is her place."

"*One* of my places," she corrected. "Sorry it's nothing much. This part of the world is so . . . bleh. Not my favorite place, but I keep it because you never know when it could come in handy. Like right now."

She gave me a kind grin, but I certainly didn't trust it. She was a faerie after all.

"So did you need something?" she asked. "It's pretty ugly in the Otherworld, and I don't want to miss anything. It's quite entertaining really. Bree sends her love, by the way. She would have come, but she's . . . a little busy."

"No, no, we're fine," I said hurriedly, squeezing my hands together before I rudely shooed her away. She seemed nice enough, but faeries equaled trouble. We didn't need any more trouble. Thankfully, she popped out of sight without another word. "Great. So we'll owe her big time for this. Now back to what you said. What do you mean still waiting? Char and them? Hopefully they're not flashing after knowing we got caught, so they're probably not even in Prague yet."

"Yes, we'll owe her, but we didn't have a choice. And it's been over a week since we saw Solomon, Char, and the rest, Alexis. They've had plenty—"

"Whoa, whoa, whoa. Another *week's* gone by?"

"Nine days actually. Since we arrived in Moscow."

I pressed my palms to my eyes. I couldn't believe we'd lost so much time. That meant it had been nearly a month since the Daemoni first attacked the Normans. A month that the Amadis hadn't been protecting them as well as we should have been. My failure counts just jumped to epic levels.

I told Tristan about everything we'd discussed in the coffeehouse—the conversation about the world going to hell with natural disasters, war preparations, bombings, and more.

"Of course, that conversation never really happened. Please tell me the world's not as bad as that."

"Mmm . . . To be honest, pretty much all of it's true, some of it worse now, from what we've been able to find out."

I threw myself back on the mattress and stared at the ceiling. "How can that be?"

"You must have heard the sorcerers talking about it, or maybe they had the television on, and you incorporated it into your subconscious."

"The parts about the Amadis and the portals?"

"Probably things you figured out yourself and attributed to us in your imagination. If you're right about the portals, Owen can get us out of here as soon as he's up to it."

"Unless it was wishful thinking."

I sat back up and stared at the curtained window, wondering what went on out in the world even as we spoke. How bad had the war become? My poor people, fighting for their lives and for the Normans out there.

"The Amadis are probably compromised," I said quietly, mentally kicking myself as the words came out. How had I not known that had been a mirage? How much had I actually said? "If I'd been talking to myself about our plans, like you're saying, that Jeana bitch probably knows them now, too."

"Guess we'll find that out soon enough, when we're back on the road."

"Does that mean we can get moving soon?" Vanessa asked from another room. Tristan and I hadn't exactly been whispering, but she'd apparently been using her vamp ears to eavesdrop.

171

"She needs to drink?" I asked.

"She's refused to leave Owen's side and has been giving him her blood to help him heal. I gave her some of mine right before we escaped, but let's just say that will only happen again in case of emergency."

I looked at him with my brow raised.

"She was like a fruit fly on crack with the strength of an elephant, hulk-smashing everything in her wake."

I laughed at the visual. "That had to have helped you guys."

"Yes, but I have no idea the extent of damage done on the way without her even meaning to. It's probably the only reason she's made it this long without more blood, though, especially with as much as she's given Owen."

"I can feed her. And yes, dear sister, we're leaving soon," I said, knowing she'd been listening to our conversation.

As soon as Owen felt up to it and the time of night was right, we said a prayer, he opened a portal, and we stepped through, hoping like hell we appeared in Prague . . . or anywhere other than Hades.

We did arrive in a dark alley near the safe house in Prague, but it was not the city I'd always dreamt of visiting.

Hell had already been here.

CHAPTER 14

"What have they done to my beautiful city?" Vanessa nearly cried the words out as we walked the silent cobblestone streets, taking in the sights. Not the kind we wanted to see.

Ever since seeing a photography book of Prague when I was in junior high school, I'd wanted to come here. I'd imagined then all the stories this place would inspire. I immediately recognized the famous Charles Bridge. Open only to pedestrians, it was where local artisans sold their goods and musicians played under the life-sized bronze statues of saints and legends. At least, that's what the photographer had written about the place. Now, half of those statues stood with no heads and a whole chunk of the south side of the bridge had been blown away. Billows of smoke rose from the towers at either end, as well as from buildings around the city. The pitched roofs of some and round domes of others looked like giants had punched holes through them.

"I used to sit up there at night and watch the tourists, picking out my dinner," Vanessa said nostalgically, pointing to the top of the tower at the end of the bridge. "This was one of my most favorite places in the world."

"Not Key West?" I asked, genuinely curious.

"Eh." She shrugged. "Key West and South Beach were fun for partying, but believe it or not, I didn't really enjoy them. They're too new. Too shiny. Nothing romantic about them. Not like this place is . . . or was."

As we walked through most of old town, my telepathy gradually returned, and we declared the city to be deserted. At least this part of it. We saw no one. We sensed no presence of life, except for a few norms huddled up in buildings here and there, too afraid to come out in the open.

"It seems to be evacuated," Tristan said.

Owen put his hands on his hips as he looked around the block. We stood in front of the hotel where Solomon had told us to meet them. What remained of it, anyway. Tendrils of black smoke still rose from a large pile of rubble and ash. The charred odor made my nose twitch. Owen's mouth twisted, and the three lines between his brows appeared, as they did when he fell into deep thought.

"Well, Solomon said something about Köln, right?" he said. "Maybe they went there next, since there seems to be no evidence of anyone here, let alone anyone on our side."

Tristan and I looked at each other, but we had no argument, and since Dorian and Vanessa went where we went, Owen created a portal. Within a few seconds, we'd left the sad state of Prague and entered an improved situation in Köln, which, I learned, was the German word for Cologne. Where we arrived, in the shadows of a huge, gothic cathedral and surrounded by a major shopping district, the area was dark, even the large train station to our right. However, lights shone in the distance, which meant the entire city hadn't been destroyed and abandoned.

We sensed nobody inside the cathedral and found no one on a search. Without knowing what else to do, we walked several eerily quiet blocks to another church and never passed a single soul. The norms hid inside the buildings, with many streets and the entrances to apartment buildings blocked off, as though they'd barricaded themselves in. As if the monsters couldn't still get to them if they really wanted.

"We're pretty much lost without Solomon," I said. "He said to see the archbishop, but since he wasn't at that cathedral, he could be anywhere."

"Including dead," Vanessa said helpfully.

A small person stepped out of a dark shadow, and all of us went into defense stance.

"Relax," Baby Cakes said. "I come on Bree's behalf. She said to go to London."

We all glanced at each other, as if none of us knew how to respond.

"How can we trust you?" Tristan finally asked.

"I helped you before, didn't I? If you didn't have my place to crash, these two would be dead." She motioned to Owen and me.

"All the more reason you wouldn't help us again," Owen pointed out.

She shook her head. "So ungrateful." But then she shrugged. "I can't blame you, of course. My kind can be a bit of a pain in the ass, can't we?"

That was an understatement.

"Anyway, you can choose to trust me, or you can wander around here like idiots, wasting more time. Your call." She disappeared.

As though her last words triggered something in Tristan's mind, he pulled his cell phone out. The electrical power in Baby Cakes' apartment had been intermittent, so we'd only been able to partially charge our phones, which hadn't mattered much anyway, because we couldn't pick up a signal.

"Can we trust her?" Owen asked.

"She talked a lot about Bree," Vanessa said. "While you two were out of it. She definitely leans toward the Amadis side."

"I trust her," Dorian said, and I wasn't sure how helpful that was. On the one hand, he was just a kid, regardless of how old he looked—older and older every day. On the other hand, he'd been through hell and back and didn't return too trusting of people. Pretty much the opposite. He had a sense for the Daemoni, too, which may extend to all darkness.

"Tristan?" I asked.

"Yeah, she seemed to know Bree," he murmured distractedly as he jacked with his phone. He held the device out to me. "Hold this for a sec."

I snatched the phone from him, more to get his attention, and the screen immediately lit up. He grabbed it right back, knowing how I usually fried the things to a crisp.

"Thanks, babe." He studied the screen before it blacked out again. "We go to London."

"Are you sure?" I asked. "We could be walking right into a trap."

"We don't have much to lose." He held the dark phone up and waved it in the air. "Besides, Solomon says so."

"You heard from Solomon?" Owen asked, moving closer as if he could see on the screen.

"He sent a text two days ago. They were headed to London. That's all I could see before the phone went down."

"Well, then, Owen, lead the way to London," I said.

We not only walked into a different country, but seemingly into a different world. We'd barely arrived when a gray-haired man swung a sword at us and blew a whistle at the same time. Another man and a woman, dressed in military uniforms, ran down the street toward us.

The older guy spit the whistle out and yelled, "Over here, over here."

The soldiers lifted their weapons, and the civilian Norman took off.

"We won't hurt you," I called out, holding my hands up and stepping in front of Dorian.

They shot anyway. We flicked the bullets away before they hit us and ran. More shots fired after us, but missed. Vanessa led the way and ducked into a shop.

"Cloak us," she hissed at Owen as two grungy-looking women in the shop held knives in each of their fists and ran for us. We disappeared right in front of them and hurried back outside.

Air raid sirens suddenly blared. People ran chaotically through the streets, yelling and wailing as they found shelters. Owen led us in a sprint through London in the direction of the safe house, the only place we knew to meet the others.

"It's just like World War II," Tristan muttered, and jet planes zoomed overhead, punctuating his point.

A few seconds later, the bombs began to drop, many too close for comfort. The ground quaked under our feet, knocking us off balance. The explosions were deafening, making my ears ring. Shots were fired from somewhere down the street, but I didn't know if they were aimed at us or not.

"It's right up here," Owen yelled, his voice muffled as he pointed to a block of row houses two streets ahead.

We came half a block closer when a bomb slammed into our destination, exploding the row houses into bits of concrete, brick, and wood. I threw my arms over my son, and Tristan dropped us both to the ground, using his body to cover us. We lifted our heads just enough to look around. A soldier came running down a cross street, blowing a whistle. No, not a soldier, a policeman.

"This way," he yelled to nobody in particular, motioning his arm toward the direction he just came from.

Normans began scurrying out of homes and shelters and running toward him. He waved them down the road and yelled at more to come.

"Hurry!" he shouted, and he looked our way, although he couldn't see us. "More planes are coming. Anyone else?"

"We should at least check it out," Tristan said. "See where they're taking the norms."

We sprang up and jogged down the street.

"I don't trust it," Owen said.

We stopped within yards of the policeman, who continued to blow his whistle and call for civilians. Only a few more stragglers came running. A crowd had gathered at the far end of the street he directed them down, where an eight-foot-high, barbed-wire-topped fence stood.

Vanessa stiffened. "Nope. Never. No fucking way."

I glanced around at the war-torn neighborhood, wondering what we should do. Familiar shapes emerged from a partially standing building, and although covered in white ash, I recognized them right away.

Blossom! Charlotte! Sheree! I mentally yelled for them and wondered at first if my telepathy had stopped working again because they didn't respond. But all three of them stopped in their tracks, causing Jax and Solomon to halt, too.

"Alexis? Is that you?" Blossom nearly squealed in my head, making me cringe.

"Owen, they can't see us." I tugged at his shirtsleeve.

He turned to see who I meant and immediately removed the cloak.

Our reunion would have been joyous if the cop didn't start blowing his whistle in a panic as he scampered down the street. Others jogged toward us—not unarmed cops, as they were in England, but well-armed soldiers. Oversized, beefed up, frightening ones. The kind that looked like they may have had some lykora blood.

"Come with us," one of them said to us as they ran. "We offer shelter and safety."

"Hell no," I muttered.

"You are *required* to come," he said, and they raised their guns to point toward us. "You come, or we'll shoot."

"Good luck with that." Owen said as he waved his hands to cloak our group. "We need to get out of here."

The heavy steps of the soldiers followed us for half a block, apparently expecting us to show again. When we didn't, they started shooting. Someone obviously watched and controlled their trigger fingers.

"This way," Solomon said, turning us down a narrow road to our left.

More planes soared overhead. The soldiers behind us stopped firing and retreated.

"To that church," Solomon said, and we began running as more bombs fell.

We crashed inside and slammed the wooden doors shut. Charlotte ran down the center aisle of the sanctuary, toward a door in the back.

"There are usually bomb shelters downstairs," she said, and we all followed her.

Through the door was a corridor with two passageways and several more doors leading off of it. We checked each one until we found steps leading downward into a cellar apparently used for storage. Metal racks lined the stone walls, the shelves stacked with boxes and cans.

"It's food!" Dorian said excitedly as his eyes scanned the boxes. He looked at me, as if actually asking for permission, but Owen didn't. He broke open a package and dug in.

"I don't see how they can eat." Blossom sidled up next to me, the ground and building trembling around us.

I looked up at her, and our eyes locked for a brief moment before we swallowed each other into hugs.

"I'm so glad you're okay," she said, her voice watery and choked.

"You, too." I squeezed her tighter.

Sheree came over and joined our group hug. "We were so worried. All of the Amadis thought we'd lost you. Solomon had to send word to make sure nobody showed signs of mourning. We just had to hope you were okay."

The building above us shook again, and chalky dust rained down. We pulled apart, and I went to join Tristan, taking a seat next to him on the floor. He ate pudding out of a plastic cup with his fingers. He held a dark brown glob out to me, but I shook my head. The chocolate tempted me, but I couldn't bring myself to suck on his fingers with everyone else around.

"These aren't biscuits, they're cookies!" Dorian said when he opened a package and looked inside. He stuffed at least three in his mouth at once before holding the bag out to me. I did take a couple of those, nibbling on the crumbly goodness, too afraid to devour them—my stomach growled and clenched at the same time.

"Please tell me these bombs aren't meant for us," I said to nobody in particular.

"It's Normans against Normans," Solomon said. "It's been going on since we've been here. An hour or two of air raids, then twelve or so of peace before they begin again."

"Who's doing them?" Tristan asked.

"Everyone. I've spotted planes from France, Germany, Italy, Iraq, China, and Japan."

"Geez," I muttered. "World War III really has started, hasn't it?"

"We haven't seen or heard anything from the U.S. or about it," Blossom said. "Information only travels by word of mouth anymore, and nobody here seems to care about the Americans. I'm hoping we can go there next, and it's not so bad. I mean, who would bomb the U.S., right?"

"The Daemoni," Solomon said.

"Yep," Vanessa agreed. "It's the Daemoni making all of this happen. The U.S. won't be safe for long."

"We need to find where Lucas has the Summoned, and that's where we're going, regardless," I said.

We caught each other up on everything we'd been through and learned while we'd been separated. Solomon had been able to reach a few other council members before the networks started failing. No region was doing great, but they managed to hold themselves together, at least as of two days ago. Conversions had increased, but not nearly at the accelerated rate the Daemoni turned Normans. Eventually they'd have to stop, though, or they'd extinguish their own food source, especially with all the norms dying by their hands, at war, or by the not-so-natural disasters.

The group had gone to Prague from Moscow, but couldn't reach Solomon's contacts before war broke out there. Then they went on to Cologne and stayed there for a few days, hoping we'd show up.

"I have not been able to reach anyone else, but we learned a lot of chatter from the Daemoni channels regarding London and the rest of England," Solomon finished. "We thought this would be the best place to start the search for the Summoned. I'd about given up that you would ever see my message to come here, and we'd left the safe house just tonight."

"Did we have people there?" I asked.

Charlotte shook her head. "No. They evacuated those in need of protection to outside the city when the bombs started dropping. The rest scattered to help the Normans, and hopefully gather some of the newly turned."

I nodded and swallowed. Tristan sat with his back against the wall, one knee bent up with an arm rested on it, and the other knee pulled in on the floor. I scooted closer to him, leaned my head back against his shoulder, and closed my eyes. Dorian sat on the other side of me and lay against me, so I draped an arm over his shoulder and across his chest.

Life sucked. War sucked. No doubt about it. But for the moment, I could be thankful to at least have my two men and my closest friends still alive and back by my side.

My people, however, were another story. And so were the Normans.

We couldn't rest here for long.

As soon as the building stopped shaking for more than thirty minutes since the last blast, we crept our way upstairs. Unable to see through the stained glass windows, Tristan and I went over to the doors, and he opened one just enough to peek through.

The street was deserted, covered in dust and ash and littered with big chunks of concrete, pieces of roofing, and shards of glass. At least, the street appeared to be empty of life, but Tristan and I looked at each other, both of us hearing the beating heart about twenty-five yards away. A whimper followed.

"We have to help them," I said.

He nodded, and we ran out without telling the others, knowing half of them would follow. Vanessa and Jax did anyway. We found a middle-aged woman more than half-buried in the rubble, so we hadn't been able to see her from the church.

She looked at us, her eyes grew wide, and she screamed.

"Shh, no," I said. "We're here to help."

I moved closer, and she yelled louder. She tried to wriggle away, but a large beam pinned her leg to the asphalt. I wasn't sure if she screamed even louder from the pain or the fear shining in her blue eyes as she stared at Vanessa and me making our way down to her because the guys were too big to fit in the small crevices.

"Shut. Up." Vanessa snapped, but the woman ignored her.

"We're trying to help you out of here," I said, "but please stop. You're going to draw attention."

"HELP ME! THEY'RE OVER HERE!" she screamed, and then she glared at us with wild animal-like eyes. "You're them. I know it. You're not touching me, you evil, horrible whores!"

Vanessa growled while at the same time lifting the beam off of the woman. I grabbed her under the pits and pulled her away, then slid one arm under her neck and the other under her legs and picked her up.

"Stop!" a man yelled the moment I crested the pile she'd been buried under.

"You stop." Tristan held his hand up, palm out. The man couldn't move, and by the look he gave the woman, I thought he must be her husband.

"We're helping her," I said as I carried her over to him.

His eyes grew as wild as hers when I approached. "No! I . . . I know who you are. Put my wife down!"

I bent over and laid her on the ground. When I came up, I stared down the barrels of several guns trained on me. Soldiers had come from nowhere—well, probably from the compound down the road, but we hadn't noticed their arrival. My damn mind was on the fritz again.

I held my hands up in the international signal of surrender, but yelled at them. "We're only trying to help, you idiots! That's what we do. We *protect* you from the true evil ones. We just saved her life!"

"Or infected her," her husband spat, still not helping the woman in front of his feet. He didn't even bend over or look at her to inspect her injuries. He feared that he'd catch what we supposedly had.

"She has a broken leg and probably internal injuries," Tristan said. "Get her some help, for fuck's sake."

He lifted his chin infinitesimally, signaling Vanessa, Jax, and me, and we all blurred away before something stupid happened. Something stupid happened anyway. The soldiers fired their mother-effin', god-forsaken guns at us. I was so tired of being shot at. And although I should have been immune to it by now, every time, my mother's bleeding body came into view. Every time, I watched her die again and again and again.

It was all I could do to not turn and shoot a few electric bolts at them.

They're just Normans. They don't know what they're doing.

I wasn't so sure about that last part—they didn't have that glazed-over look in their eyes. They didn't appear to be under control of some third entity. But I kept telling myself that anyway before I did something just as stupid as them.

We slammed the church door shut behind us, and I stomped down the center aisle, glaring at the angel statues in the corners and the image of Jesus on the cross depicted in stained glass straight in front of me, behind the altar.

"Why?" I demanded. "Why can't we just do what we're supposed to do? Why are you making this so hard?"

No answer came. Not that I expected one. I was beginning to feel like we were completely on our own down here.

"Alexis," Tristan murmured as he laid a strong, warm hand on my shoulder.

"I don't want to hear everything happens for a reason," I snapped, shrugging him off. "*We're* here for a reason. We supposedly have this purpose we're supposed to serve. But every time we turn around, we're being shot down. *Literally.* I'm so damn tired of being shot at."

I strode out of the sanctuary, into a small room to the side. I didn't know anything about Catholic churches, or churches in general. Mom taught me the Bible herself, and not just because we moved around a lot. She hadn't said so then, but I was pretty sure now she hadn't wanted my education—my training—to be tainted by human interpretation. Because humans were pretty fucking stupid sometimes.

So I sat in the middle of three short pews in whatever kind of room this was supposed to be. A table full of unlit candles stood in front of the first pew. Another image of Christ hung on the wall, this one three-dimensional. I dropped my head into my hands, covering my face, not wanting to see Him or Him to see me.

"Lex."

I jumped at the voice, thinking it belonged to Jesus at first. Sheesh. I peeked through my fingers at Tristan in the doorway.

"I need some time alone," I said. "Before I lose my sh . . ." I couldn't bring myself to say it out loud in a church, especially with Jesus still staring down at me. "My mind. We have nowhere to go and no way to get there even if we did. Every time we step outside, we're shot at. The humans don't want our help. They only want to kill us."

"Answers will come," he promised.

"Oh, I'm sure you'll figure out something brilliant, but for now, I need to be alone." I flicked my finger and shut the door. And immediately felt guilty for it, so I didn't get mad when he stopped it from closing all the way and came inside. He sat down next to me, wrapped his arms around me, and pressed his lips to my temple.

"I'll give you your space, but first I have to tell you how much I love you." He rose, strode out of the room, and shut the door behind him.

"I love you, too," I said through my tears, knowing he could still hear me.

I cried into my hands. I felt so lost. So abandoned. I pulled my hands away from my face and dug my fingers into my palm, trying to find a way into my book. Maybe the Angels had a message in there for me. They *had* to have a message for me. We were stuck, with no idea where to go.

"*Have* you abandoned us?" I said out loud, questioning my ancestors and the Angels when the book didn't appear in my palm. "Have you given up? Because I don't blame you if you did." I changed my thoughts to God himself. "Your will is supposed to be the way, and if your will is to leave us be because we don't deserve you anymore, I get it. I really do. I think it's pretty crappy, but I get it."

I didn't really know what else to say. If we'd been left here on Earth completely on our own, it's not like I could demand a signal to know this. If they were gone, they were gone. They wouldn't have been listening to me anyway.

I dropped my hands from my face and looked up at Jesus hanging on the wall. And anger began to build in my chest. "Except that you promised, you know. You promised to never abandon us—well, to never abandon your children. Maybe I don't deserve your mercy, but what about all the Normans out there? They can be ignorant, yes, but that doesn't mean they deserve to be abandoned. They're not all bad, are they? I can't believe that."

I gripped the pew in front of me, leaned my forehead against it, and stared at my boots that were no longer black, but gray, covered in dust. My breath sighed out of me. I kept trying to help and save everyone, and instead, I only brought death. Maybe this lack of support was not an abandonment of the Amadis or the norms, but only of me. Maybe that was my message, the same one I'd been saying all along, coming loud and clear now from Heaven above: I wasn't meant for this.

"Alexis."

The female voice in the room made me jump.

"Darling."

I gasped at this familiar one.

"Alexis Katerina, look up."

Only one person called me that, usually when she was angry. Now she said it with love, and tears filled my eyes as I rolled my head back and dared to look up.

And my mouth gaped open.

CHAPTER 15

J couldn't breathe. I definitely couldn't say anything. I could only stare with my mouth hanging wide open.

Three figures stood between me and the table of candles, blocking out the Jesus on the wall. Three women, all dark-haired with a tint of red, all dark-eyed with similarly shaped faces. All wearing white dresses that looked quite a bit like my wedding dress, only made of some Otherworldly material that looked like soft leather, and no fancy gems decorated the collar, giving them an overall fiercer appearance. And all with white, feathery wings tucked closely behind them. *Huge* wings, with their apexes reaching several inches above the women's heads and their tips draping on the floor by their feet.

I plastered myself against the back of the pew as I drank in the sight.

"*Mom?* Rina?" I eyed the other one. I'd known her voice from hearing it in my head several times before. My heart shook in my chest. "Cassandra?"

They all smiled at me.

"You're really here?" I asked in disbelief. Their grins only grew. I peeled myself away from the back of the pew and leaned forward. I reached out to touch Mom's hand. "Oh my god!"

"Alexis," she warned, and my eyes darted to the wall behind her, although I couldn't see Jesus anymore.

"Sorry," I murmured. "I just . . . I can't . . . *MOM!*"

I sprang from the pew, somehow hurdled over the front one, and threw myself at her. She caught me in her arms. Her familiar scent enveloped me, confirming further she really stood here, although it was mixed with an unusual freshness, like how the Sacred Archives smelled. Then I turned to Rina and hugged her, too. I stood awkwardly in front of Cassandra, but she pulled me into her arms for an embrace.

"You're *Angels?*" I demanded, reaching out to touch the top of Mom's wing. It moved when I did, and I jerked my hand back. Mom laughed. I wanted to cry. I thought I'd never hear her laugh or feel her hugs again.

"We've been promoted, in a way," she said.

"Heaven needs all the help available in these times," Cassandra added.

I laugh-snorted. "Yeah, well, so do I."

"And you have it, darling," Rina said.

I spun on her. "You're staying?"

My heart leapt with hope.

"Sorry, honey, but we cannot stay," Mom said, and I crashed back down to reality. "This is your realm. We are needed in the Otherworld."

I slumped onto the front pew.

"We have not abandoned you, though," Cassandra said. "We are still fighting for you where we are. We are still providing you guidance when you need it. The Angels and God himself are behind you, Alexis."

You could have fooled me.

"Darling, you have not needed us," Rina said. Could she still read minds? Or could they all? Well, they'd spoken in my head before, so I supposed that was my answer. I couldn't think without them hearing me, but when I pleaded for their help, they ignored me.

"We are not ignoring you," Cassandra said. "But there are some trials you must face. Some lessons you must learn on your own. Some decisions you must make for yourself. And some consequences must be suffered in order for you to become the strongest daughter you can be."

My eyes bugged. "So this has all been about training and testing? You're letting norms die so *I* can learn some kind of lesson?"

"No, dear, we are fighting for them in our own realm. Remember, their souls are what matter most."

I crossed my arms over my chest. "So as long as their souls are safe from evil, who cares if they die?"

Mom winced. "It sounds bad, but really, yes, that's how it is. Your purpose is to protect souls. Protect them from the darkness. From the Daemoni. They need to be stopped."

"I won't argue with you there. But I'm not doing such a great job. They're too strong for us, and Lucas is too cunning for me. Too experienced." I blew out a breath and shoved a hand through my hair. "I don't know how I can possibly beat him. They've always outnumbered us, and now they have the norms turned against us."

"The humans are not all against you, darling," Rina said.

I cocked my head to look at her. "Well, if there are any still on our side and still alive, where are they? Because we sure as hel-eck haven't found them."

"That is why we have come," Cassandra said. "To assure you that we are here. That we are fighting, too. You cannot see us on the other side of the veil, but we are battling alongside you. We have come to direct you to help."

I nodded. Finally, a break. "Thank you! Where are they? What do I do?"

"Go to the abbey. Find the door with the wings carved

into the wood above it. Knock twice, pause, then knock five more times."

I stared at her with a lifted brow. Was she kidding me? Go to some strange door where who knew what lurked inside and give a secret-coded knock? Did we look like school kids trying to get into the neighborhood tree house club?

"You'll find what you need there, honey." Mom reached out for my hand.

I sensed the farewell, so I grabbed hers and lurched upwards, back into her arms. I held on to her as though I held on to life. In a way, I did. "I've missed you so much. I'm so sorry, Mom. I'm so sorry I didn't stop him."

Tears flowed down my cheeks, and my whole body quaked with the weight of the pain and regret I'd been carrying around since the night she died.

"Nothing to be sorry about, Alexis. This is the way it's supposed to be, and you will stop him now. *You* are meant to do this. Not me. I am meant to be in the Otherworld, with the rest of the Amadis daughters and the Angels."

"Please don't leave me again." I held tightly to her small body, the feathers of her wings soft as they quivered under my hands.

"We're always here, Alexis. But we all have our roles. We all have our places to serve. Your place is here. Mine is not. Just know that I always love you." She pressed a kiss to my head, unable to find my face buried between her shoulder and neck.

"I love you, too," I cried, and I fell forward to my knees, nothing there to hold my weight anymore.

They were gone.

I leaned over my thighs and quietly wept, feeling more alone than ever.

A few minutes, or perhaps hours, later, the door opened. Tristan found me on my knees on the floor, probably looking as though I bowed in prayer. Except my whole body trembled, more with anger than sadness and loneliness as he sat down beside me.

"What's the matter, my love?"

"Nothing," I said before sitting up and swiping the backs of my hands over my eyes. "Everything." I threw my hands in the air and let them smack down on my thighs. "Just when I think I have answers, when we think we're doing the right thing, when we have direction, the door gets slammed in our faces."

I laughed, even as the anger burned in my chest. How could I tell him Mom, Rina, and Cassandra had been here, looking like Angels? How could I explain their instructions that seemed so ridiculous? I'd imagined the whole scene. I had to have. I *hoped* I had, and that some sorceress hadn't thrown me into another false vision. Either way, their visit could not have been real. Mom and Rina wouldn't tease me like that. Would they?

"I think I'm just tired," I said. "Tired already of all of this. Tired of being tired."

"Everyone else is resting until nightfall. Come on." He took my hand and pulled me to my feet, then led me to a small office that had probably belonged to the priest.

He sat on the suede-upholstered couch and pulled me down with him, then wrapped his arms around me and lay down. We squirmed and wiggled, getting ourselves situated, without him letting go of me.

"You smell different," he said.

"Yeah, probably gross. I need a shower."

"No. More like heaven," he murmured into my hair before we fell into a restive, regenerative sleep that I'd needed more than I expected.

"Alexis, Tristan." Blossom's voice, soft, coming through a crack in the door. "Solomon has an idea."

We both sat up simultaneously, instantly awake.

Ten minutes later, we'd all gathered into the pews in the

sanctuary, and Solomon stood in front of us, near the altar, as though ready to deliver a sermon.

"We need to go to Westminster Abbey," he announced, and I didn't know whether to laugh or scream.

"Is this some kind of joke?" I asked him. "Did they come to you, too? Tell you to find the door with the wings carved in the casing and give a special secret knock?"

Solomon leveled me with a what-the-hell look. "I know not what you mean, but we should be able to find help at the abbey."

"Nobody wants to help us," I said. "They only want to kill us."

"Surely there's somebody," Sheree said.

"Well, if there is, they're too terrorized to come out and show it," Vanessa said. "I wouldn't bank on anyone at the abbey being willing to help us—if there even is anyone. The Daemoni probably started there as they seemingly have with all the so-called religious leaders."

Solomon's cornrows grazed his shoulders as he shook his head. "No, I no longer expect anyone to be there, but there is protection on its sacred grounds. And there is a stash of weapons."

"We all have weapons," Owen pointed out. "In some form or another."

"The kinds of weapons we cannot use against the Normans," Solomon said. "The kinds of weapons that identify us as supernaturals as soon as we use them."

Tristan straightened up next to me and nodded. "Right. Yes, you're right, Solomon. We need to look and act more Norman. Carry Norman weapons. Fight like them. Even if we have to fight against them, at least it's fairer."

"Well, not exactly fair," Vanessa said as she barely flicked her wrist and a throwing star soared across the room. She suddenly stood where she'd aimed, holding the star between her fingers. "It's not like they'd have a chance against us."

"It's not like we're going to seriously fight them either," Char quipped. "They'll have the advantage because they don't care if they hurt or even kill us. Besides, not everyone here is like you."

Before we could argue any further, air-raid sirens sounded, and a nearby explosion shook the church. I grabbed Dorian's hand and ran for the cellar, where we spent four more hours taking shelter from the bombs and discussing our options. We had few. Well, only one that provided any semblance of a real plan. When our surroundings finally fell quiet, we estimated the time to be about three a.m. If we were going to head to Westminster, this was the time to do it. Hopefully, Normans slept, and the streets would be quiet.

Of course, we couldn't possibly have such good luck.

The first fifteen blocks proved to be easy as we stuck close to the buildings, dark shadows moving in a dark night. The city felt like another world—blacked out and silent with no power. No lights brightened the sky with a soft backlight for as far as we could see. No Big Ben, giant Ferris wheel, or any buildings lit up to provide a sense of location or direction. The only light came from the occasional orange glow of the fires still burning in some buildings. No motors hummed. No horns or emergency sirens. Every once in a while, I'd hear a car engine in the far distance, speeding away. Nobody—and I meant *nobody*—walked the streets. Yes, it was the middle of the night, but this was London, not some small town in Bible-belt America.

And then we found the Daemoni.

We'd been creeping along a plaza-like area right below the Eye, London's famous Ferris wheel, headed for the bridge to cross the river to Westminster. Vanessa had been running ahead of us, scoping things out and giving us the all clear when she found a place to hide us before moving on to the next point. That was how she stumbled upon a nest of vampires feasting.

"Oh, well. Hello, boys," she said about fifty yards ahead of us.

Tristan and I exchanged a look and ran ahead to catch up with her. Solomon met us there. Eight vampires were feeding on three norms, obviously against their will. We arrived in time to see Vanessa's boot land in a Daemoni vampire's head as she kicked it as though it were a soccer ball. Too distracted by his meal to realize whom he was dealing with, he looked up at us with his lips curled back to bare bloody fangs and red glowing eyes, trying to threaten us.

"I can do that, too." Vanessa displayed her true vampire look. Only, her eyes didn't glow.

"Me as well," Solomon said, and he vamped out, too, both of them snarling at the others, who'd all stopped eating.

"I can't do that, but I can do this," Tristan said, and he swept his hand out, throwing the vampires off their human meals.

They soared several yards and crashed into the ticket building for the Eye, then jumped to their feet and flew back at us. I shot electricity at them at the same time Tristan stopped them in mid-motion, paralyzing them. Vanessa blurred behind them, and with a succession of cracks, they each dropped to the ground, their heads at odd angles to the rest of their bodies.

She appeared next to me.

"You broke their necks?" I asked.

"It's not like they're dead," she retorted.

"Do you know them?" Solomon asked as he studied each one.

Vanessa walked back over to the line of still bodies. She kicked one's foot. "That's the leader of the main London nest."

"Not likely to be converted then," Charlotte said, finally joining us. "Are any of them?"

Vanessa wrinkled her nose. "Doubt it. This nest is older than dirt and one of the worst of the worst."

"Alexis, you know what to do," Charlotte said.

With a sigh, I grabbed the hilt of my dagger and walked over to the temporarily dead vamps. If they couldn't take what I was about to do, the "temporarily" part would have been, well, temporary. I swallowed hard, trying to push the lump in my throat away as I squatted next to the one Vanessa had identified as the leader. I thought he'd be an easy way to start this process, getting the worst out of the way first. Holding my dagger with both hands, I lifted it above my head, then slammed it into his chest, straight into his heart. At the same time, I pushed Amadis power through the blade.

His body immediately began convulsing from the combination of the silver blade and the power of all things good. His eyes flew open, glowing bright red. But only for a moment. They dimmed quickly and then went out completely as his skin put off a purplish-black smoke, stinking like a corpse and shriveling up against his bones. My Amadis power defeated the dark magic in him, the only thing keeping him "alive" since he had no hope or love—no *soul*—left inside him.

Mom and Charlotte had taught me the theory of killing a Daemoni who'd lost his soul completely to Satan, but this was the first time I'd actually done it. I'd delivered the final and true death to this vampire.

I moved along the line of bodies, doing the same to each one. If any of them had hope left, they would have begged for mercy. I would have been able to sense any possibility for redemption. They only needed the slightest hint of hope, of desire to be different. None of these vamps had any, and they all shriveled into dried up corpses.

My heart felt as withered as their bodies by the time I finished. I'd said numerous times how much I wanted to kill the Daemoni, but now that I'd actually done so, it didn't give me the satisfaction I'd desired. Only overwhelming sadness.

"The norms will be okay," Blossom said, putting a hand on

my arm to comfort me. "Solomon healed them and sent them on their way."

I nodded. "That's good."

Tristan shot a flame out of his palm, lighting the corpses on fire to make sure they were good and gone.

"That'll draw attention," Owen said. "We better get moving again."

We'd barely started off when someone whispered from a shadow, "Follow me."

A Norman girl wearing all black—a leather jacket, jeans, and combat boots—with a sword strapped to her back and another knife tied to her upper thigh, stepped in front of us and waved us in her direction. Tristan and I exchanged a glance.

"Come *on*," she said, "before the humans see you."

We walked in her direction, but only because she headed the same way we did anyway. She ran ahead of us, beckoning us on.

"We'll lose her on the other side of the bridge," Tristan murmured, and I nodded.

Until we'd come upon the vamps, I'd been contemplating what we were going to do after Westminster Abbey. I was pretty sure that wasn't the abbey Cassandra had meant. After Tristan had pointed out that I smelled like Mom, Rina, and Cassandra, I had to admit to myself that they hadn't been a vision, which meant I had to sincerely consider what they'd instructed me to do. And that made me wonder if Noah was still at Whitby Abbey, and they were sending us there for that reason. The whole secret door and knock was weird, though, throwing me for a loop.

The girl continued heading in the same direction we did, until right before we reached Westminster, when she turned right into an alley.

"This way," she said, but we kept on. "Alexis! This way before they see you!"

She held a door open about twenty feet into the alley. Above it, carved into the wood frame, was a pair of angel wings.

"Hold on," I murmured, grabbing Tristan's arm as I turned toward the girl. "Who are you?"

Her eyes grew big as she stared behind me. "Just come *on!*"

Several pairs of heavy footsteps ran toward us, and I glanced over my shoulder. These weren't super-sized, beefed up Normans, but they were still military, with military-issued guns pointed right at us.

"Hurry up," the girl yelled. "It's safe in here."

Guns started firing, only in the air at first. I glanced at my people, all of them looking at me as though I'd lost my mind when I jerked my head in the girl's direction.

"Let's go," I said, deciding to trust her . . . and Cassandra.

I took off for the door at the same time the soldiers lowered their guns, no longer giving us warnings. My team sprinted after me.

"In here." The girl waved us inside.

Once we ran through the entrance, she slammed and bolted the metal door shut with a thick piece of wood.

"I'll protect it," Owen said.

"Who are you?" I demanded of the girl. "How do you know my name?"

She pushed the sleeve of her jacket back, and turned the inside of her wrist upward to show what looked like a new tattoo: the same angel wings that were carved in the doorway with the initials A.K. scrolled into them.

"I'm Kristen," she said. "Second in charge of this place. Ammi, my sister, is commander, but she's out right now."

"What place?" I asked suspiciously. I assumed A.K. stood for Ammi and Kristen, and I almost laughed. Cassandra really had sent us to some kind of bizarre neighborhood clubhouse, after all.

"Relax, Alexis." She pulled her sleeve back down to cover

the tattoo and turned to lead us through the dark corridor we'd entered. After a few yards, it ended at stairs that only went down. "You're with friends. Supporters."

She moved fast for a norm, taking us down several flights before we came to the last step and walked into an enormous room lit with only two battery-powered lanterns in diagonal corners. A few dozen people were gathered, most curled on makeshift beds of blankets and sleeping bags, and some sitting or standing in small groups and whispering quietly while working on various tasks—reading, sewing, even bandaging each other up. A few others came into the room through doorways. The lighting was too dim to see where those doors led. They all fell silent, stopped what they were doing, and turned to us with excitement and awe shining in their eyes. Then they began to arouse the others. Whispers of "Wake up and look who's here!" carried across the room.

"We would have made your welcome a big party if we'd known you were coming," Kristen said. "I know it's not a castle or anything, but you and your group can call it home for now. You're safe here."

"What *is* this place?" I asked again. "Who are you people?"

Those awake enough to know what was going on held their arms up—some already bare, others having to push sleeves back—and showed the same tattoo on all of their inner wrists. *Okay, maybe not a club. More like a cult.*

"This," Kristen said, sweeping her arm out toward the room, "all of us?" She smiled proudly. "We are A.K.'s Angels."

I stared at her with bewilderment, not understanding why she seemed to expect me to be excited, or at least impressed. "A.K., as in Ammi and Kristen?"

She laughed. "No, silly. A.K. as in Alexis Katerina."

CHAPTER 16

I simply stared at the girl, too shocked to form words. Tristan, Owen, Charlotte, and Vanessa, however, pushed me backwards to stand in front of me. The rest of my team circled Dorian and me in, blocking my view of anything, although I heard the shuffles of many people in the room rising to their feet.

"How do you know her name?" Tristan demanded, and with the sharp tone of his voice, I could only imagine the frightful spark in his eyes.

"She was right?" Kristen squeaked, sounding excited and impressed just as much as scared. Her nerves showed as she babbled on. "It's really Alexis Katerina? That's what someone in one of the American cells said, but we didn't know if she really knew what she was talking about. We thought it was a guess, you know, from A.K. Emerson. I mean, we got the Alexis part from the news, before it went down, and there's been all kinds of speculation about the K. We heard more and more that it stood for Katerina, so that's kind of what we went with. No worries. It's just A.K. for all intents and purposes. Don't want those arseholes out there knowing exactly what it all means. Anyway, you, uh, don't have to worry about us. We're on your side."

"You need to explain more than that," Vanessa ordered.

"*Who* are you?" Owen asked.

I peeked around Tristan's arm. I really didn't feel like we had anything to worry about. Only norms dwelled here. Nothing we couldn't handle. And the bits and pieces I could pick up from their thoughts were far from alarming—most simply felt awe to see us here. Sasha remained hidden in Dorian's coat, so she didn't sense any danger either.

"We're A.K.'s fans," Kristen said. "*Big* fans. We had a forum on the Internet, where we would talk about the books and characters—the largest fan site for A.K. Emerson. Fans from all over would get on there all the time, even after she died . . . or when we thought she died. A lot of us didn't believe she actually had, since there was no body or anything. Anyway, we even had role-playing games and everything. So when the news said A.K. was still alive and responsible for the supernatural attacks, the forum exploded. Most of us were gobsmacked, especially the part about her leading the bad guys. Her—" She ducked to peek at me between Tristan's and Owen's arms. "*Your* books are good, as in not evil. They're dark, yes, but they're also about love and hope. How could anyone who writes stuff like that be responsible for everything going on? So we started putting together local groups and called ourselves A.K.'s Angels. It was mostly all talk at first, trying to sort how to prove to the world that you aren't bad. But then things got worse. We lost our homes, our schools, and businesses. Family members . . . Everything's changed. So we gathered here, and this has become home. There are cells around the world doing the same thing." She paused and frowned. "Last we know, that is. Since all the communication networks went down, we haven't been able to reach any of the others. We don't know who's still around. We were the third largest then, though. Two American cells were the largest. But who knows now?"

Despair colored her tone. I pushed my way between Tristan and Owen and looked out at the small crowd.

"These are all my fans?" I asked with disbelief.

"Well, not exactly, not anymore. That's how we started, but we've added other people since everything went to shit. Family, neighbors, friends . . . anyone we find still alive and can convince to come with us. Strength in numbers and all that. Ammi and a small group are out right now, looking for survivors from these latest bombings. I was out with them, but then I saw you lot and had to stop. They took off without me."

"But these are *all* A.K.'s supporters?" Charlotte asked.

Kristen grimaced. "Some don't know what to believe, but they owe us their lives. No one would be here if Ammi and I hadn't started this cell. They'd either be dead or in the camps with that bizarre-o military holding them hostage. They came with us because they know the media and the governments were full of shite when everything went bad, and they trusted us over them. So yeah, we trust them, too. So can you." She wrung her hands together as she looked over her shoulder at her people, then back at us. "So, uh, are you hungry? Thirsty? Tired? Want tea or a bath?"

She had me at bath.

Although, her idea of a bath was quite a loose definition— a soup pot of cold water and a washrag. At least a second pitcher had been provided to wash my hair. Except for Dorian, who crashed out on a cot, we'd already caught enough sleep to be wide awake when everyone else returned to bed. Everyone but Kristen.

"I'll sleep when my sister returns," she said as she led us down the hall to a room that served as the cafeteria. It apparently had been an employee break room in the not-too-distant past.

"I can't sleep either," said a girl's voice behind us.

"Same with me," said another. "I mean, A.K. Emerson's really here!"

I looked over my shoulder to find several people following us and suppressed a sigh. I'd never liked the attention when I'd lived as A.K. Emerson and still didn't like it now, but this went beyond being embarrassing. It was also very humbling. These people had come together because of their love of my books . . . and that love just might have saved their lives and many others'. I'd never believed it until now, but Rina and her council just might have been right about my stories.

Kristen lit a lantern in the dining room and set it at the center of one of the round tables, but we hadn't even sat down when two knocks, a pause, and then five more echoed down the stairs and through the hall. Kristen ran for the door, and a few moments later, hushed voices traveled to our ears, followed by Kristen and two others, a guy and a girl. The girl let out a strange little squealing noise and clapped her hand over her mouth.

"Oh gosh, I can't believe it," she said, her words muffled behind her palm. "It's really you!"

"I'm going out," Kristen announced, ignoring the girl and turning back for the door.

"Wait," I called out. "By yourself?"

"I have to find Ammi."

"You're not Ammi?" Tristan asked the girl who still stared at me with huge eyes behind square glasses. Her gaze finally pulled away when she realized he spoke to her, and when she looked at him, her face flushed the color of a ruby grapefruit.

She shook her head, and as though she just remembered herself, her hand dropped from her mouth, her expression sliding from surprise to despair with it. "We lost her and the others."

"We thought we'd lost Kristen, too," the guy said as he pulled a knit cap off his head and bunched it in his hands. "We hadn't realized she didn't run away with us when those vampires attacked those people. We thought it was too late for them, and we heard someone crying for help, so we ran off. I guess Kristen hadn't followed us. Maybe she'd seen you guys or something. And then, we got in a fight with more bloodsuckers—"

"Wait. You fought *vampires*?" I asked, not sure whether to be impressed or to yell at them for their stupidity.

He nodded. "We thought we ran them off, but then our whole group except us was gone. One second, they were next to us. The next, they weren't."

Tristan and I exchanged a glance, and he gave me a nod.

"Solomon and Char, you better go with Kristen," I said, and they took off after the girl.

"You shouldn't be out there in the middle of the night," I told the other two—and anyone else who happened to be listening—while I dropped into a seat. "That's when they *hunt*."

The girl's blue eyes widened again as she moved farther into the room and sat down at the table next to ours, facing us.

"It's really you," she whispered.

"Somebody had to look for survivors after tonight's bombings, though," the guy said. He stuck his hat in his back pocket, and then reached his hand out toward me. "Terrence. That's Olivia. I guess you're *the* A.K."

"Alexis." I shook his hand, and then he went around our group, learning everyone's names while introducing himself and Olivia. Tristan, Blossom, Sheree, and Jax joined me at the table. The others who'd followed us from the main room into the dining room leaned against tables and the wall, staring on in sleepy fascination.

"You didn't find any survivors?" Sheree asked.

Terrence pushed a hand through his longish, dark blond hair. "Everyone's dead or gone, it seems. Except the ones in the camps."

"The person we thought we heard?" Olivia spoke up. "There was nobody there."

"You were deceived," Tristan muttered.

"Wot?" the girl asked.

"That's what they do," Jax said bitterly. "They trick you, pull you in, and then go in for the attack."

I winced at his bluntness.

Olivia gasped. "Do you think they got our friends?"

"Chances are . . . yes," Vanessa said matter-of-factly.

"Maybe more of us should go out and search," Owen suggested, looking at me.

I nodded my permission before dropping my face into my hands.

"Why on earth would you try to fight vampires?" Blossom asked. "*How?*"

"With silver, of course." Olivia's voice notched up an octave with excitement. I looked up at her in disbelief, and she gave me a small grin. "Just like in your books. We've been plundering when we're out, finding as much silver as we can."

"Do you have weapons?" Jax asked.

Terrence and Olivia both flashed some kind of large gun under their coats.

"Are those paintball guns?" Tristan asked with an undertone probably only I noticed. One that subtly said, *Are you serious?*

"Not many guns in England," Terrence said. "Not ones that work. But we're legally allowed to have paintball guns, and that's what we found. We melted down silver and coated the paintballs in it."

"Huh," Tristan muttered, and I knew that sound, too. He was slightly impressed.

"We have knives, too," Olivia said. "We've raided the stores and the museums. Found a whole bunch hidden in Westminster Abbey. That's where Kristen found her fab sword."

I suppressed an inappropriate snicker. What would Solomon have done when he found out the secret stash of weapons in the abbey had been pilfered? I, personally, could only be proud of these guys for their boldness in stealing them.

"Do you know how to use them?" I asked.

Olivia grimaced. "A little. But we're just nerds. Everything we know is from books, the telly and films, and video games. Terrence and some of the guys we've brought in have taught us a tad bit, though."

"Thanks to your books, we know how to recognize the bad guys," the girl in the corner said. "We know not to be fooled by their beauty or charm, and to look for red eyes."

"The Daemoni don't always have red eyes," Sheree said.

"The who?"

My books, of course, didn't call the "bad guys" the Daemoni. When I wrote them, I knew the word, but associated it with Satanic worshippers and the like. I'd had no idea the creatures in my books made up the Daemoni . . . or the Amadis. So we explained to the group, which grew as morning approached, who the Daemoni were and who we were.

"So hold on, you're all supernaturals?" Terrence asked.

Sheree and Jax both let their fangs and claws out.

"Whoa," Olivia breathed as she stared at them. "But you're good."

It wasn't a question.

"Right. We're the Amadis. We're the good guys," Sheree confirmed after retracting her fangs.

"Our reason for existence is to protect you and the rest of the humans from the Daemoni," I said.

"But you're not," a woman accused from the corner. She was in her early thirties with a baby on her hip. "You let them attack the first time, and now they run around like they own the world. They're probably behind this worldwide war."

Tristan nodded. "You're right. They greatly outnumber and out-power us. It doesn't mean we're not doing everything we can. It hasn't helped that the majority of humans have been turned against us."

"They're turned against the Daemoni, too," Terrence said. "They were anyway. When we could still get the news, the Americans were really fighting back. I don't know if it did them much good, though."

"We need to get more humans on our side," someone said.

Olivia turned her head to look over the shoulder at the speaker. "There aren't many left that we can get to. They're all dead or locked up. Or turned into evil creatures themselves."

Several people reacted to this with noises of disgust.

"Who would have thought," Terrence mused out loud, "that the apocalypse would come by vampires and werewolves?"

Everyone at my table looked over at him.

"The apocalypse?" Blossom asked.

"Obviously," he said. "That's what everyone's saying. The horsemen are coming down on us, meting out God's punishment." He shrugged. "It's a theory. Conquest, War, Famine, and Death? We've got them all now. Last we heard, anyway, before shit hit the fan."

"Those evil creatures showed themselves and conquered the humans," someone else in the room said. The voice coming from behind me sounded older, and I turned to find a woman with a gray bun making tea. I hadn't noticed her come in. Besides the woman with the baby, she was by far the oldest we'd seen here so far. "We already have World War III. People rioted and hoarded food before, and since there's no electricity, there won't be food processed, packaged, and sold anymore. Who knows if there are even farmers left to grow it? So there's your famine."

"And people are dying everywhere," Olivia whispered.

"That man on the telly?" a girl piped up from the door.

"The one who said *you* were the bad guys? He sure looked like the Antichrist to me!"

Several people murmured in agreement, but I chuckled. Yeah, I supposed Lucas could be seen as the Antichrist. You couldn't get any more anti-God than him.

Another young woman joined in. "Me wee granny always said everyone in today's generation were antichrists because we didn't go to church anymore and did all sorts of immoral things."

"But there's been war, famine, disease, and death forever," Blossom said.

"Every generation has been able to point out signs of the end of the world," Sheree agreed.

"But nobody's seen it until now, right?" Terrence asked. "What would you call that out there? Looks rather apocalyptic to me." He chuckled, but the sound came hollow with little humor. "And here we thought the zombie apocalypse would get us before God did."

I frowned at his words. Zombies weren't completely omitted from this picture he'd painted in my mind. This image of the end of the world. Was that what this was? *Were* we witnessing the end of times? If so, I needed a word with my mother and the rest of my ancestors. They could have warned me! They could have taken me with them. Why did I have to be the one left behind to deal with this horror? I'd been left here alone with darkness trying to reign the world, and maybe there was a reason for it—because it was all hopeless in the end anyway, and I belonged here, not in the Heavens of the Otherworld. Was that what Mom had meant?

The conversation became a din in my mind as I contemplated this, my heart sinking as the minutes passed. Thank the Angels Vanessa and Solomon's mind signatures came within range, along with a Norman. Owen, Charlotte, and Kristen came in right behind them. Anxiety enveloped all of them, and I jumped from my seat and rushed for the door to the outside world, clearing the steps five at a time.

"Tell me what's wrong with her," Kristen said frantically after the door banged against the wall.

Vanessa had apparently thrown it open, and Solomon carried a limp body in his arms. The warlocks and Kristen followed after. My gaze jumped from face to face of my team members.

"*She's been turned,*" Vanessa said. My eyes shot back to her. "*I can smell the vamp's blood in her.*"

Ammi? I asked, and she gave me the slightest of nods. *Kristen doesn't know?*

"*Not yet, but she will soon.*"

I nodded. We had to tell her.

"Where can we take her?" I asked. "Where do you take the sick or the hurt?"

"Is she going to be okay?"

I clenched my jaw. "We need a private room. Where can we take her?"

Kristen pushed her way through. "This way."

She hurried down the hall, and Solomon followed after, with the rest of us on his heels. The Normans fell into step behind us, but once we reached a small office with a couch and Tristan and I joined the ones who had been out, Charlotte shut the door and muffled the room. Solomon laid the girl on the couch, and Kristen dropped to the floor next to her, taking her sister's hands in between her own.

"Tell me what's wrong with her," Kristen said. "She looks dead. Her chest doesn't even move. But you said she's not?"

She shifted to glare up at us. Knowing I needed to be the one to do this, I crouched down beside her.

"She's been turned, Kristen," I said softly.

Her eyes about jumped out of her head. "She's . . . one of *them*?" She shook her head violently. "A vampire? No. She can't be like them. Alexis, do something. *Please.* She can't handle something like this. She's too sweet and kind!"

I gently laid my hand on her arm. "We will. We can."

"You can turn her back?"

I cringed. "No, I'm sorry. But we *can* save her. We can make sure she's not like them. She's going to wake up with a crazy-insatiable thirst, but we can help her stay good."

She blinked at me as she tried to comprehend.

"Good vampires?" She didn't seem to believe the possibility at first, but then her eyes flitted over to Vanessa and Solomon who stood at the other end of the couch. "Like them?"

"Exactly like them." Char smoothed Ammi's dark hair away from her pale face. "That's what we do—convert those who've been turned against their will to the good side."

"Will it be painful?" the girl asked.

"Could be," Char said honestly. "But since she's waking up with us and not them, it won't be as bad as it could have been."

Kristen gnawed on her lip for a moment, then nodded. "What choice do I have? We can't throw her out on the streets."

"No, that would only be worse for her," I said. "And then we might eventually have to kill her."

"Like you did the ones when I found you?"

I nodded.

"Then do it. Keep her good. I can't . . . I can't imagine her going dark."

And I wondered then if Kristen was really the one who wouldn't be able to handle Ammi's change.

"You should probably leave the room," Char said. "All of you except Alexis and Tristan. Send Sheree in."

"I don't want to leave her," Kristen protested.

Tristan wrapped an arm over her shoulders and lifted her to her feet. "Trust me, you don't want to be here. She won't want you to see her like this. And you'll need to explain to your people what's going on."

Kristen looked back at me. "It'll be better coming from you, Alexis. They look up to you."

I glanced at Charlotte and Ammi.

"Go on," Char said. "We can start without you. But your power will help her most."

I nodded and followed Tristan and Kristen out with Solomon and Vanessa behind us. Questions immediately started flying.

"What's wrong with her?"

"Is she okay?"

"Where are the others?"

Kristen stuck her finger and her thumb in her mouth and whistled, quieting everyone. "She's going to be okay, but Alexis has something to tell you. Let's go to the big room."

Everyone packed into the large room, chattering and speculating, and Kristen gained all of their attention for me. As soon as the words "vampire" and "turned" came out of my mouth, panic broke out.

"Why would you bring her here?"

"She can't stay here!"

"She'll kill us!"

"We need to kill her first!"

"Enough," Tristan said, and although he didn't technically shout, the tone came out loud and frightening enough to shut everyone up. "Let Alexis explain."

A few crossed their arms over their chests or showed other signs of annoyance or confrontation, but they all listened as I told them more about who and what we were and how we could convert the turned to our side. They seemed to relax as I finished explaining.

"Ammi will be good then?" Olivia, who stood up front, asked, her voice full of hope.

"Yes. Unless she purposely gave her soul to the demons to become like one of them, she'll be good," I said.

"She would *never* do that," Kristen said.

"So I have a question," Terrence called from the back of the room. "If the Amadis side needs more numbers to be able to clobber the Daemoni side, why don't you turn humans?"

And I should have known that was coming.

"We wouldn't do that to a human's soul," Tristan said for me. "We wouldn't take that risk."

"But if we're volunteering to be on the good side?" Terrence pressed.

"Right," another guy said. "What if we *wanted* to? I've always thought it'd be brilliant to be a vampire."

"And to be immortal but not be evil? Have all that strength and speed and be able to kick those Daemoni's arses? That would be fabulous," a girl agreed.

"It would be." Terrence pointed his finger at me. "So what do you say? You could make us vampires, and we could fight for you."

Several others chimed in their agreement with Terrence's proposal.

"Trust me, you don't want this life," Vanessa said.

"But we should get to choose," Terrence insisted.

"We cannot turn anyone even if we wanted to." Solomon's deep, booming voice quieted everyone. "We would be breaking the very vows that saved our souls in the first place. It is not an option, so let it go."

I let him and the others deal with the grumblings while I returned to the office to help with the conversion. We spent over twenty-four hours with Ammi, but because she was newly turned and hadn't asked to be, she converted rather quickly. Sheree wouldn't even need to spend much time with her for faith-healing since she'd never lost any of her humanity. If only all conversions could be so easy.

She cried when we told her what happened.

"I always had a thing for vampires, thanks to you, Alexis," she said through her sniffles. "But I'd never wanted to *be* one."

"I'm sorry this happened to you."

She sighed. "I suppose it could be worse. Thank you for saving me." She let out a breathy laugh. "I can't believe I'm really talking to you. But then again . . . I'm a bloody vampire. Which is more preposterous?" Her brows pinched together. "What happened to George and the others?"

"We hoped you could tell us," Kristen said. We'd allowed her into the room once we knew Ammi would be okay—that she'd be safe around her own sister. This was a whole different situation than Sonya and Heather had been in.

Ammi shook her head, but then her eyes sparked. "I do remember one thing he said when he paused from sucking all my blood out of my body. He said, 'Don't worry. We won't kill your friends. We'll take good care of them, actually. We'll need *some* Normans around for food, after all.'"

"What? They're starting human farms or something?" Sheree asked, and I sucked in a breath.

"Kristen," I said, "you mentioned something about bizarre-o military camps. What did you mean?"

She snorted. "It's where all the *stupid* humans are going. You know, not like us. They're following the military guys like sheeple into this fenced off place over there by Parliament. They're basically being held hostage. Why? You don't really think it's a human farm, do you?"

I rubbed the back of my neck, and said, "I'm thinking we need to check it out."

CHAPTER 17

"The camp is run by the military and government, though," Kristen said. "Not the supernaturals. Not the Daemoni."

"I wouldn't be so sure there's a difference," Char muttered.

"Our queen wouldn't allow such a thing!" Ammi gasped, clapping her hand against her chest.

Your queen might not be alive . . . or human. A thought I kept to myself.

"So she'd allow concentration camps?" Char asked, and both girls frowned. "That's what this sounds like to me. You're right, Alexis. We do need to check it out."

The next day, at high noon, Owen cloaked Tristan, Vanessa, himself, and me, and the four of us followed Kristen's directions down the road and across the street toward Big Ben and the Palace of Westminster. I wanted to stop and gawk at the historical Gothic structure, but pillars of smoke rising into the sky and the sharp odor of burning buildings filling the air served as constant reminders that this was no sightseeing tour. We were on a mission.

Kristen had warned us that we wouldn't be able to see much until we moved farther down the street—seemingly farther into the heart of our enemies. As we passed an old church and a sign showing Westminster Abbey to our immediate right, though, I began to wonder if this camp, or whatever it was, possibly had nothing to do with the Daemoni after all. Maybe the norms had realized the evil ones couldn't enter sacred grounds, so they'd found refuge there. But before we reached the abbey, the barricades broke wide enough for a car to pass through, into an area where perhaps dignitaries were once dropped off, but was now full of several dozen rectangular boxes that looked like the big shipping containers used on cargo ships. A twelve-foot high fence with rounds of razor wire spiraling across the top of it surrounded the entire area, and a line of soldiers spread out along the fence, one about every fifteen feet. No other people could be seen, but we could hear their heartbeats, and I could sense their mind signatures.

Hundreds of Normans packed into the metal boxes.

As we watched, two uniformed soldiers and a man dressed in black exited the building and came into the camp. The civilian glanced up at the sun showing itself from behind scattered clouds and scowled. The show of contempt for the sun gave away his true species: vampire. The threesome walked over to one of the pods and opened the door, ordering everybody out. A couple dozen norms shuffled out of the box, blinking against the daylight. The soldiers stood on guard while the vampire inspected the people.

He pointed to an elderly man with a hunched back and bowed legs. "No. No good."

The soldiers pulled him to the side. The vamp said the same about an old woman and a younger man who hadn't stopped coughing.

"Get him out of here," the vampire ordered, and the soldiers dragged the sick man apart from the others, and without even a heartbeat of hesitancy, shot him in the head. My heart jumped into my throat.

"Oh no," I whispered as I clamped my hand over my mouth.

"They're good," the vampire said, indicating the remainder of those who'd been in the box. "Send them on."

I focused in on the norms, looking for anything helpful. Several had bite marks on their necks and wrists. They'd definitely been fed on.

"Look at that one's wrist," Tristan murmured from right next to me. "The one with the red shirt."

I zeroed in on what he saw on the guy's arm: a fresh tattoo of angel wings and the initials A.K.

"There's one accounted for," Vanessa said.

Before we could inspect anyone else's wrist, the soldiers rushed the norms back into the box. All except the two older people. The vampire dragged them both inside, presumably for lunch. I wanted to be sick.

"That definitely was not a place of refuge," I said once we returned to the bunker, and I told Ammi, Kristen, and the woman with the silver bun, all of whom seemed to have taken leadership roles here, what we had seen.

"The military and government are obviously working with the Daemoni," Tristan said.

"And it sure looked like they were harvesting humans," Vanessa added. "Weeding out the frail and keeping the strong."

Kristen and Ammi both frowned and shook their heads.

"I can't believe this has happened," Kristen said.

"Did you see Steven or Josie?" Ammi asked with a touch of hope. "George? Any of them?"

"We saw a blond guy with a red shirt and a tattoo like yours." Tristan tapped his finger against the inside of his wrist.

Ammi nodded. "Steven was wearing a red shirt. We'd argued about why he'd worn such a bright color when we'd gone out, but he'd spilt kerosene on his only black one. I'm sure he's not there alone. We have to save them!"

"We have to save all of them," I agreed.

We spent the rest of the day and the next scoping out the Norman farm and making our plan of attack. It wouldn't be easy when the House of Commons was full of military and Daemoni. We'd have to be sneaky as foxes, hoping the norms would recognize we'd come to free them and not scream for help. On the second day, we prepared to head out. Ammi joined us.

"You need to stay here," Charlotte said when she noticed the girl.

"I can help," she protested. "Those arseholes changed me. I want to hurt them!"

"You're not ready," Tristan said.

She scowled at him. "I *have* to go. I promised everyone."

I cocked my head as I looked at her. "What do you mean you promised everyone? What did you promise?"

She sucked in her bottom lip and turned her face away from me. "I promised them if they didn't come back, I'd come and get them."

"Who, Ammi? If who didn't come back?" I wracked my brain, but couldn't recall anyone being sent out for supplies or survivors. But, on closer thought, there were some people noticeably missing. Tristan realized it at the same time I did.

"Where did Terrence and the others go?" he demanded.

Ammi didn't answer.

"They've been gone for a couple of days, haven't they?" Tristan asked.

She gave the slightest nod. My stomach sank at the thought of more of their group being captured. We'd be severely outnumbered, and there was no guarantee we'd be able to help anyone escape.

Tristan jabbed a finger in her direction. "You're staying here."

She looked at me with pleading eyes. I could only shake my head.

"The last thing we need is another of you getting captured," I said as we headed for the door.

We'd barely made it up the steps, however, when the door to the outside banged open, and several bodies blocked the gray light of day. Three stumbled through, dragging two others along. I smelled them instantly.

"What have you done?" I demanded as I ran to them.

The three on their feet were mostly fine . . . except for the deep fang gashes in their shoulders. The other two—Terrence and the girl—lay unconscious, but the scent of vampire blood ran through their veins.

"Now you have to convert us," one of the guys said with a smirk that I wanted to slap right off his face. "They got the vamps, but we found the wolves."

"You idiots!" Charlotte snapped as she and Owen picked up Terrence. "You have no idea what you've done."

"Sure we do," said the girl. "You'll convert us, and we'll be able to fight for you, just like we said we would. And now we can't be killed."

"*You're* not immortal," I growled as I leaned down to pick up the unconscious girl. Tristan beat me to her and scooped her up into his arms. "Vampires aren't even immortal."

"But we're practically impossible to kill now."

"Not until you go through your first transformation," Sheree snarled, following us down the hall. I'd never heard her so mad at a patient.

"Good on us tonight's a full moon then, isn't it?" the guy said.

Charlotte dropped Terrence's feet, leaving Owen to hold him at the shoulders, and spun on the guy. "Which means *you* can't be here! You won't be able to control yourself with the smell of human flesh tempting your taste buds and your beastly needs."

"But you'll convert us," the girl said, not sounding quite as sure of herself anymore. "Right?"

Charlotte strode up to her and glared down at the shorter girl. "You don't know what you've done. By choosing this, you may not be able to convert! And certainly not between now and nightfall."

"But . . . but we still have our souls. We still have hope. You said as long as we have hope, even just a little . . ."

"It means we can't kill you. Not on purpose. It does *not* mean we'll succeed in converting you before you die." Charlotte spun on her heel and stalked back to Owen and Terrence, muttering, "Idiots."

"I don't understand," the girl whined, and it almost sounded like a puppy's whimper.

"The conversion process has been known to kill in some cases," Sheree said. "And if it doesn't kill you, your first transformation might. Or, at least, you'll wish it did."

We took them into what had apparently been a packing and shipping room before. Three long rows of tables stretched across the center of the large room and shelves of boxes lined the sides. Owen and Charlotte magically bound the five of them to the tables.

"I sure hope this holds, because they'll be a mess tonight," Charlotte muttered.

The magic binds held, although it seemed questionable at times. The conversions were grueling, taking every bit of Amadis power we managed to build. We took turns, forced to pause for breaks over the next several days, until the full moon phase passed completely. On the last night, we thought we might have succeeded in easing them through their first monthly cycle when the guy's human body exploded into were-goo and a large, red wolf appeared in his place. We'd been through many transformations over the past few nights, so this one's appearance wasn't our dilemma. The fact that dark energy and hatred still radiated from the wolf was the problem.

He stood on the metal table, still bound to it, and his

black nose sniffed the air. The huge head swung toward me, and the lips curled upwards, baring his fangs. A growl rumbled up his throat, and he lunged forward, snapping his powerful jaw at me. Although I knew he couldn't reach me, I jumped back instinctively. Hunger—a primal need for living flesh— shone in his black eyes.

"Calm down," I ordered, but he only continued to growl.

Sheree strode our way, and as soon as he caught her scent, he spun on her, snarling and snapping more intensely than ever.

"Yeah, I smell like your enemy," she said, "but I'm not. I'm here to help, remember?"

He barked and bit in her direction, either not understanding her or not caring. I silently moved up behind him, close enough to push Amadis power into him, and I turned it on full blast. The canine body reared back as he let out several yelps, twisting and turning like a mean bull with a rider on its back. His fangs nearly latched onto my hand several times, grazing my knuckles more than once, until finally his moves came slower, with less power.

The wolf collapsed. I lightened up the intensity but continued pushing Amadis power into him, even as he morphed into a naked man lying on the table.

"I . . . I lied," he panted, curling into a fetal position on his side as though he suffered tremendous pain. "I didn't do this . . . to help. I just wanted . . . to be powerful. I don't want . . . to be weak . . . like you."

His throat rumbled again, and his teeth elongated. Claws grew from his nail beds and fur popped through his skin in patches, but then the transformation stopped, leaving him halfway between human and beast. He whimpered and whined, then yelped and shouted as the sounds of bones breaking crackled throughout his body. His limbs and shoulders changed shape several times, back and forth between man and wolf. I pulled back the strength of my power even more until it dwindled into a light trickle. But his body continued twitching and cracking. He cried out in agony. I released the power completely and held my hands in the air.

Charlotte rushed over. "No, he needs more not less!"

"I don't think he can handle it," I said.

"We have to try," Sheree said, and she clasped strong hands onto his neck and hip, holding him still as she pushed positive power into him.

Char placed her hands on the wolf-man, too, and I joined them. But it was all Sheree and I could do to keep him from breaking free from our grips. Different parts of his body waved through the various stages of transfiguration at irregular rates, all of it speeding up until he became a blur underneath our hands.

"We're losing him," Char said through clenched teeth.

I couldn't possibly push any more goodness into him. My own energy depleted rapidly, and if I wasn't careful, I'd take on the dark magic that created monsters such as this. I opened my mind to call Tristan over to power me up with his love when the man fell completely still.

"Oh no!" Sheree gasped, jumping back.

I lifted my hands, pulled back, and then froze like him. Watched his face dissolve from utter agony to as slack as a sleeping baby, saw his eyes dim until only emptiness remained, and studied his chest as it fell one last time. His final breath whispered between his lips.

"No." I lunged for him again.

We tried CPR, we pushed more loving power into him, we did everything we could, but he only lay there. Still. Dead.

With my eyes burning as angry tears threatened to fall, I finally shuffled backward, a mixture of anger and grief bubbling in my chest as I glared at his body. When my back hit a shelving unit, I took my first breath in minutes, and my head snapped up. A whole crowd of people stood in the doorway and beyond, heads bobbing above other ones as those in the back tried to catch a glimpse inside the room.

"Anyone else want to be turned?" I seethed at them. "Or are we clear that this is a fucking bad idea?"

Their eyes and faces turned away from me. The crowd quickly dissipated, any conversation made in hushed tones. A few people came in, picked up the naked body, and carried him away.

"The corpse needs to be burned," Charlotte said as they passed through the door.

Those were the last words spoken in the room for another two days as the newborn vampires and the other wolves finished the conversion. They awoke with the excitement of success, but that instantly disappeared when Sheree told them what happened. But nobody could do anything about it now. He was dead. They were turned. But they were converted. We had four more Amadis, but I wasn't exactly thrilled with this development. I prayed no other norms with good intentions decided to do the same thing. Maybe it was better for them, after all, to be against us rather than for us.

"Yesterday they moved two of those metal boxes where they're keeping people," Ammi reported the day after we declared all four of them as safe. She, Kristen, and a few others had been watching the Norman farm in case anything changed, and now they briefed us in the dining room. "Put them on lorries and took them away."

"Were there people in them?" Tristan asked.

"I don't know, but we can't wait any longer. What if they're taking them to gas chambers or something?"

"They're not," Vanessa said as she perched on a table, her leg swinging back and forth. "They're doing exactly as we thought—farming them. Taking them where they won't be killed while the humans bomb the hell out of each other. They're safeguarding their food supply just like any army would."

"We still need to do something soon," Kristen said. "Before it's too late to save those people."

We couldn't argue with that, so we spent the rest of the afternoon watching the camp ourselves to see what might have changed over the past few days and the evening ironing out our plans. Right after we broke for the night, Tristan and I searched for Dorian to spend some time with him since we hadn't been able to during the conversions. We found him in his usual place—sprawled out face down on a cot in the private room Ammi and Kristen had insisted on giving to us. Actually a janitor's closet, the space barely fit a double-size mattress and a cot among the brooms, mops, and shelves of cleaning supplies.

"Why are you in here by yourself?" I asked as I sat on the floor next to the cot. Sasha, in her toy-dog size, jumped from her sleeping spot next to Dorian and bounced over to me, wagging her tail. I scratched her behind her ears.

"You haven't made any friends?" Tristan asked, sitting on our double mattress next to me.

"No." At least that was what the sound Dorian made sounded like. He didn't bother sitting up or moving at all to talk to us.

"Have you even tried?" I asked.

"I did, and nobody wants me around," he muttered into his backpack that currently served as his pillow.

"Not what I heard," Tristan said. "I know there's only a few kids your age here, but they all want to know more about you. I hear them talking."

"I hear them, too," Dorian said. "All of them. And they're just nosy. What kids are my age anyway, Dad? I don't even know what age I'm supposed to be."

Tristan and I exchanged a look. I leaned my head on his shoulder while reaching out for Dorian's leg. As soon as I touched it, though, he jerked away.

"I want to be left alone." He flipped his head over to stare at the wall.

"*We* want to be around you, Dorian," I said. "We haven't really seen you in days."

"Not my fault," he snipped.

"It's not ours, either," Tristan said. "It's nobody's fault. But we all have time right now."

He didn't say anything.

"Have you been practicing your powers?" I asked, thinking that would get him talking. I knew full well that he had been, and I couldn't blame him or stop him any longer. I'd be curious, too, if I were him, and we'd reached the point that maybe if he learned how to master and use his abilities, he could fight the Daemoni instead of joining them.

The left side of his whole body moved in what appeared to be a shrug, if a prone body could shrug. "A little."

"So what can you do?" I asked, forcing a little extra excitement in my voice. "That whole freezing thing is pretty cool. Haha! See what I did there?"

He turned over and gave me a look. "You're a dork, Mom."

"Got you to turn over and talk to us," I said. "So what else?"

He held out his hand, and a small flame appeared in his palm. "Just like Dad."

The beam I knew would come began to grow across his face. He was proud of that one.

"And this." He sat up, held his hand in front of him, closed it into a fist, and then unfolded his fingers. He kept his palm cupped, holding a pool of water. He blew lightly across the surface of it, and a cool breeze lifted my hair. Then the water solidified, becoming a chunk of ice. He squeezed his hand together once more, and the ice turned to snow, falling into his lap. I scooped up the small pile to examine it, then stared at my son with wonder.

"Looks like you can manipulate all four elements," Tristan said.

"I can create them out of nothing," Dorian corrected.

"Wow." I had no other words.

"That means you have a lot of power, son," Tristan continued. "With power comes responsibility."

Not wanting Dorian to feel like he was being lectured, which would cause him to clam up again, I was glad Blossom interrupted at that moment when she tapped on the metal frame of the door. My relief immediately floundered, though, when I caught a whiff of the steam rising from the mug in her hand.

"Are you kidding me?" I asked, my throat already closing up. "They're calling this the apocalypse, and you're bringing me that nasty tea?"

"If this is the apocalypse, then we need hope more than ever," she said, a little too cheerfully.

I rolled my eyes as I reluctantly took the mug she held out to me.

"That smells gross, Mom." Dorian wrinkled his nose. "Why would you drink it?"

I swallowed down a gulp and mirrored his disgusted look. "Blossom seems to think it's good for me." I glanced up at her, trying to give her the evil eye. "I can't believe you even have all the ingredients still."

"I had everything, but the pigeon's feet. Owen got those for me today."

Tea sprayed everywhere out of my mouth. Blossom burst into giggles, and Dorian joined her. I glared at them both. Tristan's body shook next to mine.

He touched his finger to the corner of his lip. "You have a little something there."

Dorian and Blossom laughed even harder. I narrowed my eyes at Tristan, and he reached his finger out and swiped it across my bottom lip.

"Just kidding," Blossom finally said once they settled down. "I promise there are no pigeon's feet in there." She looked over at Dorian and smiled. "I really only need their beaks."

Dorian exploded in another fit of laughter. "And don't forget their eyes."

"Gross," I said. "No wonder this tastes like ass."

"It can't be as bad as that stuff on the train," Blossom said.

"Ewwww! Nothing's that bad," Dorian said, still howling.

"I don't know." I held my mug out to them. "Why don't you try it and tell me?"

Dorian jumped back, hitting his head against the wall, which only made him laugh harder. "No way!"

Blossom shook her head and waved her hands in the air. "That's the last thing I need right now."

I eyed her more seriously. "Exactly how I feel."

"In your case, you're wrong. Drink up." She crossed her arms over her chest and stood watch over me like a warden as I drained the last of the tea. My throat felt like I'd swallowed fire.

"Blech. I half-wonder if pigeon feet would make it better." I placed the mug on a shelf.

"I'll catch one for you tomorrow, Mom, and you can find out."

I didn't doubt he could. Now that we'd lifted his mood, he talked to us non-stop until the rest of the compound fell quiet with sleep.

"See you in the morning, little man," I whispered as Dorian began to drift off in his cot.

"Not if I see you first," he murmured, and then he broke into a fit of giggles. "Just kidding, Mom. Love you both."

"Love you, too," Tristan and I said at the same time.

"Until the end of my days," I added.

Only the footsteps of the night guards and a few snores from the various rooms of sleeping bodies could be heard.

Tristan and I snuggled together in our little bed, reminding me of the first few nights we'd slept together at Mom's cottage. Saying things had changed since then was the understatement of the universe.

The next day we left the bunker to execute our plan on the Norman farm. Except things had changed again. Super-sized soldiers, standing half a foot or more taller than their counterparts and beefed up like Superman, walked the fence now.

A familiar mind signature of a Summoned son was also nearby.

Noah's here, I told everyone right before an ice pick shot into my brain.

CHAPTER 18

The sharp pain, a million times worse than a brain freeze, only lasted a few seconds this time, and I had to wonder what that meant. But I didn't have time to worry about it. I needed to find where Noah hid. This could be our chance to disarm him, and maybe even all the controls, if they were being kept together. I tried to home in on his mind signature, but the lingering pain of the ice pick blocked my reach. Bits and pieces of words wavered in and out of my mind, and it took me a moment to realize my team was trying to talk to me.

We'd split into pairs and scattered along the fence line to make our move on the fence itself. Owen had us all cloaked, of course, and my telepathy was our only mode of communication. With a concentrated effort, I pushed the last of the pain out and mentally cleared my head.

"*Where is he?*" Owen asked.

"*We need to stay on task,*" Solomon said. "*Focus on the mission.*"

"*If Noah's close enough, this would be a lot easier if we could turn off his control of these soldiers,*" Tristan pointed out. "*Alexis?*"

I'm trying, I said, and I meant it. I'd been reaching out with my mind while listening to them, searching for the mind signature I'd felt only moments ago. Finally, I pinpointed it. *He's east. A little north. By the Eye, I think?*

I wasn't sure about that last part, but only guessing based on where we'd been that night Kristen had found us.

"*Let's go,*" Owen said.

"*Hold on,*" Charlotte piped up. "*What about the people here?*"

Nobody replied at first, waiting, as though we could all feel Tristan's gears working.

"*Vanessa and Owen, come with Alexis and me,*" he said. "*The rest of you stay here, and when you see the change in the soldiers, go through with our plan.*"

"*We need you to paralyze them,*" Char said.

"*I don't think we'll need to. If we can get the stone out of Noah, these guys will probably be confused and disoriented. That's when you make your move. Surely you can hold them, Charlotte, until we get here.*"

"*And if you can't remove Noah's stone?*" Sheree asked.

"*Then we'll probably have some serious problems,*" Tristan responded, which was what I'd been thinking.

We'd brainstormed ideas for how to subdue a Summoned to cut out their stone, if we ever found one, but we didn't have a specific plan for this situation. I didn't sense any other sons or their offspring around, but perhaps they were barely beyond my mind's reach, which meant Lucas may have been lurking out of reach, too. This could have possibly been a trap, as well. If any of the soldiers had recognized us or any Daemoni had been watching, Lucas would have known we were in London. At least one of his sorcerers obviously did, based on the pain and mental jam I'd experienced a moment ago. And since Lucas always remained a step ahead of us—or two or three— he probably knew we would go after the Summoned.

In fact, he'd pretty much set it up so we would. He hadn't

spilled all his secrets that night at the abbey about the horrors he'd committed simply to brag. He knew the Normans were our weak spot, and that we'd do anything to protect them. So he knew we'd do what we could to disconnect the soldiers from their controllers.

That brought us to the question of the day: Was Noah's nearby presence a lucky coincidence or a trap?

Considering our lack of luck since the day the Daemoni came out to the world, I doubted the lady would give us a stroke of it now. But we wouldn't know until we found Noah, or at least until we could come closer to him and analyze the situation better.

Maybe we should all go, I said, worried about what we might be walking into and if we'd be enough to fight whatever we would face. On the other hand, if a trap awaited us, bringing my whole team into it probably ranked up there with worst ideas ever.

"*If we succeed in breaking the connection, we'll only have a small opportunity here to free these Normans before the Daemoni figure out something's wrong*," Tristan said.

So with that, we left the others behind to watch the camp, and the four of us set off down the road and across the bridge with the murky waters of the River Thames flowing beneath us. Moving toward Noah's mind signature, we turned left at the end of the bridge, in the direction of the London Eye. A wide and stout hotel, including a McDonald's, stood to our right, and this had no doubt been a busy tourist spot, even on drizzly days like today . . . except not now. Although it was the middle of the day, not a single soul roamed the streets or meandered around the area. No mind signatures anywhere near except the one we sought. The only others were back the way we came.

As we approached the giant Ferris wheel, Noah's mind signature felt *above* me. I halted, holding my arms out to stop the others, and tilted my head back, craning my neck and blinking against the light mist falling in my eyes. I sensed him in a pod at the top of the wheel—the wheel that hadn't moved in weeks.

Suddenly two more mind signatures popped into place— the one above with Noah belonged to Jeana, and I assumed the one behind us belonged to her partner in crime, and whatever else they partnered in. Merrick? I remembered her calling him that back at the warehouse when she'd had Owen and me chained up. No sooner had I identified them when that freaking ice pick drove into my brain. My hands flew up, clutching my head, and my jaw clenched against the agony.

"We know you're here," Merrick said from behind us, and we all turned around to face him although he couldn't see us under Owen's cloak. His stature was taller and leaner than I expected, dressed in an expensive looking suit. His dark hair was combed back, and his hand tugged at his salt-and-pepper goatee. Piercing blue eyes contrasted sharply against his olive complexion. "I feel your energy. Especially yours, Alexis. So perfect for my needs."

"Feel this," I growled through my teeth as I pushed Amadis power out of my whole body, sending it along the river of current he pulled from me.

"Fucking bitch," he snapped when it reached him, and he immediately cut off the drain on my power.

The greenish light of one of Owen's spells soared at him at the same time Tristan shot his power at the sorcerer. With a wave of his hand, both ricocheted away, but he knew where we were now. A streak of red flew at us, but Owen's shield blocked the spell—or more like absorbed it, shaking the air around us. Electrified energy made my hairs lift.

"He's too strong for me," Owen whispered. "He's breached my shields before."

"We need to split up," Tristan said. "Owen, stay with Alexis."

Owen threw a separate cloak over Tristan and Vanessa, and we ran in pairs in opposite directions around the sorcerer.

"I don't want to fight you." Merrick turned in a circle. "Jeana, on the other hand, is a tad bit angry for that false spell you provided last time. That's why she's up there with Noah. I don't how long I can keep her from killing you, though. Especially that warlock."

"Can he sense us?" I asked Owen as we continued sidling around Merrick.

"Possibly. He's a lot more powerful than me."

"What do you want then?" Tristan's voice carried from Merrick's far side. I tried to telepathically ask him what he had planned, but his answer came distorted and nonsensical. I didn't even know if it was an answer or a random thought. The pick in my brain that prevented me from hearing either sorcerers' thoughts messed with my ability.

"You still have information we need," Merrick said. "Like how to break the connection between Noah and those soldiers over at Westminster."

As if. He couldn't really believe we'd fall for that, could he?

"Jeana and I have better ideas of what to do with such power. It would involve the Daemoni vampires and shifters, and eradicating them all. Ridding the world of their uncivilized behavior and diseased existences would benefit us all, including the Amadis. Don't you agree?"

"The Amadis no longer exists," Tristan said.

Merrick let out a sick-sounding chuckle. "Somehow, I don't quite believe that. Lucas might, but I'm not so easily fooled. Now tell me what to do, and we'll take care of Noah and those soldiers over there first. Then we'll be on our way to the lovely Commonwealth for the rest of the Summoned, making them ours, not his. What do you say?"

"I say go to hell," I bit out. "If anyone takes care of Noah, it'll be us."

"You want a trade?" Merrick asked, turning in our

direction, those intense blue eyes zooming in on us. Owen and I hustled around to his left. "We might be able to do that. We'll give you Noah to do whatever you want with as soon as you tell us how Lucas is connected with the Summoned and the Norman soldiers."

Plan, Tristan? I asked, and a new shot of pain dug into my head. A garbled sound that could have been "*distraction*" came back to me.

"I think Tristan wants us to distract him," I whispered to Owen.

"Faerie stones," Owen said aloud to Merrick. The sorcerer spun toward us, his eyes lit up with curiosity. "Kali created a spell to mimic a faerie stone with the attribute of control."

"And?" Merrick asked clasping his hands together under his chin.

"And that's all," Owen lied.

The sorcerer frowned, his goatee pulling downward. "What about the lykora? What does she have to do with it?"

"Nothing," I said as we moved again. If Merrick didn't believe us, which he obviously didn't, spells could start flying any second. "They soaked the stones in the Summoned's blood, then broke them up and implanted them in the Normans. That's all."

"You're lying!" Merrick shouted, and a red streak shot toward us. We instinctively jumped out of the way, although Owen's shield held. "We know the lykora is involved."

"She's not," I said, putting as much conviction into the two words as I could muster.

"Now we told you what we know. Give us Noah," Tristan said.

Merrick laughed. "What are you going to do? *Convert* him?"

The mocking tone grated against my nerves. "It's none of your damn business."

"You can't convert the Summoned, stupid girl." He

disappeared from in front of us, and then his voice came from some distance behind us, closer to the wheel. "You lied, and so did we. Did you really think we'd give you Noah?"

Jeana and my mother's twin brother appeared next to Merrick. Noah's long, dark hair waved to his shoulders, and the scar through his eyebrow really stood out with the way he scowled at me. I couldn't get a good read on his mind, but I felt like he wanted us to help him.

We'll free you, I promised him, although I didn't know if he could hear me. *We'll find a way.*

Stabbing agony wracked through my brain, worse than ever before, accompanied by a high-pitched ringing. I clutched at my head, doubled over, and then collapsed to the ground. My eyes squeezed shut for only a moment, but when they opened, the trio was gone. Tristan's face wavered in front of me, flickering in and out of focus. His lips moved, but all I could hear was the painful tone in my head. Moisture trickled over my top lip, and my tongue swiped over it, finding the salty iron flavor of blood. I tried to say something, but I couldn't hear myself think, let alone speak.

Tristan swept me up into his arms and took off in a sprint. We crossed the bridge in a second, only to run headfirst into a battle. The sound of automatic gunfire drilled its way through the ringing in my head. More sounds of people screaming and stones breaking made their way through. The full scene came into focus as all of my senses returned.

Magic spells shot every which way as Charlotte and Blossom fought against a couple of Daemoni mages in the street. The Norman soldiers sent sprays of bullets as they ran from Westminster and the camp toward the main road where we were. Vampires swooped in on Solomon, Jax, and Sheree, who were still closer to the building. Jax and Sheree burst into their animal forms. A piece of goo splattered onto my face.

I wriggled out of Tristan's arms and shot lightning at the soldiers' feet, trying not to hit them directly, but to slow them down. Tristan waved the vampires off our friends, sending them flying backwards a dozen feet, and then turned toward the soldiers, paralyzing them all. I flicked my fingers toward each of the bullets before they hit anyone, while Vanessa yanked the guns out of their frozen grips. The vamps sprang back toward us, and Jax clamped his powerful jaws over one of them and took her into a death roll. They blocked my view just long enough for me to miss the last bullet.

It bore into Charlotte's shoulder.

She let out a sound I'd never heard before—a yowl resonating intense pain. Owen and I both ran for her, but every step made my own head scream in agony. A Daemoni vampire flew into me before I reached Char, knocking me to the ground. A big, dark blotch swooshed across my vision and crashed into my attacker. Solomon and the Daemoni leech snapped and snarled as they threw each other around. I crawled over to Charlotte, who sat propped up in Owen's lap.

"I'll be okay," she said through gritted teeth.

Her eyes narrowed as she looked over my shoulder, past me. Her hand lifted at the same time Owen's did. Knowing they witnessed something terrible, but not what, I twisted my body over and around, flipping out of their way. Their spells streaked over to the vampire fighting Solomon. The Daemoni vamp flew several feet away and burst into flames. Solomon just stood there with his back to us, as though staring at the fire in front of him. Then, as if in slow motion, his body began to lean to the side. Something was obviously wrong. Very, very wrong.

Charlotte and I both gasped.

With his cornrows swinging, Solomon's head rolled off of his neck and fell to the ground with a sickening thud.

"NO!" I screamed, scrambling to my feet as his body swayed in the opposite direction. "Oh, no. No, no, no. *Solomon!*"

Tristan turned at my scream, and his face blanched. Then

he twisted his body, swinging his arm out and blasting everyone in sight with his strongest, deadliest power—the one forbidden by the Amadis except in extreme situations. Daemoni and soldiers alike dropped to the ground, all dead. Tristan ran and caught me in his arms as I reached Solomon, which was probably good because I didn't know what I would have done as Solomon's body hit the ground, landing front down, and something dark and squishy splatted next to it. But his head. Oh god, his head.

My mind flashed back to another scene of detached vampire parts and watching Vanessa's body pieces vibrate and move toward each other to reattach, making her whole again. But Solomon's parts remained still, which I now found even more terrifying.

"Why isn't he moving?" I shrieked, trying to break free of Tristan's hold to help Solomon put himself back together. He wouldn't let me go, though.

Vanessa went over to Solomon's body, squatted, and studied it and the lump of dark red next to it. The abhorrent look in her ice-blue eyes, on her face, made my heart drop to my feet. Whatever she saw had to have been horrendous for her to react in such a way. She carefully lifted Solomon by the shoulder and turned his still body over. I couldn't help the scream.

"Oh my god, dear God, *why*?" I cried, covering my mouth with my hands but unable to tear my eyes away from the heinousness.

Solomon's entire front, from collarbone to navel, lay split open and pried apart, as though the vampire he'd been fighting had thrust a carving knife in and yanked downward. Blood and intestines spilled out to the sides. And the dark red lump next to him . . . the blob that had landed with a splat . . . was his heart.

I finally turned away and buried my face into Tristan's chest. But the image was forever emblazoned in my memory. I could never unsee that. So I opened my eyes and looked the other way around Tristan's arm, only to see Solomon's head. It still lay on its side, his empty eyes staring forward. I could only hope his last vision had been of Rina welcoming him into the Otherworld.

Tristan's arms tightened around me, and I hid my face against his chest again, trying to control the sobs. Trying to be strong. Charlotte had been shot, and I didn't know who else might be injured. I would have to deal with this grief later. My people needed me right now. But when I tried to pull away from Tristan's loving embrace, I instantly realized he needed me, too. He'd been holding on to me for strength just as much as I'd been holding on to him, and he wouldn't let go. I tightened my arms around him as he buried his face into my hair, his breaths sharp against my ear. After several grief-filled moments passed, he collected himself and pulled away.

My whole team had gathered, standing there, staring at what remained of the man who had been like a rock foundation for so many of us. I'd known him as long as I'd known Rina, when I met them both in Mom's cottage in Cape Heron, along with Stefan. They had been the heart and core of the Amadis in my mind all of this time. Now Tristan and I were the only ones in the room that night who were still alive.

My heart broke.

Solomon and Charlotte had been our ties to Rina's and Mom's generations. Now we only had Charlotte. I looked over my shoulder at her. Owen was helping her to her feet.

"I'll be okay," she said, though her face held no color and she leaned on Owen's shoulder.

"I'll take care of this." Vanessa nodded toward Char and Owen. "Go help them."

"Solomon deserves an Amadis send off." My voice was hoarse and choked by the lump in my throat.

"More Daemoni will be here any minute." She nodded

toward the parliament building where we knew dozens of Daemoni had taken up residence.

"Let's do the best we can." Tristan strode over and helped Vanessa in arranging Solomon's head near his ravaged body. He deserved so much more than being burnt in the middle of the street in downtown London. My heart cracked even more when Tristan lit him up.

"Bring him home, Rina," I whispered. "He belongs with you now."

As if in answer, the body and the flames disappeared.

CHAPTER 19

We checked the other bodies, Norman and Daemoni alike, scattered about, but found no survivors. More Normans dead. Daemoni souls that might have been saved, but not now. Vanessa was right about more Daemoni coming soon when these guys didn't return. Tristan blasted flames at the enemy corpses, but we left the Normans, hoping someone in the government remained with enough humanity to give them a proper burial. Then we hurried back to the compound, and Owen sealed it up tightly in case the Daemoni traced us back here and decided to retaliate.

"Alexis, I'm so sorry," Blossom said as she slid an arm over my shoulder once we were inside. "But you got to Noah, right?"

"Not exactly."

"Really? But . . ." She trailed off, frowning. "That must be what went wrong."

"What?" I demanded, probably sharper than I should have been. "What happened here that went so wrong?"

"A bunch of trucks arrived, and they started loading the metal boxes with the Normans inside, and we weren't sure what to do, because we were running out of time. We waited and waited, and we didn't hear from you, but then the soldiers changed from acting like puppets to behaving more normal. We thought that was the sign."

I sighed. "You thought we'd cut out Noah's stone."

"Tristan said to watch out for their reaction, and that was a reaction, and like I said, we were out of time. So Solomon gave us the go. We didn't even reach the trucks before they started taking off, and then the soldiers fired at us all at once. Like they were being controlled."

Because they were. Following Jeana's orders, Noah had obviously turned the soldiers loose on my team. I couldn't help but wonder if this had been part of Jeana and Merrick's plan. Had they distracted us on purpose? Baited us over the bridge, and then set up our people? Or had we set ourselves up for disaster by falling for it so easily? Either way, this was one more time the Daemoni were one step ahead of us.

"There was no way for you to know any differently." I picked up my pace to catch up with Owen and Vanessa, who'd carried Char inside.

They had already reached the same office where we'd brought Ammi for her conversion. Charlotte lay on the couch with Kristen hovering over her.

"I was going to be a nurse," Kristen said as she poked inside Charlotte's wound with a thin blade, presumably searching for the bullet. "I was going to uni for it before this all happened."

"You're sure you'll be okay?" I asked Char.

"Don't worry. You're stuck with me for a while longer." She forced a small smile through the pain, but then she frowned. "We couldn't save the Normans. They left while we were fighting."

I nodded, and then swung around and strode off, praying to the Angels she was right about herself. If they even listened anymore. I didn't know what I'd do if I lost her, too. But the norms . . . Noah . . . we'd accomplished zilch, coming back empty-handed.

Solomon had died for nothing.

I desperately needed to pound the crap out of something. An Aikido session with Tristan to beat my frustrations out would have been nice, but that seemed like a luxury now, so I headed to our closet-room, glad to find Dorian wasn't in it. Finally alone and surrounded by complete darkness, I let out a scream of frustration and hammered my fists against my thighs. Then I dropped to my knees on the mattress on the floor and doubled over to pound my fists into the bed.

"Please forgive me, Rina," I sobbed, my heart breaking all over again for her. "I am so, so sorry."

Tristan found me curled in a ball and staring at the wall. I didn't know how much time had passed, but enough for me to wail out my frustrations to the point of being spent. But not completely. When he sat on the bed next to me, I turned over and crawled into his lap, straddling him. I braced my hands against his face, and he held mine as I leaned in and crushed my mouth to his. I pushed my tongue between his lips with an urgent need to feel and taste and devour him. His lips were soft yet commanding, and his tangy-sweetness filled my mouth with its deliciousness.

Something about death and loss created an intense need to feel another's touch, to hold onto another living being. Except it was more than that. An overwhelming necessity to feel the life force of the one you love, to hear their heartbeat, to ensure they were still with you and you were not left alone. To become as close to them as physically possible, to connect, to join as one and let the love and passion mingle with the grief. To remind us that with all the bad in the world, there was still good, there was still love, and we had to hold on to it.

Tristan had known we both required this connection and release. He'd already planned for it and taken care of things, providing me with mental silence.

I deepened the kiss while sliding my hands down his hard chest and abs, to the hem of his shirt, and lifting it up. Our mouths parted only long enough to pull his shirt over his head before crashing into each other again. His fingers worked at my leather corset, loosening the laces until he could pull it apart and off, and then I pressed my breasts against his bare chest, needing the skin-to-skin contact. Needing the intensity, the passion, the love we shared to cradle our broken hearts and souls. His hands slid up and down my bare back, his fingers trailing along my skin, and into my hair, grasping it in his fist, and his erection grew underneath me. I rocked my hips back and forth against it, making him moan into my mouth.

"Are you sure?" he asked when I stood to remove my leather pants.

"Never been more sure in my life." I kicked off my boots and undid the button at my waist.

His fingers pushed mine away, undoing it for me, and his hands slid under the leather at my hips to cup my cheeks as his mouth found my lower belly. It quivered with the warm wetness on my skin in contrast to the coolness on my legs as he pushed my pants down. I stepped out of them and then moved backwards so he could stand and I could remove the last piece of clothing that prevented us from becoming one. As soon as his pants were off and discarded, I latched my hands onto his shoulders and climbed onto him, wrapping my legs around his waist. He held me with one hand between my shoulders and the other under my ass, gripping and teasing. I looked into his eyes, the gold sparkling and the green dark with lust.

"I need you," I said, my voice thick with desire, as I slid down, over and around him.

He moaned before his mouth captured mine, and his tongue took command of my own. My breasts rubbed against his chest, hardening my nipples into beads and sending a jolt of pleasure to my inner core. I shifted side to side, up and down, gasping as every little movement made both of us vibrate and convulse against the other. Tristan's muscles tightened and undulated underneath me, his arms and shoulders and back muscles hard as rock. I slid my hands up his neck and into his hair, grabbing it in my fists, and pulling him closer as we kissed until we both became dizzy.

His legs shook, and he dropped to the mattress. I slid down harder and deeper over him, making us both cry out. I lifted up to my knees and dropped down again. Pleasure rocked through my body. This was what I needed. To lose myself, my mind, my heart, everything, to the moment. To focus only on the physical, on the taste and smell of my man, on the feel of his skin and muscles under my touch, on the way he felt inside me, throbbing and pulsing.

His hands clamped onto my hips, and his thumbs dug into the tender area at the top of my thigh, making me squeeze him and utter another moan. Then he lifted me, and I rose up on my knees until I almost lost him before sliding down again.

"Oh, Lex," he groaned. "Again."

His hand slid forward, and his thumb circled over my center, teasing the nub of nerves as he lifted me again. I whimpered his name as I came down and he thrust upward, and then I rose again, my movements becoming faster and harder as his thumb pressed deeper and worked quicker. The sensation started in my belly, like the feeling of falling, and bloomed downward and out and in, all at the same time. My skin tightened over my breasts, and I grabbed at them to release the ache. But the pressure was building below, making me convulse around him as I started to lose control.

"Tristan," I gasped. "Oh god, baby."

I dragged myself up and slammed back down, once, twice, and a third time, and I was about to soar over the edge when he flipped us over so I lay on my back. Then he drove into me, again and again, and I completely lost it. Lost myself in the moment. In the physicality. In the complete bliss. I left this godforsaken world for our own private one, floating into oblivion, screaming my lover's name as I brought him with me. Leaving my body, with every muscle clenched down to my curling toes, if only for a moment of pure, unadulterated ecstasy.

Tristan continued pumping into me, though, and my belly trembled, my spine tingled, and my toes clenched as he sent me soaring over and over again. He plunged into me one more time as his mouth said my name like a dirty word before he exploded inside me. I grabbed him, squeezing tight with both arms and legs, milking every bit out of him. Then he collapsed on top of me, and I wrapped myself around him, melding my body to his, becoming one with him.

"I love you so much," I whispered.

"I love you more than life, sexy Lexi," he said against my ear, and then he rolled off of me. I missed him immediately and rolled over to press as much of my skin against his as I possibly could.

"I needed that."

He chuckled. "I'd say so. Not like you to let go like that."

"You know, the first time you had Owen do that, I was so embarrassed. But it's necessary, right? Like on days like today." I trailed my fingers over his chest and abs, making his muscles tighten under the light touch.

"Lexi, I didn't have Owen do anything."

My hand froze. "He didn't muffle and block our room?"

"Not this time. I hadn't expected you . . ." His voice trailed off, and his head turned slightly toward me. He stared at me with sparkling eyes, but they dimmed as the seconds ticked by. "You can't hear me?"

"I'm talking to you, aren't I?"

"In your head." He tapped his finger against my forehead.

I sucked in a breath. "Oh, no! I can't! I can't hear or sense anyone. You're sure you don't have the room blocked?"

"Even if I did, you'd be able to hear me."

I groaned.

"That explains why you didn't share everything with me like you usually do when you let go. I missed that."

I pressed my face into the soft area where his shoulder and pectoral muscle met. He meant how I could mentally share my orgasm with him and he could share his, but this development was far worse than that. I'd lost touch with my ability before, but not so thoroughly. And something as intense as that orgasm should have broken through the obstruction the sorcerers had apparently lodged into my brain.

"My telepathy is our advantage," I said. "What if it doesn't come back this time?"

He brushed a hand over my hair, pushing it back over my shoulder. "It will, *ma lykita*. The Angels gave that gift to you for a reason. They wouldn't take it away."

I hoped he was right. But I couldn't help but think that maybe this was my punishment. If the Angels planned to fire me, to throw me to the other side, they wouldn't allow me to keep such a powerful gift, would they?

Had the Angels given up on me? Had God? I couldn't blame them if they had. Maybe this had been their plan all along, and one by one, the good people of my team would make it to Heaven before it all ended. Maybe all of our bad luck really was part of the apocalypse that the Normans theorized about.

Was this really the beginning of the end?

If so, my ancestors apparently didn't want me to know, because they remained completely silent about everything.

"We have to stick with our plan, which means going to Virginia," I told my team, which had gathered in the cafeteria the next morning after breakfast had ended and everyone else had moved out. I'd called them together for a meeting to regroup on our plans. "That's what Solomon would want."

"And you want Owen to open a portal right to the DoD building?" Vanessa asked.

"No, of course not," I answered. "For one, I'm not taking Dorian into what will surely be a fight."

"So the safe house?" Blossom asked.

"We have no idea if it's really safe," Charlotte said. She sat on the edge of a table, showing no signs of being shot yesterday. Vanessa must have given her a good dose of blood to help her heal.

"Kristen said there are a few cells of A.K.'s Angels in the U.S.," Tristan said. "One of those is probably the safest place we can go first. They might panic when we arrive, but hopefully they'll see Alexis before they fire."

"We only know the exact location of two." Ammi's voice came from the opposite side of the bunker, spoken softly but carrying to our ears anyway. "Sorry, but I can't help but hear you."

"Why don't you come here then," I said, and the mages, the only ones who couldn't hear her, gave me strange looks, wondering to whom I spoke. Ammi appeared in the doorway a moment later, her dark eyes wide.

She wrung her hands in front of her. "I'm sorry. I didn't mean to eavesdrop. I'm still getting used to these new ears."

"It's okay," I said. "We need your help. Tell everyone what you just said."

She nodded and relaxed as she came farther into the room. "We only know where two of the cells' exact locations are. There was a cell in Washington, D.C., which I think is right where you want to go, but the last we heard, they hadn't found a permanent, or even semi-permanent safe place. They'd been moving around every night. We don't know if they're even still a unit."

"Where are the two you know about?" Tristan asked.

"One's in California and the other in Florida. I think Florida is nearer to Virginia? Sorry. I don't know my American geography very well."

"Florida?" I mused out loud. "Where in Florida?"

"On the left side. Cape something . . . it began with an H. I'd never heard of it before. I think it's a really small town."

Tristan and I exchanged a look. What were the odds?

"Cape Heron?" I hedged.

"Yes! That's it! How did you—oh, wait. That makes sense you would know. They said you wrote your first book there. That's why they went there."

I pressed a palm to my forehead and blew out a soft snort. My fans were lovely, but a little weird. Who goes to a town an author once lived in because they thought it would be a safe place? Especially when said author was Public Enemy Number One, or whatever ridiculous name they'd christened me?

"I guess we go there first?" I asked Tristan.

"Anywhere will be risky, but when we show up out of thin air, your supporters will be less likely to shoot at us. We'll just have to make our way up to Virginia."

"First, we have to hope they're still there and not overtaken by the Daemoni, or worse, a Norman farm," Sheree said.

"Cape Heron's too small for the Daemoni to worry about, and full of retirees," Tristan replied, and he didn't need to explain further, but the visual came to me anyway of what the Daemoni did to old people.

"You're okay to move on?" I asked Charlotte one more time before we made our final decision.

She smiled. "Good as new. Probably better than I was before I got shot. And trust me, that's not the worst thing that's ever happened to me. Your mom would . . ." She trailed off, and her smile faltered. "We had some interesting times, she and I. I'll just leave it at that."

I threw my arms around her neck, and she wrapped hers

around me. "You're the closest thing I have to a mom now, Char. Don't leave me, too."

"Like I said yesterday, I don't plan on going anywhere any time soon. You and Owen and this whole lot need me." She gave me a final squeeze, then grabbed my shoulders and pushed me away. "Now, let's get back to work and win this war."

CHAPTER 20

I mentally called out for Dorian, but my head still refused to function properly. That bitch Jeana may as well have cut off my arm. She would've wished she had if I ever saw her again, because I'd be assaulting her with lethal doses of Amadis power. I didn't know if such a thing as too much goodness existed, but I could hope so for someone like her and Merrick.

Once we were ready for our next adventure, we said goodbye to Ammi, Kristen, Olivia, and the rest.

"As soon as we're gone, seek out the other Amadis," I told them. "They'll most likely be on sacred ground, but probably more on the outskirts of the city. They'll sense Ammi is one of them when you're near, and you'll feel them, too. Give them this."

I pressed a folded up note into Ammi's palm, and she closed her fist around it. The encrypted message inside would ensure they knew the note came from me, with an order for them to come help my Angels here and train them.

"Be safe, Alexis," she said as she wrapped me in a hug. "I hope we'll get to see you again."

"Trust me, so do I. You're one of mine now, you know."

Her face broke into a huge smile, as if she'd just realized what her transformation and conversion really meant.

Tristan had figured out the coordinates to the address Ammi and Kristen had for the Cape Heron cell, and Owen opened a portal. The other side—a dark and dingy interior—didn't look like anything in Cape Heron I remembered, but I stepped through first anyway, hands up and ready to fire in case someone shot at me. Four surprised faces stared at me instead, two of them quite familiar. Now we knew who had told everyone A.K.'s real name.

"Alexis!" one of them squealed, and the young woman launched herself at me. I couldn't help but return her embrace, holding her close, happy to see her alive. And still human.

"I'm so glad you're okay, Heather," I said.

She squeezed me tighter while trying to jump up and down. "I can't believe you're here! You found us! Did you find Dorian? Oh my god, Tristan! *Blossom!*"

She released me and flew over to tackle Blossom with a hug, while her sister strode over to me and hesitated.

"How are you, Sonya?" I asked. "Still good?"

She nodded vehemently.

"Always," she said, and I swallowed her into a hug. When she stepped back, she indicated the other two young women who'd been sitting on the floor with them. The quintet had been gathered around a cardboard box with two cans of food sitting on it. "This is Teal and Teah. They're cousins, and big fans of yours, too. Not like Heather and me, though. A lot less creepy."

I couldn't help but laugh. Sonya had once been one of those fans who had my publicist worried that she'd kidnap me and break my foot so I couldn't escape. Heather wasn't quite as intense as a fan, but when she figured out we could help her sister, she'd stalked our house until I agreed to do what we could for the vampire. Sonya's initial conversion failed because of a stone Kali had given her that had been the precursor to the ones in the Summoned sons now. During our search for Dorian, we'd been able to remove the stone and convert Sonya completely. We'd lost touch with the girls when the Daemoni decided to take over the world.

The cousins unfolded themselves and rose to their feet, both tall, with brown hair, bright blue eyes, and warm smiles. They stood with shoulders touching each other, staring at us shyly. I reached my hand toward them, and when they shook my hand, I noticed their tattoos, similar to the ones everyone had in London. The taller one, I thought she was the one named Teah, caught me looking at the ink, and lifted her wrist for me to see better.

"We all have them," she said, and the other girls showed off theirs.

"They have them in London, too." I shook my head. "I can't believe—"

"Wait," Sonya said, stopping me. "You found the London group? A.K.'s Angels?"

"They were the ones who told us to come here," I replied.

"What are you doing back in Cape Heron, anyway?" Tristan asked.

"Who would have thought, right?" Heather said. She looked around the small apartment we had piled into, her nose wrinkled. "We used to live here with our asshole dad. Our mom . . ."

She bit her lip.

"She didn't make it," Sonya finished for her, and my heart broke for them. "She was showing a condo at Fort Myers Beach the night the Daemoni came out. If I'd known, I could have protected her."

I slid my arm back over her shoulders. "Their evil is not your fault. Not anymore."

She nodded, her only reply.

"What brought you here?" Tristan asked again.

"The Amadis all left Captiva," Heather said. "They said the war was starting, but Sonya wouldn't leave me."

"Some of them started acting really weird, talking about converting to the Daemoni, and no way would I take Heather into such chaos, so we stayed behind. When we saw Lucas smack-talking lies about you on TV, we knew what we could do to help. We got online on the forums and helped start A.K.'s Angels," Sonya said. "Teah and Teal had been here on vacation, and got stuck. They found us on the forums, too, so we picked them up."

"Thank god," Teal breathed. "We would have been dead if we'd tried to go home."

"This was supposed to be our meeting place for lots of people," Heather said.

"Where are they?" I asked, knowing another body couldn't possibly fit in this apartment now that we'd arrived.

"Some took off. Others . . ." Sonya frowned. "It's been really hard here, Alexis. We expected part of our group to be back three days ago. We were going to give them one more day, and then we were gonna take off."

"Where did they go?" Owen asked. Sonya looked at him as if realizing for the first time that he stood among us. Her lips twitched with a smile, but then she saw Vanessa and looked away.

"Looking for survivors. And food. There was a lot of gunfire the other night, though. I've been out searching, but haven't found them. I didn't want to get too far away, in case the gangs came back here."

"Gangs?" Blossom asked.

"Yeah," Heather said. "The gangs have been worse than any supernaturals around here. They come in and loot all the businesses and houses, stealing our food and anything else we need. That's why a bunch of our people left. We had this whole apartment building full of A.K.'s Angels, and now they're all gone."

"All except us," Teah said as she plopped down by the box-table. She looked at a can of food longingly, and then her gaze swept over us.

"Go ahead and eat," I encouraged. "We're all good."

"Mom," Dorian said quietly from the back of our group.

I rolled my eyes. "You just ate, Dorian."

"Dorian?" Heather asked, pushing her way through to him. "Oh my god! Look at you!"

She clapped a hand over her mouth, and her face flushed a bright pink. Then she threw her arms around him.

"I'm so glad you're okay! I'd been so worried about you," she cried.

His return hug appeared awkward at first, but they eventually must have remembered that they'd been each other's best friends for a while, and they both relaxed. They went off to a corner of the kitchen together, jabbering away as they caught up with each other.

I looked at Tristan. "What do you think?"

"I think we should look for their friends, then we'll take off."

I nodded my agreement.

The scene greeting me when we opened the door about knocked me to my knees. The apartment building sat on the corner of a side road that intersected with Fifth Street, the main business district of the town. Looking a little to the right from here, I could see all the way down Fifth until it ended at the beach and the Gulf of Mexico. Immediately to the left of the apartment building, a residential area of low-income housing spread out. This part of town had been occupied by some elderly who'd lived in Cape Heron for decades, but mostly by the blue-collar service personnel who'd served the snowbirds and tourists at the restaurants, bars, shops, and hotels.

Everywhere I looked, windows were broken out, and some doors hung askew from their hinges. Cars sat abandoned on the side of the road, some with jags of glass shards where their windows and windshields used to be. An older model truck was completely burnt out, nothing more than a shell, and a VW Bug sat crumpled into the trunk of an oak tree, its driver side door still open. One business' picture window had been boarded up with plywood with the words "No Food or Water" spray-painted in big red letters on it. Next to it, another piece of plywood said, "We stoled theres and its gone" with an arrow pointing to the first one and a crude image of a hand with the middle finger sticking up.

My heart grew heavier and heavier as I made my way down Fifth Street toward the block where the Book Nook, Mom's bookstore, had once been. Over ten years had passed since I'd walked this same road, and so much had changed, yet much had stayed the same. At least, it appeared that had been the case up until the last few weeks.

The October afternoon sun beat down on me and glared off the windows and metal lampposts as it had back then when my life was really just getting started. The row of bars and restaurants, including Mario's Pizza, still stood where they had then. Another block down, the shops started—clothing boutiques, antique shops, novelty stores, art galleries . . . at one time, a bookstore. If people strolled the sidewalks and cars crept slowly down the street, honking at me to get out of the way . . . if windows weren't knocked out and doors unhinged . . . this place would be exactly as I remembered. Maybe there had been some fresh coats of paint added since then, but no significant alterations.

I, however, was not the same.

I'd been a girl then. Naïve, hopeful, ignorant. A little cynical about my own life, but optimistic about the world in general. I'd seen and experienced a lot in some ways, but Mom had kept me sheltered from certain parts of life. Especially *our* parts—the Amadis, the Daemoni, the fact that supernatural beings existed, that the worst kind of darkness walked the world in human-like form. I had hopes and dreams like any other girl with plans for a future that included a career, a family, and true love.

Now, I was still naïve and ignorant in way too many ways, but definitely not that same girl. I had true love, a family, and a career, but none of it had happened the way I'd planned. I'd lost my love for seven years, given birth to a boy who should have never been born the way he was and whose life would always be in danger, and had somehow become leader of a society of creatures that went beyond human understanding. I had no more hope for my life or the world in general. Survival was the best I could offer now. I was no longer that little girl.

I was a soldier. A warrior.

A killer.

Last time I walked this street, I skipped along in shorts and flip-flops, on my way to help Mom and Owen at the store, or to meet Tristan at Mario's where I'd thrown a dart at him or at the coffee shop where he'd first called me Sexy Lexi. As I passed that shop now, the memories of innocence, hope, and excitement of first love washed over me . . . and drained away when I caught my reflection in the window.

No, I most certainly was not the girl I'd been back then. My face might have appeared to be the same age, but now I was a woman, wearing fighting leathers with a dagger on my hip and a knife in my combat boot. A variety of lethal powers sizzled at my fingertips, and my fist alone could kill somebody.

I stopped and inhaled a deep breath before turning to my right, toward the place where Mom's store had once stood. Even it looked the same, somehow, with the big picture window Heather and Sonya's sperm donor had run his car through. I walked over to it and held my hand to the glass, focused on my reflection at first, but then on the interior of the store. Not much had been ransacked here. I supposed looters had no use for books.

Tristan came up behind me and peered inside, too.

"I thought the Daemoni blew this place up," I said.

"That's what we had to tell you so you wouldn't be tempted to come back here," Owen answered from behind me. "Looks like someone's kept the old Book Nook running since then. At least, before now . . .."

I turned on him. "Mom's place?"

He pressed his lips together, and I didn't wait for more of an answer. I ran. One block north and three blocks west. I came to a halt where the driveway met the sidewalk—at about the same place Tristan would stop the bike to let me off.

Mom's cottage.

A traditional Florida-style home from the middle of the last century sitting on a block of others just like it. Ancient banyan and oak trees stood in front of most of the houses, but not Mom's, allowing me an unobstructed view of the front porch, where Tristan had given me numerous goodnight kisses. Where Mom had tried to stop us from seeing each other.

My heart seized, aching with the memories of her in this place. She'd loved it so much, along with her bookstore. Why couldn't life have stayed like it had been then? So simple, it had seemed. A bright and shiny slice of time compared to today's darkness. And now Mom was gone. In fact, everyone in this town was apparently gone.

The silence was eerie.

Part of me wanted to go inside, but I was afraid of what I might find. More memories of Mom and life as it could never be again? Or the bodies of whatever Normans had moved in when we left?

I turned for the beach instead. Tristan took my hand, and we walked in silence under the canopy of leaves until the road ended. We crossed the little boardwalk, and finally sound filled the air as waves crashed on the sand and seagulls cawed at each other. We walked out on the beach to our favorite spot. Sat down in our favorite position—Tristan behind me, my back pressed against his chest, his arms wrapped around me, and his chin resting on my shoulder. We watched the sun lower over the horizon, spraying golds, oranges, and peaches against the clouds, the light blue sky, and the water.

"It's like this little piece of the world has been left untouched," I said quietly.

"I'm sure much of the world has been," Tristan said. "We've only seen the bad parts so far."

"We can only hope." The phrase sounded empty, as hollow as the little bit of hope I held on to.

"Do you know the exact spot we're sitting in?" he whispered against my ear, sending chills over my skin.

I couldn't help my smile. "I will never forget our first kiss."

I twisted around, just like I had that October evening so many years ago, and when he leaned in and brushed his lips against mine, I let out a zap of electricity. On purpose now, unlike the first time. He pulled back and grinned before coming in again for a real kiss.

"As long as we can do that, we always have hope," he murmured once we pulled apart.

"Everyone's probably looking for us, since I can't—" I twirled my finger by my temple. "Since I'm broken."

"I can hear them from here, and you're right."

We reluctantly stood up and hurried back toward downtown. My whole team, who was supposed to have been looking for Heather and Sonya's friends, were searching the area for us. We took the brunt of a few evil eyes when we returned.

"There's absolutely nobody in this town," Vanessa said as we walked back to the apartment building. "No life, no smell of fear on the air, no heartbeats anywhere."

"Nope. Nobody," Sheree agreed.

"Unless they come back," Heather said.

She stood in front of the door of their first floor apartment, rubbing her hands over her upper arms. Since the sun had set, a light chill had come in on the air. With Sasha at his feet, Dorian leaned against the doorjamb next to Heather, standing at about the same height and no longer looking ten years her junior. I wondered if he remembered telling me that he wanted to marry her someday, back when he was a typical boy with a crush on his babysitter. Did he still feel that way? He stood with his body turned toward her, as if to say yes, but his eyes and face spoke differently. They were filled with a darkness, a sorrow that no boy his age should know. I wanted nothing more than to hug him, to comfort him, to take him back to his innocence, to the childhood stolen from him when it had barely begun.

"The gangs?" Charlotte asked, yanking me back to reality.

"Yeah," Teah said. "There are still plenty of places for them to loot, and there hasn't been enough of us to fight them off anymore."

"We should probably just get out of here," I said. "What do you think, Tristan?"

He nodded. "We need to do what we came for."

"Do you want to come with us?" I asked the four remaining members of this cell of A.K.'s Angels.

They looked at each other and shrugged.

"Where are you going?" Teah asked.

"Like it matters. We can't hide out here anymore," Teal said. "The question is *how*."

"Northern Virginia," I answered.

"Oh! The D.C. cell," Heather said excitedly.

"Would you happen to know where to find them?" Tristan asked.

"Not really," Sonya replied. "They were trying to bug out of downtown D.C., with the politicians and Daemoni being all butt buddy and BFFs with each other. Last we heard, they thought they'd found a place somewhere on the edge of the city, or maybe the suburbs."

And that was entirely helpful.

"You don't know where?" Charlotte asked.

"Not a clue," Teal said. "We lost contact with them right after that. The night the power and the phones . . . *everything* . . . went down and never came back."

"The night the world crashed and burned," Heather said.

The heaviness of the statement weighed down on all of us, and the girls seemed to have been distracted from the question. I asked them again if they wanted to come with us.

"Yeah, we'll go with you," Sonya said, making the decision for the group. "Maybe we can find them."

"Where to, boss lady?" Owen asked me. "All I can think of is the safe house, but that could expose our people there."

"*If* there's anyone there," Blossom muttered.

"It's our safest place to appear," Tristan said. "And the Amadis there were supposed to have moved out."

"Except it's a *safe* house," Sheree said. "There are all kinds of reasons for them to stay."

"Then we'll figure out something," Tristan said. "It's the only place I feel safe taking my wife, my son, and the rest of you without knowing what we're walking into. It's our best option."

He nodded at Owen who opened the portal. I couldn't help but notice the warlock seemed to strain a little, and it took him longer to create the opening this time. He hadn't rested or eaten since we left London and arrived here, and I could only imagine how much energy a portal required. After all, typically only sorcerers possessed enough power to create them.

We showed up in the foyer of the safe house mansion in Fairfax, Virginia, where we'd been less than two months ago while searching for Dorian. Only then, there had been several new converts and a staff. Now it was dark and empty. Abandoned. Other than being gloomy and quiet, it appeared to have been unscathed. Paintings still hung on the walls, the antique furniture looked undamaged, and the marble floors were clean and polished. Apparently, no looters had found it yet. Everyone but Vanessa and Sonya went straight for the gourmet island kitchen. The dark wood cabinets were still loaded with non-perishables, lifting our spirits.

Once we filled our bellies and caught a few hours of rest, we made sure Sonya and the norms, including Dorian, settled in, put Sasha on guard duty with the vampire, and left to scope out the same Department of Defense building where we'd found Dorian and the Summoned a few months ago. It was one of three five-story structures, all belonging to the DoD, that formed a squared-off U-shape with a lake in the middle of it. We stepped through the portal into the pitch black of the parking lot at the top of the horseshoe, the only light from the moon and stars overhead. I'd never seen Northern Virginia so black—usually a yellow glow from street lamps, headlights, and buildings lit up the night, obscuring the millions of stars that shone now as if someone had tossed a massive jar of glitter against the black blanket of sky.

No sooner had my eyes adjusted to the darkness when the entire building in front of us erupted into a thunderous explosion . . . and my head felt as though it exploded along with it.

CHAPTER 21

I thought at first they'd been watching us. Expecting us. Jeana and Merrick, maybe Lucas, too. The timing had been so perfect—as soon as my entire team had come through the portal and it closed behind us, the pick plunged into my brain, causing me to grab my head and double over. My team circled around me in the parking lot, and a moment later, we were knocked to our hands and knees with the explosion.

The ground shook, and heat blasted out at us. The building and the sky lit up bright as daylight as a huge ball of fire blossomed above the structure and then dimmed with an orange radiance casting over the entire area. Tristan lunged on top of me, pushing me closer to the ground, as glass, metal, concrete, and who knew what else rained down onto the asphalt of the parking lot. My ears rang and thudded, blocking out any other sound. Flames danced out of broken windows and soared high into the sky, devouring what remained of the building. The acrid smell and taste of smoke filled my nose and mouth.

And through it all, I picked up on the mind signatures. They'd been absent and my head quiet, so I noticed immediately when they returned. Besides my team, three others popped up, but two blipped out before I could latch on and identify them. The third had become familiar to me, and my heart stopped at how faint it came.

"Noah's in the fire!" I yelled. At least, I thought I did. The ringing in my ears prevented me from even hearing myself. The pain in my skull kept me from trying to mind-speak it. I pushed against Tristan's weight to rise to my hands and knees, and he sprang off of me, pulling me up with him.

"Owen and I will go," he said. "You stay here."

At least, that's what I thought he'd said, figuring it out as Owen waved his hands around the two of them, and then they raced through the parking lot toward the building. As they passed a few burning cars at the front of the lot, I could only hope Owen had shielded them with some kind of fire protectant, because they headed straight into the flames.

"Tristan!" I shouted and tried to run after him. The rest of my team tightened their circle around me, though, preventing me from passing through. They watched our surroundings carefully, but I sensed nobody around. Gritting my teeth, I pushed past the ache in my head to locate Noah's fading mind signature, as well as Tristan's and Owen's.

He's in the far, west corner, I told them, hoping they could hear me. They moved in that direction, which I took as a good sign. Then I realized Noah seemed to be above them. *On the second floor, I think? Is there still a second floor?*

Moments passed. Maybe they couldn't hear me. *Maybe we should go in.* Vanessa and I would be fast enough to run through the flames without being burnt. Maybe. My muscles bunched, ready to spring.

"*There's a second floor back here,*" Tristan finally said, followed by, "*We found him.*"

My body relaxed. Slightly. At least I could breathe again.

Is he still alive? I couldn't imagine how he would be after that explosion, and I was losing his mind signature. I couldn't latch onto any thoughts. More agony sliced into my brain as I tried harder. And then I lost them all.

"Something's wrong," I told the rest of my team, and I gripped the closest arms to me—Charlotte's and Jax's. Once again, my muscles prepared to bolt. "They're gone!"

I lunged, trying to dash for the building, but Char and Jax both grabbed at me, holding me back. When I fought against them, Vanessa put me in a chokehold.

I squirmed against her iron-like grip. "We have to go after them!"

"Whoa," Char said. "*You're* not going in there."

"The hell I'm not."

"What are you going to do, princess?" Jax asked. "Walk right into those flames? They were protected."

"And now they're gone! Vanessa and I—"

"Wait," Blossom interrupted. "*They're* gone, or all of us are? You know, in your head?"

I blinked at her. Then realized what she meant.

"All of you," I admitted when I noticed my head had gone completely blank again. At least, the part that saw the mind signatures. The rest of my brain went ninety-miles-an-hour as I wondered what happened to Tristan, wished I had Dorian's or Mom's capabilities to manipulate the water in the lake behind the building and put the fire out, and watching and praying for Tristan and Owen to come out alive, hopefully with Noah.

"So maybe they're okay," Sheree said.

"Or maybe they're dying, waiting for us to come rescue them," I bit back.

Charlotte scrunched her lips together as she stared at the fiery building. "Give them sixty seconds. Then someone will go in."

The minute passed painfully slow—it may as well have been a year—and had almost expired when finally they appeared. All three of them, Owen and Tristan dragging

Noah's unconscious body between them, their faces smudged black with soot so only their eyes showed. Vanessa freed me, and I ran to them. To Tristan, who grabbed me with one arm when I threw myself at him.

"Don't ever do that to me again," I ordered as I clung to him.

"We're fine, *ma lykita*." He turned his head enough to plant a kiss on my cheek. "But now you know how it feels."

I let out a harrumph and released my grasp on him to cross my arms over my chest as I fell in stride next to him.

"If you were trying to protect me, you know that won't work for long. I nearly went in after you."

He blew out a breath as he tugged on Noah's shoulder. "Yeah, that's why we gave up the search for anyone else. So you wouldn't do that."

I frowned. "You can't choose my life over anyone else's. Lucky for you there was no one else in there."

"Lex, I will *always* choose you over everyone else."

My heart—invariably weak when it came to him—did a little flip.

Then Owen said, "We all will. We're *sworn* to."

They dragged Noah's body farther out into the parking lot, away from the burning building, before flipping him over to lay him on his back. His heart still beat, slow and faint, and he remained unconscious, even after we tried to jostle him awake.

"Hold him, Tristan," I said as I exposed my dagger and slid it out of its sheathe at my hip. "This could be our one chance."

I kneeled next to the prone body and lifted my dagger. Noah's eyes flew open right when I was about to stab the blade into his chest to dig out the stone. They were dark and murderous, and his body strained, but even as big and strong as he looked, he couldn't budge against Tristan's power.

"Do. It." The words came out in pants through a clenched jaw, sounding as though he had to force each one out against his own will. Then his eyes rolled into the back of his head, and his body twitched and convulsed.

"They're trying to control him," I said, "but I think he's fighting them off."

Since I couldn't read his mind, I wasn't exactly certain about that, but that was how it looked.

"Then hurry, before they win control," Tristan said.

I grasped my dagger with both hands and plunged it into Noah's chest, right above his heart. He groaned, and his body jerked just the slightest bit. If I didn't hurry, he could possibly break through Tristan's power, especially if he had the force of the sorcerers working on it. I twisted the tip, poking around, then finally it hit against something hard. With another twist and a flick of my wrist, the stone popped out and rolled across the asphalt.

Noah's body immediately fell still. His eyes lost focus, the lids fluttered closed, and his face went slack. But his heart still beat, slowly but steadily.

"Let's get him to the safe house," I said.

"I don't know if that's a good idea," Charlotte said.

"We can chain him up. Bind him with magic." I flicked my hand toward Owen. "If he can hold Tristan down like he has before, he can surely contain Noah."

"I don't know if we can convert him, Alexis," Sheree said.

"Not against his will, but he *wanted* me to cut that stone out. I've seen hope in Noah. We have to try! For Rina, if nothing else."

I'd already lost Solomon, her true love. I'd do everything I could to save her son. To save Mom's brother.

Owen grunted and groaned as he made the portal that took us back to the safe house. As soon as I passed through, I immediately ran up the stairs to check on Dorian, Heather, and the others. Everyone but Sonya and Sasha were asleep in the luxurious beds. The vampire sat by a fire, reading, and

Sasha lay on Dorian's bed with one ear lifted and her tail twitching when she saw me.

Not wanting to disturb them, I tiptoed away and went downstairs to wait with the others for Noah to regain consciousness.

Tristan and Jax had taken Noah to the basement, to a room used for conversions where he could be chained up. The seemingly barbaric treatment was for everyone's protection, including his own. Although he was passed out now, he'd likely be irate and violent when he woke.

In the meantime, we all sat in darkness, in the same living room where we'd gathered years before, when the men left for the fight that took Tristan away from me. I remembered the powder blue carpet, the darker blue, velvet upholstered couch and chairs that nobody had sat in then, the sounds of a battle behind the heavily draped picture window. That had been the last time I'd seen Stefan alive, and the last time I'd see Tristan for seven years. I stared at the door to the library off the side of the room, where Tristan had said goodbye to me and our unborn baby.

We'd been discussing our next plans and how we might extract information out of Noah, when we'd fallen into one of those thick silences as everyone became lost in their own thoughts.

"What's that sound?" I suddenly blurted, a faint rhythm catching my attention. I sat up on Tristan's lap, listening for signs from the basement, but this strange *dut-dut-dut-dut* came from the very room we sat in.

Sitting next to Owen on the couch on the far side of the room, Vanessa cocked her head. "I hear it, too. It's over by you."

I jumped off Tristan's lap and to my feet, and he joined me.

"Sounds like a really fast heartbeat," he said. "A bird?"

"A cloaked shifter?" I asked, and I spun in a circle,

swatting at the air in case an invisible bat or Jax's friend the eagle, who'd spied on us before, watched us now.

"Hold on." Vanessa said as she moved nearer to me. The sound was so close to me, but my fists didn't land on anything. Owen and Char both flipped a spell in my direction, but nothing showed itself. Vanessa crouched lower, placed her hands on my shoulders to stop me, and leaned her head down further. She bit her lip. "Tristan, come down here."

He knelt on one knee, and we all fell stone-still to let him listen. He tilted his head and leaned closer to me. Pressed his ear against my lower belly. His brows furrowed for a moment, and then he looked up at me, his eyes full of awe and adoration . . . and hope. He smiled.

"No way," I squeaked.

He beamed brighter as he sprang up and scooped me into a hug, swinging me around in circles. Everyone jumped to their feet, whooping and cheering and congratulating each other. As if they were all a part of it. I supposed they were.

Tristan finally set me down, and I pressed my hands to my abdomen, still not able to believe it. The enthusiastic commotion around me faded so all I could hear was my baby's heartbeat and my own. Tears filled my eyes, threatening to spill over the rims, and not tears of joy. While everyone else apparently wanted to celebrate, I couldn't bring myself to be thrilled with this major change in circumstances like they obviously were. I just wanted to run away. To hide. To be by myself and think. Because my mind, my heart, my soul remained stuck on one question.

How the hell could we bring an innocent baby into *this* world?

As if to emphasize this predicament, a loud crack cut through the air over us, and the roof fell to the floor.

CHAPTER 22

*T*he walls shook, and screams came from the upstairs bedrooms.

"Dorian!" I yelled as I ran up the stairs. The ceiling caved in over me, and a beam dropped on the steps ahead. I hurdled it, swinging my arms as I ran to knock away the plaster and pieces of wood falling around me. I grabbed the doorknob and shoved my whole body into it, pulling it off its hinges as the wall it had been attached to fell over. I threw the door to the side and swept my arms around my son who'd been stumbling toward the door.

"You two get out of here," Tristan yelled at us over the blasts that kept hitting the mansion, knocking more parts of it down.

"I got you, Mom," Dorian said, and he lifted us out of the wreckage.

"Noah!" I yelled at Tristan as we soared higher in the air. I watched him run for the basement, Jax meeting him at the door, and when they disappeared down the stairs, I feared I'd never see them again.

The lights of magic spells, in various colors, streaked through the night as Daemoni mages attacked the mansion, and Owen, Charlotte, and Blossom fought back. My mind still remained blank, but Jeana and Merrick played a role in this, no doubt. If not them, then another sorcerer, because Owen and Char had had the mansion shielded.

Dorian set us down on a branch at the top of a tall pine. Right below us stood two young women wearing leather jackets, jeans, and knee-high boots, with hair down to their butts, one raven-haired and the other blonde. I recognized the dark-haired one—a were-cheetah who'd chased after Vanessa and me in Hades. Rene was her name.

"What do you think, Cruz?" she asked. "Shall we join the fun?"

The blonde purred. "I've always wanted a taste of Seth."

They both ran into the clearing, transforming on the way. Cruz, the blond, changed into a lithe jaguar as they ran toward the mansion, presumably after Tristan. I shot a bolt of lightning at Rene's feet, sending her rolling across the overgrown lawn. Dorian threw a stream of water at them that immediately iced over on contact, freezing them in place, with Cruz's mouth wide open in a roar.

Someone had seen where our powers came from, though, because a spell shot in our direction, hitting the trunk two feet below us. Dorian grabbed me again and flew up and away right before the tree split in two. Another spell soared at us, but Owen threw a shield around us just in time, and the light ricocheted off the bubble and into what remained of the mansion.

"By the garage," I said to Dorian, pointing at three figures running from the mansion toward the detached building. Tristan and Jax, with Noah slung between them.

Dorian swooped downward. As our feet hit the ground, that god-awful *ta-ta-ta-ta-ta-ta* sound of automatic gunfire ripped through the night. Jax threw the door to the garage open and ushered Dorian and me in. Tristan followed and set

Noah on the floor before running back outside. I lunged for the door to follow him, but Jax held me back.

"No way, princess," he said.

I pushed against the solid bar of his arm that blocked my way, watching as Vanessa grabbed Blossom, Sonya snatched up Heather, and they blurred toward us. Tristan followed with Teah and Teal under his arms like oversized footballs. Owen and Char sprinted across the mansion's lawn with Sheree right behind them. I gasped in horror as her body launched forward in the air, her spine arching backward as if she'd been hit, but then she burst into tiger form and bounded for us.

Jax slammed the door after her. I watched through the window as the soldiers and the mages turned their attention to the mansion, blasting at it continuously until it was demolished so completely, it couldn't be rebuilt by magic. The ice on the were-cats dripped as they began to thaw.

"There's the van and enough bikes to get us out of here if we pair up," Tristan said, and I spun away from the window to see what he meant. A bullet pierced through the glass and soared over my head. We all dropped to the floor as more gunfire blasted into the garage. "Let's go!"

Tristan and Jax shoved Noah's unconscious body into the back of the van, and Sheree, still a tiger, climbed in to guard him. Sonya hopped into the back, too, and the Norman girls huddled together on the center seat. Blossom claimed the driver's side and had the van started before Jax had even hopped into the passenger seat. I ordered Dorian to ride with Charlotte, and the rest of us jumped on the motorcycles. Owen and Charlotte cloaked and shielded us, I grabbed hold of Tristan's waist, and he blasted the garage door open. Blossom pealed through it, and the rest of us followed, barely escaping before the garage's roof collapsed.

Because Owen and Char had us under a single cloak and shield rather than separate ones for each vehicle, we had to ride close together as a group. At least there was no traffic to dodge on the roads because the other drivers couldn't see us. We had no plan, and Blossom only knew the area from when we'd searched for Dorian, so she followed the same main streets we'd traveled then, taking us closer to Washington, D.C. Eventually, Tristan sped up and around the van to take the lead, pulling in front before he moved too far ahead to keep us hidden. I tried to break through the block in my head so we could communicate and form a plan without stopping, but the best I could do was pick up a stray thought here and there from any of them, like a crappy radio unable to tune into a specific station.

"Where should we go?" I asked Tristan.

We passed a shopping plaza where a handful of people ran in and out of stores, carrying what looked like old-fashioned torches to light their way as they scavenged for goods.

"Any idea where your fans might hideout? Any clues in your books?"

I wracked my brain, trying to remember everything about the stories, the characters, and the settings. Writing those books felt like a whole other lifetime. It really had been a different life then.

"When the human's in danger, there's the part where the vamp tells him the safest place for him to hide would be a convent, monastery, or a religious boarding school. A church, if nothing else."

Headlights and flashlights shone ahead of us, pointed in our direction. Armed soldiers marched toward us, accompanied by a Hummer and a tank. A freakin' tank! Down Main-Street Suburbia! Although they couldn't see us, Tristan leaned the bike into a left turn, taking us away from what would probably be a bloodbath between the looters and the so-called militia police. I'd thought things would be different here in the States than they'd been in Europe and that coming home would bring a sense of familiarity and peace. But nothing familiar remained in this world anymore, even in these places where I'd lived before. And definitely no sense of peace.

After ensuring our group had stayed with us, Tristan stayed silent for a few minutes, and I assumed he contemplated what I told him. "Thinking about your readers' age group," he finally said, "there's one place I'd expect them to go."

"Where's that?" I asked, because I could think of many options with all of the churches and private schools in the area. Did he plan to visit each one, hoping to find the A.K.'s Angels group? "The National Cathedral is the most well-known, but too many politicians and government officials would probably go there. If there were any good ones left . . ."

"Right. I don't see a group like A.K.'s Angels going there. Your younger readers would be in college now, right, like Heather? Or close to that age, like Sonya or the two cousins? And there happens to be a Jesuit-Catholic university that fits your suggestion perfectly."

I knew exactly which one he meant. "Oh, you're right. Good thinking!"

"From what I know of the campus and the school, it should be considered sacred grounds. And it would have everything these people would need."

"True. But is it far enough from the Capitol? From all of the military bases around here? You know they're all controlled by Lucas."

"The cell in London made their new home right across the street from Parliament. They stayed to help people."

The squawk of braking tires on asphalt stopped me from replying, and I looked over my shoulder. The black van swerved all over the road, and Blossom's face blanched white as snow as she tried to regain control. Tristan turned us to the side and hopped the curb to the sidewalk before she ran over us. The van spun as though on ice, leaned too much to the outside, and flipped on its side. The grinding of metal against road screeched through the night until the van finally came to a stop when the back end plowed into a light post with a definitive crunch. My head snapped to the right to make sure Dorian and the others were okay before I sprang off the bike and ran for the van.

Jax crawled out through his window first and helped Blossom who was already bawling.

"Are you okay?" I yelled.

"I'm so sorry!" she cried, obviously shaken, but physically okay. "I was worried about Sheree and turned to look at her but then I almost ran over Tristan and Alexis so I tried to avoid them by swerving and hitting the brakes, but that sent me into a tailspin and now, ohmygod, are the girls okay? Is everyone okay?"

Vanessa yanked the side door completely off the van and threw it behind her, while Charlotte jumped onto the vehicle's side to help Sonya, Heather, Teal, and Teah out.

"Sheree and Noah are stuck in the back," Char said with her body half in and half out of the van. "I can't get to them."

"Hang on," Tristan said from the rear at the light post, and he shoved on the van's back end. The vehicle stayed attached to the post, pulling the entire street lamp with it as it skidded across the pavement several yards. He grasped hold of the post, and I ran to the van and gave it another push as he jerked the pole out of the bumper's grip. The metal pole clanged on the ground when he tossed it aside, and a loud creak and crack followed as I pulled open the scrunched up back doors.

"Oh, no," I gasped.

Noah lay crumpled up against the side window that now pressed against the street, and Sheree's naked and bloody body was sprawled out on top of him.

"I'm afraid to move her," I said, backing out of the van, my heart growing heavy. "Tristan . . ."

He pushed past me and gently lifted her out of the vehicle.

"Blossom, do you have clothes for her?" I asked. The girl deserved some dignity.

Blossom shook her head. "I don't have my bag."

"There's a blanket up front," Heather said, and she jogged around the van.

The vehicle moaned as she climbed onto it, but a moment later she returned with a black, wool blanket. I wrapped it around Sheree the best I could before Tristan laid her on the street. Her brows pushed together, and her closed eyes winced.

"Anything broken?" I asked her while Tristan and Jax pulled Noah from the wreckage.

"I . . . don't . . . think so," she whispered. Her eyes fluttered open. "Just my lower spine. Can't feel my legs very well."

"What?"

"She was shot, Alexis," Blossom said tearfully from behind me. "That's what started all this."

Tristan gently pulled the blanket back and turned Sheree to her side to inspect her back. He frowned, looked at me, and gave a small shake of his head.

"She changed back to human, and that's when Sonya noticed," Heather said.

"The blood started really gushing then," Sonya clarified. "I guess her tiger scent masked it before."

"I was . . . trying to . . . heal myself . . ."

The sounds of boots marching on pavement and heavy wheels rolling over anything in its path approached.

"We need to get out of here," Char said. "Owen?"

"Where are we going?"

Tristan told everyone his idea as he slid his arms under Sheree. "Just get us on campus, and we'll get Sheree somewhere safe where we can heal her."

Owen rubbed his hands together and slowly pulled them apart to create the portal. Only, nothing happened. Usually we could see the air tremble and then the scene of the other side would gradually begin to show itself. Owen pressed his lips into a line, shook his head, then clasped his hands together again and tried once more. Still nothing.

His shoulders slumped, and his hands dropped to his sides. "I can't do it. It's been too much too fast. I need some recovery time. I'm sorry."

Nobody could blame him—he'd done so much for us in the last twelve hours, saving our butts many times. But we couldn't flash, and now we couldn't portal. The van was useless, and no way could we all ride on the motorcycles. Not that Sheree, or Noah, for that matter, could make the ride.

"We only have one option," Tristan said. "Find a place to hide."

"There's a motel a half-block back," Vanessa said. "Not exactly five-star, but—"

"It'll work," I replied.

When we managed to break into the first room, I questioned whether I said that too soon. Some kind of rodent scuttled into the far corner, and I swore the entire floor rippled with movement. A crunch under Tristan's boot with his first step inside confirmed the infestation of cockroaches.

"Oh, that's just nasty," Char said, but with a few magical twists and thrusts of her hands, the room was cleaned up. Maybe not hospital-quality, but better than being on the streets. Especially as the SWAT team, or whatever they were, approached.

Tristan laid Sheree onto one of the double beds, and Jax dropped Noah on the other one. Noah's head lolled to the side on the orange quilted bedspread, and he let out a quiet moan, but he otherwise remained unconscious. I stayed nearby, ready to act if and when he finally came to, while Tristan tried to inspect Sheree's injury as best as he could in the darkness with Vanessa standing by. She'd once said she'd studied medicine for a while out of sheer boredom, but it didn't hold her interest long enough for her to earn a degree. She knew enough, though, to help Tristan if he needed her.

Meanwhile, Char used her magic to cut doorways through the walls, connecting several rooms together, which she and Blossom cleaned up one by one. Sonya took the girls to one of them. After standing in the corner for a few minutes watching his dad, Dorian sulked off to another room. Owen followed him, and I hoped both were headed to catch some needed sleep.

Tristan looked at me and tapped his finger to his temple. Once again, I tried to push through the block in my mind, but whatever Jeana or Merrick had done, they'd done it well. I could only pick up on a few words Tristan tried to convey. They were all I needed. "*Lodged*," "*spine*," "*another*," and "*bleed out*."

Heal her! I ordered him, not knowing if he could hear me. Even when he shook his head, I didn't know if he responded to my words or to the look on my face, which had to be one of anguish and desperation. I rushed over to Sheree's side.

"I'm so cold," she whispered. "I'm . . . dying . . . aren't I?"

"No," I barked out. "You won't die. That's an order from your matriarch."

She gave me a faint smile. "You're so bossy."

Her eyes fluttered closed, and she passed out. Tristan and I moved to the corner of the room.

"What are we going to do?" I asked him. Tears stung my eyes at the thought of losing Sheree. She'd been my first convert, and I'd almost killed her then. She'd become a friend and a special addition to the Amadis with a heart bigger and warmer than anyone I knew. I owed her so much. "We have to save her."

"I don't know if a fully trained medical team in the most advanced operating room could save her," Tristan said quietly. "Did you understand what I said?"

"Telepathically? No. My head's still broken. But we're *more* than a Norman medical team, Tristan. Surely between you, Vanessa, and Sonya, there's enough healing powers to help her, and she has her own."

He shook his head. "I don't think so, *ma lykita*. It's impossible to tell without the right equipment, but I think the bullet is lodged very close to her spinal cord. Too close for me to even try to remove it. There's another one, though, a little higher. All I can see is the entry point, so it could be somewhere in her kidney or liver. Even her heart. She could be bleeding out internally. I closed up the wounds to stop the external bleeding, but I don't know if she can heal past this, Lex."

I rubbed the back of my neck as I stared at her sleeping body, blinking against the tears, then squatted down and leaned against the wall. My heart ached so badly. How could I cope with another loss? How could any of us? Our morale was slowly deteriorating, and this would make it plummet. All because of the fucking Daemoni and their damned soldiers.

I dropped my head into my hands and pressed the heels of my palms against my eyes. I felt so helpless. So hopeless.

So powerless.

Here I was, supposed to be the matriarch of a powerful society that served as the Angels' army on Earth. But my society had to disband in order for the individuals to survive. My warriors still fought, but we were losing every battle and likely the war. And the Angels we served? They seemed to have forgotten we even existed, abandoning us when we needed them most. No messages of wisdom and direction came from them. They'd said they'd always be near. They'd promised I would never be alone. But I sure as hell felt alone.

CHAPTER 23

*E*xcept for gunfire in the far distance, the rest of the night passed uneventfully. Sheree made it through, but she wasn't doing too well. If the first hours were the most critical, though, maybe, just maybe she'd make it. I awoke to the gray morning light seeping under the curtains and Noah stirring. Tristan immediately awoke, too. We'd apparently dozed off as we leaned against the wall and each other.

Noah sat up in the far bed, his face contorted and his eyes glowing red. He sniffed the air, and his nostrils flared.

"Amadis," he growled.

Tristan and I both sprang to our feet, and he instantly paralyzed Noah before he did anything threatening.

"Easy, Noah," I said calmly. His eyes swung to me and narrowed. "Do you remember why you're here?"

He looked around the room, and when his gaze returned to me, he seemed to be more confused than anything else.

"I mean with us," I said. "We cut the stone out of you, remember? You wanted me to do it so they couldn't control you anymore."

"What? You want a cookie for it?" he snarled, although his eyes showed a tiny hint of gratitude.

"Actually, I'm really hoping you might want to convert."

He barked out a laugh. "You're as stupid as Kali said, aren't you?"

I stepped closer to him, trusting Tristan's hold on him. "I've felt hope in you, Noah. Especially when you saw Rina and Mom—your mother and twin sister. You still have feelings for them."

"Yeah. It's called hatred."

"Hatred is a feeling. A pretty passionate one, at that." I tilted my head. "But I don't think that's what you really feel for them. What you really feel is love, isn't it? But maybe you don't remember what it feels like."

"And maybe I don't *want* to remember what it feels like." His upper lip curled. "What does it matter what I feel for them? They're dead."

He probably meant the reminder to hurt me, but I heard the undertone in his voice. I was onto him. "Except I think you *do* want to remember. You miss love—feeling it, having it. Know what else I think? I think you don't really want to be Daemoni, do you? Whatever choice you made so long ago, you regret it. I can feel that in you."

He rolled his eyes away from me. "Fuck off," he muttered.

"I can help you, Noah. All you have to do is ask." I held my hand up, palm facing him. His eyes darted back to me, filled with fear and anxiety, and his body twitched and convulsed against Tristan's power.

"Leave me alone, you Amadis whore," he growled.

His body flew backward, and the back of his head slammed against the wall with a crack. He lost consciousness again.

"Tristan!" I said with a gasp.

"Nobody talks to my wife like that," he replied simply.

Owen came running into the room with Dorian on his heels.

"What's going on?" Owen asked. He eyed Noah who was plastered against the wall. "Need some help?"

"Nope," Tristan said. "We're good. Unless you can make a portal now and get us out of this rathole."

Owen rubbed a hand over his stomach. "Just need some food first. And everyone to wake up."

Tristan nodded his head toward Noah. "Let's take him to his own room before he hurts someone, and bind him up nice and tight. Then we'll find food."

He flicked his hand, and Noah's body came away from the wall, hovering over the floor. He came to again, snarling and snapping like a wild animal as he tried to fight against Tristan's hold. Owen led the way as Tristan directed Noah out of the room. Dorian looked at me with wide eyes and his brow lifted. I held my arm out to him to hug him. He slipped past me and dropped on the bed.

"You should let him go," he said as he stared at the floor.

"We can't just let him go." I plopped down next to him. "We can't take the chance. Especially if there's any possibility he'll convert."

"He won't, though. He *can't*."

"We don't know that for sure. There's hope for him."

"It doesn't matter."

I ducked my head down to get a good look at his downturned face. "How do you know?"

He scowled at the floor, as if it had committed some personal offense against him. His hands twisted together in his lap, and he scuffed the toe of his shoe into the threadbare carpet.

"I just know," he said, and he bolted up and out of the room.

Everyone but Sheree awoke when Tristan and Owen returned with a few measly packages of crackers and beef jerky they'd found stuffed in a desk drawer in the motel office. The looters who'd broken into all the vending machines apparently hadn't thought to look there. The food wasn't much once split between all of us, but it at least took the edge off of the hunger. Being the strongest out of all of us, Tristan and I offered up some blood for the vampires. Vanessa grinned like the Cheshire cat when I held my wrist out to her, knowing the powerful rush she was about to receive. Sonya, however, wasn't prepared for it, nor had any tolerance, so only a couple of drops of Tristan's blood had her chomping at the bit like an abused dog ready for a fight.

"Let's fuck some Daemoni up!" she said with the growly enthusiasm of a pro wrestler as she bounced on the balls of her feet and punched at the air. Apparently she didn't realize how close she stood to the wall or her strength, but her fist pushed right through the plaster. She yanked her hand free and laughed.

I closed my hands over hers, trying to calm her down. "We're going to look for A.K.'s Angels, remember?"

"Okay. Cool." She nodded, though she couldn't keep still. "But if we see any Daemoni, I'm gonna fu—"

"Yeah, okay, we know," I said.

With our bodies somewhat rested and our bellies not quite empty anymore, we gathered together in Sheree's room. After taking a bathroom door off its hinges, we used sheets to strap Sheree to it, trying to keep her as still as possible. She woke up when we first moved her and passed out again as soon as she was strapped to the door. Tristan used his power to move Noah into the room against his will.

"Sonya and Jax, carry Sheree," Char said. "Tristan and Vanessa, you better grab Noah. Going through the portal may interfere with your hold on him."

Once we were ready, Owen made the portal with no problems, and we stepped through, onto the street in front of the entrance to the university's campus. As soon as we did, arrows soared through the air at us from the school's direction. Everyone dropped to the ground, the stronger of us covering Sheree and the norms. Tristan, the mages, and I used our powers to bat the arrows away. At least this time they weren't bullets. Which probably meant these weren't soldiers.

"We have more," a man called from somewhere right behind the gray brick wall of the gate to campus. "All covered in silver."

"Silver won't hurt us," Tristan said.

"Liar," a female voice yelled. "We've watched many of you die from it. You're next."

More arrows shot at us. They bounced off the shield one of the mages created, and Vanessa sprang up and blurred away. A second later, she stood behind the gate, holding a Norman by the neck in each hand—a girl and a guy. We all stood, leaving Sheree on the ground. Jax held a tight grip on Noah.

"How many more are there?" Vanessa demanded.

"Enough to kill you," the girl spat.

The guy, looking to be around thirty years old, with black hair and a crooked nose, seemed somewhat familiar to me as he stared at Vanessa, but I couldn't place him.

"How are you here?" he asked. "Behind the gate? This is sacred grounds."

"Because I'm not evil, dumbass," Vanessa snapped. "We *protect* idiots like you."

"You're not human, though," the girl said, "of course you're evil."

She twisted and whipped her body, trying to break free of Vanessa's hold.

I stepped forward. "You don't know what you think you do."

"We're hunters," the guy snarled. "We know enough."

Oh, yay. More hunters, like the ones we'd run into in Russia. I sensed several dozen Normans beyond the gates, many in the big, gray building ahead of us with a clock tower that reached above the autumn-colored trees for the sky. A handful stood out here, by the gate—the other hunters, I presumed.

The guy had been appraising our group, his gaze traveling over everyone until it fell on me for the first time. His black eyes narrowed as they lingered. Then he let out an unattractive snort-chuckle. I could guarantee his nose had been broken in the past.

"Alexis," he said to me. "The very reason I became a hunter. I knew you weren't normal then, and since you haven't aged more than a year or two, I was obviously right."

I cocked my head. "Do I know you?"

The look he gave me made my skin crawl. "Oh, you used to know me pretty well. Babbled on and on, talking my ear off with all your stupid secrets when all I wanted was a piece of your ass."

Tristan growled next to me. I placed a hand on his arm, his muscles tense under my touch.

"Good thing I didn't, since you really are a freak. How's that whore of a mother of yours, anyway?" the guy asked, and I immediately knew who he was. Yep, his nose had most definitely been broken in the past. And I'd been the one to break it.

"James," I said, striding closer to him. "How long did it take for you to heal the last time you said that to me? Do you need a reminder?"

"What the hell, James?" the girl asked, still squirming in vain as Vanessa held her, watching us, seemingly bored. "Is this the bitch you've been looking for?"

James lifted his arm straight up in the air, his hand balled in a fist over his head. "After she and her mom ran away from the assault charges, the real monsters showed up, looking for them. Killed my best friend. Or so I thought. They turned him into a disgusting leech. Then *I* had to kill him. Yeah, this is the bitch. About time."

As soon as he finished, his arm chopped downward.

Arrows flew from various directions. These guys weren't the brightest bulbs in the box. All of their arrows dropped to the asphalt before hitting any of us.

"Stop!" A blond woman came running out of the building, sprinting in our direction. The weird reunion became even weirder. "It's Alexis! We told you to leave her alone!"

I'd recognize that voice anywhere. Besides Tristan, who I hadn't been able to figure out that night we met, she was the first person to have been nice to me in ages. Unlike James, she hadn't changed much. Sure, she'd grown older, around thirty now, but still had that cute girl-next-door look to her.

"Carlie?" I asked in disbelief.

"It's really you!" She looked like she was going to run out to me, but she stopped at the gate. At the edge of the sacred grounds. She waved her hand at us. "Come in here where it's safe."

"Carlie," James snarled.

"This is *my* place," she snapped at him. "If you don't like it, you and your so-called hunters can leave. We don't need you. Especially not now."

I led my team over, easily crossing onto sacred grounds.

"See?" Carlie said to James. "I told you they were good. Not all of these guys are bad. And these," she ushered Heather, Teah, and Teal all the way through to stand by her, "are *humans*, James. And they're still alive. Taken care of by Alexis and Tristan here, no doubt." She held up Heather and Teah's arms to show their tattoos. "And they're part of us."

James eyed them, then moved his glare to Sonya, Char, Owen, and me as we stood inside the gate. The girl stared at us, too, and then relaxed in Vanessa's grip as she cut her eyes over to her comrade.

"Let me go," she said. "I get it. *He's* the dumbass."

Vanessa looked at me, and I nodded. She released her hold on the self-described hunter, who strode over to stand by

Carlie. Both women crossed their arms over their chests and glared at James. As did we all.

He jerked himself out of Vanessa's loosened hold. "If they kill anyone, Carlie, that's on you."

When the tension in the air lightened, dozens of people poured out of the building, as though they'd been watching the whole thing and waiting for it to be safe. They gathered around us with an almost celebratory air, corralling us all the way through the gate.

But then we had trouble.

When Tristan and Jax tried to walk through with Noah between them, they couldn't pull him across the line. He began shouting obscenities, and smoke rose from his flesh. Little patches of skin peeled away all over his body, exposing muscles and tendon underneath. Several of the hunters who'd gathered around us suddenly had their weapons drawn. Tristan and Jax stepped back, away from the grounds. The rest of us gathered in front of them.

"Don't shoot!" I said, my arms held out protectively.

"I thought you said you were all good," James said.

"We're working on him," I admitted.

James shook his head. "Not good enough. Kill him!"

"NO!" I yelled before any more arrows flew. "We obviously can't bring him on the grounds. Just leave him alone. We'll take care of him. *We* know how."

"And let him murder how many of our own?" James demanded.

"None. We'll keep him locked down."

"Like I should believe *your* lying ass."

The next thing I knew, Tristan held James by the neck three feet off the ground. "I've had enough of you. You show my wife some damn respect, and maybe we'll try to keep you alive. If you don't, well, then your death is on *you*."

James' eyes bulged out of his face, and his feet kicked at the air. Tristan tossed him to the ground.

"Asshole," he muttered as he strode back over and relieved Jax from his hold on Noah. Vanessa held him from the other arm. She'd apparently moved in when Tristan had let go to give his mine's-bigger-than-yours warning to James. "You take the others inside," Tristan said to me. "Owen, Vanessa, and I will handle Noah."

They pulled Noah to the other side of the street where a row of townhomes stood. The crowd began to swallow us up, excitement rising again.

And then screams.

Something blurred by Sonya and me. A couple of norms who'd been standing in the street—away from the line of consecration—fell to the ground, blood gushing from their throats. We spun around, and it blurred toward us again. Sonya punched her arm out, clotheslining the vampire. Reddish-blue eyes glared at us from under a curtain of blonde waves.

"Lesley?" Sonya asked, in shock.

Where the hell were all of these people coming from? Had *everyone* we'd ever known decided to converge on D.C.? Lesley, a vampire who Sonya had been staying with in Tallahassee after she'd massacred our mages, bared her fangs in an unfriendly smile. Then she punched Sonya in the cheek. Sonya returned the swing, but Lesley blurred away, and Sonya went after her. The two vampires streaked this way and that, stopping only when one's fist or foot landed on the other. From the roof of one of the townhomes, Lesley let out a trill of laughter, enjoying the game. Then she launched herself off the building. I lunged for her, but she kicked me in the head, flipped over me, and landed with a Norman girl in her arms.

"I'm tired of being so damn *thirsty*," she growled, and she dove for the girl's throat.

The next moment, her head rolled to the ground. A hunter stood behind her, holding a bloodied sword. Several people screamed, and others joined them when two more figures shot out of nowhere, appearing in front of the hunter. Two women with yellow, cat-like eyes, long, curved fangs, and claw-like fingernails. Rene and Cruz again. They both hissed at the hunter, and he ran for the gate. As they crouched down to gather Lesley's two separate body parts, their gazes swept over the crowd. When they landed on me, they hissed again.

"We'll see you again soon," Cruz promised before disappearing with Lesley's body, Rene following with the vamp's head.

Chaos broke out. Above it all, a wail of "Noooo!" came from down the street. Another vamp streaked toward us.

"Go!" I yelled at the norms, waving my arms frantically at them, and they ran for the building, a few gathering their injured friends and helping them across the sacred line.

I held my hands out, about to shoot my powers, as did Char and Blossom.

"Wait! It's me!" The vamp stopped running, showing herself. Nearly six-feet tall, long blonde hair, and blue eyes I knew.

"It's okay," I breathed, thankful to finally have a break. "She's one of us."

Recognizing Alys from when we converted her in Charlotte, South Carolina, my team relaxed.

"We need to get Sheree inside," Char said after a quick greeting to Alys, and I nodded.

Sonya and Jax lifted Sheree and carried her toward the building with Blossom and Dorian following after. Heather and the other norms had already gone inside. I stared after them, pushing my hands through my hair and wondering what the hell just happened. James and Carlie. Lesley. Daemoni collecting their fallen? Of course, Lesley wasn't necessarily dead for good. She was a vamp, after all, and her torso hadn't been fileted like Solomon's had. The shudder that wracked up my spine came from both the memory and the craziness that had just occurred.

Once everyone but Char had walked off, Alys lifted her hands in the direction of where Lesley's blood still pooled on the pavement.

"Shit," she said, sounding defeated. "I tried to stop her. I really did, Alexis."

"What are you even doing here?" I asked.

"What are you doing with *her*?" Char demanded.

Alys sighed. "I'd found her involved with a vamp nest in Richmond. She's always had this wild streak, but she's good deep down. She still had hope, and I'd had her convinced to convert. I've been looking for help for days, but I can't find Amadis anywhere. Then I sensed you guys here." She groaned with frustration. "We were so close! I just made her go too long without drinking. We've been so thirsty."

Someone in a tree grunted. An arrow swooshed through the air toward Alys' head. I caught it in my hand.

"She's one of us," I snapped again as I threw their stupid arrow back at them. I took Alys' arm and dragged her through the gate, onto the sacred grounds. "See?"

Without waiting for a response, we strode across the semicircular driveway for the large, gray, Gothic-style structure ahead of us where everyone else had gone. Everyone but hunters, who still hid in trees and behind walls. I wondered how much we could trust them, and hoped no other Amadis headed this way. Those hunters needed some serious training before they killed any of us. Assuming they hadn't already nailed an Amadis, which they probably had. We'd almost reached the steps when Carlie ran out to us.

"Your friend is hurt pretty bad," she said after we finally managed to give each other a hug in greeting.

"I know," I said miserably. "I don't know if she's going to make it."

"We have the hospital," Carlie said. "Part of it anyway. We have to be careful so we don't show signs that we're here, but we have access to an operating room and a generator."

I looked over my shoulder at Tristan, who stood in the second-floor window of one of the townhomes, watching us. Probably listening, too.

"With the right tools, Tristan can at least try—"

"I can do it," Carlie said. "I'm a surgeon now. Was, anyway. Finally finished everything about two months before shit hit the fan."

I twisted my head to stare at her. "Really? How'd that happen? When?"

"Second year of college, after you left. I decided to go pre-med, then came up here for med school. I've been here ever since."

I grasped her arm. "Do you think you can save Sheree? She's not exactly normal."

Carlie lifted a brow over her caring blue eyes. "What is she?"

"Um . . . a were-tiger?"

Carlie chuckled, and then shook her head. "I can try."

"I don't know what that means about her anatomy," I said. "I know it means she runs hot, so don't be alarmed unless she gets to like 120 or something."

"I'll do what I can, Alexis. But I can't guarantee anything."

I nodded. "I know. I'm just asking you to try. Whatever you have to do."

We entered the building where Blossom and Jax waited with Sheree just inside. Carlie went off to find some help, and I squatted down next to Sheree. Her brown eyes rolled up to look at me, and her purple lips turned slightly upward.

"They're going to take care of you," I said. "You'll be good as new in no time."

Carlie and two men in their twenties arrived. The guys lifted the door Sheree lay on, ready to take her away.

"We'll be on the other side of campus," Carlie said to me. "But don't worry. I'll take care of her as best as I can. We have plenty of room for all of you here. Some food, too. Not an abundance, but we're more than happy to share what we have."

"Thanks, Carlie," I said. "It's good to see you. Bye, Sheree. See you soon."

Her fingers twitched in a little wave. When they carried her away, Blossom and Jax following, I had to bite my lip to keep the tears at bay. Char let out a worried sigh.

"You should go with them," I said to her. "Keep them shielded, just in case."

"They'll still be on holy grounds. And I'm not leaving you. Nobody else is here to protect you."

I rolled my eyes. "I'm on sacred grounds, too. I'll be fine." I pressed my hand to my belly, knowing Char probably worried more about the baby's safety since she knew I'd fight her about my own. "We'll both be fine."

"I'm sure we all will. But I'm not taking any chances." She walked around and gave Alys a hug. "You're looking good, girl. Sorry I couldn't do that before."

"That . . . was insane out there," Alys said. "It happened so fast. She just took off . . ."

Char stopped her with a hand on the vamp's shoulder. "We can't control them. We can only try to lead them, and you did the best you could."

Alys blew out a heavy breath and nodded. Then she looked at me, down at my belly, up at my face, and squinted. "Are you . . .?"

I nodded, and she let out a squeal as she hugged me. Once again, I pretended to be happy about it.

The chatter of girls' voices came down the long hall.

"We're going to stay in a dorm," Heather said as she led the rest of the girls and Dorian toward us, walking ahead with a little spring in her step. She slowed when she saw Alys by my side, though. I wasn't sure, but I thought the last time she might have seen the vampire was when she and Lesley had been trying to turn the girl into one.

"Alys is one of us now," I said.

Heather nodded as she walked toward us. "She must be if she's here, right?"

I thought she'd be a little more wary than that. She *should* have been a little more wary. Sometimes I worried about the girl and her comfort level among monsters.

"It's so weird that you knew that Carlie chick before," Heather continued while we waited for the rest of her group to join us. Dorian really dragged his feet behind the girls.

"Yeah, it's a small world," I said, snorting at the understatement. Carlie, James, Lesley, Alys . . . who else from my past would end up here? The rhetorical question made me frown. I wasn't sure how many other people were alive anymore.

"So," Heather said, "I guess this is like the headquarters building now. They said there's a big auditorium upstairs where they gather for meetings and stuff. The dorms are next door. And here I thought the end of the world meant I'd never know what it was like to live in a dorm."

"Way to see the bright side, kid," Charlotte muttered.

This campus seemed like the perfect place for escape when the Daemoni attacked, but obviously not too many people thought of it, because we didn't pass a single person on the short walk to the residence hall. We entered the massive stone building through an archway, and when we walked the hallway, we had a hard time determining which rooms were already claimed. Every one looked like someone had been there recently. As though the students had had no chance to pack or anything, but had run away in a panic. Perhaps they had. We'd been cut off from the rest of the world, making our way across freakin' Siberia, when civilization fell, so I only had my imagination for how people had reacted.

I wondered if we could have made any difference if we'd been more in the middle of it all. Probably not. So far, it seemed like I'd only made things worse. For every step forward

I thought we were making, we were pushed back two or three by Lucas and his army.

The girls settled on two adjoining rooms, and Dorian and I entered the next set of double rooms. They were boys' rooms —and smelled like it. Even Dorian wrinkled his nose.

"This is gross," he said. So we crossed the hall to another pair that had belonged to girls. He looked around at the bra hanging on a chair back and a box of tampons sitting on a dresser. "Ugh. This is even worse."

I picked up the bra and the tampons and anything else "gross" I could find and tossed them all into the closet. "Better?"

He shrugged as he dropped onto a bed made with a hot-pink-and-zebra-print comforter.

"At least it doesn't stink."

He nodded as Sasha crawled out of his coat and curled into his lap. "It's fine."

"But you're not." I sat on the bed next to him. His mood hadn't changed since we'd left the motel room, but he didn't respond. I glanced out the window. "You can see where Dad is from here."

He barely looked up to see. "I feel bad for Noah. He shouldn't be locked up like that. It's not fair."

"Dorian, we talked about this already. We're going to try to convert him."

"He doesn't belong here, Mom." He sighed and stared at Sasha's back as he dug his fingers into her thick fur. "Neither do I."

"Little Man, I know it sucks to have to be in a girls' room, but the whole world sucks right now. You have a safe place to stay, though. There's food. And I'm sure there are people somewhere."

"I don't get along with people."

"What about Heather? You get along with her."

He ignored me. "I don't belong here, Mom. Not with

Normans and not with the Amadis. Not even with you and Dad."

"Dorian," I gasped, and I moved closer to him and wrapped my arms around his stiff shoulders. Sasha moved over to my lap and licked my arm. "Don't ever say that. You belong right here with Dad and me. Wherever we are is where you should be."

He didn't respond at first, but then said, "Nobody wants me here."

"I do! I always will, forever and ever. Until the end of days. Dad does, too, of course. And Uncle Owen, Blossom . . . and Heather—"

"Haven't you noticed? Heather doesn't give a crap about me anymore."

"Of course she does!"

He shrugged my arms off of him. "Not really. She barely even talks to me. Treats me like I'm a totally different person than I used to be. And I am."

"No, Dorian—"

He pulled completely away and jumped off the bed then turned to face me. He lifted his arms out and flicked his hands toward himself.

"Look at me, Mom. Really look at me! I *am* different. Different than the kid I was. Different from all of you. I'm not Norman. I'm not Amadis." He tossed his hand toward the window. "I'm more like Noah than anyone."

Shaking my head in denial, I moved Sasha to the bed and stood in front of my son. I placed my hands on each side of his face and tilted it down, forcing him to look at me.

"You *are* Amadis, Dorian. You are my son. Don't you ever forget that. You are *nothing* like them."

"Do you really believe that?" he seethed, his eyes hard as he glared at me, his nostrils flaring. "Do you seriously fool yourself with that bullshit? Or do you know deep down inside that I'm *exactly* like him?"

"Dorian," I whispered.

He yanked himself free from my grip and glared at me. When he spoke, his voice came quieter and more forlorn than a child his age should ever sound. "He doesn't belong here. I don't, either. We both know it. *You* just have to admit it."

He strode out of the room, Sasha on his heels, and I could only stand there, staring after him with tears spilling over my cheeks. He didn't even talk like a child anymore. His words, his tone . . . the despair in his voice. He spoke as though *he* carried the weight of the world on his shoulders.

He sounded like me.

And it was up to me to keep him protected. To keep him safe from the clutches of the Daemoni. Those six months earlier this year had been excruciating, and now I feared I was about to lose him for good.

After all, I was losing everybody else. Why not him, too?

CHAPTER 24

"*D*orian," I yelled as I ran out of the room after him.

"Let him go." Char placed a hand on my shoulder to stop me in the corridor, and my whole body sort of sank. "He won't go far, but he wants to be alone."

I scrubbed at the tears on my face. "You heard?"

She frowned. "I'm sorry, Alexis. I know you don't want to hear it, but he's kind of right."

I shook my head. "I won't accept it. There has to be a way to stop it."

With that thought, I strode down the hall toward the door, down the steps, across the driveway, and through the gate with Char keeping pace next to me. We entered the townhome where Tristan, Owen, and Vanessa had brought Noah, and I took the stairs two at a time to the front bedroom. I found them in there with Noah spread eagle on a four-poster bed, his wrists and ankles magically bound to it. I frowned, remembering what it'd felt like not too long ago to be held against my will. Maybe Dorian was right about it not being fair. But I didn't care at the moment.

"How do we break the curse?" I demanded of Noah.

He lifted his head off the pillow, peered at me, and smirked. That was his only answer.

"Tell me how to save my son, damn it!"

He only stared at me with the stupid half-smile that probably made some girls' panties melt, but irritated me. I wanted to throw myself at him and beat the answers out of his arrogant ass. With anger, fear, and despair about Dorian roiling through me, constraining myself from doing so took every bit of self-control I possessed.

"Where are the rest of the Summoned?" I asked, my fists clenched at my side, and now he looked away from me. "You know, don't you?"

He didn't answer me. I asked him more questions about the curse and the Summoned, and he ignored every one. After pacing the room several times, I joined Tristan, who leaned against the wall opposite the bed. Vanessa was perched on the edge of the large wooden dresser, picking at her cuticles. Owen sat in a reading chair next to some bookshelves. We all stared ruthlessly at Noah. He didn't bother fighting against the invisible constraints, but only lay there.

"Why do you want to know?" he asked a good thirty minutes later.

"Know what?" Tristan asked.

"About Santa Claus's naughty and nice list," Noah snarked. "About the Summoned, Seth. What do you think?"

"So we can free them, too," I said.

Noah's gaze came to me, and he seemed to really look at me for the first time. "Why would you even bother?"

I shrugged. "Lots of reasons. Like winning this war."

He chuckled. "You *can't* win. There's no place for *good* in a war."

"Well, we all know that nobody here is *entirely* good, don't we?" I pushed myself away from the wall and took a step closer to him. Something flickered in his eyes. He seemed to appreciate that statement of truth. "But we can all choose to do the right thing. And you, Noah, know that what Lucas is doing to all of the Summoned and their children is *not* right. Even for evil."

"So what are you going to do? Take control yourself and *force* them to be good?"

I ignored his mocking tone. "We're going to remove the stones from them just like we did you and let them make their own decisions. If they want to be good, then we'll help them."

"So young. So naïve." He let out an honest-to-god laugh now. "Don't you understand, stupid girl? You *can't* convert us. Not me. Not any of us. We're cursed!"

I tilted my head. "Then tell me how to break it."

He didn't answer.

I threw my arms in the air. "We'll figure it out on our own then. We *will* break it."

Noah sighed. "It's not up to you, Alexis. Not even the matriarch of the oh-so-wonderful Amadis can break it. You can't even order it to be done. But even if you could . . . even if it *was* up to you . . . I don't think you could make that decision."

I narrowed my eyes and stepped even closer to him. "You don't know me or what kind of decisions I'm willing to make to protect my son."

"That's just it," he said, holding my gaze. "You're not strong enough to break the curse. Not mentally or emotionally. You would never do what needs to be done."

I glared at him for a long, drawn-out moment. His brow lifted as I did, but then he broke our connection and looked away, his mouth clamped shut. All kinds of emotions and questions ran through me, but I wouldn't let him see any of them. I turned on my heel and strode for the door.

"They're under The Mall," he said when I reached the doorway. I paused and looked over my shoulder at him. "The Summoned, their descendants . . . all of them. Hidden in the underground tunnels."

Owen and Tristan both stood up, straightening themselves with attention.

"Which mall?" Char asked.

"*The* Mall. The National Mall."

"You're sure?" Tristan asked.

"That's where they'd had me, still controlling those English soldiers from here. Until they used me as bait to pull you in, then tried to burn me to a crisp before I could tell you."

"Why should we believe you?" Owen asked.

Noah rolled his eyes. "You don't have to. But what if I'm telling the truth? What's the risk worth to you? To the Amadis? To humanity?"

I tried poking into his mind and barely caught a glimpse of his memory before my own brain cut it off. From what I could tell, he told the truth about being there, but that didn't mean the others still were. Maybe this was another trap—Lucas or the sorcerers trying to reel us in again. Maybe he was even part of it, lying about their attempted murder of him. Unfortunately, I couldn't reach those thoughts with my worthless power. And he was right. The Amadis counted on us to accomplish this mission. All of humanity was at stake. The risk would be worth it.

I turned to the others. "I say we have to check it out."

Tristan nodded. "He's right about the tunnels under there. They connect all the important buildings and sites. The Daemoni have been focused on those for ages. Lucas had me studying them all the time."

"Victor and me, too," Vanessa said. "But Lucas had never gained access to them before."

"We know he can now, though," I said. "He's probably sitting in the damn Oval Office this minute, telling the president what to do."

"Or having him turned," Vanessa muttered, the bitterness of her own turning leaking through her tone.

"When are we going?" I asked.

Tristan's eyes narrowed for a moment. "Tomorrow, late afternoon. Gives us time to rest up and regenerate. We'll scope it out in daylight and watch for the Daemoni to leave for their nightly hunt. I don't know how much security they'll really have in place since they're pretty much in control anyway."

"Except they know we're close," Owen pointed out.

"I don't think we should all go," I said. "Blossom and Jax will want to stay with Sheree and the norms, just in case something happens. They prefer helping like that."

"I'm not so sure Jax does, but he'll stick with Blossom regardless," Tristan said. "Charlotte, are you willing to stay behind? Keep this place locked down?"

She grimaced. "I'd rather not. I'm one of your strongest fighters."

"Which is why we need you here," Tristan said. "If the Daemoni know we're here and then we show up there, they'll know this place is vulnerable."

"They haven't attacked these people yet. It's sacred," I reminded him.

"They can still shoot spells and fire inside from beyond the line," Owen said.

"And they didn't know these people had any ties to us before," Tristan countered. "Now they do. Now they know this place and the people here are our weakness. They need a shield."

Char pressed her lips together and blew air out of her nose. "Fine. I'll stay. Blossom and I will shield it."

"Can you keep an eye out on Dorian, too?" I asked. "I'm worried about him."

"Yes. Of course."

"Thank you," I said. "So it's the four of us?"

"Three of us," Tristan corrected. "Owen, Vanessa, and me. You can keep an eye on Dorian yourself."

"Hey!" I protested. He glanced down at my abdomen. I

narrowed my eyes and shook my head. "Don't you even go there."

"Lex—"

"Don't *Lex* me. I'm going with you. You need me and my mind."

His brows lifted as his gaze locked on mine. "You're broken, remember?"

I frowned. "Not completely. And maybe my power will come back."

"You'll need more than three of you," Noah said.

"Shut up," everyone but me replied at the same time.

"You're not leaving me here, Tristan. I swore to my people I would not cower and hide. That I would be out there, like everyone else. That I would not send anyone off to do what I would not do myself."

"You weren't pregnant then," Char said unhelpfully. "You probably should—" She cut herself off when I gave her a death-glare, and she sighed. "You're as stubborn as your mother, you know that? But you're the matriarch. If you think it's best for the Amadis and humanity for you to go, by all means, go."

I scowled as I considered this very valid point, but then made up my mind. If we didn't succeed in disconnecting the Summoned and the Norman soldiers from Lucas, we'd never have a chance of defeating him. There would be no Amadis or humanity to worry about. No future for a baby. I was one of our strongest fighters, and we needed all we could get, especially if Char stayed here, where she was needed more than I was.

"We each have our role to play," I said. "Mine is to be a warrior. And I *will* be there to cut those stones out."

I looked to each one of them, challenging them, but nobody argued with me further.

"I'm going to let the others know, including Carlie," I said.

"I'll come with you." Tristan looked at Owen. "You're good here, Scarecrow?"

Owen rubbed his stomach. "Just bring me some grub."

Char stayed with her son and Vanessa, in case Noah decided to give them a hard time. I told Tristan about Dorian's attitude as we crossed back over to campus.

"He obviously knows who Noah is," I said. "He knows what's expected of him in the future. Kali probably brainwashed him while she had him, and now he thinks he has no choice."

Tristan took my hand into his. "We don't know what the future holds anymore, *ma lykita*. The best we can do right now is to take one day at a time. And for the rest of today and tomorrow morning, I say we try to have a little peace as a family."

We didn't know where to look for Dorian, but our noses and stomachs led us to the cafeteria. He wasn't there and didn't show up while we each ate a bowl of pasta from a can, but when we stepped outside, Tristan lifted his chin as he gazed across the quad. Dorian sat on the ground, leaning against a tree trunk and playing with Sasha, who ran through the fallen leaves. We descended the stairs to join him.

"Alexis!"

I turned to Carlie jogging across the greenway, her blond ponytail bobbing behind her head. She panted as she ran up. "I've been looking all over for you."

"Is Sheree okay?" I asked immediately.

She drew in a deep breath and nodded. "She is for now. We did what we could, and the rest is up to her. Does she . . . you know . . . heal fast? Is that true about her . . . kind?"

I nodded. "Depending on the injury, yeah."

"Then she might make it."

I blew out a breath of relief. "Thank you!"

"Hey, Carlie. I don't know if you remember me—"

Carlie burst into laughter as she stared at Tristan's

outstretched hand. "Are you serious? It's been a long time, and I've met a lot of people, but Tristan, you don't exactly have a forgettable face."

He looked at me as though he didn't understand. Yeah, right.

"Uh, anyway," he said, "what do you know about what's happened? Anything about the rest of the city? Like the Mall?"

"The Mall's infested with zombies," James said from behind us.

I choked down a gag just at the sound of his voice. Of all the people to emerge from the past, why him? Tristan took my hand, squeezing it harder than usual.

"How do you know this douche canoe?" he asked me under his breath, only loud enough for me to hear. I giggled. I'd never heard him use that word before. "Learned it from Dorian. It fits."

I nodded. "Remember how I had a hard time trusting you in the beginning? This asshole is one of many reasons why. That crooked nose of his is from my fist."

He chuckled. "Ah. I remember the story now. Good girl."

"Zombies, huh?" I asked, turning toward James and wishing someone else could give us this crucial information, but he seemed to be our only choice. Him and a couple of other hunters standing with him, all dressed in black cargo pants, black t-shirts, and black combat boots, with weapons hanging on their backs and belts.

"Something like that," said one of his friends, a black guy. "They ain't alive, that's for sure. But they ain't dead, because they move around, mostly just wanderin' around like they're drunk. Until they smell fresh meat. Then they get all worked up."

I cut my eyes sideways to look at Tristan and spoke under my breath again. "I thought the outbreaks were limited to the other side of the world."

"Apparently not."

"What else is going on out there?" I asked the others.

"Pretty much hell," James said.

I suppressed the urge to roll my eyes. Or slam my fist into his face again.

"We need details," Tristan said. "We have a mission, and the more we know, the better."

Carlie stared at us with huge blue eyes. "You want to go out there?"

"We don't have a choice," I said. "It's something only we can do."

"I bet we can handle it." James smirked. "Better than you. You seem to have a soft spot for the supes. Besides, what are you going to do? Punch them?"

My hand balled into a fist, ready to remind him of the power in said punch, which was even more than it had been last time his nose had met my fist. Instead, I threw a bolt of electricity at his feet, making him jump backwards. Carlie gasped and covered her mouth with her palm.

"You are going out there, aren't you?" she asked, her voice muffled behind her hand.

"We have to. It's the whole reason we're even here."

She pressed her lips together as she studied me, and then she grabbed my hand.

"Come with me." She tugged me along as she headed toward the big building at the front of campus.

James and the other hunters didn't follow, thank the Angels.

"I can't stand being around him," Carlie said as she led Tristan and me inside the arched doorway. We went up some wide steps, turned a corner, then entered an enclosed stairwell. "Some of the hunters are okay, but he and his friends are dicks. Unfortunately, he seems to think he's in charge. Did you date him or something?"

"Hell no! He wanted something, though, that I wouldn't give. When he pushed it, I punched him."

Carlie laughed. "Good for you!"

I shrugged. "It was a long time ago, but he hasn't changed. Maybe grown worse."

We continued climbing the steps to the top of the stairwell. She took us through the door, a short ways down the top floor hall, and through another door that led outside. Four columns surrounded us with more steps. I looked up as we climbed, into the bottom of a huge bell, its clapper looking like a long, bulbous tongue. When we reached the top of the clock tower, Carlie turned to look out.

"I thought you should see this," she said.

I followed her gaze and gasped at the view of the city spread out before me. What should have been a beautiful landscape of trees in autumn and interesting architecture broke my heart and soul with the utter destruction.

Buildings were demolished or only half-standing. Several pillars of black smoke rose to the sky all around the city. The top of the Washington Monument in the distance ended at jagged edges instead of its normal point. Cars and buses littered the streets, some in the middle of the roads, many with their doors hanging open. The tops of some trees had been broken off, and others were only blackened trunks, their leaves and branches fried.

And dead bodies lay scattered everywhere.

Legs and other body parts protruded from underneath fallen buildings. Charred corpses lay in the ashes of burning piles of rubbish. And mounds of bodies were piled on street corners, as though waiting for the trash service to collect them. Bile rose in my throat, and my eyes watered.

Buildings that hadn't been destroyed suffered broken windows with half their contents spilling out, what looters had left behind. Were they really even looters anymore or scavengers simply trying to feed themselves? Whoever they'd been, they were long gone now. The only living beings roaming the streets were Daemoni and military. From what we could see from here, the humans were locked up in a camp like the one in London—another Norman farm, about halfway between here and the National Mall.

"I . . ." I shook my head, unable to form words in my shock. "What happened? What do you know?"

Carlie pressed her lips together as she gazed out at the devastating scene in front of us. "I was here, working the night shift as the surgeon on call when the evil creatures attacked. All of the injuries coming in . . . it was insane. And what the people were saying? I mean, the news had been reporting all day on what was happening everywhere else, but you just don't think it'll happen to you, you know?" She sighed. "People locked themselves up in their homes, which didn't do a lot of good if the monsters really wanted in, but they backed off a little. Like they'd swooped in for their shock-and-awe and then knew they had us by the balls. My sister called me when the news showed that part about you being the head of all this. She just couldn't believe it. She knew I'd known you before, and I told her I couldn't believe it either. That's when she started talking to the others about this A.K.'s Angels idea. When the bombs started dropping, the phones went out, and I didn't hear from her again. I was so scared."

"Bombs dropped here, too?" I saw the destruction before me, but I just couldn't believe it.

"It was horrible, Alexis. You don't think it can happen here. I mean, when it comes to bombs and war, this city is the number one place the military's supposed to protect, right? But there were no F16s scaring off the planes that came in, even when they entered the no-fly zone. There weren't any land-to-air missiles being shot off to destroy the bombs in midair. It's like the government and military abandoned the rest of the city, leaving us for dead."

"No warnings?" Tristan asked. "Nobody fighting back?"

She hunched her shoulders as she crossed her arms over her stomach. "The news was all over the place with bombings and assassinations and war breaking out everywhere. I had a hard time keeping track of everything going on. It was like the civilized world fell into a free-for-all street brawl." She shook her head, the ends of her ponytail whisking over her neck. "There were militias here trying to make sure we were protected, but our president and leaders kept saying everything was under control. Whatever the hell that means. Does that look like everything was under control?"

Despair colored her tone, and her bottom lip trembled with emotion. I put an arm around her shoulders. She sighed.

"After the bombings, there was no power, no water, no phones. Nothing. We went from capitol of the free world to a third-world country in days. Chaos broke out. Looters were everywhere. Ex-military guys tried to settle things down, but people fought back, and then the so-called real military came in and killed them! Their former comrades and civilians alike." She paused to take another deep breath and shook her head again. "The monsters sat back and watched as humans killed each other over a carton of milk or a loaf of bread. Some people formed gangs to protect themselves against others, and their fights were deadlier than ever. But then people began leaving in droves, running for the hills, I guess. I stayed, still hoping to find my sister."

"Did you?" I asked, bracing for more bad news.

She nodded. "Yeah, she showed up here a week ago, with about thirty friends and neighbors, calling themselves A.K.'s Angels. She knew to come here because of the holy grounds. She'd learned that from your books. I'd noticed the vampires and other monsters wouldn't come on campus, but didn't know why." She glanced at me and blushed. "I hadn't had time to read your books yet, with med school and everything."

"I'd say you had more important reading to do."

She chuckled, the sound flat and hollow. "Did I? If I'd read your books instead of medical textbooks, I might have saved more lives than I ever will as a surgeon. I could've tried to keep everyone here. But the entire campus cleared out the day after the monsters attacked, running for families and home. They would have survived here. They most likely didn't out there." Her voice had become watery, and she paused to suck in a ragged breath. "Do you know the last we heard anything, a quarter of the world's population had been killed? They estimated another quarter had been infected and turned into those monsters. And look out there." She waved at the city before us, where cars should have been clogging the roads and people crowding the sidewalks—live people, not corpses. "Anyone left is in those camps or have gone underground, except for the few here or in the gangs. One-fourth of humans dead. Gone. Wiped out. Just like it says in the Bible. I can't wrap my mind around that many people. And pretty much everyone I know is included in that. My sister's the only family I know who's still alive. The rest probably died trying to get out of here."

"We have people out there who could have helped them," Tristan said.

"Did you ever see any good creatures?" I asked. "Supernaturals like us, trying to help?"

She stuffed her hands into her pockets. "I did at first. That's how I knew my sister was right about everything she believed. But the humans went after them, especially the gangs. They killed some, but I think the rest just bolted."

My heart shriveled at the thought of some of my people dying out there in the streets before me. Murdered when they'd only been trying to save lives and souls. And where were the rest? Had any escaped? Did any work covertly, still trying to help, or had they all given up?

"It's not safe out there, Alexis," Carlie said as she turned for the steps. "No matter what special things you can do. It's not safe *anywhere*. Some people here think help is coming, but it's not. There's nobody left to help us. We stayed to find survivors and give them a safe place, but there are none of those left. Now we stay because there's nowhere to go. We have enough food to last us another week or so, and then what? We become one of them?" She blew out a heavy breath. "Supernatural or human, they're all monsters out there."

She descended the stairs, disappearing from sight. I turned back to the view before us. Besides the destruction and weird emptiness, which were bad enough in themselves, the sight was marred by strange symbols everywhere. Burnt into grass. Spray-painted on buildings and streets. Smeared in blood. Ugly lines that I couldn't interpret, but nevertheless made the hairs on my arms stand up.

"Dark magic sigils and signs of the devil," Tristan said. "Symbols calling out to Satan."

And they were everywhere.

Lucas and his Daemoni *owned* this city. And who knew where else? How long had they been infiltrating, worming their ways in like the snakes they were? How far did they plan to go still? The Satanic symbols sent my body into a full shudder.

My legs nearly gave out by the weight of it all. The death and destruction. The loss of lives, of hope, of humanity. The promise of a future filled with only darkness. The reality that Dorian could be headed straight into it, and that the baby in my womb would never know differently.

I collapsed to my knees and buried my head in my hands.

I'd completely and utterly failed. I hadn't protected the humans, and now their souls were already lost or would be soon to the evil still coming, for Lucas wasn't done yet, I knew. Anything left of humanity was barely worth fighting for. The Amadis showed no signs of existence anymore. They'd probably given up on us ever accomplishing our mission. And I couldn't blame them. I'd failed them, too. Solomon had been killed, and Sheree lingered in death's grip. How many more loved ones would I lose?

Tristan crouched beside me and wrapped his arms around me.

"We've lost, Tristan. I've failed everyone, and we've lost. There's no hope of us winning. There's no *us* to win. It's . . ." I blew out a harsh, tearful breath, and whispered with a soul-crushing sense of hopelessness, "It's all over."

CHAPTER 25

"As long as you and I are alive to fight, it's not over," Tristan said. "Remember what we promised each other? We fight together, hand in hand . . . ? The ultimate warrior and fierce protector . . ."

"Nobody can beat us. Yeah, I remember. That's back when I was stupid enough to believe that good always wins. That the Amadis were all-powerful. But we don't have the power, Tristan."

"No, *we* don't," he admitted. "But we have everything to fight for."

I shook my head. "How can you say that? There's hardly anything left fighting for."

"But there's this." He took my hands and pulled me to my feet, and then he walked me around the steps in the center of the tower, to the far side that looked out over campus instead of the city. "This is how I can say that. This is what's worth fighting for."

Down below, a couple dozen people were busy at work. Some chopped wood while others hauled armfuls of it off to the buildings. A small handful of college-aged guys had gathered around some kind of mechanical contraption, studying it, and tinkering. I didn't know what the object was, but the vague clips of thoughts I managed to grab told me that whatever it had been before, they wanted to turn it into a water purifier now. A few hunters with compound bows or swords on their backs jogged into the quad carrying pillowcases stuffed full of something bulky. One reached in his bag, pulled out a package of Twinkies and tossed it at Heather who sat with Teal, Teah, and some other Norman girls about their ages. They ripped the package open and divided the two snacks to share among them. Dorian still sat under the tree while Sasha and a couple of little kids ran circles around him and threw dead leaves in the air. Their laughter carried up to us.

Tristan stood behind me as I watched and slid his arms around me. He leaned down and murmured in my ear, "You were so focused on the devastation out there, you missed the beautiful part of the view."

I knew what he meant, but I could only sigh. "Except they won't be around much longer. You heard Carlie—they don't have enough food to last forever. The odds are stacked against their survival."

"Yeah, you're right," he said. "If we give up and roll over. If we don't fight for them, they have little chance of making it. But if we do, we increase their odds greatly. If we can free the Norman soldiers from the Daemoni's control, they'll fight for the right side. They'll protect their fellow humans instead of locking them up to be served for dinner. These people will have hope, Alexis. But only if we do our part. Only if we don't give up. They need us."

I leaned back against him, trying to soak up his positive energy by osmosis.

"The Amadis need you, too," said a female voice from the top of the stairs behind us. "Sorry, but I'd been sitting on the roof over there and couldn't help but overhear."

Alys came over and stood next to us, gazing down at the scene below.

"I'm afraid the Amadis have given up on us," I said dejectedly. "We've had no way of communicating with anyone. No way of telling my council we're still alive. Half of them didn't believe in me anyway, and they were right not to. I've failed them. And now they're just trying to do their best to survive."

Alys turned toward me and tilted her head. "You're wrong, Alexis. They're still out there, fighting the Daemoni and protecting the norms. They're still doing all they can to convert the newly turned. I hadn't come across any for several days before today, but that doesn't mean they aren't out there—that *we* aren't out there. We're scattered around the world, making it hard to be detected even by each other, but that was the point of your orders, right? They're still expecting you to succeed at whatever it is you need to do and to give them new directives. In the meantime, they're fighting like they're supposed to. Don't give up on them. I promise they haven't given up on you."

My brows pushed together, and I scowled as I considered this news. "When was the last time you saw the Amadis actually fighting?"

"About a week ago, in the mountains. Right before I found Lesley. I went back to find those guys, thinking they could help me with her, but they'd moved on. Staying under the radar, just like we'd been told to do. If they knew you were pregnant, Alexis, you'd probably see them everywhere, showing their commitment to you and each other. So please, *please* don't give up."

I gazed down at the scene below as I let this sink in and imagined it being replayed all over the country, all over the world. Were there other pockets of norms like this, simply trying to survive and help others and not trying to kill each other? Were my Amadis truly still out there, following my orders? Or, at least, serving their purpose of protecting souls? *Of course they are.*

I wished we'd developed some old-school way for the Amadis to stay in communication with each other, such as using messengers. Of course, when we'd given the orders, we hadn't expected the world to fall apart at the seams as it had. And perhaps such a scheme to keep us in contact would have only made things worse by jeopardizing the messengers if they'd ever been caught by the Daemoni. So relying on accidental run-ins, such as Alys with the others and now with us, had become our only means of passing on news. And I appreciated the coincidence of her finding us while chasing Lesley, because her update was exactly what I needed to hear to be reminded of my own commitment.

Nothing is coincidental. The words echoed in my mind, a quiet whisper no doubt from Mom or Rina or Cassandra. Perhaps a hint that Alys was meant to deliver this news to keep me going.

"Well, then," I said, trying to sound more chipper than I felt deep down, "we promised our people that this would all be worth it. We'd better give it our damnedest, since they've given theirs."

The three of us leapt off the tower straight to the ground, catching everyone's attention, which was the point. At Tristan's direction, Carlie gathered them into the auditorium inside the gray-stoned building, sending a few to round up those who were scattered across the grounds. Only patients in the hospital were left alone. Forty, maybe fifty people had come out of the woodwork and stood in the aisles and in front of the seats, nobody bothering to sit down.

Physically, they'd obviously seen better days. Many faces were smudged with dirt, some scratched and bruised from flying debris. Bandages covered arms and hands, probably burnt from the bombings and resulting fires. Knit hats and baseball caps covered some heads, but everyone's hair could use a good washing. So could their clothes, which could also use some mending, already showing lots of wear and tear. I couldn't imagine everything these people had been through to make it this far and everything they'd still have to face.

Yet, they looked up at us on the stage through eyes lit with hope.

It was up to us to ensure they had the best chances of survival we could possibly provide. It was up to us to give them that hope for a future.

Tristan had Carlie introduce me, but introductions proved to be unnecessary. As soon as she said my name, everyone began clapping and wolf whistling. I wanted to throw up. This felt worse than the coronation, because then I'd been too wrapped up in grief to care. At least Tristan kept hold of my hand and walked out on stage with me, standing by my side as I cleared my throat and began.

"I'm, uh, pretty overwhelmed by all of this," I admitted, trying to make my voice loud enough to be heard, but it was impossible over the lump in my throat that wicked all of the moisture from my mouth. Blossom waved her hands at me, and my voice suddenly amplified across the auditorium as though I spoke into a microphone.

"You all are truly amazing," I started again. A few people cheered when they could hear me this time. "You've really blown my mind. When I wrote those books, I honestly had no idea about all of this. I thought I wrote fantasy, nothing more than fiction. I'd just needed an escape from my own real life and had hoped my stories would provide an escape for others, too. I had no clue my tales would lead to this."

I paused to swallow, and the audience took the opportunity to clap and cheer.

"*You* deserve the applause," I said. "You've made it this far. By working together, hopefully you'll get through this insanity and be able to restart the world."

"As long as you're here, we can do anything," someone in the back yelled.

I sighed. "That's actually why I wanted to talk to you tonight. The people I came with, we're like the elite team of our kind, and we have a mission to accomplish. Some will be staying to protect you, but I and a few others will be leaving tomorrow afternoon. We're hoping by accomplishing our mission, we can free the people in those camps, including the soldiers keeping them there. They're not in their right minds, but our mission will return them to normal. When that happens, they'll need you, but you'll also need them. They can protect you and train you. We plan to give you all a fighting chance."

Excited chatter waved over the room. My sensitive ears caught whispers about family and friends being held like prisoners in the camps. Tristan lifted his hands to quiet them down.

"I just have to ask you one thing," I said. "There are others like us out there. They've had to remain covert because of the lies humans were told about us. Not all supernaturals are dark, though, as you can see before your eyes right now. Our people are waiting for us to accomplish our mission. When we do and when the time is right, we'll be calling them out to fight more overtly. We're going to need all the support and help we can get. We'll train you. We'll help you. We'll protect you. And eventually, we may need you to help us fight the real monsters that are out there. I just ask that you give *us* a chance."

"We're on your side, A.K.," somebody yelled, and the audience burst into chants of "A.K.'s Angels! A.K.'s Angels!"

Even the hunters in attendance got caught up into the chant and shouts of support. James and his besties were noticeably absent, though, probably on guard outside. I wondered if they'd be a part of this now, or if they'd be standing by the door, arms crossed over their chests, smirking as they rolled their eyes. Then I decided I didn't care. He'd either learn eventually or he never would, but one thing I knew for sure. Stupid people didn't stand a chance against the Daemoni.

We spent the rest of the evening by candlelight with Dorian in his room that shared a bathroom with ours. Since we hadn't been able to sit down together and officially tell him until now, we delivered the news about the baby.

"Yeah, I heard," he said with a small smile. "That's really awesome."

"I'm so glad you're happy about it," Tristan said.

"Why wouldn't I be?" he asked, and Tristan and I exchanged a look. We'd been worried about Dorian's reaction, hoping it wouldn't send him into one of his broody mood swings. Or worse, shove him along the path to the Daemoni. "I've always wanted a baby sister. And I know you've wanted her for a long time."

I threw my arms around him. "You're going to be an amazing big brother."

"I know." He beamed.

We talked for a while about what it would mean to have a baby, and Dorian promised he'd be the protective big brother and always look out for her. Unavoidably, our conversation turned darker as we discussed what it would be like to take care of a baby in this new world we lived in. Dorian's mood darkened along with it until he fell out of the conversation completely.

Trying to bring him back, we asked him to play cards with us, using a deck we'd found in one of the desk drawers, but he didn't get into the game. Then we made up stories about the girls who'd lived in the room before, looking at their photos and other belongings pinned to bulletin boards or left out on the desks and dressers. Well, Tristan and I did. Dorian just sat there, petting Sasha and scowling at the zebra print comforter.

"I know one thing for certain about them," he finally said after Tristan and I had spent an hour playing the game between the two of us. We both stopped looking at a pile of pictures by the candle flame and turned our attention to our son, glad to have him involved. His hazel eyes cut over to us, and he said flatly, "They and all their friends are dead."

Tristan and I stared at him in silence. What could we say to that? As much as I hoped he was wrong and most humans still lived, I knew the chances were slim. Some had survived, yes. But not all. Any denial to Dorian's statement was probably an outright lie.

Sleep eluded me, as usual, but not because of memories of Mom keeping me awake. Worries of what the next day and night would bring had my brain whirring in a hundred different directions. I was thankful when morning finally came, and we could sit down with my team at the dining table in the townhouse to make more solid plans.

Once we'd gone over everything, Charlotte stood and braced her hands on the table, leaning toward Tristan, Owen, Vanessa, and me. Her gaze traveled over each of us, her lips pressed into a hard, thin line. Something weighed heavily on her mind.

"What?" I demanded.

Her words came out as an order. "You have to *promise* to be back before midnight."

"What's at midnight?" I asked. After all, a deadline hadn't been discussed before. Was there some kind of curfew we hadn't known about? Who was even policing that, anyway?

Char pierced me with her sapphire eyes, bringing all thoughts to a halt. "According to the Normans who've been keeping track, today is Halloween."

I immediately turned toward Tristan, my mouth opening, but he held up his hand and shook his head. For once, I didn't ignore him. This wasn't the time to be celebrating his birthday.

"So . . . what's at midnight?" I asked again, turning back toward Char. It's not like we had to worry about partiers, crowds, or drunk drivers.

"It's when the veil to the Otherworld is thinnest," Blossom answered from Char's side. "And with those Satanic symbols you said were everywhere . . ."

Vanessa's hands slapped the table, the force making me jump. "It won't be good, that's for damn sure."

Her tone and the meaning of it all sent a chill down my spine. Noah's chuckle coming from upstairs brought on a full shiver. I'd known about the theory that the veil was thinnest on Halloween night, but hadn't realized how seriously the Amadis took it. Blossom's point—and Char's, too—was very valid.

"Should we wait until tomorrow?" I asked. Not that I really wanted to, but the situation was risky enough. Too many lives were on the line. Pretty much the whole world's future.

"If anything happens with the veil, tomorrow may be too late," Tristan said grimly.

"Just make sure you make it back before midnight," Char said again. "Back on sacred grounds, just in case Lucas does something even more atrocious than he already has."

Once we finalized our plans, we spent the rest of our time eating, resting, and feeding the vampires to ensure we all were powered up. I tried not to let this extra threat about the veil get to me. After all, Lucas had lived through hundreds of Halloweens and had never done anything outrageous before, as far as I knew. Hopefully, this one wouldn't be any different. And if it was? We'd cross that bridge later tonight. For now, we had to do what we could to minimize the consequences.

Carlie allowed us a visit with Sheree, who was barely conscious, but alert enough to at least say goodbye. I prayed we'd come back to find her healthy and raring to go. Or roaring to go. That would be even better.

By late afternoon, my insides were even more of a wreck as nervous energy, anticipation to finally accomplish our mission, and an overwhelming desire to stay here with our son battled within me. As I approached Dorian's room to say goodbye, I overheard him talking to someone.

"I have a sister coming, and I have to do everything I can to protect her," Dorian said. "And you have to protect her, too, Sasha. So you're going to go with Mom and Dad. And no matter what *anyone* commands you to do—I don't care if it's Mom, Dad, or even me—you protect my parents and my baby sister. Okay? You understand?"

I peeked around the doorway to see Sasha's blue tongue lick his cheek.

"Good. And if anything ever happens and I can't be your master anymore, my sister will be. Okay?"

I smiled, enjoying the little bit of happiness I could grasp on to in knowing that, although he'd been so moody since he'd come back to us, his heart remained big, soft, and warm. And that would keep him safe from the Daemoni's clutches. But then realization of what he'd just done set in, making my stomach sink. I strode into his room and sat on the floor next to him.

"Dorian," I said, "Sasha needs to stay here and protect you."

He shook his head. "I've given her orders, and she's loyal to me before anyone else."

I swallowed and nodded. At the moment, that was exactly the problem. "Right. So you need to tell her to stay here with you. She can't go with us."

"No, Mom. You need her more than I do. My sister needs her more."

My throat closed, and tears pricked at my eyes. I'd never been so proud of his compassion and tormented with what it meant. I pulled him into an embrace.

"Dad and I will be fine," I said. "Uncle Owen will keep us

protected. We need to know that Sasha is here, doing her job —protecting you. That will help us focus on *our* job better so we can get back as soon as possible."

He returned my hug for the first time in a long time and rested his head on my shoulder. "You don't have to worry about me, Mom. I promise I'll be fine. But I'm scared for you and Dad, and I'll feel better if Sasha is there to help you. I won't change my mind, and you can't make me. It's not like you can take my Xbox or any other toys away from me."

I frowned, and then let out a growl. "You're too smart for your own good."

"But you'll always love me anyway, right?"

"Always," I said quickly and automatically. I gave him a hard squeeze, then pulled back and braced my hands against his cheeks. I stared into his hazel eyes, trying to reach his soul with my touch and my words. "You never have to question that. No matter what, Dorian, I'll *always* love you. Until the end of forever."

He nodded, his eyes glistening, and his mouth tilted up in a smile. "I love you, too, Mom. Until the end of forever. And Dad, too." He tentatively laid a hand on my stomach. "And her, too. I promise to be the best big brother I can be. What are we going to name her?"

"I don't know. Maybe we can discuss it tonight when we get back." I planted a kiss on his forehead before pulling both of us to our feet. "We'll see you soon, okay? We'll be back here as soon as we finish the mission."

"I hope . . ." He trailed off, and his face darkened. "I hope it's all worth it."

"Me, too, Dorian. Me, too."

Tristan met us outside the door, and they had a moment together, then Dorian, along with several others, walked us outside. Hugs and pats on the back were exchanged along with a bunch of "good lucks."

"You guys be safe," Blossom said as we held each other in a tight hug.

"You, too," I said. "I expect when I come back that you'll have figured out how to make a cake without a working oven."

"Oh, I've been thinking about it. I'm sure I can figure out how to make the oven work. It's the ingredients that might be the problem. Even if Tristan doesn't want a birthday cake, we could all use some yumminess, yeah?"

"Yes, we can." I squeezed her one more time. "I love you, Blossom."

"Love you, too, girl. Now go kick some Daemoni ass and get yours back here in time."

Before we turned for the townhome across the street, I gave Dorian one last hug, not caring if the public display of affection embarrassed him.

"Until the end," I whispered into his ear. "No matter what."

"Until the end," he echoed, holding me tight and eventually letting go with a sigh.

Damn, I was going to break down right here in front of everyone. I internally questioned my decision to go on this mission. "Maybe I should stay here with you."

Dorian rolled his eyes. "Mom, I'll be fine. You gave Charlotte, Blossom, Jax, Sonya, and Alys strict orders to watch me, right?"

He ticked them off his fingers as he stated their names, and although the number seemed excessive as he did so, I didn't feel one iota of guilt about it. If any other Amadis had been around, they'd have received the same orders. Blossom slid an arm over Dorian's shoulders, and Sonya and Alys both stepped in front of him to guard him.

"Okay. I'll see you tonight."

"Not if I see you first," he joked.

I forced a smile for him, and then Tristan and I headed for

the street and the townhomes on the other side to where Owen, Vanessa, and Char waited.

"Go, Sasha, and protect," Dorian said from behind us, and I glanced over my shoulder at them. Sasha started trotting after us.

"Go back to Dorian, Sasha," I said. "Protect *him*."

She grew to the size of a large Great Dane, but she didn't return to her master. He'd given her a command, and she'd listen to him over anyone else. At least I'd tried.

We passed James and his buds, all armed up, as we walked through the gate. They didn't wish us luck, offer up help like the other hunters had, or anything. They stayed at attention—all of it on the townhome we approached.

"I don't trust them," Tristan said as he opened the front door for me.

"Neither do I. I'm pretty sure they'll be all over Noah as soon as we leave. I'm glad Char's staying here to protect him."

"I think we should take him with us."

I climbed the stairs ahead of him and looked back as he closed the door. "What?"

"Charlotte needs to focus on the campus and the people there. If they're attacked, we can't have her attention and her powers divided."

"What are we going to do with him?"

"We'll leave him with T.J."

I hit the landing and turned toward him again to get a read on his face. He was dead serious.

Owen and Char must have been saying their goodbyes when we entered, because her reddened eyes blinked rapidly, and she threw her arms around me.

"You guys be safe, you hear me?" she said, her voice tight and firm. "Don't do anything stupid. If you can't get to them, then you come back here, and we figure out a new plan. And no matter what, you be back here by midnight. You understand?"

A small grin tried to reach my lips. "You sound like my mom."

"Good. She'd want me to." She tightened her embrace. "We need you, Alexis. The Amadis do. Humanity . . . *I* do. You and that baby are our hope. Maybe our last hope."

I nodded against her shoulder. "We'll be careful, Char. I promise. And we'll be back in time. Then maybe you'll finally tell me the story about why Mom called you Charred sometimes."

She chuckled. "We get through this, kiddo, I'll tell you, as frightfully embarrassing as it is. I promise."

Owen redid the bindings on Noah so Tristan could use his power to force him along with us, and then he created the portal. A moment later, we left our little refuge—and what remained of our family—behind and stepped through the portal. We'd decided earlier that appearing at the Lincoln Memorial, the Washington Monument, or anywhere else directly on the Mall would be too conspicuous, so we'd picked the Thomas Jefferson Memorial, which happened to have an entrance to the tunnels underneath it. And, overlooking the calm waters of the Potomac Tidal Basin, still happened to be my favorite site of them all.

Although, I didn't appreciate the Satanic symbols graffitied on the walls, the colonnades, and even the interior of the shallow dome of the pantheon-like structure. The peace I used to come here for was snuffed out by the black magic that hung heavily in the air, singeing my nose hairs, prickling my skin, and making my stomach clench. Sasha let out a low growl, feeling it, too. I wondered how long anyone could be surrounded by such darkness before their soul dissolved into a black, oozing pool. I could only hope ours were strong enough to withstand it for as long as it would take to complete our mission.

While Tristan and Owen situated Noah—they really were going to bind him to old Thomas' statue that stood in the center of the domed portico—my eyes fell on the quotes inscribed on the walls. I knew the excerpts from the Declaration of Independence and letters to prominent statesmen by heart from when I used to come here all the time. Certain parts stood out to me now, though, as if a soft light illuminated them especially for this moment.

Vanessa must have noticed them, too, because she read aloud, "I have sworn upon the altar of God eternal hostility against every form of tyranny over the mind of man." She paused before saying, "I can't imagine a worse form of tyranny than Lucas controlling the world."

With a nod, I turned to the next one, my eyes skimming over the words: "We hold these truths to be self-evident: that all men are created equal . . ." Mr. Jefferson and the rest of our founding fathers must not have known about supernatural creatures posing as men. Or, maybe they had, and this line had more than one meaning—a statement to the Daemoni that they would not bow down. That supernaturals were equal to them. That evil would hold no power over them.

Unfortunately, the dark force held as much power as people would give it, and today's world had given it too much. They'd fed the bad sides of themselves, and not enough of the good, creating a gross imbalance. And now the darkness would rule, and they would lose their liberties, if not their lives, if we weren't able to free them first.

With a heart growing heavier by the moment, I read the next one out loud: ". . .with a firm reliance on the protection of divine providence, we mutually pledge our lives, our fortunes, and our sacred honor."

The phrase felt like a prayer, or perhaps an oath I was taking this very moment. I *hoped* we truly had the protection of God and the Angels. With no word from Mom, Rina, or Cassandra, I had to believe they saw us on the right path, doing what was necessary to win this war. Otherwise, they really had abandoned us.

Owen continued casting binding spells while Tristan held Noah in place, so with these thoughts and ideals tumbling around in my mind, I wandered outside. Both Vanessa and Sasha stuck close to my side, and we stopped at the top of the marble steps that circled the monument, this side leading down to the water. The memory of the last time I'd been here came vividly. It'd been the night I'd first met Tristan, Owen, and Vanessa, but I hadn't known it at the time. I'd been sitting here on these very steps, feeling as though someone watched me. I knew now it had been them.

How the world had changed since that night.

I lifted my gaze from the smooth surface of the water reflecting the blue, late afternoon sky and tried to peer across the basin to the Mall, toward the Washington Monument and beyond it, the White House. My vision was good enough to see that far, but trees still held onto enough of their red, orange, and yellow leaves to block my view. The autumn scene would have normally been breathtaking, but the yellow, hellish haze blanketing the area diminished the beauty. As did the feeling of trepidation that hugged me like a second skin, making both my insides and outsides tremor with electrified nerves.

"They don't look right," Vanessa said from right next to me, with her hands on her hips as she also gazed across the water to the other side. A few people meandered around the trees to the edge of the basin. "Look how they walk."

I nodded. "Must be those zombies James mentioned."

"Want me to run over there and check it out?"

"Nah. We're not going that way. From what I can see through the trees, though, it looks like there's a bunch more on the Mall. I wonder why they're all here, but there weren't any by the campus or in Virginia."

Vanessa tapped her fingers against her hip. "My guess would be Lucas has them contained here by choice."

"To keep Normans out of the area?"

"Bingo."

"Heh," I said, shaking my head. "Zombie boobie traps. Who would have thought?"

"Lucas would."

I snorted. "Of course. He's such a sick freak."

Her head turned for the first time as she looked down at me. "You don't know the half of it, sister."

"Let's go," Tristan said from behind us.

CHAPTER 26

$\mathcal{W}$ith a last glance at the zombies, we turned toward the shadowed interior of the monument, where Noah was bound to the statue, back-to-back with Thomas, only able to move his eyes and mouth. Owen shielded and cloaked the four of us and Sasha, and we passed Noah as he glared at the red symbols on the walls with a mix of hatred and awe in his eyes. He didn't give us so much as a cursory glance as we walked by, headed to the door that led downstairs.

"Alexis," he suddenly murmured, and I turned to look at him from the doorway. "Aim for directly under the right ear. It will put them to sleep."

"What?" I asked.

He clamped his mouth shut and stared straight ahead again.

Whatever, I thought as we went downstairs to the gift shop, which had been left in a shambles. Shelves lay on their sides, and miniature replicas of various monuments and several snow globes littered the floor. Postcards and other pieces of memorabilia lay scattered everywhere, too, never to be seen by another tourist again. I paused for a moment to pick up a postcard of the sun setting over the monument with cherry blossoms surrounding it, before it had been vandalized. I stuffed it into my backpack as my own souvenir for how the world used to be.

At the back of the shop was a door to stairs that led downward. One flight down, we entered what appeared to be an office under the monument with another door leading off of it. Through there came more stairs, another two flights downward, and then we entered the tunnel with a concrete floor and white tiled walls displaying more offensive graffiti. If the dark energy felt thick above ground, it was positively suffocating down here. Sasha let out a soft whine.

"I know, girl." I reached up and rubbed the back of her head. "It hurts all the way to the bones, doesn't it?"

After Owen gave himself a magical boost and provided a tiny point of light in the pitch blackness, we sprinted through the tunnel that stretched far into the darkness beyond. My internal compass felt as though we headed north, which meant we ran under the Tidal Basin. Then we reached a few forks that I figured meant we were under or near the Washington Monument.

"This way," Tristan said, turning right.

We ran for only a moment when he stopped and the rest of us plowed into him. A horde of Daemoni gathered not too far ahead, their voices carrying to us. The stink of more zombies floated on the air. I assumed they guarded the Capitol building. When I tried to reach out for mind signatures with my faulty ability, I could barely grasp on to vampires and werewolves, as well as a couple of were-felines.

"No Summoned or Lucas here," I whispered, unable to mind-talk.

"Let's go back and try a different way," Tristan said.

We followed him through the tunnels, finding a similar

crowd of Daemoni and zombies at the entrance to the White House, but still no Lucas or Summoned. Same with the tunnel that led to the Lincoln Memorial.

"There's another way to the other side of the Capitol building," Tristan said. "They must be over there."

"Do you think it's safe to flash?" Owen asked.

"Flash or portal—if they want to trap us, they will. At this point, what do we have to lose?" He took my hand and Vanessa's. "Sasha, hide." The lykora shrunk down to her toy-dog size, leapt into my arm, and then crawled into my jacket. "I'll lead the flash."

We arrived in a grand, round room with marble walls and columns that reached upwards toward a dome that arced high overhead. The ceiling stretched down to large, semicircular windows, separated by statues between them. Below the windows were two rows of balconies displaying more statues and archways, and then tall, rounded doorways on our level. We stood among three rows of tables encircling the room with a round counter and what appeared to be a service desk in the center, all made of dark, polished wood. The extent of the room's beauty and majesty exceeded anywhere I'd ever been, including the Amadis mansion.

"Where are we?" I whispered.

"The vastest collection of knowledge on Earth," Tristan answered. "The Library of Congress."

Vanessa sniffed the air. "Holding a vast collection of the Summoned and their descendants in its belly."

Reader-and-writer-girl inhaled the intoxicating pulp-and-leather smell of old books and wanted so badly to geek out. We were in the freakin' Library of Congress, surrounded by more books than my head could wrap itself around. Unfortunately, I didn't have the luxury to bathe in its glory. In fact, I'd probably never have such luxury again.

Vanessa, whose sense of smell was even stronger than

Tristan's and mine, led us to the far side of the room, through double doors, and across a corridor that stretched to our right and left. Ahead, we entered a utilitarian stairwell meant for employees and definitely not Congressmen and dignitaries who visited the library. We left the polished marble and wood behind for plain gray walls, darker gray rails, and concrete stairs. Once again, we headed downward. Three flights down, we entered another tunnel, but only walked a few yards before Vanessa's nose led us through a doorway and into a space that appeared to have been a conference room.

Unlike the rooms and halls of yesteryear above with their ornate murals, beautiful sculptures, and fine details, this room belonged in today's world. The contrast reminded me of the difference between the media room and the rest of the matriarch's mansion. Much like our media room, huge flat screens lined the walls of this room, but rather than comfortable home-theater type seating, the rest of the space was devoid of any furniture. Towers of stackable chairs stood in one corner, leaving an expanse of gray commercial-grade carpet stretching from wall to wall. In a time when the rest of the world, or at least what we'd seen of it, had lost electrical power, overhead fluorescent lights somehow illuminated the room.

Like the lights, the monitors were somehow powered on and somehow connected to cameras around the world. I figured the "somehow" must have been magic, in the same way Amadis Island was powered. All of the screens showed a similar scene, but at different locations with different backgrounds. Norman super-soldiers lined up on the left side with guns pointing at masses of human men, women, and children on the right. The people on the screens appeared to be of various nationalities, wailing, pleading, and crying for help in a multitude of languages. One camera showed the Eiffel Tower in the background, another the Egyptian pyramids, one snow-capped mountains, and yet another what was obviously an American mall.

When I peered closer, I recognized a few faces among the Normans on each screen: Chandra in India, Minh's second-in-command in front of the Sydney Opera House, and there were Trevor, Sundae, and their whole pack of Amadis werewolves in a crowd of norms with Stone Mountain, Georgia, in the background. My heart leapt into my already tight throat.

The weirdest part of the whole situation, though, was what brought Vanessa to this room: A few dozen men, dressed in various styles of clothes from jeans and t-shirts to thousand-dollar suits, standing in perfectly lined rows and staring glassy-eyed at the front of the room. They all appeared to be in their early to mid-twenties, most with various shades of brown and reddish-brown hair, although a few blonds were mixed in, many with dark eyes and olive-toned skin. Enough shared features to show that they were not only related to each other and Noah, but also to me.

We'd found the Summoned and their offspring.

Vanessa stepped farther into the room and snapped her fingers in front of the face of the man closest to us. He showed no reaction. I'd expected them to attack us on Lucas's orders the instant we arrived, but they only stood there, still as statues. Would this really be so easy? I doubted it.

As if in response to my silent inquiry, a man's head turned toward me, and he gave me a creepy grin that didn't reach his glazed eyes. Then he looked forward again while his lips moved, as though he spoke, but no sound came. Suddenly, gunfire erupted on a monitor close to him. My eyes to flew to it. The people on the screen screamed and some tried to run, but they were all gunned down, eventually falling into a bloody mass of bodies.

I clamped my hand over my mouth before I screamed, too.

"Thought you'd like that little demonstration," a familiar female voice said from between two of the Summoned where she'd appeared from thin air.

The two men didn't move as Jeana, dressed in her dominatrix costume, pushed her way past them. A moment later, Merrick showed himself, too. Sasha jumped from my jacket and grew to stand nearly a foot taller than me before her paws even hit the ground. Her wings sprouted from her back, her stripes came out, and her upper lip curled away from her fangs.

"Oh, good. She's exactly why we brought you here," Jeana said as she appraised the lykora.

"Shit," we all muttered under our collective breath. This had all been a trap for Sasha?

"Yes, shit for you, but not for us," Jeana sing-songed as she swaggered back and forth in front of Sasha, as though inspecting the lykora like she planned to make an offer of purchase. Except Jeana wouldn't bother with an offer. That wasn't who she was. She would simply take.

"So you finally pulled your two brain cells together and figured out Lucas's secret sauce?" I asked, trying to mask my fear for the lykora—and the world—behind snark.

Jeana laughed. "Oh, child, we've always known his secret. Do you really think we're as stupid as Kali and tried to overtake Lucas? He's our master. He'll soon be our Lord. That whole interrogation skit was a ruse. What we really needed to know then was the extent of the connection between the lykora and the Norman soldiers, and we learned when she was shot how they all felt her pain. That's a weakness as long as we don't have possession of the mutt. So thank you for making this special delivery. Maybe if you'd played London a little smarter and handed the lykora over then, the last matriarch-whore's vampire mate would still be around."

At the mention of Rina and Solomon, anger blossomed

within me, and I lunged at her. She dropped her arms to her sides, splayed out her hands, and I froze in place as intense power jolted through me. Only for a moment, though, before it began streaming the other way. She'd created a connection that sucked the electrical energy from my body and straight into hers, locking my muscles up. I tried to push her off with a shove of my Amadis power, but she easily dismissed it with a wave of her hand. Tristan moved between us to block her access to me, severing the connection, and he lifted his hand, raising Jeana up with it. But Merrick shot a spell at Tristan, blasting him into the wall. Cracks splintered across the plaster, and a screen fell and shattered on the floor. Several of the Summoned sons suddenly sprang into action, and chaos erupted.

While Merrick and Jeana plastered themselves against the wall and controlled some of the men to move in front of them in a protective half-circle, they apparently ordered others to divvy up and attack us. They didn't use any powers, only fists and feet as they punched and kicked. Tristan had anticipated this, although we'd expected Lucas to be the one controlling them, and we'd agreed that we didn't want to hurt the Summoned. They'd hopefully be on our side soon. So I only fought back enough to minimize the blows that landed on my body.

Jeana and Merrick were our real targets.

I couldn't use my electric power, though, because they'd only latch onto it and charge their own magic with the energy. So while swinging my arms and legs to parry the Summoned's attacks, I gathered my Amadis power within me and created a bubble of energy, letting it expand within my body. And then I pushed it outward in an explosion of power. The wave hit the Summoned closest to me, knocking them off their feet. The ones in front of Merrick and Jeana fell, too.

Owen took the opportunity and shot a spell at Merrick, but the sorcerer shoved it back at him, sending Owen flying into one of the Summoned. Spells and powers started flying, most deflected into the floor and walls. Another screen exploded with impact. With no real powers but her body, Vanessa launched herself at Merrick, but he already flew for Sasha. The lykora snapped and bit at him, crunching her jaw around his arm. He blasted a spell that not only sent her flying, but everyone else in the room, too. I crashed into the wall, and my head banged against the corner of a screen, but the gash that it left healed up right away.

Merrick and Jeana stood in the center of the room. Everyone else jumped to their feet. The Summoned sprang at us, but Tristan, Owen, and I swished our hands all at the same time, throwing them back, away from us, as we advanced on the sorcerers. My glare remained on Jeana, specifically. I drew my dagger, still concealed, and lifted it for the throw. The sorceress twisted her hands in front of her and pulled them to her hip, as though yanking on a rope. My energy flowed like a river out to her, bringing me to my knees in a nanosecond. Tristan twisted his hand, and the sorceress flew back several feet, but she stopped herself in midair with her own magic, her hold on me never loosening. Using the bit of strength I could hold on to, I threw the dagger, thumbing the amethyst at the last moment to reveal the blade before it arced end-over-end in the air and drove into Jeana's shoulder right above her heart. She fell to the floor on her ass.

The energy drain stopped, and my mind exploded, clearing out what felt like cotton stuffing clogging my brain. I hadn't noticed the filling in my head until everyone's thoughts came loud and clear, the onslaught momentarily blacking out my physical surroundings. Hundreds of dots of mind signatures in the distance filled my head, but when I tried to latch on to most of those in the room, their thoughts came up blank. But I had no problem hearing Jeana's and Merrick's, which I shared with Tristan, Owen, and Vanessa.

Owen and Merrick had continued trading spells back and

forth, Owen holding his own, but Merrick was about to let one go that aimed for me rather than the warlock. Owen shot a spell at him first, while Tristan full on charged at him like a pissed off bull.

I did my own charging, right toward Jeana who tried once again to pull on my energy. The silver blade still protruding from her shoulder weakened her, though. At the same time she tried to suck me dry, she ordered the Summoned to attack again. Focused solely on Jeana, I absently punched at the men who lunged at me, knocking them away, as I pushed my other powers against Jeana, blocking her pull as I ran for her. Vanessa blurred over to the sorceress, looped her arm around Jeana's neck, and locked her in a chokehold for me. I plowed into the bitch with my left palm lifted and shoved Amadis power into her as hard as I could. Her body arched and convulsed against Vanessa, and she screamed obscenities at me, yelling over the sounds of Tristan and Owen fighting with Merrick and the Summoned.

Then Jeana fell suddenly silent, and she gave me an agony-filled grin before looking up to the Summoned standing closest to her and giving him a slight nod. I picked up on no exchange of thoughts, but she somehow communicated with him.

Gunfire erupted on the screen right behind her. Normans and Amadis slumped to the ground.

"Stop!" I shouted, and everyone in the room froze, presumably under Tristan's power.

"You *can't* stop them," Merrick said, his voice full of glee, and another Summoned's lips moved, followed by more shooting and Normans and Amadis dropping execution style. I shared a thought with Vanessa, her fangs slid fully out, and she pierced them into Jeana's throat, drawing a trickle of blood. Merrick let out a sound of disinterest. "Even if you kill us, Lucas will take over."

More gunfire. My stomach lurched as another group was

mowed down by the Norman super-soldiers. My eyes stung as my gaze bounced between the three screens showing piles of dead bodies and soldiers standing there, just staring, with no understanding or awareness of what they'd done to their fellow humans. About thirty or so more monitors still displayed small crowds begging for their lives. Jeana and Merrick—and if not them, Lucas—would keep going until they'd all been executed, or we gave them Sasha. And probably our own lives, too. We needed to stop them. But how?

"You could kill the controllers here," Jeana suggested, her tone snide as she guessed at my thoughts. I certainly wasn't sharing them with her. She flicked her hand toward the Summoned and their offspring. "But I imagine there's still *hope* for some of them. Isn't that what you're always looking for?"

"Not that it would matter much," Merrick added. "With the lykora's blood in them, Lucas still has those soldiers' loyalty."

I wasn't so sure about that. The soldiers seemed to be more loyal to Sasha than Lucas, which could be our advantage when the time came. But first, we had to address the Summoned and their offspring. And killing them wasn't an option. We weren't here just to save the Normans, but to save the Summoned, as well. Not only did we plan to protect their souls from damnation when we figured out how to break the curse, but we also hoped they would fight with us, helping us to win this war.

"Of course, you could kill Sasha," Jeana purred, and my heart immediately recoiled at the thought. I glared at her with pure hatred. "That's the name Dorian gave the mutt, right? If you kill her, the soldiers will immediately go down, too."

I narrowed my eyes at her.

"Like we said before, she's their weakness," Merrick said. "But *can* you do it? That's the question."

Jeana stared at me with a smirk on her lips and excitement

alight in her dark eyes, igniting the red glow of the Daemoni. I didn't think it possible, but this little bitch held more darkness in her soul than Kali ever dreamed of. It pulsed out of her in waves that rippled over me . . . into me. If she couldn't drain me of my power, she would fill me with her own black energy.

"Those are your options, poppet," she said, her voice dark and gravelly. "What ever are you going to do?"

I stared at her for a long moment before returning her smirk as my mind ran through all the things I'd wanted to do to her from the moment she dared to touch my son. I *did* share those thoughts with her.

"*Those are not our only options,*" Tristan mind-spoke to me. I nodded, knowing he was right, and Jeana's brows furrowed. I closed off my mind from hers at the same time Norman soldiers shot down another group.

Let's end this, I growled into my team's heads. *Before anyone else dies. Jeana's and Merrick's souls are black. There is no hope. Vanessa and Owen, put the controllers to sleep. Tristan, you can have Merrick, but I get this bitch.*

Vanessa released the sorceress and blurred around the room, and before they could react, the Summoned and their offspring fell unconscious as Owen raced to catch them and lay them on the floor. Jeana's mouth fell open with shock at first, and then her eyes filled with panic. I didn't pay attention to what Tristan did to Merrick, but based on the sounds of the sorcerer's wails, I knew he suffered terrifically. I had my own evil wretch to take care of.

I narrowed my eyes, lifted one corner of my mouth in a half-smile, and lunged at Jeana's paralyzed body. She cried out when I yanked my dagger out of her shoulder and tried to mumble a spell at me, but I swung around and kicked her in the face. Her head snapped to the side, and her teeth smashed together, shutting her up. Before she could try another spell, I threw myself at her again, my dagger pointed at her heart. But I didn't stab her with it. Instead, I fisted the hilt and drew the sharp tip through her skin, gritting my teeth against her siren screams of pain as I twisted and pulled artfully. Blood filled the lines between the flesh and spilled over the edges, leaving a trail over the curve of her breasts and into her blouse. When I finished my etching, I paused for a brief moment to admire my artwork. Unfortunately, too much blood flowed through my crude rendition of the Amadis symbol carved into her chest.

With Jeana's body trembling under mine, but her eyes hard as steel, I held my palm over the crimson engraving and shoved Amadis power through the open wound. Along with it, I used my other hand to push the full strength of my electrical energy into her, charging her higher than her body could handle. Dark purple blotches bloomed over her skin and smoke rose, accompanied by the acrid odor of burning hair and flesh. Merrick's cries fell silent. Jeana's eyes widened at the sight of his dead body that fell next to her and fear overcame her mind. Along with revenge.

You wish, I thought. *But you won't have that chance.*

At the same moment I aimed my dagger at her heart, her hand twitched, then lifted against Tristan's hold on her. She flipped it up, exposing her palm to me. If she was asking for help or showing surrender, it was too little too late. I felt not one smidgen of sincere hope for her soul. I plunged my blade into her, and simultaneously, her fingers folded and squeezed into a tight fist.

I keeled over in pain.

It felt as though her hand had been in my very uterus when she squeezed it. My belly tightened and cramped, sending waves of agony throughout my torso and legs. At the same time, the ice pick slammed into my mind again, so hard I saw lights flashing before my eyes. But with gasping breaths, I pushed beyond the pain and focused, collecting all of my Amadis power into a ball and ramming it into her until the life left her eyes.

The pain in my belly lessened, but I instinctively pressed my hand against it as though I could hold it together and keep everything inside, while I freed my dagger from Jeana's corpse and stumbled for the closest Summoned son.

"We have to get the stones out," I said through a clenched jaw.

My whole lower body ached and burned as I dropped to the floor and dug my knife into the man's chest, searching for the stone. The tip of the blade found the solid piece, and I twisted it out. He remained unconscious as his skin healed up, but his heart held a steady rhythm in his chest, so I crawled over to the next man. Vanessa, Owen, and Tristan each went to work. By the time I reached my sixth or seventh one, the others began to stir. I watched this one's face as I popped the stone out, finding it even more familiar than the others. My mind flashed back to Tristan's house in Cape Heron, darkened because of the hurricane blowing outside.

"Edmund," I whispered.

His eyes flew open, glowing bright red. "Hello, sweetheart."

Faster than I could react, his hands clamped around my neck and squeezed. I swung my fists at him, slicing his arms and chest more than once with the silver blade, but he barely reacted. He began to rise from the floor, lifting me by the throat as I choked, trying to grab air. A streak of someone blurred at us, whether Tristan or Vanessa I didn't know, and Edmund dropped to the floor again, bringing me down with him. I crashed to my knees while slamming Amadis power into him until he fell unconscious.

Tristan grabbed me by the waist and lifted me to my feet. I wobbled at first, my body still aching from whatever Jeana had done to me in her final seconds, and I glanced around the room. All of the controllers had been freed, many of them waking and looking around with confusion in their eyes. Some sprang to their feet right away, crouching into fighting stances.

"Amadis," one man hissed.

"Do you want to join us?" I asked, my voice heavy yet hopeful.

He laughed maniacally. "Never! But it wouldn't matter if I did. We can't convert."

He sprang into the air and flew straight toward me. Tristan waved his hand, and he soared across the room and smashed into the tower of stacking chairs. Others attacked, too, but they moved slowly, having spent too much time under Lucas's control. An arm to the throat by Vanessa, an easy blocking spell by Owen, or a wave of Tristan's hand stopped every single one. Sasha growled and snapped at them, holding them off. I could barely stand there, hunched over, my arms crossed over my belly as wetness seeped under my leather pants.

One of the screens on the wall caught my attention, distracting me from thoughts I didn't want to explore yet anyway. The Norman super-soldiers simply stood on their sides of the monitors, their guns hanging from their hands at their sides. Chandra slowly approached them, and they didn't react, but remained still like powered-down robots. Others followed behind her. She nodded, and then began to remove one of the soldier's stones, and other Amadis there did the same. The scene played out similarly on all of the screens, some of the norms joining in to cut the stones out.

"We did it," I murmured, trying to grasp onto the hope of what this meant.

Realizing they couldn't fight us—and most looking like they didn't even want to—the Summoned and their offspring in the room ran out of the door and up the stairs. All except those who still remained unconscious.

"Wait!" I yelled at the last one to leave. "Let us help you!"

He stopped in the doorway and looked over his shoulder. "Impossible."

With that one word, he disappeared.

"At least they're free," Tristan murmured from my side.

"Now we just need to break the curse and get them back," I said, still clutching at my abdomen as I turned toward him, Owen, and Vanessa. Their eyes filled with worry when they looked at me. I forced myself to ignore the pain and straighten up. We didn't have time for them to fawn over whatever was wrong with me.

"Right now, we need to get our butts to the camp," I said. "Get those norms to A.K.'s Angels before the Daemoni beat us to them."

"And before midnight," Vanessa reminded us.

"Do you have enough strength to make a portal?" Tristan asked Owen.

The warlock nodded and went to work creating an opening.

"What about them?" I asked, indicating the few remaining Summoned, including Edmund.

"If they want to convert, they'll find us." Tristan took my hand and led me to the portal.

Once we passed through, though, we didn't arrive in front of the Norman camp we had seen from the campus clock tower. Rather, we stood on an expanse of marble, facing a light-colored building with a row of arched windows and a series of pillars above them. I craned my neck and stared up at the tall dome of the United States Capitol building, not lit up as it should have been, but a light gray against the dark of night.

"What are we doing here?" Tristan demanded.

Owen groaned. "We were rerouted."

"And I don't think we're getting out of here," Vanessa muttered as she turned around.

My telepathy had disappeared again, and I only sensed the Daemoni behind me by the evil in the air and the stench hitting my nose. Slowly, I turned around, hoping against all odds to find that the Summoned had reconsidered. I even held a little hope that they'd come back to tell us how to break the curse because they wanted to join us. But that wasn't who I found standing on the railing of the balcony against the backdrop of the broken Washington Monument. What felt like enough dark power belonging to a horde of Daemoni waved off of a single man in an Armani suit.

Lucas.

CHAPTER 27

"*S*asha, hide!" I hissed before Lucas made a move for her. She didn't shrink and hide in my coat, but jumped into the air and flew away. Unfortunately, I knew she hadn't gone far—she'd wait and watch until she was needed.

I grabbed Tristan's hand, using him for strength as I pulled up to my full height next to him, both of us standing with our feet shoulder-width apart and our shoulders squared. Vanessa stepped up to stand next to me, Owen took his place on Tristan's other side, and we faced the man who, in some way or another, had played a role in creating each one of us. Even Owen, whose father had been possessed by Kali, the sorceress who at once had been Lucas's pet, acting on his orders, while also trying to overpower him.

"I seem to remember we already discussed how I feel about others taking what belongs to me," Lucas said, his icy voice matching his cold blue eyes as he stood perfectly balanced on the marble rail. To each side, a broad staircase descended to street level and the Mall below Capitol Hill. The moon shone down on the reflecting pool far behind him that stretched toward the Washington Monument, damaged buildings of the Smithsonian museums lining each side.

My sperm donor and my enemy crossed his arms over his chest. One hand twisted and tugged at his snow-white goatee as he studied us. His gaze barely stopped on Vanessa or Owen, but it lingered for a long moment on Tristan, and the blue of his eyes turned a bright red. When they fell on our clasped hands, his nostrils flared, then his gaze traveled up to me. I wanted to recoil, to run away, to escape the evil, murderous look in his eyes. The blackness in him felt so much stronger than it had the last time I'd seen him.

"You've taken my number-one warrior," he said with a glance at Tristan, and then his eyes slid to Vanessa. "And my daughter, too, although you can have that worthless cunt. And now you've taken my soldiers and my favorite weapon against the Normans." His eyes traveled upward and glanced around, likely searching for Sasha, knowing she wouldn't have gone far. His gaze came back to me, glowing with a mix of anger and excitement. "I guess my payment's coming soon, though, in the form of your son."

Tristan growled and lifted his hand. A flame flew out of his palm at Lucas. Lucas's fingers barely twitched, and Tristan's hand yanked out of mine as he flew backwards. He crashed into the marble wall of the building behind us with a loud crack and dropped to the ground. Vanessa and I ran to his side while Owen shot a spell at Lucas, but again, he easily deflected it, the green light shattering a window to our left. Tristan seemed to be okay, although angrier now as he rose to his feet, shaking off our offers to help.

"He's gained strength," Vanessa murmured under her breath as we followed Tristan back to Owen's side.

Lucas laughed. "That I have! You're actually right for once, but even a monkey guesses the correct answer once in a while. Now that evil outweighs the little bit of good that remains in the world, the Ancients have grown stronger, and they've passed that power onto me, preparing me. Want to see?"

Not waiting for our answer, he lifted his hand above his

hand and flicked his wrist as though tossing a ball into the air. A small explosion sounded behind us. We automatically looked over our shoulders. The top of the Capitol, including part of the dome, was gone, looking as though a can opener had peeled it apart. Flames licked at the jagged edges. Lucas gave us a wicked grin when we turned our attention back to him.

"But fear not," he said. "I don't want to fight you right now. I don't want to annihilate you yet. I don't really need those soldiers or the Summoned sons anyway. Not anymore. The apocalypse is here, and you, darling Alexis, weren't able to stop it. And now you're out of time."

He wiggled his fingers, and four figures, two on each staircase, blurred up toward us, then stopped at the landing. They each turned toward Lucas and dropped to a knee, their heads bowed. When they rose to their feet, they remained planted at the tops of the marble stairs, guarding them, as though to prevent us from escaping. Edmund and Rene on one side, and Victor and Cruz on the other.

Vanessa made a noise in her throat when she saw her brother—*our* brother—and her body coiled. Owen grabbed her arm and took her hand, stilling her.

"It's not over yet," I said, and while Lucas was distracted with Owen's gesture toward Vanessa, I shot a powered-up jolt of electricity at him.

Edmund twitched, as if to attack, but Lucas stopped him, shrugging off my power and returning his gaze to me. The Summoned son, the vampire, and the two were-cats didn't worry me. The evil man before us did, though. If only my stupid mind worked right, I could possibly pull his plans out of his head. Instead, I could only keep him talking, hoping that in the meantime, Tristan formulated our method of escape. Or better yet, method of attack. It would be awesome to put this whole thing to an end tonight.

"Even if it is *the* apocalypse," I continued, "we have a few years to stop you. Seven, according to the Bible."

"Don't believe everything you read," Lucas said with another chuckle. "Besides, do you even know how long this has been in motion, young Alexis? Centuries, if you really think about it. I brought on the Four Horsemen *years* ago. Conquest? My Daemoni army has been walking the world for millennium, conquering the feeble Normans, especially over the last several years. War? Well, when has there not been war? Famine? The wealthy have been oppressing the poor forever, but how much more so in recent times? Even the ignorant humans talk about how the rich get richer while the poor starve at their feet. And now we have Death. Plenty of it, wouldn't you say? At least a quarter of the human population, just as the Bible says. That part is true. So now it's time for the final battle. Armageddon. It's just a matter of me opening the veil and letting Satan and his Demons in. I'm ready for him! And then I'll watch you bow down to me, like all of my followers."

"Never," I spat, and I launched a stream of Amadis power at him this time. He easily diffused it, dousing it with a wave of darkness that made my skin crawl.

"Oh, you will," he said as though it were a promise. "The veil is at its thinnest tonight, making it easy to rip a few tears into it. Enough to let the Demons come through first and possess what the stupid Normans call zombies." He flicked his hand backwards to indicate the walking dead on the Mall. "They're simply bodies we've been keeping functional until the spirits of my lord can come and save this world from itself. Humans are so eager to destroy their home and themselves. He will be a good king over them. The *true* god who will empower them and give them everything their hearts desire. So I will drop the veil for him, and he will come and take me." His voice rose, booming with excitement. "And *you* two will watch, and you *will* bow down to me. That's the *only* reason

I'm keeping you alive this very moment. Because I've been waiting for this day forever."

Tristan shot another fireball at him, and Lucas chuckled once again as he caught it in his hand. He grew the ball of flames between his palms until it became big enough to engulf him. Then he and the fire rose off the railing and into the air.

"I wonder, Alexis, who you're going to try to save first this time. Not that there's a chance in hell that anyone will survive in the long run, but for now, who will you run to first? Your people? The Normans? Or your son?" His voice deepened even more and crackled with the fire, sounding almost demonic. "And don't fool yourself for a moment that Dorian stayed with the Normans. He's not that stupid. I'd say he's reached Noah by now."

He rose higher into the air, his eyes glowing brightly and his white-blond hair curling upwards to look more like horns jutting out of his head. And the way he hung there, the way the flames danced around him so that you could almost see the shape of bat wings for a moment, and then a tail the next, he took on the appearance of Satan himself. With a wicked grin, he clapped his hands together, and the sound thundered loudly over the earth. The ground rumbled and buildings along the Mall began to crumble and fall.

A flash of light shone in the far distance, faint and small from here, but probably blinding up close.

"There goes Richmond," Lucas said, his tone sharp, filled with a demented thrill. Another flash sparked to our right. "And Baltimore. See what I mean about the Normans? So eager to destroy. Like I said, you can't stop this."

And then he disappeared.

Orange glows dotted the horizon all around us, illuminating several mushroom clouds rising into the air.

"Oh, fuck," Vanessa breathed.

"Cruz and Rene, you know what to do," Victor said as he pierced us with his ice-blue eyes.

The two women nodded, spun, and launched themselves down the stairs, their bodies exploding into their were-forms before their paws hit the ground. The jaguar and the cheetah ran toward the Mall and the Washington Monument.

"Who are you going to save, *sisters*?" Victor asked, saying that last word as though his tongue molested it. "Don't worry about the humans we have. They're tucked safely away. Of course . . . there's *your* norms halfway across the city. I wonder if they have any clue what's coming for them. And then there's the boy and Noah."

"Dorian," I whispered.

"Don't worry. Edmund and I will get them." The words had barely left his lips when a large, white shape swooped down, grabbed him in her mouth and shook her head like a normal dog shakes a toy. Sasha flung Victor off the landing, and his body soared into a tree below. She picked up a shocked Edmund next and flew off with him clamped tightly in her jaw.

I turned to Tristan. "Do you think Dorian's—"

"GO!" Tristan barked at Vanessa and Owen, cutting me off as he grabbed my hand. "Go to the others and take them underground. Hurry! We'll get Noah—and Dorian if he's really there."

Owen and Vanessa disappeared with two pops, and Tristan led me for the flash. We left the steps of the Capitol building and appeared at the bottom of the stairs of the Jefferson Monument. Balls of fire streaked across the sky and slammed into Earth, sending chunks of dirt and grass flying. What looked like black crystals also shot out of the air. Two crashed into the ground thirty yards away from us and shattered on impact with two creatures exploding from the shards.

My heart stopped in my chest.

Their horned heads twisted on their human-like bodies as they looked around, as though orienting themselves. Thickly muscled arms, powerful looking chests, and trunk-sized legs were covered in mottled skin that changed colors, as though they'd been bathing in motor oil. Their glowing red eyes landed on Tristan and me, huge leathery wings rose from their backs, and their mouths stretched open, revealing rows of sharp teeth. The darkest depths of evil poured out of them, as if they'd risen from the pits of Hell itself. I had a feeling they had. Fear wrapped itself around me.

With two flaps each, the creatures rose from the ground and flew at us.

"Get Dorian," Tristan barked, snapping me out of my frozen state, and he shoved me up the steps before turning to fight the Demons.

Ignoring the warmth of pain still pulsing in my belly, I sprinted up the stairs, and although my telepathy refused to work again, I sensed the two souls inside. When I reached the top of the stairs, a fireball blasted into the domed roof. Chunks of stone rained down.

"Dorian!" I yelled as I swerved to avoid the falling debris. I ran into the portico. Two bodies stood on the far side, one much bigger than the other. The smaller one, still taller than me, grabbed the other one and launched himself straight upward. "NO! Dorian!"

He soared over the top of the building with Noah in his arms, narrowly missing a hunk of black ice that slammed into the far side of the memorial. The ground shook. More debris fell. I sprinted across the portico, but new words painted in blood on one of the walls stopped me in my tracks.

"We don't belong with you. I have to do this. Don't try to follow."

Oh, no. Oh god, no! Please don't do this to me.

I wanted to drop to the ground, to shrivel up and die, but I ran back for the other side. Halfway down the steps, Tristan fought with three Demons as he tried to make his way up here.

"Dorian!" I screamed desperately at the top of my lungs as

I searched the sky for my son, but I knew in my breaking heart that I wouldn't find him. He was gone. My son had done the inevitable that I'd fought against for so long.

Sasha landed next to me, the fur around her muzzle stained red.

"Go after Dorian," I ordered her, pointing to the sky, but she ignored me. Instead she went after one of the Demons Tristan fought, following it into the sky when it flew away.

I ran down several steps, shooting electricity at one of the others still fighting my husband. With a noisy flap of wings, it launched itself at me. Its powerful claws grabbed my shoulders, digging into my skin as it flew upward several feet, and then it threw me back to the ground. I crashed into the rotunda and rolled across the marble floor with the impact reverberating through every bone. With a grunt, I pushed myself to my hands and knees. A loud sound thundered overhead, shaking the whole stone and marble building, and I looked up.

The far side of the roof collapsed, boulder-sized chunks of marble falling to the floor. Cracks splintered across the ceiling and down the walls. I pushed myself to my feet and spun back toward the steps and Tristan. A huge piece of marble fell from the ceiling in front of me, breaking into pieces on impact, destroying the phrase I'd read earlier so only "god," "hostility," and "tyranny" could be read. More snapping and cracking in the walls, and the words "all men are created equal" crumbled before me, along with "life, liberty, and the pursuit of happiness."

The world and everything I knew was falling apart around me.

I tried to move again, to run for Tristan, but a heavy weight immobilized me—the weight of total failure. My heart and soul broke for all that had been lost, shattering along with the pieces of marble that crashed down around me, knocking me to the floor. Despair wracked through my every cell, ripping me apart from within. I looked outward at the blazing sky as I collapsed facedown, unable to fight the truth anymore. The sensation that engulfed me was not one I could easily brush my fingers over, drag off and flick away. This girdle of misery was something I'd live with until my dying day and beyond.

I'd be tormented forever, not by what Lucas had done, but by my own failure to stop him. Because I could do nothing now. Nothing for the world. Nothing for my people. Nothing for myself nor my son nor my husband, who still fought, trying to protect us from evil to the bitter end.

I'd tried, and I'd failed.

It took me a long moment to realize that more than the heaviness of my emotions weighed me down. A chunk of roof had fallen, crushing my body to the floor and pinning me facedown. Not even with my inhuman strength could I move it from this position, and I called for Tristan, but my voice came out weak. He'd never hear me over his battle with the Demons. I let my head fall, my cheek pressing against the cool marble floor.

Barely conscious, I lay at the top of the stone steps with the stately Thomas Jefferson behind me, and gazed over the Potomac River Tidal Basin at the scene of annihilation before me. I tried one more time to scream my love's name as fire and ice fell from the sky.

Hell stormed down on Earth, ending life as we knew it.

EPILOGUE

"*A*lexis! Dorian!" Tristan's voice carried from what sounded like far away, although I knew he was close.

I opened my mouth to answer him, but could only scream from the excruciating agony that tore through my back and shoulders. My bones felt as though they were breaking, and my skin was shredding to pieces. Clenching my jaw, I pushed myself to my hands and knees, and focused on trying to breathe as the pain momentarily subsided.

"Tristan," I gasped as my muscles tensed, readying for another onslaught I felt rippling from the inside out.

"Alexis! Dorian!" he yelled again, panic filling his voice now.

A wail ripped from my insides, my only answer. My back arched up like a cat's and then down as more pain exploded from my spine. Panting, I fought to catch my breath. The pain rolled away again, and I rocked back on my heels and pressed my palms to my thighs to stand. My entire body ached, and I felt like a two-ton weight was strapped to my back.

"Alexis!" Tristan's voice came closer, yet still muffled and distant. "Dorian!"

"Here," I called out to him. He finally ran into what

remained of the rotunda, hurdling over the piles of rubble that had once been the domed roof. The sky lightened above us with dawn, illuminating his fretful face, bruised and battered, as were his arms.

"Dorian! Alexis!" he yelled again as his eyes darted around the demolished building.

"I'm right here," I repeated, trying to yell louder. "I'm okay!"

Sort of. I was sure I would be after my body healed whatever back injury I'd suffered. It seemed to be already on its way.

Tristan's gaze swept everywhere but failed to land on me. Instead, it fell on the pile of marble and stone at my feet.

"Oh, no. Oh, fuck. Alexis!" He lifted a boulder and threw it to the side. "God, no. *Please* no."

"What are you doing? What's wrong?" The fear and anguish in his voice scared the hell out of me.

He threw off another chunk of stone and boomed out, "NOOOO!"

The desperate sound broke me. Tears streamed down my face, and I didn't know why. Dorian had flown away. Right? Wherever he'd gone, I was positive that he couldn't possibly be buried under this pile. So what did Tristan see that had him so devastated? It couldn't be what he thought. I wanted to hold him and hug him and tell him it would be okay. But I couldn't move, and he couldn't hear me. And then I looked away from his desperate yet lovely face and down at what he had found. My breath caught in my throat.

Legs with familiar boots pinned under another slab of marble. A midsection soaking in a pool of blood. A small, pale hand.

Tristan lifted the last two pieces and threw them to the side. He bent down in an unusually disgraceful way, slipped in the blood, and fell next to her. His whole body trembling, he slid his arms under her, wrapped them around her torso, and pulled her limp body to his chest, one hand against the back of her head, holding her tightly.

I shook my head in denial at the sight, straightening up as I tried to make sense of it all. Movement behind me made me jump and spin on my heel. Whatever had been back there disappeared, but something white moved behind me once more. I spun again, but every time I moved, it did, too. I looked over my shoulder, turning in place, but it remained in my peripheral vision. Realizing I acted like a puppy chasing its tail, I stopped. The movement behind me ceased, too.

But in front of me stood three women, looking all angel-like with their huge wings lifted and spread as though they were about to take flight. I grinned at first, happy to see Mom, Rina, and Cassandra, but almost immediately my smile faltered, and then slid away. Behind them, in the distance, standing with other people in a white mist that faded in and out, were Winston, Stefan, and Solomon. I shook my head, not understanding, and my gaze came back to Mom. My heart stuttered and tilted as I glanced at her wings, and my brow furrowed as I looked over my shoulder again. Now I knew what I'd seen moving before. As though appreciating the acknowledgement of their existence, my own wings lifted from my back and spread wide.

What the hell? I thought but didn't dare to voice.

I noticed the clean freshness of the air for the first time and inhaled its clear, crisp scent. It didn't match the scene of fire and destruction surrounding us. My frown deepened as I looked at my wings again, then at my mom and my grandmother, and then at my sobbing husband.

"Tristan," I breathed, falling to my knees and trying to reach out for him, but unable to touch him, to comfort him.

He rocked back and forth, holding her body close with the most devastating and heart-wrenching expression I'd ever seen. Her chestnut colored hair spilled over his hand and arm as he clutched her to his chest as though if he let go, he'd fall completely apart.

"Alexis, my love," he sobbed. "Don't leave me, *ma lykita.*"

"Never," I cried. "I'm here, Tristan. Always with you."

His voice broke into a howl filled with a pain unlike anything I'd ever heard, sending wracks of grief all the way through my soul, shattering it into tiny shards. I lunged for him, needing to hold him, to return his embrace, to tell him I loved him, but I couldn't push through to him, no matter how hard I tried or how many times I threw myself at him.

A hand landed on my shoulder, stilling me, and squeezed. "Alexis."

I shook my head. "No."

"Honey."

"NO!" I yelled at her.

This could not be happening. I could not be watching my husband, my soul mate, my one and only true love who owned a piece of my heart and soul through the veil. We could *not* be on opposite sides of it. I could no longer breathe as I looked up at my mother, pressing my hand against the stone embedded in my chest—a piece of Tristan's heart. I opened my mouth to speak, but the words became lodged in my throat. I could only shake my head and look back to Tristan's dirt-smudged, tear-stained face that was still the most beautiful thing I'd ever seen.

"Am I . . ." I glanced up at Mom, whose face appeared as forlorn as my husband's, and then back at Tristan. I swallowed, hard, and tried again. Blinking against the tears that flowed with each of my love's sobs, I finally managed to push the question out. "Am I really . . . *dead?*"

Read on for an excerpt of *Fractured Faith.* For some extra fun, enjoy *Wonder: A Soul Savers Collection of Holiday Short Stories*

& Recipes, including fun tales about Alexis, Tristan, and the gang, as well as new characters from both the Amadis and Daemoni. Available to read for free by joining my reader newsletter group, where you'll also get other exclusive content and be the first to know about releases, sales, and special events.

GLOSSARY & CAST

A.K. Emerson – Alexis's famous pen name.

Alexis Ames Knight – Amadis matriarch. Married to Tristan Knight and mother of Dorian. Youngest daughter to ever go through the Ang'dora and to become matriarch. Her bio father is the leader of the Daemoni. Known abilities include telepathy, electricity, telekinesis, super strength, speed and senses, Amadis power.

Alys – Recently converted Amadis vampire.

Amadis (uh-MAH-dees) – Secret matriarchal society that serves as the Angels' army on Earth, currently led by Alexis Ames Knight. Their purpose is to defend human souls from the Daemoni and to convert Daemoni souls to Amadis. Consist of a variety of supernatural beings.

Amadis daughters – Women of the bloodline of the original creator of the Amadis. Each daughter eventually serves as the matriarch.

Amadis power – A special power of love and light gifted to the Amadis by the Angels. The Amadis daughters receive it during the Ang'dora. Other society members are granted a lower level of power upon conversion and official acceptance into the Amadis.

Ammi – Started the London cell of AK's Angels with her sister Kristen. Turned into a vampire and converted immediately by Char and Alexis.

Andrew – The Angel who fell from Heaven and fathered Cassandra and Jordan before eventually ascending (read about it in *Genesis: A Soul Savers Novella*).

Ang'dora – Literally means "gift of the Angels" (Ang = angels, dora = Greek word for gifts). An enigmatic change all Amadis daughters go through to receive their powers and supernatural abilities. Usually happens in middle age, after the daughter has experienced major milestones of life as a human, but Alexis went through it quite early. Except for Sophia, no Amadis daughter has given birth after the Ang'dora.

Armand – French vampire on Rina's council, he oversees Amadis police force and is anti-Tristan. Killed by Daemoni.

Attair – Amadis warlock from Arabia who's on Rina's council and is anti-Tristan.

Baby Cakes – Faerie who's a friend of Bree, so she's helped Tristan and Alexis. For a price, surely.

Blossom – Alexis's best friend and council member. Amadis witch from the Daytona coven.

Bree – Tristan's birth mother. Fae.

Carlie – Alexis's human classmate during her first year at college. Now a doctor in D.C.

Cassandra – Half angel, half human who started the Amadis (read her story in *Genesis: A Soul Savers Novella*).

Chandra – Amadis were-tiger and member of the matriarch's council who oversees the region of India.

Charlotte Allbright – Amadis warlock, Owen's mother, Sophia's best friend, and overall badass aunt figure to Alexis.

Cloak – A magic spell performed by mages that hides or makes invisible its subject. Often used in conjunction with a shield.

Conversion – The process of eliminating dark or light energy and replacing it with the opposite, then indoctrinating the supernatural being into the new society. The Amadis purpose is to convert Daemoni souls before they become damned, destroyed, or forever lost. However, on occasion, Amadis members will convert to the Daemoni (e.g., Ian).

Cruz – A Daemoni were-jaguar.

Daemoni (day-MAH-nee) – Satan's servants as the Demons' army on Earth, currently led by Lucas. They turn humans to harvest their souls and build their army. The Amadis try to stop them.

Debbie – Faerie in England who helps Alexis and Tristan from time to time. Cohorts with Stacey, another faerie.

Dorian Knight – Son of Alexis and Tristan, unknown creature but currently human. Known abilities include self-healing and flying. Converting to Daemoni?

Edmund – Summoned son and member of the Daemoni. Known abilities include flashing, super strength and speed, idiocy, and being an overall douche-canoe.

Eris – Daemoni witch from ancient times who helped Jordan create the potion that changed everything (read about it in *Genesis: A Soul Savers Novella*).

Faeries/Fae – Little is known about the fae as they tend to stay away from human affairs, as well as those of the Amadis and Daemoni. A handful do enjoy wreaking havoc in the Earthly realm, and sometimes they may even help out. They're considered Otherworldly creatures, because their world is not exactly part of Earth. They closely guard their secrets about the Faerie realm.

Ferrer – Blacksmith mage who lives on Amadis Island.

Fertility Stone – The faerie stone Bree gave Tristan when he was a young boy, embedding it in his heart with the instructions to give it to his true mate. Only when she has possession of it can he father children. The stone also allows the holder to share their emotions so he could feel his mate's love—but also the possessor's darker emotions.

Flashing – The supernatural ability to transport to

another location up to a hundred miles away (give or take) in the blink of an eye. While objects can be held or attached to the body during a flash, Tristan is the only known creature who can flash while carrying another person. While both Daemoni and Amadis can flash, it's not necessarily a natural ability for all—some creatures have to be assisted by mages.

Galina – Russian Amadis warlock and a member of the matriarch's council, she favors Tristan and Alexis.

Hades – Daemoni HQ, an underground city in the Taymyr Peninsula of Siberia.

Heather – Human girl, Dorian's babysitter and friend, daughter of Phil and sister to Sonya.

Hunters – Humans (or are they?) who know about the supernatural creatures and kill them.

Ian – Member of the Daemoni, converted from the Amadis. Known abilities include compensating for his miniscule junk by spilling secrets, causing problems with the Amadis, and ruining Alexis's life.

James – The boy Alexis punched in the nose when she was a teenager. Later became a hunter, and they met up again in D.C.

Jaxon – Were-croc from the Australian Outback who's become part of Alexis's team. Blossom's beau.

Jeana – Sorceress who tortured Alexis and Owen to learn Lucas and Kali's secret about the Norman soldiers. Mate of Merrick. Dead.

Jelani – Wizard from Africa who is one of the matriarch's council members.

Jessica – Faerie with a southern accent, calls Lisa her sister.

Jordan – Early leader of the Daemoni who sought power over all, inadvertently helping to create the Amadis (read his story in *Genesis: A Soul Savers Novella*).

Julia Acerbi – Vampire and Amadis matriarch's council member. She'd been one of Rina's closest advisors and friends.

Kali – Daemoni sorceress who took over Martin Allbright's body. Dead.

Katerina "Rina" Ames – Past matriarch of the Amadis. Known abilities included telepathy, super strength and speed, flashing, bonding souls, converting souls to Amadis, making ballgowns everyday attire. Ascended.

Kristen – Human girl who started the London branch of AK's Angels with her sister, Ammi.

Kuckaroo – Amadis village in Australia.

Lesley – Daemoni vampire. Companion of Sonya and Alys.

Lilith – Bree's daughter and Tristan's sister. Dead.

Lisa – Faerie with a southern accent, calls Jessica her sister.

Lucas – Alexis's sperm donor and leader of the Daemoni. Often (but not always) uses the last name Emerson.

Lykora – An Angelic being that is extremely loyal and highly protective of its master. When in hidden form, looks like a small white dog, but when in defensive mode, can grow as large as necessary to protect, has a wolf head and body, tiger stripes on a white coat, and feathered wings.

Mages – The wide classification of supernatural beings that can wield magic, including witches/wizards, warlocks, and Sorcerers/sorceresses. These general sub-classifications are based on strength of power. Some may call themselves by other names, depending on the type of magic they use, preference, or other reasons (e.g., Shamans, Druids, etc.).

Martin Allbright – Powerful warlock, Charlotte's husband and Owen's father.

Merrick – Sorcerer who tortured Alexis and Owen to learn the secret about the stones that control the Norman soldiers. Jeana's mate. Dead.

Minh – Vietnamese witch, member of the matriarch's council, oversees the Asian region.

Noah – Sophia's twin brother, Rina's son, a Summoned son with the Daemoni and controlled by Kali.

Norms/Normans – Normal humans.

Oliver Winston Chambers – Sophia's true love who was turned to a vampire then buried under a building in Charlotte, North Carolina, for a century. Dead again.

Ophelia – Witch who serves as head of staff at the Amadis matriarch's mansion.

Otherworld – Currently unknown but seems to refer to Heaven and Hell, as well as Faerie.

Owen Allbright – Warlock and Alexis's so-called protector. Also like a brother to her and Tristan's best friend. Known abilities include shielding, cloaking, magical bindings, flashing, and pushing everyone's limits.

Phillip Jones – Human wife beater, child abuser, and overall scum of the earth who drove an older orange Camaro. Heather and Sonya's father. Dead.

Portals – Magical doorways that can only be created and controlled by sorcerers/sorceresses and extremely powerful warlocks like Owen. They allow teleportation to anywhere in the world just by stepping through.

Rene – Daemoni were-cheetah who chases Alexis down in Hades.

Safe House – Homes, lodges, and other accommodations scattered around the world where Amadis can retreat to when under attack or when going through the conversion or transformation process.

Sasha – Dorian's lykora.

Savio – Italian were-shark who was on Rina's council and was anti-Tristan.

Seth – Tristan's former name when he was Daemoni. The Daemoni still call him that.

Sheree – An Amadis were-tiger who'd been bitten and turned against her will by the Daemoni. She was Alexis's first ever conversion from Daemoni to Amadis. Now she helps with conversions of others and is a close friend to Alexis.

Shield – A magic spell performed by mages that puts a

protective barrier around its subject. If the subject is not also cloaked, the subject can still be seen, so it's often used in conjunction with a cloaking spell.

Shihab – Wizard from Arabia who sat on Rina's council.

Solomon – Vampire, Katerina's partner, and Amadis council member. Known abilities include being scary AF. Dead.

Sonya – Recently turned vampire, now converted to Amadis. Heather's sister. A.K. Emerson's "biggest fan" (a/k/a stalker).

Sophia Ames (a/k/a Mom a/k/a Mimi) – Alexis's mother and Amadis daughter. Known abilities included telekinesis, summoning and manipulating water, persuading others to do as she likes, sensing the truth of a situation, super strength and speed, flashing, converting souls to Amadis. Ascended.

Sorcerers/Sorceresses – The most powerful of the mages that can boost their energy by siphoning more from the earth and everything around them. Their greed for power, narcissism, and general disdain for pretty much everyone make them loners and also not part of the Amadis.

Stacey – A faerie in England who helps Alexis and Tristan from time to time. Cohorts with Debbie.

Stefan – Warlock, council member, and Sophia's former protector. Known abilities included creating a protective shield, flashing, serving as Alexis's only father figure. Dead.

Summoned Sons – Amadis sons, twins of Amadis daughters/matriarchs, who always go to the Daemoni, as though magically summoned. Include Noah, Edmund, and Dorian.

Sundae – Alpha of the Georgia wolf pack. Trevor's mate.

Sylvie (Aunt Sylvie) – Blossom's aunt and leader of the Daytona Beach witch coven.

Trevor – Amadis werewolf and leader of the main Florida wolf pack. Sundae's mate.

Tristan Knight – Former Daemoni converted to Amadis

by Sophia. Matriarch's second, best friend, and husband. Dorian's dad. Sexy AF warrior. Known abilities include shooting fire from his palm, quickly determining the best solution if he knows enough of the facts, telekinesis, paralysis, instant killing power, super-duper strength and speed, brooding with guilt, giving a girl multiple Os.

Vampires – Supernatural beings that are sustained by blood. They can also feed on fear and other emotional energy. There are vampires on both the Amadis and the Daemoni sides.

Vanessa – Formerly one of the Daemoni's star vampires recently converted to Amadis. Alexis's half-sister, Victor's twin, and Lucas's daughter. Known abilities include stirring up trouble and pissing everyone off.

Victor – Vanessa's twin brother, Alexis's half-brother, Lucas's son and Daemoni vampire who's not too bright.

Warlocks – Part of the mage classification, supernatural beings who are born with the ability to wield magic and physically endowed with strength and speed, making them excellent warriors. They are not gender specific and are on both the Amadis and Daemoni sides.

Whitby Abbey – Ancient abbey on the northeastern coast of England. The place where Dorian was found, where Alexis faced off with Lucas, and where Sophia, Rina, and Winston died.

Witches/Wizards – Part of the mage classification, supernatural beings who are born with the ability to wield magic, usually using a wand as well as spells, incantations, potions, elemental energy, etc. While they can be quite powerful, their powers and physical strengths aren't as strong as Warlocks or Sorcerers. Using the term Witch or Wizard was traditionally by gender, but really is up to each individual's preference. There are Witches and Wizards on both the Amadis and Daemoni sides.

Were-creatures/animals (a/k/a Shifters) – Supernatural

beings with two combined spirits—human and animal—and they can physically shift between their two forms. There is a were-creature/shifter for nearly every predatory species on Earth, and they're on both the Amadis and the Daemoni sides.

Zombies – Reanimated corpses with deadly bites. Created by mixing necromancy magic with fatal and highly contagious viruses, such as Ebola. Lucas made them as an experiment and to provide meatsuits for the Demons he planned to let loose on Earth.

UNHOLY TORMENT PLAYLIST

(Songs I listened to on repeat while writing this book.)

As You Go by Red
This Is War by 30 Seconds to Mars
My Songs Know What You Did in the Dark by Fall Out Boy
Indestructible by Disturbed
Evil Never Sleeps by Above Only
Where Did the Angels Go? By Papa Roach
Lights Out by Breaking Benjamin
Blow Me Away by Breaking Benjamin
Warriors by Imagine Dragons
Cry for Help by Shinedown
Rebellion by Linkin Park
Final Masquerade by Linkin Park
Hopeless by Breaking Benjamin
Hold Me Now by Red

ABOUT THE AUTHOR

Kristie Cook is a lifelong, award-winning writer in various genres, primarily New Adult paranormal romance and contemporary fantasy. Her internationally bestselling, award-winning Soul Savers Series includes seven books, as well as several companion novellas and short stories. Over 1.2 million Soul Savers books have been downloaded. She has also written The Book of Phoenix trilogy, a New Adult paranormal romance series. Her books have been featured in *USA Today's* HEA section, on Good Morning America, and in the Emmy's Gifting Suite.

Kristie also created, writes in, and publishes the award-winning Havenwood Falls shared world, a collaborative project with multiple series, dozens of authors, and countless stories.

Besides writing, Kristie enjoys reading, cooking, traveling, getting her hippie on, and feeding her addictions to coffee, chocolate, cheese, and her latest TV obsession. She has lived in eleven states, but currently calls Florida home.

CONNECT WITH ME ONLINE

I love to hear from and connect with readers. Please don't be shy.

Facebook Reader Group: https://www.facebook.com/
groups/KristieCook.AKAngels.KnightRiders/

Email: kristie@kristiecook.com

Author's Website & Blog: http://www.KristieCook.com

Facebook: http://www.facebook.com/AuthorKristieCook

Twitter: http://twitter.com/kristiecookauth

Goodreads: https://www.goodreads.com/KristieCook

Instagram: http://instagram.com/kristiecookauth

BookBub: https://www.bookbub.com/authors/kristie-cook

Word of mouth is very important for any author. If you enjoyed the book, please consider leaving a review, even if it's only a sentence or two. This is one of the most important and appreciated things you can do for an author.

ACKNOWLEDGMENTS

First and always, my gratitude goes to my Maker.

I thank my family, too, for being so understanding and supportive of my writing career, even when it takes me away from them more than it should. Especially to Shawn, Zakary, Austin, and Nathan.

Thank you to Brenda Pandos for being such a good friend. Much appreciation to S.T. Bende for all of your help with blurbs and endings, but most of all for your friendship. I'm so blessed to know both of you. Many thanks to Kristen and Tammi for keeping me on track and saving my sanity.

Thank you to Lily Rowserein for the incredible covers. Kristen, Jen, and Chrissi for giving my words your critical eyes, and more thanks to the entire writing and book community.

I have so much gratitude for my beta readers—Jessie, Heather, Debbie, Rissa, Jewels, Stacey, Claire, Mindy, and Inga—who worked on a tight deadline through the holiday season to make this book a reality. Many thanks to the rest of the Crew and to Kristie's Warriors, who mean the world to me.

And thank you, reader, for once again choosing to spend your time with my characters. Because of you, I am living a dream and able to share it with the world. God bless you all. (And please don't hate me when you finish this book. All I can say is, "Have a little faith.")

AN EXCERPT

SOUL SAVERS BOOK 7

FRACTURED
FAITH

KRISTIE COOK

Evil reigns the world. Earth's been ravaged. The only signs humans survived the war come from those who serve the Demons' army. To continue his conquest of humanity, Lucas prepares to open the gates of Hell and bring Satan himself to the physical realm.

With a soul that's been battered and beaten by both Heaven and Hell, I hold on to a single conviction—my love for my family. My only mission now is to save their souls. But the Angels have other plans for us all.

My faith in them, in everything is fractured . . . broken. Possibly gone forever.

I mean, after everything, after all of the loss, who can blame me? Tristan and everyone else still believe—in the Angels and in me. I have to dig deep, though, for the tiniest bit of faith in order to defeat Lucas and win back the world. But first, I must answer the question that's haunted me for years: How far will I go to save the souls I love—and those I do not?

FRACTURED FAITH

AN EXCERPT

TRISTAN

*A*s the world destructed upon itself, the last thing I wanted to be doing was staring into the black abyss of a Demon's eye. Yet, here I was, standing on the marble steps of the Thomas Jefferson Memorial doing just that, while bombs exploded throughout the city and chunks of black ice crashed into the ground, transporting more Demons into this realm. Along with the ice came a rain of fire. It ignited the dry, autumn landscape, creating an orange glow in the night sky that added to the imagery of Hell on Earth.

The only thing I *did* want to be doing at this moment was to be holding my wife and son, or better yet, sweeping them off to safety. But first, I had to finish off this last son of a bitch who blocked my way to the rotunda above. The first few Demons had given me quite the beating, but I learned with each one, and had sent six, so far, chasing after their heads.

Seven had always been my lucky number. If I believed in such a thing.

I watched the Demon's horned head as its membranous

wings beat at the air and its barbed tail swished to and fro, while I calculated its next move. Its green and yellow dappled skin seemed to undulate like a separate being with each movement, creating a distraction for the inexperienced. But I focused on its obsidian eyes. And when it glanced to my left, I knew it would actually go right, so I feigned that way too. Then I ducked and weaved to its left and swung my foot up. My boot slammed into its lizard-like nose, shoving its face into its head with a squishing, spurting sound as if it were made out of gelatin.

Its thick neck twisted, and a fang jutting out of its jaw hooked into my boot. When it gave a shake of its head, as though trying to throw its face back into place, it jerked me off the ground. I flew into the air, bits of black matter from its head flying with me. I flipped in midair and landed on my feet three steps above the Demon. At least I headed in the right direction.

The Demon let out a screeching, wheezing sound through its smashed nose and mouth, and then it dove at me. Its sharp claws lashed out at my face, and I arched backward out of its reach. Then I sprang back on my hands and launched myself upward, feet first. My thick-soled boots plowed into its barrel chest. The force should have sent it tumbling away, but the powerful beast barely budged a few feet before its wings caught the air. It hung there for a moment, screaming evil curses in the old language as its eyes bulged from the pressure of its crushed nose.

I glanced at the portico only a dozen steps above me now, straining to listen for heartbeats while trying not to draw the Demon's attention toward that direction. I'd heard Alexis screaming what must have been hours ago, but she'd been quiet since, and I hoped she'd been hiding somewhere safe with Dorian. Hiding wasn't like her, not for this long, but I had to hope. I could hear nothing, though, over the squawk of the Demon.

Almost there, my love. Almost there. Her telepathy had become unreliable, so I prayed that she even heard my thoughts.

While sliding a shuriken from a hidden pocket inside my jacket's sleeve, I refocused on the shrieking Demon, analyzing it again so I could seize the perfect opportunity. Since they had no hearts—their bodies weren't permanently physical—my killing power had no effect on these creatures straight from the depths of Hell. Every time I tried to paralyze them, they broke free in seconds with powerful black magic. The Ancients had once divulged to me, during my previous life when I was their pet, that most Demons were too simpleminded to use the powers they possessed. They preferred the thrill of a physical brawl.

Which was fortunate for me.

Because there was only one way to decommission a Demon: decapitate it. It wouldn't die permanently, of course. It was a spirit of the Otherworld. But it would have to return to that other realm, to Hell specifically, to heal before it could take a physical form again. And decapitation required a closeness their magic would never allow if they chose to use it.

Shaking its deformed head again, the Demon batted its wings, lifting it higher in the air so it was once again above me. And that was its mistake. It probably thought it had gained a vantage point, but instead, it exposed its vulnerable throat. At the same moment it twitched to lunge at me, I flicked my wrist, sending the shuriken across its neck. It grinned for a moment, likely believing I'd tried another of my powers on it. But the grin faded along with the inky shine in its eyes. A moment later, the head fell from the body, and then both parts disappeared.

My legs pumped up the steps toward the rotunda as I shouted for my family. "Alexis! Dorian!"

I continued calling for them, but no answer came. Where the hell were they? Why weren't they responding? Panic rose and filled my voice as I yelled their names. My heart pounded with the unfamiliar feeling of fear as I reached the center of the portico. Only broken pillars remained, the roof and walls gone. The statue of Thomas Jefferson, where Noah had been magically bound, lay on its side. On a broken piece of wall, written in what appeared to be dried blood and taking the form of Dorian's handwriting, were the words, "We don't belong with you. I have to do this. Don't try to follow."

Fuck! Dorian had taken Noah and left, possibly for the Daemoni. That must have been what had Alexis screaming earlier. But where was she now?

My pulse raced even faster as my eyes swept over the piles of jagged marble and stone until they caught on something a few yards in front of me. My heart came to a screeching halt. Locks of dark coppery hair. A pale hand. A pool of crimson. And I could see nothing else of her under the rubble.

"Oh, no." A string of profanities poured out of my mouth as I heaved a large chunk of marble to the side. I lifted another, making my way to her still body, my stomach dropping further with each stone I moved. "God, no. Please no."

I couldn't lose her. I couldn't fucking lose her, damn it!

When I cleared another boulder from the pile, my worst nightmare became reality.

The word ripped out of my chest, taking my heart with it. "NO!"

I tossed the last two chunks away and lurched forward, still refusing to believe what I saw. My boots splashed in the blood and slid on the wet marble until I crashed down next to her. My fingers automatically darted for her wrist, but I felt no pulse. No breath warmed my fingertips against her pale lips.

No, Lexi, no. Damn it, no!

I carefully lifted her broken body and pulled her into my lap. My arms wrapped tightly around her, probably crushing her further as I held her against my chest. But it didn't matter.

Because she remained so still. So cold. So . . . lifeless.

The horrific feeling that exploded within me was unbearable. Unimaginable. Unlike anything I'd ever felt before. I knew physical pain. From all of the wars I'd been in, all of the suffering at the hands of Lucas and the Daemoni Ancients, all of the times they'd tried to take my heart but couldn't, I knew physical pain very well. I knew emotional pain. I knew misery and regret when my son had been taken. I knew grief and sorrow from others' deaths, especially Rina's and Sophia's, because I'd come to love them. But this . . .

This unfathomable sensation inside me . . .

This agony of my heart being bludgeoned by a dull machete with each beat it made that hers did not echo . . .

This torture of my soul clawing and scrabbling, tearing itself apart as it searched for hers . . .

I did not know this kind of internal mutilation. I didn't know how to handle it, what to do with it.

Senseless words blubbered out of me as I buried my face in her soft hair and sobbed incoherently for my beautiful bride. For my soul mate. For the one person who had loved me unconditionally. Who had taught me what love felt like. Who had warmed this heart of mine that had been cold for centuries. Whose soul had completed mine, making me whole for the first time ever.

"Alexis, my love, don't leave me." My words morphed into some kind of wail mixed with a howl. A sound of desperation that made me recoil, but I couldn't help it. I couldn't quell it. The pain, the anger, the overwhelming grief! Emotions that were too violent to be held inside. They erupted in shouts and screams and sobs. But still, the agony remained, ripping me apart from the inside.

When I could no longer muster the energy to yell, I silently rocked her in my arms as I recalled our lives together. The first time I'd seen her as an adult—young, barely eighteen and still very human, but nonetheless the most beautiful sight

I'd known in my many years. I couldn't pinpoint exactly what it was about her, but she'd captured me and enraptured me from the moment I set eyes on her at this very monument. Her laugh had been medicine for my damaged heart. Her love a salve for my wrecked soul.

And when I thought I couldn't possibly hold more love in my heart, I met our son for the first time. I'd never imagined I could produce such beauty, but of course, it had come from her. With the many hardships our poor child had suffered, he'd grown into a fine young man. But now . . . Although I'd been expecting this since the day I learned of his birth, a father could never be prepared to lose his son. I could only hope, for his soul's sake, he'd perished in the bombs before he ever reached the Daemoni.

They were both gone. I was left alone. With nothing left to live for.

I pressed my lips into Alexis's hair and murmured in her ear, praying she heard me. Or that *someone* heard me. "Lexi, *ma lykita*, I need you. Don't leave me here alone. Come back to me, my love. Please come back."

I closed my eyes against the brightening sky of morning and slumped backward against a large chunk of marble with my wife still in my arms, her head pressed against my chest as though she were only sleeping. I wanted to sleep with her. The night of fighting the dark magic of the sorcerers and Lucas, and then the Demons that had kept coming, combined with more grief than any one man should have to bear, drained me.

I'd lost my son. I'd lost my wife and our unborn child. The world seemed to have lost anything still good in it.

Take me, too.

"Is that what you really want? Would you come back home if that's where she is?" The deep, Otherworldly voice spoke the old language of the Daemoni Ancients as evil blanketed over me. I peeled one eye open. An orangish-yellow Demon balanced on the edge of a slab of marble a few feet away. I was too exhausted to fight. Too drained to give a shit anymore. "Shall I find her for you?"

My eyes fell closed again. I tightened my hold on Alexis's small body. The word came out as a whisper. "Yes."

The Demon's evil presence disappeared. As the sun rose higher, the odor of burning ozone filled the air. A distant part of my brain urged me to get up, to find shelter from the fallout that would likely blow this way from the mushroom clouds we'd seen near Baltimore and Richmond. Hell, Lucas probably planned a direct hit here in Washington, D.C., at any moment. If I knew him at all, which I did too well, he certainly had. But I couldn't bring myself to care. I slipped off into a doze.

"You will follow her where she goes?" The Demon's voice startled me partially awake.

I sighed. It didn't need me to answer. As a spirit, even an evil one, it already knew.

"Even into the dark?"

Again, it required no verbal reply. But I knew she wasn't there. Not my Alexis. She'd be in Heaven with the rest of the Amadis matriarchs.

"Come with me and make your choice."

I went with the Demon.

Read Fractured Faith where books are sold.

BOOKS BY KRISTIE COOK

SOUL SAVERS

Recommended Reading Order:

A Demon's Promise

An Angel's Purpose

Genesis: A Soul Savers Novella

Dangerous Devotion

Dark Power

Sacred Wrath

Unholy Torment

Fractured Faith

Age of Angels Part I: Awakened

Age of Angels Part II: Lost

Age of Angels Part III: Marked

Prophecy of the Wolves: (A Soul Savers Tie-In Novella)

Wonder: A Soul Savers Collection of Holiday Short Stories & Recipes

HAVENWOOD FALLS

Recommended Reading Order:

Forget You Not

Lose You Not

Break Me Not

The Collector: Awakening

Savage Salvation (Sin & Silk)

Sun & Moon Academy Book One: Fall Semester

Sun & Moon Academy Book Two: Fall Semester

The Winged & the Wicked (with T.V. Hahn)

Havenwood Falls Short Story Anthology 2018

Havenwood Falls Short Story Anthology 2019

Havenwood Falls Short Story Anthology 2020

BOOK OF PHOENIX

The Space Between

The Space Beyond

The Space Within

* 9 7 8 1 9 5 0 4 5 5 6 6 9 *